CIRCLE OF
INFLUENCE

CIRCLE OF INFLUENCE

A ZOE CHAMBERS MYSTERY

ANNETTE DASHOFY

HENERY PRESS

CIRCLE OF INFLUENCE
A Zoe Chambers Mystery
Part of the Henery Press Mystery Collection

First Edition
Trade paperback edition | March 2014

Henery Press
www.henerypress.com

ISBN-13: 978-1-940976-00-6

Printed in the United States of America

To Ray,
for always being the wind beneath my wings.

ACKNOWLEDGMENTS

It has truly taken a village to bring this story to fruition. I know I'm going to leave out some very important participants in the process, and for that I'm truly sorry.

The words "thank you" seem woefully inadequate to express my heartfelt appreciation to Donnell Ann Bell for being my longest-running critique partner, the president of my fan club, the one person who could talk me down from the bridge when the writer's life was wearing me down, and for taking on the role of my agent (even though you still aren't getting 15%!). Love you, girlfriend.

The same goes for Hank Phillippi Ryan. I don't know where she finds the time to write her own incredible novels on top of her day job of investigative reporter, yet she never fails to eagerly offer to help me anytime, anywhere. Hugs, Hank!

Thank you thank you thank you to Nancy Martin who has kicked my butt on any number of occasions, who has taught me more about writing a compelling story than any book or course could, and who played matchmaker one summer a couple of years ago, putting together a group of local writers from which developed my beloved critique circle.

Since I'm on the subject, thanks so much to my three friends and wonderfully brutal critiquers Judith Schneider, Jeff Boarts, and Tamara Girardi. They've suffered and celebrated along with me. And trust me when I say no one ever wants to incur the Wrath of Jeff.

To my online Fatal Four critique group, as well. Donnell, Mike Befeler, and L.C. Hayden. Thanks, guys!

I also lay claim to the best team of "beta readers" imaginable. Thanks to Kristine Coblitz, Paula Matter, Meredith Mileti, Jessi Pizzurro, Stephanie Szramowski, and Joyce Tremel for taking the time to pick apart the entire manuscript.

A big shout-out to my keen-eyed friend Mary Sutton for being my proofreader extraordinaire.

Many thanks to the experts at Crime Scene Writers for answering those pesky research questions. And while I'm on the topic of research, thanks to the Pittsburgh Bureau of Police Citizen's Academy and to Robin Mungo and the Pennsylvania State Police Citizen's Academy. Any errors in procedure within these pages are strictly my fault, not theirs.

I would not have survived the years of trial and error and rejection without the support and guidance of the Pennwriters and Sisters in Crime. Most of the names I've just listed are folks I met through one or both of these fabulous organizations.

Last but far from least, thank you to my Henery Press Hen House family, especially my incredible editor Kendel Flaum. You have made the process of converting a manuscript to a novel a true pleasure. Henery Press rocks!

ONE

Zoe Chambers eased the Monongahela County EMS ambulance to a stop next to a heap of dirty snow. The overhead dusk-to-dawn light revealed a fire hydrant poking through the mound, which explained why that spot remained vacant on a street otherwise packed with cars, trucks and SUVs. No one would ticket an emergency vehicle, though. At least, no one had in the dozen years she'd been a paramedic. She hoped tonight wouldn't be a first.

"This meeting is gonna be a disaster," Zoe said. But she and Earl were going only as observers, not medics. She hoped. "Look at the parking lot. Everyone in town is here. Who doesn't love a good riot, right?"

"It's our civic duty to stay informed. That's what I say." Earl fingered the radio mic and reported their location and in-service status to the Emergency Operations Center. "Especially when you never know what the local tyrant is going to pull next."

Zoe zipped her coat. "The Steelers didn't make the playoffs, and the Penguins don't have a game tonight. What else is there to do around here?" Personally, she'd rather return to the station and crash on the lumpy sofa. With the weathermen forecasting eight to ten inches of snow overnight, down time might be at a premium for a while.

"The way Jerry McBirney has the township residents pissed off, I still think this would be the big draw of the night."

That bastard Jerry McBirney. Another good reason to avoid the meeting. Earl was going to owe her. Big time.

A blast of frigid air smacked Zoe in the face as she opened the driver's door and stepped down, her work boots splashing in the slush. Winter in southwestern Pennsylvania bounced back and forth between snow and slushy slop. Icy white pellets swirled in the wind, reinforcing her trepidation that the winter storm advisory might not be an exaggeration.

Pulling the fur-trimmed hood of her parka over her head, Zoe jogged toward the meeting hall. Earl caught up to her and reached out to open the door. A cacophony of discontent blasted them as they stepped inside. He nudged her with an elbow and leaned closer so she could hear him above the clamor. "I'll catch you later."

She nodded, and he disappeared into the throng.

At an ordinary meeting, attendance might top out at a dozen residents. This evening, the room was filled to capacity. At the front of the hall, the rural township's three supervisors sat behind a long table, facing a few hundred angry locals.

The chairman, Jerry McBirney, pounded his gavel. "I demand order," he bellowed, glowering at his constituents.

Even the sound of his voice sent the muscles in Zoe's neck into spasms. From the back of the room, a slender woman waved both arms. Zoe lifted a hand in response and made her way through the crowd toward her best friend, Rose Bassi.

A man in a quilted flannel shirt stood. "You're claiming perks that no supervisor has ever gotten in the past."

The chairman tipped his head at a well-dressed woman seated to one side of the table. "Our township solicitor says otherwise."

"A solicitor you hired against the residents' wishes," another man said.

"This is getting us nowhere." McBirney cracked the gavel again. "Next order of business."

Zoe side stepped through a crowded row, avoiding knees and feet.

Rose moved her coat and purse from an empty chair beside her. "I didn't expect to see you here. Aren't you on duty?" she whispered.

Zoe settled into the cleared seat. "Earl loves political drama and just had to check out the action."

"Are you placing bets on who throws the first punch at Jerry?"

Zoe bit back a laugh. "Maybe. Where's your husband? If there are punches to be thrown at McBirney, I'd think he'd want to be in on it."

Rose checked her watch. "Ted must have gotten hung up at the fire station. He'll be here."

An older man with deep crevices carved in his leather-brown skin was on his feet. "Nothing's been done yet about that sign on the new four-lane. Folks keep exiting there, thinking it's the road to town, but they just end up stuck in the mud back in the game lands. I have to haul at least one car a week outta there with my tractor. And diesel ain't cheap no more."

McBirney waved a hand, dismissing him. "Joe, I've told you before, that's up to the state. You need to talk to PennDOT, not me. Next order of business." The chairman narrowed his eyes at the crowd. "Since I'm serving this township full time, I feel it's only fair that the township covers my health insurance costs."

A man Zoe recognized as the owner of the feed store leaped to his feet. "Are you kidding me? Vance Township supervisors don't qualify for township funded insurance coverage until they've been in office for two years. What you're proposing is clearly against the law."

McBirney again slammed his gavel against the table's surface. "Everything we do is legal and above board." He puffed up his barreled chest. "You people are just too stupid to understand the law."

"Oh, good way to make friends, Jerry," Zoe muttered under her breath.

McBirney continued as if everyone were in total agreement with him. "I move that we waive the two-year service requirement for the chairman to receive health coverage from the township insurance providers."

"I second the motion," said Matt Doaks, the supervisor seated next to McBirney, although the crowd all but drowned him out.

"I have a second. All in favor?" McBirney said.

"Aye," said McBirney and Doaks.

"Opposed?"

"Nay," said Howard Rankin, the third supervisor.

"Motion carries," McBirney shouted over the protests of the residents.

"Terrific." Rose huffed. "Anymore, it's not *if* he's going to pull something at each meeting. It's more a matter of *what* he's going to pull."

"I know. That's why we're all here," Zoe whispered back. "How does he keep getting away with this?"

Rankin stood up and winged an empty water bottle toward a trash can. He missed, and the plastic bottle skittered across the floor. He kicked his chair back and stomped into the VFW's kitchen.

McBirney glared after him. "We'll take a five minute recess while everyone regains their composure."

Zoe shrugged her shoulders, popping a knot of tension. "Who voted for McBirney, anyway?"

"Look around." Rose motioned to the crowd. "All these fine citizens fell for his line of bull about bringing change to the township. Well, we got change for sure. We now have a supervisor who's lining his pockets at our expense and acts as if the entire township was put here to do his bidding."

Dark memories she'd tried to forget for years swirled too close to the surface. "He's a beast." Zoe spoke the words so softly she didn't think anyone, even Rose, heard her.

But the look Rose gave her indicated otherwise. "You would know."

The room quieted except for the creak and scrape of folding chairs as some folks moved to gather in small groups. Others remained in their seats, fuming in silence. McBirney shuffled through a pile of papers on table in front of him.

Zoe forced her thoughts onto a different path. "How are the kids? Allison hasn't called me for a riding lesson in over two months."

Rose heaved an exaggerated sigh. "She's driving us nuts. It's like she's suddenly become possessed by the demon hormones. Have you seen her since she dyed her hair?"

"No." The girl had a perfect long auburn mane. Why in the world would she dye it?

Rose tugged at her own short red tresses. "Black. She's gone Goth. But that's not the worst of it." Rose leaned closer, speaking in hushed tones. "A month ago, we caught her with one of those high school jocks. A senior. And Allison was stripped down to her bra." Rose shook her head. "She didn't even seem embarrassed when we busted her."

"What did you do?"

"Ted tossed Mr. Football Star out on his ass. Then we took the door off Allison's room."

Zoe snickered. "Taking away her privacy? That's capital punishment to a teenage girl."

"She finally got her door back two days ago. It remains to be seen how long it stays. Oh. Here comes Ted now."

Rose sprang to her feet, waving. Zoe followed her friend's gaze. Near the door, Ted Bassi managed to spot his wife's vigorous flagging. He threaded his way through the crowd, toward them.

"Evening, ladies." Ted bussed his wife on the cheek before squeezing into the seat next to her. "Did I miss anything?"

"Just Jerry being his usual pushy self," Rose said.

Ted removed his fogged eyeglasses and wiped them with a bandana. "I saw the ambulance out front. I thought maybe something had happened."

"Not yet," Zoe said. "We're just hanging out here in case someone spills blood."

"Could happen. The way Commandant McBirney's been treating my mom lately, could even be me spilling his."

Rose patted his knee. "You promised to keep your cool this time, remember?"

Ted shrugged. "Did I? I don't recall."

Howard Rankin returned with a fresh bottle of water. Zoe noticed he hadn't brought any for his two compatriots.

McBirney cracked his gavel. "Next order of business." A smirk crossed his face. "I hereby call for the dismissal of township police secretary, Sylvia Bassi."

Ted's chair crashed to the floor as he leapt to his feet. "On what grounds?"

The smirk blossomed into a smug smile. "Theft of township property."

"*What* township property? My mother's never stolen anything in her life."

Zoe spotted Sylvia Bassi near the front, as the white-haired woman looked back at her son. Even from her seat in the back row, Zoe could see the shock in Sylvia's eyes.

"She stole a computer from the police department."

"I did not." Sylvia looked more like the township grandma than the township thief. "It was a junk computer. They told me to dispose of it, so I took it home for Ted's kids to play with when they come to visit."

"There. You heard it from her own lips. She admits taking it."

"But not *stealing* it," Ted said, his words drowned by the roar of outrage coming from the crowd.

"This is absurd," Rose said to Zoe over the din. "Why on earth would he..."

Ted and everyone else in the hall were on their feet. Their words crashed into each other so that Zoe could hear nothing clearly. Jerry McBirney's face was as red as the letters on the exit sign above the door to his left.

Rose nudged her with an elbow. "Look who just walked in."

Zoe had to weave and bob to see around the people standing in front of her. Just inside the door, Police Chief Pete Adams dusted snow from his black jacket. Her pulse quickened. Tall, rugged, and impressive, if anyone could handle Jerry McBirney's idiocy, it was Pete.

The chairman also noticed the new arrival. "Chief Adams. I'm glad you're here."

You are? Zoe thought.

The room fell silent.

Pete Adams wore his poker face. The one with those unreadable clear blue eyes Zoe had studied at many Saturday night card games. They'd worked side-by-side in the years since he'd taken over as chief, dealing with everything from the mangled remains of traffic accidents to gunshot wounds to drunks passed out in the street. Theirs was a friendship forged of mutual respect and admiration.

"Take this woman into custody." McBirney pointed at Sylvia who clutched a tissue to her face.

"I have to get back to work," Zoe whispered to Rose. In truth, she hoped to catch a moment alone with Pete.

"Uh-huh." Rose gave her a knowing look. "Say hello to the chief for me. And tell him to trump up some charges against that maggot, McBirney."

Zoe's cheeks warmed. So much for hiding ulterior motives from her best friend. She edged her way out of the row, hoping to work her way toward Pete before things got ugly again.

"Now, Jerry." Pete fixed the chairman with an icy stare. "Why would I want to arrest Mrs. Bassi?"

"I want her charged with theft of township property."

"I'm sure we can talk about this." Pete's gaze swept the room, and most of the irate citizens lowered into their chairs.

"There's been enough talking. Arrest her. Arrest her now." McBirney's face had deepened from red to almost violet.

Pete looked weary. "Jerry—"

"Chief, must I remind you that you work for me? You follow my orders."

Zoe froze. The ugly history between Pete Adams and his new "boss" was no secret. Besides, throwing Sylvia Bassi in jail would be akin to arresting the police department's own personal den mother.

A soft rumble rolled over the room, as everyone murmured their theories and waited.

Then Pete stepped over to Sylvia and extended a hand. "Let's go outside and talk," he said with a sad smile.

McBirney stood rooted in his spot behind the table and appeared on the verge of stomping his foot. "I want her arrested," he boomed.

Pete fixed him with a steely stare and replied in a voice only those closest to him could hear. Whatever he said finally silenced McBirney.

Sylvia took Pete's hand and climbed to her feet. The police chief helped her with her coat and then held the heavy steel door for her. As soon as it drifted closed, the room erupted.

Zoe maneuvered her way along the wall. Noise and heat pressed in on her from all sides. When she slipped through the same doors that Pete and Sylvia had used moments earlier, the quiet and the cold of the January night offered glorious relief. The ice pellets had softened into white snowflakes. They drifted through the night air, dusting the grass with a powdered sugar coating and melting where they fell on salted concrete.

Zoe spotted Pete helping Sylvia into the passenger seat of his SUV. She broke into a jog toward them.

"What's going on?" Her breath created a cloud in front of her face.

Sylvia was twisting the strap of her purse. Pete met Zoe's gaze and rolled his eyes. He turned back to the older woman. "So tell me about this computer. And why is Jerry McBirney in such an uproar over it?"

"I've always been responsible for getting rid of the junk the township doesn't need anymore. That computer's been sitting in the back room for two years—since you replaced them with the new ones, remember?"

"Did the supervisors say you could take it?"

"No." Both Sylvia's lower lip and voice trembled. "But I didn't think I needed permission. No one had touched the thing in ages."

The doors of the township building burst open. Four people and a few hundred angry voices spilled out into the snow. Ted Bassi led the brigade toward the police vehicle. On his heels marched McBirney and Matt Doaks. Bringing up the rear, wobbling on stilettos not designed for rural townships' gravel parking lots, came Elizabeth Sunday, the well-dressed township solicitor. Zoe had only seen the woman sitting in meetings, calm, reserved and arrogant. In a stylish, but lightweight jacket—too lightweight for any winter night, but especially this one—and the kind of shoes that Zoe had only seen on television shows about cities and sex, Elizabeth Sunday had stepped out of her element the moment she'd exited the building.

"Terrific," Pete said with an exasperated sigh. "Here we go again."

Zoe motioned to two teenagers loping toward them from the opposite direction. "That's only the half of it."

TWO

The tall, scrawny boy jogged across the snowy parking lot toward them, holding up his oversized jeans with both hands. Logan Bassi reminded Zoe of the ladies in old western movies, hoisting their skirts and petticoats.

Behind Logan came an equally thin, but somewhat shorter, girl with long jet-black hair. Allison wore a bulky blue and white jacket with the high school's Blue Demons decal stitched to the front, and her faded jeans were as tight as her brother's were huge.

"Here come your grandkids, Sylvia," Zoe said.

The woman leaned out from her perch in Pete's passenger seat, looking wild-eyed toward the kids.

"Damn," Pete said with a growl. "This just gets better and better."

Ted reached the Vance Township Police vehicle first. "Don't you dare arrest my mother, Pete."

Huffing, McBirney trudged up behind Ted. "That computer contains vital township records."

"What?" Sylvia's voice creaked. Zoe wondered if the flush in the woman's chubby cheeks was a result of embarrassment or the cold.

"What are you doing with my grandma?" Logan demanded.

And then everyone, except Zoe and Pete, spoke at once. There hadn't been a mob scene like this in the VFW's parking lot since the drunken brawl last summer at the Morgan-Platt wedding.

Pete brought his thumb and middle finger to his lips. Knowing what was coming next, Zoe jammed her hands against her ears.

His whistle sliced the cold night air and probably stopped traffic all the way to the far end of town. It also brought a halt to the bickering.

"Look, guys." Pete struck his take-charge pose, one hand on his hip, the other resting on his sidearm. "We aren't going to solve any of this tonight."

McBirney opened his mouth, but Pete raised an authoritative hand to silence him then turned to Sylvia. "I'm sorry, but I'll have to file papers with the magistrate in the morning. You should probably call a lawyer to help you sort this mess out. Ted, do you know an attorney or do you need me to recommend one?"

Ted's breath hung like fog around his head. "I have one, Pete. Thanks."

Who else besides Pete Adams could have someone thank him for arresting their mother?

McBirney took a step closer to Pete. "Aren't you going to throw her in jail?"

"No. I can write her up a citation if you insist, but I'd rather save a tree."

Elizabeth Sunday rested a manicured hand on McBirney's arm. "That will do for now, Jerry. The magistrate will issue the arrest warrant, and we can proceed from there."

McBirney drew in a deep breath. Then he blew it out, reminding Zoe of a deflating balloon. "Fine." He glared at Pete. "This isn't over by a long shot."

"I never expected it was."

McBirney's gaze settled on Zoe. The chairman might have been considered attractive by some with his outdoorsman physique and chiseled features, but she only saw pockmarked skin and the deep creases lining his face. And his eyes. Those dark, soulless eyes.

He leaned toward her until she could smell the stale cigarette smoke on his breath. "How you doin', blondie?" He winked.

Sickened by the breath, the voice, and the memories they stirred, Zoe clenched a fist, fighting a desire to use it on him.

McBirney ambled back toward the VFW with Elizabeth Sunday tottering after him.

Matt Doaks watched them go, but instead of following them, moved closer to Pete's SUV.

Logan bent forward next to Sylvia, the bottoms of his baggy jeans wicking moisture from the wet pavement. "Are you all right, Grandma?"

Allison hugged herself against the cold, her eyes darting from face to face and settling on Matt.

"I'm fine, dear," Sylvia said. "This is all just a big mistake. We'll get it straightened out."

Logan's gaze shifted to Pete. "Can I take Grandma home now?"

Pete nodded.

"I can give you a lift in the ambulance." Zoe didn't want Sylvia walking in the cold, especially after the stress of a theft accusation. She turned to Ted. "Unless you want to take them?"

He shook his head. "I'm going back to the meeting. Someone ought to just kill that guy and put him out of my misery."

"You probably shouldn't say stuff like that when the cops are around," Pete said with a crooked smile.

Ted sniffed. "Allison. Go with your brother and grandmother."

The teenager with the Goth-black hair had wandered over to stand near Matt Doaks. She stared at him with the kind of star-struck, come-hither smiles girls generally reserve for some hot, young movie star. Matt, tall, thin, and rakishly handsome, had a reputation as the local non-celebrity heartthrob. Zoe understood his appeal all too well, having spent a large chunk of her own youth caught in his orbit.

But no father wanted to see his teenaged daughter getting horny, especially over a thirty-five-year-old man who obviously enjoyed the attention. "*Allison.*" Ted's voice took on that sharp, no-nonsense parental tone that all kids recognize.

"Coming, Dad." She batted her dark eyelashes at Matt one last time and swaggered toward Zoe, her narrow teenaged backside doing an impressive little bump-and-grind.

"Breathe, Ted," Zoe whispered.

"I'm going to lock her in her closet until she's forty," he said before following McBirney and the lady lawyer.

"I'd like to see that." Pete chuckled. "You make sure they get home, okay?"

"Yeah." Zoe dug her cell phone from her pocket. "I'd better tell Earl I'll pick him up when I swing back around."

"With this snowstorm blowing in, it'll be an interesting evening."

Logan helped his grandmother from Pete's vehicle.

Pete and Zoe tipped their heads in silent goodbyes. As she guided

Sylvia and the kids toward the ambulance, she noticed Matt still watching them.

Pete scanned the computer screen through his reading glasses. After fixing two typos, he clicked *print*. The HP all-in-one whirred into action. Ordinarily, his secretary would type up the affidavit requesting an arrest warrant. But considering that his secretary, Sylvia Bassi, was also the arrestee, having her do the paperwork might be a little crass.

While he waited for the pages to print, he whipped off the readers and poured the dregs from the coffee maker into his monster-sized mug. Sipping the bitter, hours-old brew, he renewed his silent wish for a Starbucks to open in Dillard. Or even Phillipsburg, two miles away.

The bells on the police station's front door jingled. Pete checked his watch. Five after eleven at night. Expecting a resident with a dire emergency and an aversion to telephones, he stood and stretched. Before he made it to his door, Sylvia appeared. Fat snowflakes nestled in her gray hair, melting into droplets glittering in the overhead fluorescent lighting.

"I saw the lights on," she said. "What are you doing here so late?"

"I could ask you the same thing."

"Yeah, but I asked first. Your insomnia kicking up again?"

"It takes an insomniac to know one."

Sylvia nodded at the coffee cup in his hand. "Maybe, but I can't blame caffeine. That stuff doesn't help, you know."

Pete set the mug down and side-stepped to the printer. He hoped to appear nonchalant as he scooped the pages from its tray.

The carefree attitude didn't work. "Is that for Judge Mitchell?"

He hated this whole ordeal. He hated that he had to put Sylvia through what was obviously nothing more than a waste of time. He hated that he had to kiss that son-of-a-bitch Jerry McBirney's ass. And while he was running over his personal hate list in his head, he decided to add that he just plain hated Jerry McBirney.

"It is, isn't it? And it's about me." Sylvia heaved a massive sigh and moved to her desk caressing its old oak surface with her fingers. "I know I shouldn't be here, seeing as I've been fired."

"McBirney made the motion. I didn't hear it pass."

"It did. After we left. Ted phoned and told me. They called the meeting back to order. Then Matt Doaks seconded the motion. His and McBirney's votes overrode Howard's dissension. You know, I used to like that Doaks kid."

Pete smiled. Matt Doaks was a long way from being a kid. But Pete, at forty-five, had ten years on the guy, and Sylvia still called *him* a kid, too. "Don't worry about it. McBirney's just trying to throw his weight around. Give it a few days and I'm sure this will all go away."

"Like it did when he got involved with your Marcy?"

Ouch.

"I'm sorry. I shouldn't have said that."

Pete waved her off. He had plenty of reasons to despise Jerry McBirney. Granted, the fact that the guy was now married to Pete's ex ranked pretty high.

"You know, Pete, I used to think the worst day I'd ever had on this job was way back when the township's receipts went missing. But this definitely beats all." Sylvia's voice cracked. "I'll get Ted to help me pack up my things tomorrow."

"I'd rather you didn't. These charges will never stick. McBirney's just making noise."

"But I don't know if I want to work in this township anymore." Tears welled in her eyes. "Things have changed so much in the last few months, and I don't see them getting better anytime soon."

Pete wished he could argue with her, but he knew how she felt. Only he wasn't about to give that bastard McBirney what he wanted. Not without a fight. As if that had made any difference before.

"Ted is in a fury over all this," Sylvia said. "He's been in a foul mood a lot lately what with the kids being typical teenagers and all. Now this business with my job and stealing township property...I've never seen him so angry. And that crack he made in front of you was...well..."

"Stupid," Pete finished for her with a grin. How many times had he heard someone say they wished someone else dead? "But understandable considering the circumstances."

The phone on Sylvia's desk rang. She reached for it and then hesitated. "Oh. I guess I shouldn't answer that."

"Sylvia, get the damned phone."

A smile flashed across her face, and she picked up the receiver. "Vance Township Police Department."

Pete watched as she said "Uh-huh" a couple of times before picking up her pen. "How long has it been there? Uh-huh. No, no, Joe, you're absolutely right. Something needs to be done. Uh-huh. Yes, I'll send somebody out there right away. Uh-huh. Thanks, Joe." She hung up. "That was Joe Mendez."

"Let me guess. Someone's stuck out in the game lands by his property again."

"You got it. He says he doesn't see anyone around, so they likely got out and started hiking. But with the weather as bad as it is..."

"Yeah. We might have someone wandering around lost in the snow in the middle of the night." Pete reached for his jacket hanging on the coat tree in the corner.

"Don't you want me to radio Seth?"

"He's already working a traffic accident out on Babcock Road."

"How about Kevin?"

"Home with the flu. It's all right. I'll check it out."

Sylvia wiggled out of her long wool coat and tossed it onto the peg Pete's jacket had just vacated. Then she slid into her chair. Pete almost told her to go home, but changed his mind. If McBirney had his way, this might be the last evening of overtime the two of them put in together.

In the two and a half hours that Pete had been inside, the snow showers had turned into a blizzard. He grabbed a broom and swept almost four inches of white stuff from the black and white SUV the township had recently purchased, secondhand, for him. At least it started when he finally dug his way inside. That was never a given with the old Crown Victoria he'd been driving since he left his job as a homicide detective in Pittsburgh eight years ago, and moved here.

Either the snow plows hadn't been out yet or the snow was keeping ahead of them, because the roads were covered. Tire tracks indicated a few brave souls were out and about. But Pete didn't see another vehicle as he drove through town and out into the dark country night.

At least the need to focus on his driving kept his mind from wandering to Sylvia. Or McBirney. Or Ted. Or Marcy. If Route 15 was this treacherous, he knew better than to tackle the back roads. So he took the longer way around to the new highway. The one with the confusing signage. He understood why so many people, unfamiliar with the newly completed expanse of road, mistakenly took the wrong exit. It was clearly marked "Phillipsburg." And while it was true that one could eventually arrive there by taking that road, it required traveling some rather rugged dirt roads through the state game lands.

Pete doubted anything shy of the most serious four-wheel-drive vehicles could manage that trip that night. And he really hoped whoever had made the wrong turn was not wandering around in the dark, snowy woods.

It occurred to Pete that the call had come from Joe Mendez and not from the stranded motorist's own cell phone. Maybe their phone's battery was dead.

The exit loomed ahead. Pete eased off the gas and coasted around the loop of the ramp, steering gingerly to keep his vehicle on the road. Had there been tire tracks here earlier, the snow had since filled them in. He was only about three hundred feet off the ramp when his headlights flashed off a car sitting next to the dirt road, tipping precariously toward the passenger side. Stuck in a ditch. And covered in snow.

Pete parked several car-lengths behind the stranded vehicle and hit it with his spotting light, illuminating the license plate.

Something wasn't right. This was not the car of someone who didn't know the area. The vanity plate read BIGJMC.

What the hell was Jerry McBirney doing out here on a night like this?

Pete grabbed his flashlight and climbed out of the SUV. Ankle deep in snow, he approached the car, shining the flashlight into the interior with his left hand while his right hand rested on his sidearm. The beam revealed an empty backseat. The passenger seat likewise appeared vacant. But a dark figure sat behind the wheel. Keeping his breath slow and even, Pete stepped up to the driver's side window, swiped it clear, and shined his light through it.

After all these years as a cop, dead bodies still made his stomach knot.

"Damn it, Ted," he muttered.

THREE

The wind had picked up. The cold penetrated Zoe's bomber jacket, bit at her cheeks and fingers, and numbed her toes. Adrenalin kept a person warm for only so long under these conditions.

"I don't need an ambulance." Their patient hiccupped between sobs and held a gob of 2x2 gauze squares to her bloody nose. "My husband is gonna kill me." Her car faced eastbound on southbound Babcock Road. The vehicle's front end was mashed from an encounter with a tree. And from the extent of damage, Zoe guessed the driver had gone way over any sensible speed on the snow-coated roads.

"Miss, I have to recommend that you see a doctor," Earl said. "Your nose is likely broken."

The woman drew the gauze away from her face. She blanched at the sight of blood and dissolved into another round of hysterical weeping.

A contingent of volunteer firefighters attempted to clean up the debris scattered across the snowy road. Zoe noticed Ted wasn't with them.

Officer Seth Metzger approached, fumbling to slip his cell phone into his pocket with fingers buried in bulky gloves. "Mrs. Lyle? I just spoke to your husband. He's on his way to pick you up. That is if you're sure you don't want the paramedics to take you to the hospital."

"I'm sure."

"You can sit in the back of the squad car if you want. To keep warm."

Mrs. Lyle shivered. "No, thanks. I'm fine."

"Suit yourself." Seth shrugged and trudged away.

"We'll need you to sign this." Zoe held out the aluminum clipboard and a pen to the woman.

She shook her head. "I'm not signing anything. My husband's always pointing out those commercials where the lawyers say—"

"Miss, it only states you're refusing treatment," Earl said. "You either sign it, or you get in the ambulance and let us take you to the hospital."

Mrs. Lyle looked around, as if searching for legal advice in the blizzard. Sniffling, she accepted the clipboard and scrawled an illegible signature with a trembling hand before returning it to Zoe.

"You must be freezing. Maybe you ought to take Officer Metzger up on his offer."

The woman's cheeks glowed pink in the emergency lighting. She gave her head another shake, pressed the gauze to her face, and picked her way through the snow and the ice, toward the wreckage of her car.

Zoe handed the blood-smudged report to Earl. "Do you get the feeling there's a story there?"

"Yeah, but I don't want to hear it. Let's get out of here. My feet are frozen."

Mine, too, Zoe thought. "I'll go tell Seth we're leaving."

"Meet you in the unit."

Zoe patted her gloved hands together as if that might help. She scuffed through the snow toward the police officer, who was lighting another flare to replace one that had burnt down.

"Hey, Zoe." Seth gave her a grin. "Can't you and Earl charm that poor girl into taking a ride in your nice warm ambulance?"

"She seems more concerned about how her husband's going to react. There's nothing else we can do here, so we're pulling out."

"I'll stick around until this mess is cleaned up." Seth's cell phone rang. "With the looks of the weather, I'll probably see you again before the night's over."

"Wouldn't doubt it." Zoe left him digging for his phone.

When she climbed into the passenger seat, Earl was scribbling notes on the call report. Zoe unclipped the mic from the dashboard. "Control, this is Medic Three. Show us back in service."

"Copy that, Medic Three. Your time is twenty-three forty-one," responded the voice from the Emergency Operations Center.

Earl heaved a growling sigh. "Damn it. It's almost midnight already. I was hoping to get some sleep."

Zoe clipped the mic back in place. "Well, if our local residents are smart and stay home, we might have a quiet night from here on."

Someone thumped on the driver's side window. Earl flinched. "Shit. Now what?" He rolled it down.

Seth stood there, a grim look on his face. "Chief just called. He wants us all to meet him at the game lands exit on new Route 33 for a DOA. He said not to put it over the air, so you might want to phone it in to the EOC."

"Gotcha. See you there." Earl rolled the window up and glared at Zoe. "You just had to jinx it, didn't you?"

"Me? You were the one wishing for sleep." She dug her phone from one of the pockets in her cargo pants and called the dispatcher to report their status.

"I wonder why the chief doesn't want this going over the air," Earl said.

She wondered the same thing.

The ambulance's headlights glared off the wall of white snow blowing sideways across the road in front of them. High beams only made it worse. Zoe clutched at the armrest, knowing that Earl was making an educated guess as to where the edge of the road was. Thank goodness for tire chains.

"At least the victim's already dead," he said. "We don't have to worry about being in a rush."

"That's the exit everyone's been complaining about."

"Yeah. If someone got lost out in the game lands and died of exposure in this weather, there could be a lawsuit in the making. Might be what it takes to get those signs changed."

Zoe thought of old Joe Mendez at the next supervisors' meeting. He would be wagging his finger at everyone now, saying, "I told you so."

But mostly she was thinking of the call ahead. She had taken on the duties of deputy coroner three years ago. What she'd imagined would be an intriguing job involving sleuthing and mystery-solving instead mostly involved calling the official time of death for elderly or drunk corpses discovered days after the fact. Monongahela County Coroner Franklin Marshall always made it a point to show up in person for all the interesting cases. This time she figured she'd have to pronounce a lost stranger dead. Cause of death: hypothermia. Manner of death: accidental.

A trip that should have taken ten minutes took over half an hour. As Earl wheeled the unit around the exit ramp, Zoe spotted the amber lights of a PennDOT salt truck beside the red and blue flashing lights of Pete's vehicle. The headlamps of both vehicles were aimed in the same direction, away from the ambulance's approach. Strategically placed flares provided additional illumination.

Earl parked alongside the idling yellow dump truck, adding yet another set of headlights to the scene. "At least we won't get stuck trying to get out."

Zoe phoned the EOC dispatcher before climbing out of the ambulance and following her partner toward the scene.

He pointed to the snow-covered vehicle in front of the police cruiser. "I don't see the chief."

The driver's side door was open on the victim's car, and Zoe could make out the glow of the dome light through the iced windows. As she and Earl approached, a strobe briefly lit the night.

Something wasn't right. Pete was photographing the car. So the victim hadn't gotten out and frozen to death trying to find help as she'd assumed.

Then, Zoe spotted the license plate.

"Hey," Earl said. "Isn't that Jerry McBirney's car?"

Oh, God, no. Jerry knew this area better than anyone. He would never have attempted the game lands road on a night like this. It would have been suicidal. And Jerry wasn't the suicidal type.

Ted's words rang in her ears. Someone ought to just kill that guy and put him out of my misery.

Ted, what the hell did you do?

She broke into a jog toward the car, her heart pounding in her ears. Before she got to the open driver's door, someone grabbed her. She looked up into Pete's grave face.

"Ted did not do this." Her voice created a veil of mist between them. "He couldn't kill anyone."

"He didn't." Pete slipped a supportive arm around her waist and walked the last few steps with her. "Are you going to be able to do this?"

She barely heard him. The white mist of her breath enveloped her. Her eyes were playing tricks on her. She blinked to clear the fog. But the body behind the wheel remained the same.

The body in the front seat of the Buick wasn't Jerry McBirney.

It was Ted.

Pete feared Zoe might do something uncharacteristic, like faint, when she saw the victim. Instead, she renewed his admiration for her by taking a deep breath of cold air and shaking it off. Literally. Through layers of parkas and winter gear, he felt her tremor, but then she drew herself up even taller than usual.

"I'm fine." Her teeth chattered as she pushed away from him.

"Good. Marshall's at a fatality in Buffalo Township. The county detectives are delayed because of road conditions. It looks like it's up to us on this one."

Behind them, Seth's car, emergency lights flashing, eased around the ramp from the highway.

"I'm ready." Zoe exchanged her winter gloves for Latex ones.

Pete wasn't sure he believed her. "I've taken photographs and processed the scene as much as I can here. The snow has pretty much obliterated any evidence we might have found outside the car. I called for a tow—get this car out of the weather—but I suspect it may take a while."

Earl stood behind the car, hugging himself against the bitter wind and bouncing from one foot to the other. "Is there anything I can do?"

Seth had parked his cruiser and was doing his best attempt to jog toward them in the deep snow. Pete motioned to him and said to Earl, "You two get the tarps out of the back of my vehicle. I want as much of the area around McBirney's car covered as possible. The county crime scene guys will want to go over it once they get here."

The pair headed off, and Pete turned to Zoe. "Let's do it."

He held the flashlight while she leaned into the driver's side of the Buick. She slid her fingers into the crease at Ted's throat. After several moments, she pulled her stethoscope from one of her jacket pockets and listened to his chest. Pete knew as well as she did that she wasn't going to hear anything.

She slid a penlight from her shirt pocket, only to have it slip from her fingers and drop into Ted's lap.

Pete couldn't make out the words she muttered, but had a good idea they weren't suitable for polite company. He caught her hand, giving it a squeeze. "It's okay. I've got it." He retrieved the penlight from between Ted's dead legs and passed it to her.

What a night for the coroner to be stuck elsewhere.

Zoe reached for Ted's eyeglasses, but paused. "Did you already photograph his face?"

"Of course."

She pointed at Ted's eyes. "Did you notice that?"

Pete moved in closer. Ted's eyeglass frames were bent. Yeah, he'd noticed. But he'd missed what Zoe was pointing at. One of the lenses was missing. He turned his flashlight downward and leaned further into the car, searching Ted's lap, the car seat, and the floor. Nothing.

"He might be sitting on it," Zoe offered.

"We'll find out." Pete dug his digital camera from inside his coat and snapped several additional close-ups.

Zoe gingerly removed the glasses and deposited them into an evidence bag. She scrawled her initials and the date on it before handing it to Pete.

Then she went back to work, flicking the penlight in both of Ted's eyes. "Fixed and dilated." She checked her watch then dug a notepad from her hip pocket and a pen from inside her coat. Pete shone the light on the paper as she scribbled her findings.

She handed the pad and pen to him. "You write. I'll examine."

He tugged off his gloves and tucked the flashlight under one arm. "Got it."

One at a time, she picked up Ted's hands and examined them. Then she secured each in two more paper bags. She took several minutes to study his face. Pete knew why.

"Multiple contusions and abrasions on his face." She scowled. "Note possible broken nose, too."

He wrote it all down.

She worked her way through Ted's hair and her frown deepened. "I can't tell for sure, but it feels like there may be a compressed skull fracture. Help me lean him forward."

Zoe supported Ted's head and neck while Pete grasped the shoulders and tipped the body toward the steering wheel. He considered reminding her that Ted's cervical spine was in no danger of injury at this point, but decided to keep quiet instead.

She finished her exam with a quick once-over of the body, back and then front. Marshall and his forensic pathologist would do a more thorough external examination and x-rays once Ted was in the morgue.

Easing out of the car, Zoe turned to Pete. "Rigor mortis is already setting into his extremities and his face."

"Can you guestimate his time of death?" Pete was fairly certain of what her answer would be.

"I wouldn't want to venture a guess based on anything here. But we know he died sometime after seven-thirty p.m. That's when we saw him—" Her voice cracked.

That's when they saw him outside the supervisors' meeting, threatening Jerry McBirney.

Pete pulled her into his arms. She clung to him, shivering and sniffing back sobs. Zoe liked to play tough, but he knew she cared deeply about those close to her. And she and Ted had been friends since before he'd married Rose. Pete suspected they'd possibly been more than *just friends* way back when, but he'd never asked, and she'd never told.

"What the hell happened to him, Pete?" she said with a shuddering breath.

"I don't know yet. But I will find out."

She pushed free from him. "We," she said. "*We* will find out." Zoe blew her warm breath onto her fingers and then reclaimed her notepad and pen. "Did you notice the ice crystals in his hair?"

"I did."

"His clothes are frozen, too. It's as though he went swimming fully dressed."

Pete touched the coating of snow melting in her blonde hair. "Or he was out in a snow storm."

Zoe met his gaze. "I think it's more than that. Look at his face. And there's a tear in the front of his jacket, but the back is fine. I think he was dragged face down."

Pete pondered her theory. "Dragged? Maybe. But I'd think his clothes would be a little more ripped than they are."

Chewing her lip, she studied Ted's body.

Flashing amber lights swept over the expanse of snow. A large flatbed truck advanced toward them from the exit ramp.

"Are you done here?" Pete asked.

"I guess so."

"Good. Here comes the tow truck."

He studied the gray, icy face of what had once been Ted Bassi. How had he come to be way out here on this bitter night in Jerry McBirney's Buick? Had he and Jerry gotten into a fight and Ted escaped, mortally wounded, in Jerry's car? And if he hadn't driven himself, who left him here and why?

So many questions burned in his mind. Not the least of which was where had McBirney been in the hours after the supervisor's meeting?

First things first. He wanted the Buick secured inside the township garage before the weather further ruined any evidence he might find.

Zoe doubted she'd ever be warm again. Earl blasted the heater inside the ambulance's cab during the long, treacherous drive from the game lands to the morgue in Brunswick. While the heat managed to penetrate her parka, it failed to chase the chill from her bones. She clamped her gloved hands under her armpits, but her fingers still ached from the cold.

They wasted no time delivering their charge to the attendant and filling out the paperwork. As soon as Ted's body was wheeled into the cooler, Zoe bolted for the door.

In all her years as a paramedic, and more recently as deputy coroner, the worst thing was arriving on scene to discover she knew the patient. Or victim. But she'd never before dealt with the death of a close friend.

Poor Rose. And the kids.

"You okay?" Earl asked as he steered out of the parking lot.

"What do you think?" Zoe snapped.

"Sorry. Stupid question."

She stared out the front window at the fat snowflakes, like a swarm of insects flying into their headlights.

Had Pete talked to Rose yet? When they'd parted company at the game lands, he had left Seth and Nate Williamson, one of his part-time officers who'd arrived with the tow truck, to secure the crime scene until County arrived. Pete had been on his way to talk to Joe Mendez. But after that, he'd have to notify Ted's family. His next of kin.

Zoe's cell phone rang, and she tugged off her gloves to answer it.

"Where are you?" Pete's voice asked.

"On our way back from the morgue. Have you seen Rose?"

"I'm heading there next."

There was a moment of silence on the line, and Zoe feared they'd been disconnected.

But then he continued. "I thought you'd like to be there when I talked to her."

The word "Yes" came off her tongue before she had a chance to think. "But—I'm still on duty for another five hours or so."

Earl never took his eyes off the snow-covered road. "Do what you need to do," he said. "All things considered, no one'll say anything about you taking the rest of the night off."

If her partner wasn't married with three kids, she'd have kissed him right then and there. "We're a good ten, maybe twelve miles from Dillard," she told Pete, "and we're making lousy time on these roads."

"I'll meet you next to the old Convenient Mart. Take your time."

Forty-five minutes later, Earl eased into the unplowed parking lot of what had been Dillard's only grocery store. Snow clung to the Real Estate For Sale sign concealing the details of the available retail space. Pete's SUV sat next to the building.

Zoe thanked her partner as she stepped out of the ambulance. He waved and pulled out, the tire chains biting into the snow and ice.

"How about we stop at the house first," Pete said as Zoe settled into the passenger seat. "Then you can stay with Rose and the kids while I go break the news to Sylvia. I'll bring her over afterwards."

"Sylvia doesn't know yet?"

"That's one reason I kept all communications off the air. She's manning the radio back at the station."

"Oh." Learning your son was dead over a police radio transmission would be horrific. Not that there was any good way of receiving news like that.

Pete wheeled the SUV out of the parking lot and coasted down the snow-covered hill, easing around the sharp bend at the bottom. Ted and Rose Bassi's house sat at the end of a narrow side street. The porch light was on, but otherwise the house was dark.

"I'm surprised," Zoe said. "You'd think Rose would be waiting up." She pictured her friend wearing a hole in the kitchen floor, pacing, wondering where her husband was. A deeper chill ran up her spine. "Something isn't right."

"She probably just fell asleep waiting for Ted to come home."

Zoe studied Pete's face, searching for a sign that he really believed what he said and wasn't just trying to keep her calm. But he'd been a cop too long to give away his true thoughts.

Fierce winds drove a swirl of snow into the car as soon as they opened the doors. Zoe pulled her collar closer around her neck and flipped the oversized hood over her head until they stepped onto the porch.

Pete held out an arm, directing her behind him. With his right hand resting on his sidearm, he pounded on the door with his left.

She listened for movement—footsteps indicating someone was home. All the time she'd been examining Ted's body, it had never occurred to her that he might not be the only victim. Had someone killed the entire Bassi family? Had Ted been trying to get help?

Pete banged on the door again. "Rose," he called. "It's Pete Adams. Open up. I need to talk to you."

This time a light flicked on behind the closed curtains followed by the thump-thump of feet on the floor. Zoe's knees went weak with relief.

The blinds on the door's window parted and an eyeball appeared between them. Then the deadbolt creaked and clicked and the door was yanked open.

Instead of Rose, a bleary-eyed Logan stood before them in flannel pajama bottoms that threatened to drop off his narrow hips.

He rubbed his eyes like a child. "What's going on?"

"May we come in?" Pete said.

"Yeah. Sure. I guess." He unlatched the storm door and stepped back.

Zoe followed Pete into what she'd always thought of as a cheery kitchen. "Logan, where's your mom?"

The boy sniffed as if he had a cold. "Mom? I guess she's still over at grandma's. Why?"

"Sylvia's?" Pete asked. She lived two doors over, but spent most of her waking time right here.

"No. My other grandma. Mom's mom. Grandma Bert. She's got the flu, so Mom's spending the night over there. Do you want me to get my dad?"

Zoe and Pete exchanged looks.

Logan sniffed again and glanced around the kitchen before grabbing a paper napkin from the table. "He must be sleeping. I waited for him to get the door when you knocked, but..."

"No," Zoe said as the boy turned toward the hall. Then she winced. She'd heard the anguish in her own voice and knew from the look on Logan's face that he'd heard it, too.

Pete caught her arm. "Go back out to my car and call Rose," he said into Zoe's ear. "Tell her she's needed at home." He drew away enough to meet her eye.

Zoe understood the intense gaze, the unspoken request. Try not to alarm. "Okay."

"Good." He turned to Logan, his tone professional. "Let's make some coffee while we wait for your mom to get home."

The kid was buying none of it. "What's going on?"

As Zoe stepped outside, she heard Pete's soothing voice calming the boy without using words like *everything's all right*. It wasn't.

She climbed back into the SUV and tugged off her gloves to fish her cell phone out of her pocket. It took a moment for her trembling fingers to locate Mrs. Bertolotti's number in her cell's address book.

On the fourth ring, Rose picked up with a sleep-fogged, "Hello?"

Words jammed in Zoe's throat, leaving her choking for the right ones.

"Hello?" Rose said again. "Is anyone there?"

"It's me," Zoe said, her voice raspy.

The fog was gone. "What's wrong?"

"I—I can't say on the phone. You need to get home. Now."

"Oh my God. Is it Logan?"

Zoe considered saying no, Logan's fine. But in her mind she played out the rest of the conversation. Rose would ask about Allison. And then

Ted. "Just come home." Zoe hung up before her friend had a chance to ask anything else. *Try not to alarm.* Well, she'd seriously failed at that one.

Now what? Should she stay in Pete's vehicle and wait for Rose? Or should she go inside and try to avoid a teenaged boy's inquisition? She could see Pete through the kitchen window. Filling the coffee pot from the sink, she presumed. Calm. Professional. In control. A shadow swept behind him. Logan. Pete would be giving him tasks to do to keep him occupied.

If she joined them, the balance of composure Pete was establishing would crumble into panic, concern, and frantic questions. No, she should stay right where she was.

Minutes passed. Zoe shoved her fists deeper into her pockets and slouched inside her coat, like a turtle in its shell hiding from the world. She closed her eyes, trying to block out reality, but Ted's battered face floated behind her eyelids. Blinking away the vision, she caught the sweep of headlights approaching from the rear of the police SUV and twisted in her seat. The car pulled up behind her.

Rose.

Zoe bounded from Pete's car and intercepted her friend as she staggered toward the sidewalk to her house.

"Zoe? What the hell's going on? Why's Pete here? What's happened?" Rose's voice faltered.

Maybe Zoe should have waited inside with Pete and Logan. She wrapped an arm around her friend's shoulders. "Let's go in the house."

Rose shook her off. "No. Tell me now. What's happened to my kids?"

A lump wedged in Zoe's throat. "The kids are fine. Pete's in there with Logan now."

"Then what?" Rose's gaze bored into hers.

"It's Ted."

Tears filled Rose's green eyes. "How bad is it? Is he..."

Zoe couldn't speak the words. *He's dead* refused to pass her lips.

It didn't matter. Rose knew. Her wail pierced the snowy night's silence.

FOUR

The scream jolted Pete into full alert. "Stay back," he barked at Logan. Two strides carried him to the door. He fingered his sidearm, ready to snap it free from the holster. With the other hand, he edged aside the curtain hanging on the door's window. Outside, two women knelt in the snow at the end of the sidewalk. Zoe had her arms around Rose. He relaxed his stance.

"What is it?" Logan asked.

Pete signaled him with a raised closed fist, but then remembered the kid didn't know what that meant. "Stay here. Keep an eye on the coffee." He snatched his coat from the back of the chair where he'd draped it and stepped out onto the porch.

Zoe looked up at him, panic in her eyes. Rose had collapsed, and Zoe was all that kept her from going face-down in the snow. Pete approached them, thinking Rose had passed out, but her keening told him otherwise. He dropped to his knees beside them.

"I should have let you break the news," Zoe whispered. Her face was damp with tears.

"Yes. You should have," he said, but kept his voice gentle. She didn't need to be chastised right now.

He scooped Rose up in his arms and carried her back to the house with Zoe trudging behind him.

What the hell was the kid going to do when he saw his mother in hysterics? So much for keeping everything low key. But to Pete's surprise, Rose thumped him on the shoulder when they reached the stoop.

"Put me down. I can't have my kids seeing me like this."

Atta girl, Rose. He lowered her to her feet, and she straightened to her full height, which barely reached five feet.

She swiped her arm across her face and sniffed a couple of times. "Was it a traffic accident? What happened to him?"

"We're not sure what happened just yet. I need you to answer some questions for me."

Rose gave him a quick scowl. "Are you sure it was Ted? Maybe there's been some mistake."

He squeezed her shoulder. "I'm sorry, Rose. There's no mistake."

She looked past him to Zoe. He didn't break eye contact with her to see Zoe's reaction, but she obviously backed him up. Rose's shoulders slumped. "I have to talk to my kids."

As they stepped into the kitchen, Logan launched out of his chair and caught his mother by her arms. "Mom, what's going on? No one will tell me anything."

"In a minute. Where's your sister?"

"Upstairs asleep."

Rose eyed Pete. "If it's all right with you, I'd like a few minutes alone with them."

"Absolutely. Take all the time you need."

She led her son into the darkened living room, and they disappeared down the hall.

Pete turned to face Zoe. Her face was streaked with tear-smudged mascara, and she hugged herself as if she were still out in the blizzard.

"Now what?" she said.

"Now we have coffee. It's going to be a long night."

They sat across from each other at the kitchen table for almost a half an hour, nursing their respective mugs of caffeine and not saying a word. Finally Rose shuffled into the room followed by Logan, and the Goth daughter...what was her name? Madison? Addison? Allison? Yes, that was it. Allison.

"Okay, Pete," Rose said, "I want to know exactly what happened."

"Is there someplace we can talk alone?"

He left Zoe in the kitchen with the kids and followed Rose down the hall to a small home office. Not much larger than a walk-in closet, the room contained two desks, two chairs, and two laptops. Shelves over one of them held assorted fire department memorabilia. That would be Ted's. The other desk was cluttered with real estate flyers. Pete had noticed Rose's name on several property for sale signs around the area.

Sinking into one of the chairs, she covered her face with her hands.

Pete removed his notebook and pen from his coat pocket. "I know this is lousy timing, but I need to ask you a few questions."

She dropped her hands into her lap. "First, I need to know what happened. Was it a car accident or not?"

"I'm hoping you can help me figure out the answer to that." He went through the usual questions, and she responded without hesitation. The last time she'd seen Ted was when they parted company after the supervisors' meeting around a quarter after eight. He was still pretty steamed and said he was going home. She was going to check on her mom who'd been ill.

"You were there all evening?"

"Yeah. Mom's flu seems worse. I was afraid she'd be too weak to get to the phone to call me if she needed help."

"Did Ted know you were staying?"

"I called the house, but got the machine. I figured Ted was in the shower."

"What time was that?"

"I dunno. About nine-thirty, I guess." Rose's voice broke into a sob. "What's this all got to do with what happened to Ted?"

All of her answers would be easy enough to confirm. Time to shift to the difficult questions. "I need you to think hard about this," Pete said. "Is there any reason at all that Ted would be driving Jerry McBirney's car?"

Rose blanched. "What?"

He waited for her to process his question.

"What the hell does Jerry McBirney have to do with this?" Her eyes shifted from Pete to the empty chair at Ted's desk and back to Pete. "Did they get into a fight? Did—did Jerry kill—"

"We don't know what happened yet. The car, Rose. Can you think of why Ted might be driving it?"

"No!"

"Did he have access to McBirney's keys?"

"*No!* Pete. What the hell is going on?"

* * *

Zoe sat in Ted and Rose's living room in one of the camel-back chairs. She had offered to make hot chocolate or even coffee for the kids, but was met with sullen rejection.

Logan had changed into baggy jeans and a sweatshirt. He paced the floor in his bare feet with one fist pressed to his mouth, attempting to tough it out, fighting tears that he was too old to shed. She longed to hug the boy she'd known his entire life and tell him everything would be okay. But she knew it wouldn't.

Slumped on the couch, Allison sat catty-corner from Zoe. Still wearing her pale blue pajamas, the girl was doing a great impersonation of a zombie. How was a fifteen-year-old supposed to react to the shock of losing her dad? Allison apparently chose to internalize her grief.

Zoe moved closer to Allison. What should she do? Pull her into a hug? Try to get her to talk? Try to get her mind off this terrible night?

She opted for the latter. "Hey, kiddo. You haven't called me to go riding in a while."

Without looking at her, Allison shrugged.

Zoe reached out to place a hand on her knee, but Allison pulled away, withdrawing into the seated equivalent of the fetal position.

Zoe sighed. She'd always been so close to these kids. Watching them grow into happy, feisty teens had been a blessing. Watching them agonize over Ted's death was torture.

The sound of footsteps coming from the hall drew her attention. Rose, looking as if she'd aged twenty years, followed Pete into the living room.

"You stay with them," Pete told Zoe. "I'm going to the station to talk to Sylvia."

"Grandma?" Logan stopped his pacing. "I should go with you."

"Thanks, but you're needed here." Pete clapped him on the arm. "Take care of your mother and your sister." He brushed passed Zoe, through the kitchen, and was gone.

"Mom?" Logan's strained tone snapped Zoe's attention away from Pete's back disappearing through the door.

Rose gripped the back of one of the living room chairs so tight, her knuckles went white. She tipped forward and Zoe thought she would tumble face first onto the floor, but Logan caught her. Sobs racked Rose's thin frame and she collapsed against him. Logan towered head and shoulders above his mother, but when his face twisted in despair, he reminded Zoe of the nine-year-old boy whose puppy had slipped its leash and been hit by a car so many years before.

Tears warmed Zoe's cheeks, too. She looked at Allison who had at least lifted her eyes and was watching the scene, though her face remained emotionless.

Stop fighting it, little one, Zoe wanted to say. You don't need to be tough for us.

"He's gone?" Rose hiccupped. "Zoe? Tell me it's not true."

Zoe crossed the room and drew mother and son into her embrace. "I wish I could," she whispered into Rose's hair. "I really wish I could."

The snow had finally stopped by the time Pete parked next to the station's front door and checked the dashboard clock. Three fifty-four.

Bells on the door jingled, announcing his return. Sylvia popped up behind the half wall, her faded blue eyes glazed with concern. "Well, it's about time. What the hell's been going on? Why wouldn't you tell me over the phone? I was afraid something had happened to you."

"I'm fine." Pete ran several possible versions of the upcoming conversation through his mind. "Come into my office. I need to talk to you about something."

She squinted at him. "What about?"

"Just come into my damned office already." Without waiting for more questions from her, he passed her door and hoped she would follow.

She did. Sylvia took a seat facing his desk and leaned her forearms on its edge.

Pete sunk into his well-worn chair. He met her curious gaze for a moment before looking away.

"All right, Pete. What's up? You get into trouble for not throwing my old ass into lock-up?"

"Nothing like that. But I'm afraid I have some bad news. It's about Ted."

"What about Ted? Oh, God. He beat the crap out of Jerry

McBirney, didn't he? I knew something like this was going to happen. That boy has got a temper—"

Pete reached over and put a hand on her arm. "Sylvia. That call about the car stuck in the game lands? There was a body inside. It was Ted."

The room grew quiet. Sylvia's mouth hung open. Her gaze slid from Pete to the desktop. "I don't think I heard you right. You mean Ted was on the fire crew at the scene."

"No, Sylvia. I mean Ted was the victim."

For several moments, the only sound in the office was the soft tick of the clock on the wall, counting off seconds. When she spoke, her words were little more than a squeak. "He's dead?"

"Yes."

Pete didn't notice her breathing. She slumped against the back of the chair.

"Sylvia?"

She blinked. And choked back a moan. "That son-of-a-bitch McBirney," she said, her voice low and deliberate. "That son-of-a-bitch killed my boy."

By eight o'clock in the morning, the sun was shimmering across a blinding white landscape. Bone weary, Zoe slipped on her sunglasses as she climbed into her battered Chevy pickup truck outside the ambulance garage, where Pete had dropped her off after taking Sylvia back to the house to watch over what was left of the Bassi family.

Zoe was glad there hadn't been any more calls in those last few hours before the daylight guys came staggering in to relieve her, Earl, and the four other members of her shift. Not that she'd gotten any sleep. She'd lain on the lumpy mattress and stared at the underside of the bunk above her, Ted's ghastly gray face fixed to the inside of her eyelids every time she ventured to close them.

The salt trucks were out, and while the roads weren't entirely clear, at least they were sloppy rather than slick. No sooner had Zoe pulled onto Phillipsburg's narrow Main Street than a car passed going the other way, splashing brownish, salty slush on her windshield. She cursed to herself for forgetting to fill the washer fluid reservoir and hoped she had enough to make it home.

Ten minutes later, when she pulled into the farm lane, she realized she didn't remember a thing about the trip. Her mind kept replaying the events from last night. Ted's body. Logan looking like a little boy trying to be a man. Allison withdrawing into herself, pushing her emotions into an unreachable cubby. And Rose, pale and in shock, then hysterical after Pete disclosed the details of where Ted's body had been found. He was her entire life. They were what all married couples should be—a team in every way. How would Rose get along without him?

Zoe was glad to see the farm lane had been plowed. She didn't feel like fighting with the transfer case to shift her twenty-year-old truck into four-wheel-drive. She braked as she approached the huge old white farmhouse, then opted to continue on to the barn.

The house—circa 1850s—boasted a wide center hall and staircase that split it in two. She rented one half—two rooms and a kitchen downstairs, a bedroom and bath upstairs—from Mr. and Mrs. Kroll, who were well into retirement age. When Zoe had approached them about the ad offering a portion of their house for rent as well as a stall for her horse, the timing had been perfect. They offered her both at a discount if she agreed to manage the barn. Considering her small-town paramedic's income barely covered the cost of gas for her truck and food for her and her critters, the deal was perfect. She made up the difference by giving riding lessons. Some months she even made enough for extravagances. Like clothes.

She trudged through the snow from her truck to the big barn—the new one with an indoor riding arena lined by stalls on two sides. Massive double doors on both ends were currently closed against the bitter wind. She slipped in through the standard-sized one facing the driveway.

Soft nickers greeted her. One of the boarders must have fed the horses or the whinnies would've been much more insistent. When she checked the dry-erase whiteboard on the wall by the feed and tack room, as predicted, Patsy Greene had left a note stating that she'd fed them an hour earlier. Patsy also noted that her horse, Jazzel, was to be kept in. The vet would be there late morning to check on the mare's mysterious lameness.

The familiar sounds of horses shuffling in their stalls, eager to be released and smells of warm manure mingling with hay and wood shavings should have soothed Zoe. But instead, the barn's peacefulness felt bizarre to her. How could the world just go on as if nothing had happened? Her body was stuck doing routine chores while her mind raced. She needed to do something. But what?

She checked her watch. Pete would be on his way to Jerry McBirney's house by now. Damn. She wanted to be there when Pete questioned that bastard. She wanted it so bad, she ached. But Pete had forbidden it. Claimed she might say or do something that would jeopardize any case he built against McBirney.

What annoyed her the most was that he was probably right. She preferred to think she could restrain herself when facing the man likely responsible for Ted's death—and so much more. But if she was honest with herself, she wasn't so sure she could hold back her anger.

George, the school pony, nudged her over his stall door, rousting her from her thoughts. Smiling, Zoe rubbed his furry ears. She decided to leave the pony in his stall next to Jazzel's to keep the fidgety Arabian mare company. After tossing both of them an extra flake of hay, Zoe put a shoulder into the huge sliding back door that opened into the pasture. It rebelled, then released with a loud, metallic grumble. Starting at the first stall, she unlatched and opened each one, stepping out of the way as the horses charged out and into the snow. Several immediately dropped and rolled in the white powder. One gave an impromptu bucking demonstration. The older ones simply ambled off, nose to the ground, sniffing out bits of grass beneath the snow.

The last horse she released to the outdoors was her own twelve-year-old Quarter Horse gelding, Windstar. He pawed at the stall door as she approached.

"Patience, Windy," she said, sliding the latch.

He snorted in response.

"Whoa." She used her firm, no-nonsense voice.

As if understanding the trouble he would be in if he misbehaved, he stood motionless, but alert, when Zoe opened the door.

She stepped to one side. "Okay."

He half-crouched and launched from the stall as if it were a starting gate, kicking up his heels as he charged across the empty arena and out of the barn.

Zoe followed him at a more subdued pace.

She checked her watch again. Ten whole minutes had passed. Pete was probably talking to McBirney. Rose was probably making phone calls.

There had to be something she could do. Franklin Marshall and Doc Abercrombie, the forensic pathologist, would perform the autopsy later today. She considered driving back into Brunswick for it, but no way did she want to watch Doc cutting into Ted. She should just finish her morning chores and get some sleep. Later there would be stalls to clean, water buckets to fill. Mundane daily tasks took no vacation because of a tragic thing like the death of a friend.

As she reached the door, her cell phone chirped. The name Logan appeared on the small screen..

"Aunt Zoe?" The teenager's voice trembled. "I need your help. I think I've done something really bad."

FIVE

Pete took another hit from his travel mug of strong, black coffee as he steered his vehicle into the long driveway leading to the McBirney house. Caffeine. What he really needed was an antacid to quell the churning in his gut. The thought of interrogating Jerry McBirney didn't bother him. In fact, to remain professional, he'd have to mask his satisfaction at the idea of arresting the asshole. No, Jerry wasn't the McBirney Pete dreaded. Marcy McBirney, formerly Marcy Adams, his ex-wife... He'd made it a point to avoid running into her. Until now.

The glare of the sun off the snow forced Pete to squint behind his sunglasses. The sputtering rumble of a tractor filtered through the Explorer's closed windows. As he topped the hill and eased down the other side, the farmhouse, barns and sheds stretched out before him. Odd shaped mounds of snow surrounded the outbuildings, indicating buried pieces of machinery and shrubbery.

What the hell had Ted Bassi been doing in Jerry McBirney's car? Had he driven out to the game lands alone? Or did someone drive him there and place his body behind the wheel? How and where had he sustained those injuries? Rose hadn't been able to give Pete any answers to his questions. Nor did she claim to have any knowledge of where Ted's old Ford F-150 pickup was.

Pete spotted the tractor maneuvering around the outside of the older barn below the house. A man he assumed was McBirney sat perched on top of it, bundled in brown Carhartt coveralls. The driver hadn't noticed Pete's arrival or perhaps chose to ignore him. Either was fine with Pete. He preferred to do a little quiet snooping before dealing with the questions anyway.

He'd spent the better part of an afternoon at the farm last summer investigating a wildfire, and he still recalled in which shed McBirney usually kept his Buick. He parked the Explorer in front of that building, cut the engine, and climbed out.

The wind had died down, but the January sun lacked the strength to warm the icy air. He looked at his travel mug. The contents would likely be cold or at least lukewarm by the time he returned to it. But he wanted his hands free so the coffee stayed behind.

He approached the shed that housed a baler, some tools, a John Deere lawn and garden tractor, and usually the pale blue Buick. Today, however, that bay stood empty.

"Hello, Pete."

Every muscle in his back clenched at the familiar voice. He pictured her face before he even turned. And when he did, his memory hadn't failed him. Marcy remained as drop-dead lovely as he recalled, even bundled in a hooded parka with her face half-hidden by a woolen scarf. She tucked her hands under her arms for warmth. Jeans hugged those incredible legs down to a pair of furry mukluks.

"Marcy," he said, trying to keep the chill from his voice. He wasn't sure he succeeded.

She tipped her head to one side. "What brings you out here?"

"Business."

"Well, I figured it wasn't pleasure." She looked toward the tractor moving snow from around the old barn. "Jerry will be up in a few minutes. I was just heading out to an appointment in town."

Perfect. "Don't let me stop you."

But she didn't move.

"It's okay. You can go." Pete made a shooing motion with his hand.

"I'm not in a hurry."

Damn. Marcy never did make life easy for him. "Do you mind if I look around?"

A scowl crossed her dark eyes. "Why?"

He shrugged, avoiding her gaze. "Why not?" He tried to sound flippant.

But she knew him too well. "I think maybe you should wait for Jerry."

"Fine." He swung his gaze to the shed as casually as he could. "Where's the Buick?"

Pete had caught her off-guard. "Huh?"

"Jerry's Buick. The one he parks over there." He motioned to the empty spot in the shed.

Marcy's eyebrows rose. The scarf failed to obscure the questioning frown. "I..." Her voice trailed off, and for a moment she was silent. Except for the wheels Pete swore he heard grinding in her head. "I suppose Jerry loaned it to one of his buddies," was the best she could come up with.

He hid his smile behind a forced frown, but noticed his ex-wife watching him. She was trying to read him as only she could. Turning his back to her, Pete spotted McBirney making his way up the hill toward them. The tractor roared as he hit the throttle and bounced up the rutted lane.

Pete wanted to be the first one to pose the question of the missing Buick to McBirney, but he knew that given a chance, Marcy would try to beat him to it.

"Thanks, Marcy. I'll let you get to your appointment while I talk to your husband." Those last two words grated on his tongue.

"I have plenty of time."

Obviously, being clever wasn't going to work. He'd have to shift into official-mode. "I'm sorry. I really need to talk to him alone. You know. Business."

"As in official business. I get it. What's this all about, Pete? What's going on?"

Before he could insist she leave, McBirney and his tractor pulled up beside them. The tractor sputtered to a stop.

"Chief Adams," McBirney called out as he climbed down. "Once again, your timing is impeccable. I was just about to go inside and call you."

This wasn't how Pete expected the conversation to begin. But it was more intriguing than what he'd planned, so what the hell. "Really?"

McBirney sidled over to Marcy and slipped an arm around her waist. "Hello, darling." He planted a kiss on her lips.

Clenching his jaw, Pete tried not to look away. Of course, this little show was all for his benefit. Knowing it, however, didn't make it any less painful.

"Yes." McBirney held Marcy close to his side and turned his attention back to Pete. "I need to report a stolen vehicle."

He seemed serious. Marcy appeared startled. Interesting.

"A stolen vehicle? Which one?" Pete loved playing dumb.

"My Buick." McBirney waved an arm at the shed. "I parked it last night and when I came out this morning, it was gone."

Pete pulled his notebook from his pocket and clicked his pen. "Any idea who might have taken it?"

McBirney frowned, his gaze shifting to his left. "Do I have any idea who might have taken my car?" he repeated.

"That was the question, yes."

"Not really."

"What's that mean? Either you have an idea or you don't."

"No. I have no idea." McBirney rubbed his nose with the back of his hand.

Pete nodded. He didn't believe a word of it. "Mind if I take a look?"

"Not at all."

Pete headed toward the shed, knowing that McBirney and Marcy trailed behind. "You said you parked it last night. When was that?"

"About eight-thirty, quarter of nine. After the supervisors' meeting broke up. By the way, have you thrown Sylvia Bassi in jail yet?"

A pain shot through Pete's right temple. "Not yet."

"I don't know what you're waiting for. And I want that computer confiscated, too."

"Right now, I'm busy taking your stolen vehicle report. Why don't we focus on that, okay? What did you do after you parked the car?"

"I went inside. Why?"

Pete shrugged. "Did you hear anything? Like someone hanging around outside? Maybe you heard the motor starting."

"No. I didn't hear anything. I was watching TV."

"Yeah? What was on?"

"A movie. *The Good, the Bad and the Ugly.* I just love Clint Eastwood. Don't you?"

"Uh huh." Pete jotted a note to check the television listings.

He studied the interior of the shed. The building was constructed of rough-hewn timber. The sides and roof consisted of corrugated tin. No frills. The equipment inside seemed well cared for. A pegboard held an assortment of tools. Rakes, a hoe, and several shovels hung from sets of nails pounded into the support posts. Other nails held bundles of twine, old license plates, and rolls of tape. An uncluttered workbench ran the length of the back wall.

"I wonder how they got it started." Pete hoped he sounded as if he were merely thinking out loud.

"Probably hot-wired it. Isn't that what car thieves do?"

"Sometimes." Except Pete already knew the ignition hadn't been tampered with. "Where are the keys?"

McBirney reached into his pocket and pulled out a ring with at least a dozen keys on it. He fingered them and held up one. "Here."

"Do you keep a spare?"

"I do." McBirney pocketed the keys and stepped to the workbench. He removed one glove and slipped his hand under the bench. "I keep an extra hidden right—" He frowned. "It's missing."

How convenient.

"Oh, wait. Here it is. I was feeling in the wrong spot." McBirney extracted his hand. A key on a ring dangled from his finger.

Of course it was. Pete looked at the key, wondering if it had really been an accidental find or just a sleight of hand to keep him from knowing McBirney had had it on his person all along.

"Do you mind?" Not that it mattered whether he minded or not. Pete speared the ring with his pen, while digging a paper bag from his coat pocket that he kept for just-in-case moments when he needed to hold onto evidence. He deposited the key into the bag and labeled the evidence. He doubted he'd be able to lift a usable print from it, but he'd try. "Who else knows where you hide this?"

"No one who would use it to steal the damned car. Shouldn't you get on your radio and put out a BOLO on it?" McBirney demanded.

Pete didn't need to be on the lookout for the Buick. He knew exactly where it was. He just wasn't quite ready to play that card yet.

The wind and snow had obliterated any signs of tire tracks. However, there was a trail of the white stuff leading into the bay as if someone had tracked it in. Pete knelt to study it. No discernible boot prints, only clumps. Traces of snow grew fainter toward the rear of the shed.

"Did you have the car pulled in headfirst or backed in?"

"Huh?" McBirney scowled. "Backed in. What the hell difference does that make?"

"Probably none." Pete stood up and strolled around the shed, taking in every detail. Nothing seemed out of place. The man was anal regarding his tools.

A small flash of blue caught his eye. Squinting, he moved toward one of the nails hammered into the wall. No tool hung on it. But a miniscule scrap of blue fabric with frayed edges clung to it.

"Do not move," he ordered and headed back to his SUV.

Marcy and McBirney appeared baffled by his actions. "What's going on?" Marcy called after him.

Pete hoisted a black nylon bag containing his evidence collecting gear from the back of the Explorer and trudged back to the shed. After digging his camera from the kit, he snapped a series of photos to show the location and size of the fabric and noted a description of each shot in his notebook. Then he pulled out another paper bag and a pair of tweezers, which he used to carefully remove the shred of blue. He dropped it into the bag and labeled it. "What the hell are you doing?" McBirney's expression had shifted from perplexed to annoyed to outraged in a matter of seconds. "My car was stolen. Plain and simple. Get on the horn and report it, damn it."

Pete tucked his camera and the evidence back into the kit. "No need. Your car is back at the township garage."

McBirney's mouth hung open, his brows furrowed into a sharp V with matching creases across his forehead.

Marcy put a hand on her husband's arm. "Pete, stop with the games. Just tell us what's going on."

"Fine. Your car was found last night in the game lands."

"Great." McBirney rubbed his hands together. "When I can pick it up?"

"You can't. It's being held as evidence in a murder."

The color drained from Marcy's face.

"Murder?" McBirney grunted. "Whose murder?"

"Ted Bassi's. He was found dead behind the wheel of your Buick."

Marcy doubled over. Pete expected McBirney to reach for her, but instead he shot a look at her that Pete couldn't quite interpret. Shock? Anger, perhaps? Whatever it was, it sure wasn't loving concern for his wife.

SIX

Sitting in the McBirneys' kitchen felt like a bad episode of *The Twilight Zone*. Pete recognized many of Marcy's touches from his own kitchen and made a mental note to have his house redecorated. At the very least, he intended to toss the vintage advertisements for Coca-Cola and Campbell's Soup. Similar tin signs hung on the backsplash in this kitchen as well. Funny. He thought *he* had been the one to pick those out.

At least Marcy had finally left for that appointment of hers.

"You can't possibly think I had anything to do with this." McBirney's words cut through Pete's reverie.

"Why wouldn't I? You and Bassi weren't exactly friends."

McBirney leaned back against the kitchen counter with his arms crossed. He opened his mouth, but reconsidered whatever retort he had been about to make and closed it again.

"You say you were here all last night?"

"After the meeting, yeah."

"Alone?"

"No, of course not. Marcy was with me."

Pete jotted a note to verify that with her later. "Do you have any idea who might have wanted Ted Bassi dead?"

"Bassi was an asshole."

Sylvia would have snapped McBirney's head off for that one. "Just because he didn't appreciate you having his mother arrested?"

McBirney raised a finger. "Speaking of that—"

"No, we're not," Pete interrupted. "We're speaking of Ted and your car and murder."

McBirney clamped his mouth shut so hard his lips turned white.

He lowered his hand. "There are a lot of people out there who would want Bassi dead. He was a hothead."

"Care to name names?"

"No."

No? Something wasn't right with this picture. "You sure? Because as far as I'm aware, you're the only one who had a shouting match with the victim just hours before he turned up dead. In your car. I don't suppose you have any thoughts on how else Ted got there if not for you."

McBirney's face reddened. "Look, Chief, I have an alibi. Finding out who killed that SOB is your job, not mine. And I think it's time for you to go serve that arrest warrant on our computer thief. If you want to talk to me anymore, you'll have to do it through my attorney." He stepped to the door and opened it, letting a rush of frigid air into the house. "Good day, Chief Adams."

Pete smelled guilt in this room the way a wolf smelled blood from wounded prey. But he knew he'd gotten all he was going to for now. He rose, picked up his hat, and tucked his notebook into his pocket. As he passed McBirney in the doorway, he paused to stare into his eyes—eyes that shifted ever-so-slightly under the scrutiny. Pete smiled and headed out into the bitter cold.

The snow crunched beneath his boots and his mind gnawed through McBirney's responses as Pete headed for his car. McBirney was hiding something. If he hadn't killed Ted—and Pete wasn't convinced he hadn't—then he knew damned well who had.

Pete slid behind the wheel and cranked the engine. He started out the lane, casting another long look at the empty spot in the shed.

Zoe passed a Channel 11 News truck parked at the end of the street as she approached Ted and Rose's house. Make that Rose's house. The combination—Ted and Rose—had always flowed off her tongue with such ease. As if they were one entity. TedandRose.

But no more.

Zoe recognized Sylvia's white Ford Escort in the driveway, but not the black Lincoln.

When Sylvia greeted her at the door she swept her into an

embrace. "Zoe, dear, thank goodness. I'm so glad you're here. I've asked my attorney to meet me here instead of my house so I can help Rose with the kids. You'll be a good distraction for her."

"Your attorney?" That explained the Lincoln.

"Yes. I'm going to turn myself in to the magistrate."

"Oh." Zoe motioned toward the street. "What's with the news truck?"

Sylvia blew a disgusted puff of air. "Damned vultures. They're interviewing our neighbors. Can you imagine? They knocked on the door here about an hour ago, but we didn't answer. As if Rose and the kids haven't been through enough without the media asking stupid questions." She shook her head. "Why, if my husband were still alive..."

A tall, rotund, silver-haired man in a pinstriped suit stood in the middle of the kitchen, a cup of coffee in his hand. A briefcase sat open on the table with a legal pad covered in scrawls next to it. Sylvia introduced him as Anthony Imperatore, attorney-at-law. They exchanged polite greetings before he went back to frowning at his notes.

Zoe and Sylvia found Rose in the living room with the blinds drawn. She sat on the couch, her telephone in her lap, her head in her hands. Zoe eased down beside her.

Rose sat upright, as if awakened from a sound sleep. "Zoe," she whispered. And then she burst into tears. Zoe pulled her against her shoulder and held her while she wept.

Sylvia blinked away tears of her own. "I'll get you girls some coffee. Or would you prefer tea?"

"Whatever Rose is having is fine," Zoe said.

Once Sylvia had left the room, Rose sniffed and disengaged herself from Zoe's arms. "I'm all right."

"No, you're not."

She huffed a short laugh. "No. I'm not. What am I going to do? I haven't been a single mom since the kids were little. I don't remember how to do things on my own. Ted promised he'd never leave us. Hell, the kids don't even remember a life before Ted became their dad." And with that, she leaned toward Zoe and again dissolved into tears.

Zoe held her close, fighting her own tears, while flashing back fourteen years to a time when she and Ted had been dating. She and Rose were best friends all through high school and had been known as party girls. Zoe was lucky and never had to pay the price of stupidity and backseat rendezvous.

Rose, on the other hand, became pregnant for the first time before she turned eighteen and again two years later. Rose's mother and Zoe stuck by her and the babies, helping the young mother who was little more than a baby herself.

Ted was a rebound romance for Zoe. They hung out together and went to the occasional movie. But he never set off fireworks for her the way her first real love had. So when Ted fell hard for her best friend, Zoe stepped aside and watched their love and passion grow. Within six months, they married and Ted adopted Logan and Allison as soon as the legal system allowed.

It was a love story that wasn't supposed to end. Especially not like this.

Rose drew a deep trembling breath. "I really need you to do me a favor."

"Anything. You know that."

"Can you take the kids? I'm trying to make arrangements. *Arrangements*. What a crappy word. Arrange my husband's funeral. Arrange my life without him."

Zoe took her hand and squeezed it.

"Anyhow, Logan is like a raw nerve. And Allison has withdrawn worse than I've ever seen her. They need to get away from here. I hate to ask. I know you...well, you had a rough night last night, too."

Zoe didn't mention the phone call from Logan. Whatever the boy had gotten himself into, his mother had enough to deal with. "Don't be silly. I'll be happy to take them. Maybe getting Allison out at the farm and around the horses will get her mind off...things."

Rose managed a weepy smile. "I was thinking that, too. Thank you." She flung her arms around Zoe.

Without waiting for the tea or coffee that Sylvia had been preparing, Zoe loaded the teens and their overstuffed backpacks into the old Chevy and rode to the farm in silence. Allison, in the middle, stared at her hands clenched in her lap while Logan gazed out the passenger-side window.

The truck jounced up the farm lane, which circled around to the rear of the house. No one ever came or went through the front door. Zoe parked in her usual spot, and they poured out of the truck, shuffling down the gentle slope of the backyard to the screened-in porch. From there three doors accessed the house—one to the Krolls' side, one to the center hallway that split the house, and the one for the half Zoe called home. The kids stood waiting as she fumbled with the keys. When the door clicked open, two orange tabbies greeted them.

Logan stooped to stroke the back of the larger cat. "Hey, Jade."

Jade meowed a response.

Crossing the room, Logan flopped onto the overstuffed sofa and started digging into his backpack.

Allison scooped the smaller cat into her arms and buried her face into Merlin's thick fur. Zoe smiled. Feline therapy. Maybe that was just what the girl needed.

Cradling the cat, Allison dumped her backpack by the door. "It's cold in here. Do you have any hot chocolate?"

Those were the first words Zoe had heard out of the girl since this nightmare began.

"Of course." Zoe tossed the keys onto a small table next to the door. "You know where the pantry is. Help yourself."

Allison blew out an irritated breath, but with Merlin snuggled in her arms, she trudged to the swinging door, bumped it with her hip, and disappeared into the kitchen. Jade trotted after her.

Zoe tugged off her boots. "Okay, Logan, what was that phone call about? All you said was that you'd done something that was going to get you into big trouble. But if you want my help, you're going to have to spill it."

He paused in his rummaging and sighed. His expression was a mix of sheepish and determined. "You know about Gram and the computer, right?"

Visions of Jerry McBirney ranting at last night's meeting flashed through her mind followed by Ted raging over the accusations against his mother. Had it just been last night? It felt like a lifetime ago.

Ted's lifetime.

"Some of it," Zoe said. "It was an old one that the township had replaced, and your grandma took it home for you guys to use."

Logan rolled his eyes. "Yeah. Gram meant well, but jeez. The thing is a dinosaur. Anyway," Logan went on, "so, yeah, this old computer's been sitting over at Gram's house for a couple months now. Then that dude last night—"

"Jerry McBirney," Zoe offered.

"Yeah. He starts screaming about it and making threats to have Gram arrested."

"I know all this. What I want to know is what did you do?"

Logan nodded, keeping one hand in his backpack.

"I got to thinking...I mean, what's going on? What's got this dude all bent out of shape? So I start...you know...messing around on it. Like, maybe there's something on there that McBirney guy doesn't want anyone to know about."

Zoe's chest tightened. *Of course.* That had to be it. "Did you find anything?"

"I didn't get a chance. I mean, Dad got—you know—last night." He took a deep, ragged breath and stared down at his backpack. "Are they still going to arrest Gram?"

"I don't know. Probably."

"That's what I figured, too. And they're going to take the computer, and I won't get a chance to find out what's on it. What that McBirney guy wants to keep secret."

A secret he might have killed to keep. Zoe found it hard to breathe.

"So, I called you. I need your computer."

"Huh? What?"

Logan pulled a small, black metal box from his backpack and held it up. "I stole the hard drive from that computer Gram took. I need to install it in your computer so I can keep trying to find out what's on it."

Zoe's knees buckled, and she sank down onto the couch next to him. She stared at the innocuous little box. Could this hold the answer to Ted's death?

"I know you and Chief Adams are good friends." Logan wrinkled his nose. "I'm kind of putting you in a weird spot. I mean, you're not going to turn me in, are you?"

Sylvia being guilty of "stealing" the computer was highly questionable. However, knowing the situation, taking the hard drive and keeping its location a secret...there was no question about it. She and Logan would both be in deep shit if they were caught. Pete would have no choice except to arrest both of them.

She'd never kept a secret from Pete before, with the exception of what cards she held in her hand when they played poker together on the odd Saturday night. And the fact that she occasionally entertained fantasies which involved him. Still, this might be her best chance to find out why Ted had been killed.

And to get something on Jerry McBirney.

Jerry McBirney. Okay, so she *had* kept secrets from Pete.

"No, I'm not going to turn you in."

Logan released a huge sigh.

"I do have one question," she said.

"What?"

"When you put this thing in my computer, is it going to keep me from checking my e-mail?"

Logan laughed. "No. I'll set it as a slave drive. Your old hard drive will still be the master. You'll be able to use your computer same as always. In fact, unless you let someone else play around on it, no one will ever know this extra hard drive is in there."

Good enough. "Well, what are you just sitting there for? You know where my computer is. Go do whatever it is you have to do."

A half hour later, and revived by a hot shower, Zoe went downstairs to find her living room empty except for Merlin snoozing on one of the chairs. Zoe scuffed across the hardwood floor in her stocking feet to peer into the front room, which served as her office and reading nook. Mismatched bookshelves overflowing with tomes she hoped to get to someday lined most of two walls. Her favorite recliner, backlit by one of the three nine-over-nine windows, perched next to an ancient fireplace.

Logan sat on the floor by her long computer desk, a do-it-yourself deal from IKEA. It wasn't fancy, but it had been within her price range. In other words, cheap.

The boy had removed the front of her computer tower and was tinkering with the insides.

"You okay?" Personally, Zoe'd rather deal with the blood and guts of her paramedic life than deal with the innards of a computer.

"Yeah." He looked up and flashed a smile. "I'm just finishing."

"Where's Allison?"

He glanced around and shrugged. "I haven't seen her." Then he went back to his work.

Zoe left him to it and crossed the living room with its came-with-the-house used furniture and a small, round dining room table from another excursion to IKEA. She peeked into the kitchen. A century-old add-on to the original circa 1850 farmhouse, the room was long and narrow, but well lit. The refrigerator and stove still worked even though they might easily be considered antiques. An empty mug with chocolate stains on the rim sat on the counter.

But no Allison.

Noticing the kitchen door was unlatched, Zoe peered outside. Boot prints in the snow led away from the door toward the barn. Donning her Muck Boots and goose down barn jacket, she followed the tracks across the yard and down the footpath to the barn.

The veterinarian's truck sat backed into one of the big open doors. Zoe slipped between the truck and the doorframe. Inside, Dr. Benton crouched next to Jazzel, working on her foot, while his assistant, a young woman—probably a vet student, held the fidgety mare's head. There was no sign of Allison.

"Hey, Dr. Benton," Zoe said.

He returned her greeting.

"Have you seen a teenage girl out here?"

"In the feed room," the assistant said.

"How's Jazzel?"

Dr. Benton shook his head. "So far, I can give you a three-page list of what *isn't* wrong with her. I figure we must be getting close."

Zoe left them with the mare and opened the feed room door. Allison sat on the floor with her back against the wall. Her gloves lay next to her as she tapped out a text message.

"You could do that in the house, you know." Zoe moved to her side and joined her on the dusty floor.

Allison shoved the phone in her pocket. "I know."

"How are you holding up?"

Allison shrugged.

"You know if you need to talk—"

"I don't. I'm fine."

"Well, in case you change your mind, I'm here."

Allison jumped to her feet. "I said I'm fine. I just wish everyone would leave me alone."

Zoe's climb to her feet was a little slower. She longed to scoop the girl up and hug her the way she'd done when Allison was younger. That hadn't been all that long ago, had it? At what point had hormones transformed the sugar and spice into venom and ice?

She decided to try a different tactic. "You remember Jazzel, don't you? Dr. Benton is working on her. Wanna watch?" At one time Allison had wanted to be a veterinarian when she grew up.

Allison responded with another infamous teenage shrug of indifference. But her expression had softened.

A crack in the tough veneer? Zoe jumped on it. "Come on. Let's see what's going on. Just for a minute, okay?"

"Whatever."

Zoe led the way across the riding arena to where Dr. Benton was now setting up a portable x-ray machine.

"You guys need help?" Zoe asked.

"Now that you mention it, yeah," the assistant said. "One of you want to hold Jazzel while I help the doc?"

Zoe looked at Allison. Jazzel could be a handful, but the teen had good hands and enough experience to control the mare's antics. Besides, Allison's dead eyes suddenly held a spark of interest.

"Go ahead," Zoe said.

Allison didn't quite smile, but her face brightened as she took the lead rope from the assistant's hands.

Zoe turned away to hide her pleasure from the girl. But her joy at seeing a tiny flicker of life in Allison faded as she remembered what Logan was working on back at the house. What secrets might he unlock from that innocent-looking little black box?

Pete glared at the Buick, willing it to speak to him. But it stood before him in the Vance Township Police garage, a silent witness to the events of the previous night.

He'd done a quick once-over on it in the game lands. Here, in the warmth and light, he'd completed a thorough inspection. The evidence he'd gleaned from the Buick's interior had been bagged and labeled and waited in the box at his feet.

"Were you planning on doing all my work for me?" came a voice from behind him.

Pete turned. "Were *you* planning on waiting until spring thaw to process the vehicle?"

Detective Wayne Baronick of the Monongahela County Police Department grinned from the doorway. Young, good-looking, and cocky, Baronick was a constant source of irritation to Pete. Most annoying was the fact that he reminded Pete of someone. Himself.

"Relax, Chief. I come bearing gifts." He held out a venti Starbucks. "I know you can't get these out here in the boondocks, so I brought one from civilization."

Baronick had always been good at sucking up, even as an over-eager cadet at the Pittsburgh Police Academy when Pete had taught the crime scene processing module more than a decade ago. Now, as a county detective, he not only irritated Pete with his ability to charm, but by the fact he was a damned good—and extremely determined—investigator.

Pete snatched the cup and took a long hit of the not-quite-hot-enough brew. What could he expect? The nearest Starbucks was fifteen miles away.

"I was surprised you called us in." Baronick stalked toward the Buick as if it were prey. "I know how much you hate admitting you need help."

The detective thrived on pushing Pete's buttons. Ignoring the effort to rile him, Pete scooped up the box, which held the fruit of his morning's work. "Did your boys find anything in the snow?"

"Yeah. More snow. You had the only viable source of evidence towed here." Baronick tipped his head toward the Buick. "What did you find?"

"The usual. Hair. Fibers. Nothing I can't handle."

"Prints?"

Pete hesitated. Baronick had been right about him not wanting help. He coveted the idea of being the one to bust McBirney. But a small department on an even smaller budget didn't have the kind of crime lab that Monongahela County possessed. "Nothing on the steering wheel."

"Nothing?" Baronick's eyes sparked with interest. "The car was wiped clean?"

"Mostly."

"What do you mean? Mostly? Come on, Chief. Don't make me pull teeth. What'd you find?"

"There was nothing on the steering wheel, the seat belts, or the door handle. But I lifted a partial from the rearview mirror."

Baronick chuckled. "I love it. Do you mind if I take a look?"

The arrogant son-of-a-bitch thought he'd be able to find something Pete had missed. Damned kids. "Sure. Be my guest."

Toting the box of bagged evidence samples in one hand and Starbucks in the other, he left the county detective with the Buick and headed into the office. Instead of Sylvia manning the front desk, Seth Metzger sat there, scowling at the computer screen.

"I thought you were off duty today," Pete said.

"I am. But these reports need to be filed and Sylvia..."

"Is Kevin still sick?"

"Yeah. I talked to him a while ago. He sounded bad. Real bad."

"Well, call next door and get one of the township secretaries over here to fill in for Sylvia. I need you out on the street. I want you to question Ted Bassi's neighbors. Find out if they heard or saw anything last night. Talk to his mother-in-law's neighbors, too." He'd have had Seth questioning Jerry McBirney's neighbors, too, except McBirney didn't have any.

"Yes, sir." Seth spun in the chair and reached for the phone.

"And after that, make a new pot of coffee."

"Yes, sir."

As Seth punched in the number for the township offices, the other line rang. He jabbed at the blinking button and listened for a moment. "Right away, sir," he said and hung up.

"That was Judge Mitchell. He said you'd better get over there. Sylvia just turned herself in, and Jerry McBirney showed up. It sounds ugly."

SEVEN

"Aunt Zoe. Wake up."

The words filtered into the middle of a horrendous nightmare in which Jerry McBirney loomed over Zoe. She tried in vain to scream for help. Fingers clutched her arm, and she jerked away.

Bolting upright in her recliner chair, Zoe blinked and looked at the teenage girl. The slender fingers gripping her arm didn't belong to McBirney. They belonged to Allison.

Zoe forced her breath to slow as panic drained away. It had been a dream. Only a dream.

"Aunt Zoe? Are you all right?" Allison asked.

Zoe patted her hand. "I was having a nightmare. I'm fine." She brought the chair back to a sitting position. She had only intended to close her eyes for a moment. What time was it? How long had she slept? Her mouth felt like parchment. Rancid parchment.

Logan remained bent over her computer keyboard, right where he'd been before she'd dozed off.

She climbed out of the recliner and moved to his side. "Find anything yet?"

Allison dove into the deserted chair and started thumbing her cell phone's keypad.

Logan blew a puff of air from his lips. "Not yet. Someone reformatted the hard drive. Probably when they switched over to the new computers."

"So there's nothing left on it?"

He looked at her over his shoulder with a grin and wiggled his eyebrows. "Stuff is never really deleted from a hard drive. I'm downloading some software that will let me restore the old files."

"You can do that?"

"Yep," Logan said. "It'd be easier if you had a faster Internet connection."

Zoe thumped him playfully on the head. "Beggars can't be choosers, dude."

He snickered without looking up. "Hey, are you gonna feed us lunch or what?"

"Yeah. I'm starved," Allison piped up.

"What time is it?" Zoe squinted at the clock on the bottom of the monitor screen. Jeez. Almost one o'clock. She really did pass out. "Okay. Let me see what I've got in the fridge."

"Can't we just order pizza? I bet Mario's would deliver out here," Logan said.

Allison made a face. "Mario's isn't open for lunch, moron."

"You're the moron."

"Dweeb."

"Goth."

Zoe cleared her throat. "Enough already, you two. How do hot dogs sound?"

"Woof, woof," Logan said followed by a pretty good impersonation of a panting hound, complete with tongue lolling out of his mouth. Allison tried to hide a small smile.

Zoe closed her eyes and shook her head. "Sorry I asked." But she wasn't. The kids were laughing. For a few brief minutes, they'd escaped the horror of reality.

She was half way to the kitchen when Allison's alarmed cry brought her back into the room.

"What?" Logan demanded of his sister, who was staring at her phone.

"It's about Gram. She's in jail."

"Are you sure?" Zoe suspected the girl had misunderstood whatever message she'd received. "I know she was going to turn herself in this morning. But I can't believe Judge Mitchell would lock her up."

Allison had been texting nonstop and paused only to read the response. "It's not about the computer thing. She attacked Mr. McBirney."

* * *

Against her better judgment, Zoe succumbed to Logan's demand that she drive the kids to the Vance Township Police Station to find out what was going on with their grandmother.

The parking lot was packed. Channel 11's news truck had been joined by vans from the other two Pittsburgh stations. Zoe suspected several of the other cars belonged to print reporters. No way did she want to march Sylvia's grandkids through a media gauntlet.

She dug her cell phone out of her pocket, and within a few minutes of placing a call to Pete, she and the teens were escorted into the back entrance by Seth Metzger.

"The Chief's not too happy that you guys are here," the young officer told Zoe as they made their way through the storage room. "We're having a hard enough time keeping the lid on this powder keg."

"I'll bet." She caught Logan's sleeve. "Did you hear that? Don't make me regret bringing you here more than I already do."

He met her gaze, but said nothing.

The door at the far end of the storage room opened into a narrow hallway with a low acoustical tile ceiling, dimly lit with fluorescent panels. They passed a couple of empty interrogation rooms before coming to a T-shaped intersection in the hall. Instead of turning left and heading toward the offices at the front of the station, Logan bolted straight toward the holding cell. And Sylvia.

Seth muttered something under his breath as Zoe loped after the boy.

She'd expected to find Sylvia cowering and weeping inside the sterile cage-like cell. Instead, the old woman appeared to have grown taller. Her jaw jutted and her eyes narrowed to match the determined crease in her forehead. She took her grandson's hands through the bars and held them tight.

"Don't you worry about your old grandma," Sylvia told him. "I'm fine. You need to take care of your mom and sister, you hear?"

Where was Rose?

Logan sniffed back tears and chewed on his lower lip, but nodded. "I will. But I'm going to make things right for you, too. Aunt Zoe's helping me—"

Zoe caught his elbow and squeezed. Hard. He winced, but shut up.

From behind her a voice boomed, "Aunt Zoe's helping you with what?"

She wheeled around to face Pete. Gauging from the scowl on his face and the dark circles under his eyes, she could have guessed he'd had a rough, sleepless night even if she didn't already know it for a fact. She hoped exhaustion dimmed his observational skills enough that he missed the panic on her face at nearly being busted.

"I'm helping him watch his sister so Rose can take care of some things."

"Yeah," Logan said. "We're—ah—yeah. What she said."

Pete pinned her with a stare, and Zoe made a mental note to strangle the kid later.

"Is that right?" Pete sounded skeptical.

A door slammed. Footsteps and raised voices interrupted the conversation.

She might have been grateful for the diversion, except she recognized one of the voices as belonging to Jerry McBirney.

"Right this way, folks," McBirney bellowed as he appeared around the corner, leading a small army consisting of Elizabeth Sunday and four reporters armed with notepads and cameras.

Pete approached the group, his arms spread wide. "Metzger!" he shouted. Then to McBirney and his entourage, he commanded, "*No.*"

The reporters froze, mid-stride. The attorney, in her high heels and tailored skirt and jacket, snapped to attention. Even McBirney hesitated in his advance.

Zoe noticed the red swelling on the left side of McBirney's face and the slight discoloration below his eye. What the hell had Sylvia done? Zoe eyed her and raised an eyebrow in a silent question. The older woman gave her a smug wink.

"Step aside, Chief," McBirney said. "These fine reporters want photographs of the thief."

The reporters exchanged uncertain glances with each other.

"What you mean," Sylvia said, "is they want pictures of the little old lady who cleaned your clock, you son-of-a-bitch."

The rest of McBirney's face reddened to match the welt.

"Shut up, Sylvia," Pete said through his clenched jaw.

Seth Metzger appeared around the corner behind the reporters. The creases in his forehead indicated he knew he'd screwed up.

"Metzger, get these people out of here," Pete ordered.

"Yes, sir, Chief. Folks, you'll have to leave. Now."

"Hold on there." McBirney held up an arm, as though stopping traffic. "I told them they could have pictures to go with the interview I just gave them. And I intend to see that they get their photo op."

Pete stepped closer to McBirney until their faces were mere inches apart. Zoe strained to hear Pete's whisper. "And I'm telling you. Get the hell out of my police station before I decide to lock you in that cell with Sylvia and let her finish the job she started."

"You think I'm scared of an old lady?"

"I think you ought to be."

McBirney glowered at him. Zoe wished she could see Pete's face.

Silence hung between them for several long moments. Two reporters scribbled madly on their notepads. A third raised his camera, and the flash lit the hallway.

At that moment, Elizabeth Sunday stepped in and placed a hand on McBirney's arm. "Jerry, I told you this was a bad idea. Let Chief Adams do his job. Mrs. Bassi is under arrest. That's what you wanted. Leave it at that."

"What I want is to have the computer confiscated," he snapped at her.

Zoe looked at Logan who met her gaze with an expression that said *I told you so.*

"Detective Baronick is with Rose over at Sylvia's house right now picking it up," Pete said.

Logan stood outside Sylvia's cell, still holding hands with his grandmother. But Allison was nowhere to be seen. Zoe looked around, but couldn't find the dark-haired girl anywhere. When was the last time she'd seen the girl? They'd come into the station together. They'd all slipped through the door from the storage room into the hallway together. After that, she wasn't so sure.

A commotion drew Seth's attention back to the front offices.

"The murder victim's wife just pulled in," came a shout.

Three of the four reporters spun in unison and charged past Seth, flattening him against the wall.

"I got it, Chief," he said before Pete had a chance to bark orders again. Then he disappeared after the group.

The one remaining reporter thrust a small digital recorder in Pete's direction.

"Excuse me, Chief Adams, but would you like to comment about the Bassi homicide or the skirmish at the magistrate's office this morning?"

Pete fixed him with a stare. The reporter's hand started to quiver. Then he withdrew the recorder and turned to follow his colleagues toward a potentially more talkative subject.

"Is it safe to assume," Elizabeth Sunday said, her hand still resting on McBirney's arm, "since Mrs. Bassi has returned that your detective is also back with the evidence?"

"You can assume whatever you like," Pete said. "But you'll have to do it somewhere else."

McBirney's grin turned into a broad, victorious smile. Zoe was glad she hadn't had a chance to eat lunch.

"Yes, of course," McBirney said. "Ms. Sunday, let's go see what kind of interview the widow Bassi is giving the reporters."

"You're a pig," Logan said, his voice cracking.

Sylvia patted his hand, while Zoe put an arm around his shoulders and shushed him.

McBirney chuckled and turned to leave. But before he and the attorney took a step, a tall, rather attractive man appeared in the hallway. Wearing a long, dark wool coat and an exuberant grin, the new arrival seemed familiar to Zoe. She'd seen him before. But where?

"Chief, I figured you'd want to log that computer into the evidence room yourself," the man said.

McBirney extended a hand toward the newcomer. "You must be Chief Adams' detective. Baronick, is it? I'm Township Supervisor Jerry McBirney."

The man raised an eyebrow at Pete, who gave a slight nod. "Mr. McBirney." He took the offered hand. "Yes, I'm Detective Wayne Baronick. But I'm afraid you've got it wrong. I'm not Chief Adams' detective. I'm with the Monongahela County PD."

Of course. That's why he looked familiar. His picture had been in the newspaper a few weeks back, escorting a drug dealer he'd arrested.

"And I find it very interesting that our homicide victim was found in your car," Baronick continued. "Don't you find it interesting, Mr. McBirney?"

The color drained out of McBirney's face. Even the red, swollen blotch faded to a pale pink. "That car was stolen."

"Yes, so I hear. But I still think it's interesting." Baronick turned his attention to Pete. "The flatbed will be here in an hour or so to pick up the car."

"Pick it up?" McBirney stuttered. "The car? *My car?*"

"*My* evidence in a homicide," Baronick corrected. "County will be taking over the case from here."

McBirney leaned toward Elizabeth Sunday's ear, but his harsh whisper carried all the way back to Zoe, Logan, and Sylvia. "What about the computer?"

"Oh, Chief Adams can keep the computer," Baronick said. "I'm not interested in evidence from a simple theft case."

Some of the color seeped back into McBirney's complexion.

"Of course," Baronick went on, "if it turns out that the theft and the homicide are related—and when you consider the theft suspect and the homicide victim are mother and son, it does seem likely—then I'll be back to claim it, too."

McBirney's face turned white again. "Let's get out of here," he said to the attorney and stomped away with her sashaying behind him.

"Gee, Wayne," Pete said, "if I didn't dislike you so much, I'd keep you around just to repel the pests."

"Baronick Asshole Control, at your service," the detective said, displaying a mouthful of brilliant white teeth.

Pete turned toward Zoe and Logan. "I need you two out of here."

"But what about Gram?" Logan demanded.

Sylvia squeezed his hand. "I told you not to worry about me. I'll be out of here soon. Won't I, Pete?"

He squirmed, something Zoe rarely saw him do. "You know I don't have anything to do with that. For chrissakes, you slammed McBirney with that lethal weapon you call a purse. In front of the judge, no less. You're damned lucky he just cited you with contempt of court. He could have charged you with assault."

Zoe suppressed a laugh. "You hit him with your purse?"

"Damned right. Only way I could shut that mouth of his. Judge Mitchell should have given me a medal."

"He probably wanted to," Pete said. "That's why it was only contempt."

Baronick stepped forward. "You mean this is our computer thief?"

Sylvia puffed out her ample chest. "I didn't steal it."

Pete introduced Baronick to everyone.

"You have my condolences," the detective said, shaking hands all around. "I'll need to talk to all of you in the next day or so."

Logan stuffed his hands deep into his baggy jeans pockets. "Chief Adams already asked us questions."

"Yes, well. That's how it works." Baronick seemed apologetic, but Zoe suspected it was a practiced response. "He asks you questions. Then I ask you questions. And there will no doubt be twenty more people asking you the same damned questions. Do yourself a favor, kid, and get used to it."

Pete touched Zoe's arm, and a little flutter raced beneath her skin. "Get him out of here."

"Yeah. Come on, Logan. We need to find your sister and your mom."

Logan's eyes widened as he looked at Sylvia. "Gram?"

"You go on, now. I'll be out of here before you know it."

He gave a half-hearted nod and turned away from the cell, pressing past Zoe, Pete, and Baronick with his hands still in his pockets and his shoulders hunched.

Before Zoe could follow him, Pete closed his fingers around her elbow and leaned in toward her ear. "We have to talk," he whispered. "Soon."

"You know how to reach me."

He released her arm. "Okay, Baronick, let's go log in that evidence."

As Zoe rounded the corner toward the front offices, she heard Sylvia's plaintive voice behind her. "Pete, you make sure I get out of here. I have to bury my son. After that, I don't care what you do to me."

EIGHT

Hurricane Jerry had swept through the police station, leaving the front alcove in stillness. First, Zoe had managed to lose Allison and now Logan had vanished, too. Certainly he wouldn't have followed McBirney and the attorney outside.

Would he?

Crap. The kid wasn't even armed with his grandmother's purse.

The only human she found was Matt Doaks, standing with his back to her as he peered through the vertical blinds hanging on the station's front door.

It had been years since she and Matt had shared a life. And love. He'd been her first true romance, her high school sweetheart. Their perfect world began to unravel when he blew out his knee and lost his basketball scholarship to Penn State. The resulting depression and addiction to pain killers further frayed the relationship. And when she'd walked into their house and found him in bed with that slut from the Tastee Freez, her world hit a brick wall that shattered her heart.

Fifteen years had passed. But seeing him always stirred those old aching memories.

"Hi, Matt." Zoe made a concerted effort to keep all emotion from her voice.

He spun around. "Zoe. I didn't hear you coming."

"What's going on out there?"

He shrugged. "More of the Jerry McBirney Show. He's preening for the media."

A rush of anger engulfed her. "How can you keep doing this?"

His eyes narrowed. "Me? Doing what?"

"Don't act stupid. You know what I mean. How can you support that bastard? It doesn't matter what he's voting on or pushing through the board, you back him up. Is he paying you? Exactly how much does it cost him for you to be his lap dog?"

The outburst took her by surprise, and she took a deep breath to regain her composure.

Matt studied his boots for a moment. "Jerry's not so bad. He has some great plans for the township if folks'd just give him a chance."

"A chance? To do what? Bankrupt us? What about Sylvia? How can you sit by and let him railroad her into jail?"

"I had nothing to do with that."

If she didn't know better, she'd have thought he was about to shed a tear. "You sure aren't doing anything to stop it."

"She clubbed Jerry with her purse in front of the judge. You can't blame me."

"You could have ended it before any of this happened." Heat simmered around her collar. "You knew he was going to call for her arrest and have her fired. You had to know."

"I swear. I didn't."

Yeah, right. "You're lying." Again. Zoe heard the quiver in her voice. She turned her back to Matt before her anger reduced her to tears.

Silence closed around them.

Finally, he drew a deep, audible breath. "Look. If there was anything I could do, I would. I like Sylvia."

Zoe pinched the bridge of her nose, hoping the physical pain would keep the emotional tears at bay. "You have a damned funny way of showing it. What about Ted?"

"What about him?"

She spun to face him, clenching her fists. "Sylvia's son is dead and that bastard McBirney is probably the one who killed him. Why? And don't tell me you don't know. You live in McBirney's hip pocket, for crying out loud. You have to know something."

Matt's eyes shifted side to side under his furrowed brow, as if the possibility that McBirney were guilty of murder had never occurred to him, and he needed to process the news. "Huh."

"That's it? That's all you're going to say? 'Huh.'"

Matt tipped his head to check the hall behind Zoe then glanced over his shoulder at the group gathered outside. He took her arm and drew her close to him. She resisted, but curiosity overcame her anger. "I hadn't given it much thought before, but now that you mention it, there is something."

He paused, and she waited for him to continue. In the quiet, her heart pounded loud enough that she feared even the reporters in the parking lot would hear.

"Jerry..." Matt licked his lips. "Jerry thinks Marcy is fooling around on him. And..." He glanced around again. "He was pretty sure that the guy she was messing around with was Ted."

By the time Seth Metzger showed up to inform Zoe that Rose and the kids had been stashed in the conference room, she'd gained control over the tremors that wracked her body. Matt's bombshell left her weak-kneed, but the coward hadn't stuck around to comfort her. Not that he could have anyway. Don't murder the messenger, they said. But she desperately wanted to beat the crap out of Matt Doaks.

Ted loved Rose. He'd never cheat on her. The way Matt had cheated on Zoe. Never.

"Are you all right?" Seth said as Zoe hesitated outside the conference room, her hand on the knob. "Can I get you some water or a pop?"

Bourbon maybe. "Okay. Yeah. That would be great. Whatever you have is fine. Thanks."

As Seth headed down the hall to score a beverage, Zoe took a deep breath and entered the room.

Rose sat at the long table with Logan next to her, holding her hand. Allison reprised her seated fetal position on the floor, her back against the corner of the room. Only Logan looked up when Zoe closed the door behind her.

"There you are," Zoe said, her voice not as light as she had tried to make it. "I've been looking all over."

"That cop herded us all in here so McBirney couldn't bug us anymore," Logan said.

"And to keep me from killing him," Rose muttered.

Zoe pushed a mental image of Ted with Marcy out of her brain. It wasn't true. Matt was a liar.

But what if he wasn't? Marcy and Ted. Maybe McBirney found them together in the Buick. Maybe that's what Ted was doing in McBirney's car. It might also explain the vendetta against Sylvia—Ted's mother.

Did Sylvia know? Or suspect? Did Rose?

Zoe shook her head, squeezing her eyes shut tight. Stop it. Stop thinking about it.

"What's wrong with you?" Rose asked.

"Nothing," Zoe said. "Headache."

"You need some sleep." The dark bags under Rose's eyes indicated she had personal experience with this diagnosis.

"Yeah? Look who's talking."

"There's no way in hell I'm going to sleep. But you stand a chance of getting a nap if I stop dumping my kids on you."

Logan met Zoe's gaze. "We'll be quiet," he said.

Rose drew a deep breath and stretched, arching back in the chair until her shoulders popped. "Actually, I want you guys home with me anyhow. I thought I could get more done with the house to myself. But the place is too quiet."

Logan glanced between Zoe and his mom. "Take Allison home with you, then. I was in the middle of helping Aunt Zoe with her computer and—and it's almost fixed and—"

"It's okay," Zoe interrupted before the kid babbled them both into the holding cell next to Sylvia. "My computer isn't going anywhere. You can fix it later. Your mom needs you now."

Logan's face contorted in frustration. Zoe sent him a look that she hoped said *cool it*. He must have received the message because he sighed and dropped his gaze to the table.

Rose gave Zoe a sad, but appreciative smile. "Thanks. By the way, Ted's viewing is tomorrow. The funeral is Thursday."

The door opened, and Seth entered holding a can of Coke, which Zoe accepted. "Looks like the circus out front is breaking up," he said to Rose. "I'll let you know when it's clear to leave."

Rose thanked him, and the young officer closed the door on his way out.

Zoe reached for a chair. "I'll sit with you."

Rose waved her off. "No, no. You should go home and rest. We're fine here. Pete and Seth are taking good care of us. Pete's a good guy, you know." Her tone suggested more than just an offhand comment.

Zoe knew. But as attracted as she might be to him, it would never work. Between the two of them, they lugged enough baggage into a relationship to sink a small yacht.

She hugged Rose and Logan. Allison had retreated into her shell and didn't even look up when Zoe stood in front of her.

"Allison," Rose said with an authoritative edge to her voice.

"It's okay," Zoe assured her. Then she knelt and touched the girl's knee. "Anytime you want to come out to the farm, Merlin would love to snuggle with you. And the horses are always ready for a ride."

Allison almost lifted her eyes to meet Zoe's, but lowered them again. Crap. She thought she was making progress with the girl. But she recalled her own struggle with the grief of losing a dad. Time. Just give Allison time.

Zoe left the station through the same back door as she and the kids had arrived. Temperatures were dropping and gray clouds rolled in, crowding out the blue sky. She pulled her collar tighter around her neck and lowered her head against the wind. As her cold fingers fumbled with the keys, she became aware of a gnawing in her gut. And it wasn't the soda on her empty stomach. She felt eyes on her. Someone was watching.

She looked up. The wind bit at her face drawing icy tears. At the front corner of the building, Jerry McBirney stood staring at her, expressionless. The chill that rushed through her had nothing to do with the weather. McBirney's face morphed into a self-satisfied grin. He winked at her.

Zoe started shaking. She couldn't breathe. Her keys slipped from her gloved fingers and fell into the wet slop on the ground. She bent down to retrieve them. Clutching the keys, she lifted her gaze to search for McBirney, but he was gone. For a moment, she wondered if he'd really been there. Or had she only imagined him?

Pete managed to get maybe an hour of sleep after he'd gone home from the station. Thoughts of Sylvia behind bars mingled with annoyance over Wayne Baronick taking charge of the homicide investigation. Pete wanted this one. Nothing would give him more satisfaction right now than tossing that sanctimonious bastard Jerry McBirney into lockup.

Giving up on his bed, he slipped into a pair of rumpled jeans he found draped over the chair in the corner of the room. He dug an equally rumpled sweatshirt from the dresser drawer and tugged it over his head.

In the kitchen, he drained a half cup of nasty looking brew from the coffee maker into a clean mug, rinsed the pot, and started a new batch. In the meantime, he nuked the day-old stuff. As he waited for the microwave timer, he thought of Zoe.

She was lying to him.

He wasn't sure what she was lying about, but she definitely was. Or at the very least, she was keeping something from him.

The microwave beeped, and he pulled the cup of murky black sludge from it. He took a sip. And winced. God, that was awful. But the fresh pot wasn't near ready yet. He carried the cup to the round oak table and sank into a chair.

Pete had long ago grown used to Marcy lying to him. Like the big one. 'Til death do us part. What a load of bull.

But Zoe was different. Or so he'd thought. She was painfully honest. Oh, sure, there were parts of her life she kept to herself. Her past relationships for example. He sensed she didn't want to talk about them, so he didn't ask. And it wasn't as though they were dating, much as he'd contemplated the idea.

Even so, if he did ask, he knew she'd tell him. The truth was he didn't *want* to know. He already thought Matt Doaks was a huge waste of flesh and bone. Beyond the obvious—even Pete had to admit Doaks was a good-looking son-of-a-bitch—there seemed little to attract someone like Zoe to him.

And he long suspected there had been something between Zoe and Ted before Ted and Rose married. But no one involved seemed stressed over it, so he guessed it hadn't been much. Ted and Zoe acted more like siblings than past lovers.

The coffee maker stopped dripping. Pete got up to dump the old stuff in the sink, but noticed his cup was empty. He'd drained it without realizing. He poured a fresh cup and carried it to the basement. His workshop was his favorite spot in the house. It was the one area that carried no memories of Marcy. She'd hated it and never went down there. Too many spiders.

He flipped the light switch. His vast collection of wood carving tools sat on shelves in plastic boxes. The ones he had used most recently lay on the workbench next to his current project—a reproduction Jaeger flintlock muzzleloader. He touched the bare wood of the chunky gun stock, tracing the swells and grooves of his past work. Slipping on a pair of cheap reading glasses, he selected a chisel and bent over the workbench. The curved blade shaved a sliver of maple from the stock.

Pete attempted to focus on his work, but instead of the mental picture of the finished engraving that he tried to hold in front of him, his mind's eye conjured up Marcy. The way she'd nearly pitched forward on her face at the news of Ted's death.

The blade slipped and gouged a deeper crevice than Pete had intended. Swearing under his breath, he returned the chisel to its box. Instead of whittling away at the Jaeger's stock, he decided he needed to be whittling at McBirney's story. The truth remained buried somewhere under the surface. He needed to gouge out the lies to find it.

He had to talk to Marcy.

Zoe stared at her computer. She longed to continue with Logan's snooping. If only she knew how. She should've had him show her what he was doing.

She didn't dare phone him and risk having Rose overhear what they were up to, so for now, Zoe was stuck. She checked the clock on the mantle. Maybe not.

After a quick call confirmed that Ted's autopsy had been completed, Zoe grabbed her coat and made the half hour drive to the county seat where the Marshall Funeral Home was located across the road from the Brunswick Hospital. Convenient, Zoe mused. The hospital's failures didn't have far to travel.

She pulled into the funeral home's parking lot and entered via the back door. Bells jingled, announcing her arrival. Inside, the scent of lilies and carnations and other assorted flowers assaulted her nose. The fragrance brought back memories of long ago, when her dad had been in a similar building. Different mortuary. Same aroma. Grief smelled like floral arrangements.

Zoe shivered off the memory just as a round-faced woman appeared at the end of the hall and came to meet her. The woman's hair was pulled back so tight it gave her face the look of bad plastic surgery. She wore a dark burgundy skirt and blazer and black comfortable shoes.

"Zoe, dear, how lovely to see you."

"Hi, Paulette. Is Franklin around?"

Franklin's secretary escorted Zoe into a large room. Shelves bearing urns, boxed thank you notes, and guest books stood against one wall. In a dark corner, three caskets, one brass, one platinum, and one wood-grained, displayed their comfortable, silk-lined interiors.

The Monongahela County Coroner sat at an Early American desk, bent over a stack of papers. He lifted his head and offered a tight smile, extending a slender hand in Zoe's direction.

"Zoe. I see you made the trip even when I told you not to."

She smiled as she clasped his hand. "This one's special."

"All the more reason you should stay out of it." Franklin Marshall was thin and pale with equally thin and pale hair swept into a comb-over. Zoe suspected he was much younger than he appeared but the old-fashioned half-glasses he wore low on his beak didn't help.

"You know I can't do that," she said. "What did you find out?"

Franklin heaved a sigh and used one finger to bump the readers higher on his nose. He thumbed through a neat stack of papers in an organizer tray, gingerly removing two paper-clipped pages. "Ted Bassi died from massive brain trauma. He suffered multiple skull fractures including his nasal and frontal bones." He placed the palm of his hand on the top of his forehead. "A blow right here compressed the skull into the frontal lobe. That's your cause of death."

"A blow? Someone hit him?"

Franklin shrugged. "Or a boulder fell on him. The damage was extensive. Whatever struck him was large. Flat, would be my guess. Not like a baseball bat. And it would take considerable force to create that kind of trauma."

Zoe's mind raced. Large and flat? Considerable force? She held out a hand. "May I?"

He hesitated. "You're too close to this case. I really shouldn't."

"Come on, Franklin. I'm the one who processed the body at the scene. I brought him in." Somehow, she kept her voice from wavering.

His mouth drew to one side of his face, and he squinted. "Fine."

Zoe snatched the papers and studied the notations. Ted had also suffered assorted abrasions on his face, which she'd seen for herself. There was some bruising to the front of his body and a number of his teeth had been broken. What the hell had happened to him? "Do you have any theories about what might have caused all these injuries?"

"Not a clue. Sorry." Franklin wiggled his fingers, indicating he wanted his report back.

She ignored him. "I assume Chief Adams attended the autopsy and knows about this."

Franklin shook his head. "Detective Baronick observed, and County homicide gets the report." He did the finger wiggle thing again. "Please."

"I'd like a copy of this."

"You know I can't do that."

Crap. "Can't you just make a photocopy for me? Please. I won't tell."

For a moment he said nothing. Then, he ran his bony fingers through his sparse hair and glanced toward a dark corner where a copier sat next to a set of file cabinets. "I can't. Sorry. Now, if you'll pardon me, I need to visit the little boy's room." He rose and shuffled out of the room, closing the door behind him.

Zoe grinned. She owed Franklin. But what kind of gift do you send a coroner/mortician? Flowers? Not likely. She decided to think about it later. Right now, she had copies to make.

And then, she needed to track down Pete. She hoped he'd have some ideas about what Ted's injuries meant. Because right now, the coroner's report raised more questions than it answered.

NINE

The aroma of roasting chicken wafted through the closed door at the McBirney farm and set Pete's mouth to watering. Regardless of her other failings as a wife, Marcy had been a terrific cook. He raised a fist and knocked.

The curtains parted revealing a sliver of his ex-wife's face and one of her dark brown eyes. Her scowl was evident even on that small glimpse. The door swung open.

"I told you on the phone to stay away," she said.

"And I told you we need to talk. You wouldn't agree to meet me somewhere else, so what was I supposed to do?" He slid past her into the kitchen. Pots simmered on the stove. Silverware graced two places at the table. "Besides, you mentioned Jerry would be late."

"As far as I know. He might have changed his plans. He might be on his way here right now." She hadn't closed the door.

"If he shows up, I'll leave." Pete took a seat without waiting for an invitation.

Marcy's sigh was audible over the bubbling pots. She shut the door and moved to the oven. "I don't have anything to tell you."

He pulled out his notebook and pen. "Where were you last night?"

She kept her back to him. "I was here, of course. Just like my husband told you."

"I'd like to hear your version of the evening."

"It's like he said. I was here when he got home."

"Marcy, look at me."

She fidgeted with a towel, opened the oven and peered inside, and then shut it. Dropping the towel on the counter, she picked up a spoon and stirred the aromatic contents of a large cast iron skillet. Gravy. "I'm busy. I don't want to burn dinner."

Pete stood and moved to her side. If she wouldn't turn around to face him, he'd position himself where she had no choice. "Okay. Now you can look at me *and* keep an eye on your cooking."

"It doesn't matter. I was still here. You can't change that."

"I know. The part I question is when your husband got home."

"Whenever he said he did. Really, Pete, you should leave."

"If you keep evading my questions, I could be here all night."

For the first time since she'd let him in the door, she met his gaze. He read a mixture of terror and pleading in her eyes. What the hell was she hiding?

"Are you all right?"

"I'm fine. Ask your damned questions."

"Where were you last night?"

She went back to stirring the bubbling gravy. "Here."

"At the stove?" He said it with a grin, meaning to lighten the mood, but his humor missed its mark.

"No," she snapped. "In the living room. I was reading."

"Okay. What time did Jerry return home?"

Her eyes narrowed. "I didn't look at the clock. It must have been eight thirty, quarter to nine."

"Are you sure?"

"I'm sure he came home. But as to exactly the time, no. The roads were bad. It may have taken him longer than usual."

"That's odd. I'd think you'd have been keeping an eye on the clock. Don't you worry when your husband's out on a bad night?"

"It wasn't that bad earlier. I didn't know the roads were getting icy until later."

"Later? When?"

She gave him an exasperated look. "After Jerry got home and told me how slick they were."

Pete thumbed through his notes. He needed to trip her up. To locate the point where Jerry's and Marcy's stories parted company. "Did he leave the house again after he arrived home?"

"No." Her voice carried a note of uncertainty, as if she were asking a question rather than answering one.

"Did you hear any noises outside?"

"No."

"Nothing? You didn't hear another car pull in?"

"No."

"Or the Buick start?"

"No. I told you a thousand times, *no*. I didn't hear anything."

"But you're so isolated out here, it's not like you'd mistake it for traffic passing by. If someone pulled in and stole the Buick, you must have heard them."

"Maybe they didn't drive in. Maybe they walked in."

"So you did hear the Buick start up?"

"I didn't hear anything."

No one ever hears anything. The world was full of deaf and blind witnesses to crime. But Pete wasn't buying it this time.

"How can that be, Marcy? Where were you? What were you doing?"

The spoon in her hand quivered. "I was here. Reading."

He leaned toward her. "What book?"

Her mouth opened almost as wide as her eyes. "I—um—"

Got her. "Guess it wasn't that good, huh?"

"I need to finish setting the table. Please go."

Pete ignored her. "Are you sure Jerry didn't leave again? If you didn't hear anyone pull in, maybe it was Jerry who took the car."

The spoon slipped from her fingers and flopped into the skillet, splattering gravy over the stovetop. Marcy swore under her breath and grabbed the towel.

He waited until she'd mopped up the mess before continuing. "What really happened, Marcy? Did you go upstairs to take a shower? Take a load of laundry to the basement? Get involved in a phone call? Couldn't Jerry have slipped out when you weren't looking?"

She clutched the towel, her hands trembling. "I don't know. He could have. But he didn't. I'm sure he didn't."

"How are you sure?"

"Because I am. That's it. No more questions."

"Because you are? That's bullshit, Marcy, and you know it." He wanted to grab her and shake the truth out of her. Make her admit she was covering for her husband. After all, it wouldn't be the first time McBirney had encouraged her to deceive Pete.

"No, Pete. I'm serious. If you want to ask me anything else, you'll have to arrest me. And then I would demand a lawyer. I know the rules, remember? And right now, I want you to leave."

From her tone, she meant it. He tucked his notebook back in his coat pocket and gave her a sad smile. He'd really hoped to reach her. As he crossed the kitchen to the door, one last question formed in his mind. He paused with his hand on the knob and turned back to face her. "Just tell me one thing, Marcy."

She brushed the back of her hand across her forehead. "What?"

"What's Jerry done that has you so frightened?"

Her face went white.

Zoe stood in the middle of the pantry, studying the meager offerings stored on the shelves. She really needed to go shopping. As she reached for a can of tomato soup, her phone rang. It had to be Pete. She'd left messages for him on his cell phone, his home phone, and at the station.

"What's up?" Yes, it was indeed Pete.

She bit back a smile at the sound of his voice and informed him she had a copy of the coroner's report. And some other important information. She didn't elaborate. Matt's tale of McBirney's suspicions was better not shared over the phone.

"Have you eaten yet?"

She thought of the soup. "No."

"Meet me at Parson's"

"I'll be there in a half hour."

Folks didn't just happen across Parson's Roadhouse. The crowd consisted of regulars, familiar with the township's back roads. The gravel parking lot was full of four-wheel-drive trucks and SUVs. Zoe added her Chevy to the collection and spotted the Vance Township police vehicle parked well away from the rest.

Inside, the rumble of conversation and the clink of glassware and dishes mingled with the strains of country music filtering through ancient speakers. The aromas of grilled meat blended with that of beer and overused cooking oil.

She spotted Pete chatting up some locals at one of the booths in the dining room, and her heart warmed. He'd shed his uniform for jeans and a sweatshirt. She wished the jeans were a little tighter, but her imagination had no problems filling in the gaps. She valued the easy comfort of their friendship. But, sometimes...

She drew a deep breath and made her way to Pete's side. "Hey," she said.

"Hey, yourself." He smiled. "I got us a booth over here."

She followed him to a secluded corner. His jacket had been folded and stowed on one of the benches. She slipped out of her parka and settled into the other seat. No sooner had Pete taken his place across from Zoe than a waitress in a grease-spotted brown uniform appeared with menus and a pot of coffee. "Regular or decaf?"

Zoe weighed her need for sleep against her desire to stay awake long enough to make it home after dinner. "Regular."

The waitress poured. "I know better 'n to ask you," she said, winking at Pete.

"It's high-test or nothing." He gave her a crooked smile.

After the waitress had left them to study their menus, Zoe pulled the crumpled copies of the coroner's report from her purse and set them on the table.

Pete snatched them and squinted as he read. "So what does this tell us?"

"I was hoping you'd know."

He rummaged through his jacket before coming up with his reading glasses. "Fracture of the frontal bone. Cause of death, blunt-force trauma to the frontal lobe."

"Franklin said he was probably hit with something large and flat."

"Large and flat? Like a two-by-four?"

"Maybe. I hadn't thought of that, but I suppose it could be."

Pete studied the papers, flipping back and forth between the pages. "No mention of wood fragments."

"Or anything else embedded in the wound." Zoe could almost hear his brain processing the report. "Has Baronick called you with an update on the investigation?"

Pete gave a short laugh. "Hell, no. As far as County is concerned, we're out of it."

"And as far as you're concerned?"

"What do you think?"

The waitress reappeared, pad and pen at the ready.

Without consulting either the menu or Zoe, Pete ordered. "I'll have a large order of ribs with fries. The lady will have a cheeseburger with the works and a side of coleslaw."

The waitress scribbled on the pad and left with a nod.

Zoe suppressed a laugh. "Either I'm entirely too predictable or you know me too well."

"Did I order the wrong thing?"

"Of course not. That's my point."

Pete stuffed his glasses back into his jacket and took another sip from his cup. "I talked to Marcy this afternoon."

"Oh? Why?" Zoe flashed on Matt at the police station, revealing Marcy's secret.

"She's lying to me."

"How can you tell?"

He rolled his eyes at her. "I was married to the woman. I can tell."

"What did you find out?" Zoe dreaded the answer. What if Marcy confirmed Matt's vicious gossip?

"Not much. She parrots exactly what McBirney said when I talked to him earlier. But she's hiding something. It's in her eyes."

Zoe's stomach did a slow roll. "I think I may know what she's keeping from you."

Pete lowered the cup to the table. "What?"

The intensity of his blue eyes made her squirm. "I was talking to Matt at the station today—"

"Matt Doaks? I wouldn't exactly consider him a reliable source."

She shook off the hope that Pete's bitter tone carried a hint of jealousy. "He's McBirney's lapdog. Who would know better what's going on with him?"

Pete shrugged. "What did he say?"

"Apparently McBirney suspects Marcy has been having an affair."

Pete leaned back in his seat and scowled. Zoe wondered if he was thinking back to the moment he learned about another of Marcy's affairs.

Zoe inhaled deeply to brace for the rest. Lowering her voice, she said, "He thinks the affair was with Ted."

Pete stiffened. "Son-of-a-bitch," he muttered through a clenched jaw. "Do you believe him?"

Good question. "I've been trying not to," she admitted. "But whether or not it's true, what if McBirney believed it?"

Pete leaned forward and cupped his chin in his fist. His gaze burned into her brain until she had to look away. If he knew what she wanted to order for dinner, maybe he really could read her thoughts and see her doubts.

The waitress's arrival with two heavy, steaming stoneware plates saved Zoe from Pete's scrutiny. For a few moments there was blessed silence between them as they both organized silverware and napkins.

Pete inspected one of his barbecued ribs. "If Ted and Marcy were having an affair—that might explain a lot."

"But they weren't having an affair." Zoe prayed the words coming off her lips were true.

"And you know this because?"

She stirred her coleslaw to buy time before answering. "I don't know. But I can't believe Ted would do that."

"Marcy would." He bit into the rib.

The poignancy of his voice touched her heart. "I'm sorry."

He spun the meat between his fingers as if determining his next plan of attack. "It's just the truth. She would. So if they were having an affair—"

Zoe's protest died on her lips when he held up one sauce-smudged finger.

"I said if. *If* they were, then perhaps they were together Monday night after the meeting. Maybe Marcy was lying about McBirney's whereabouts because she wasn't home either."

"That might explain why Ted was in McBirney's car." Zoe hated herself as soon as she said it.

"McBirney came home, found his wife gone, and he went looking for her."

Zoe put down the fork and picked up the burger. Too bad she'd lost her appetite. "But the game lands? In the middle of a blizzard? They wouldn't be parking out there. Too cold."

"And they aren't kids. Kids park in the game lands to make out. Adults get a room." Pete polished off the rib and started on another. The prospect of an affair between Ted and Marcy and the motive it provided appeared to bolster his appetite. "Or maybe McBirney came home and caught them together. Killed Ted and drove him out there to cover up the crime scene."

Zoe took a bite. She loved Parson's cheeseburgers, but the juicy meat and the salty cheese held no appeal to her right then. "I don't think they'd have been stupid enough to get caught at the house. Marcy would be expecting McBirney." God, she hated the whole scenario.

Pete dropped another bare bone on his plate with a *clink* and wiped his fingers on a napkin. "You're probably right. But he still could have found them at a motel. I'll start asking around. Not that many places they could have gone. Are you all right?"

She looked up from the burger. "Yeah. Why?"

He tipped his head at her plate. "You've barely touched your food. That's not like you."

True. She rarely left a crumb behind. "I can't stomach this whole idea of Ted cheating on Rose. I don't buy it. Ted's not like that." She caught her mistake, and her voice broke. "He *wasn't* like that."

Pete reached across the table and took her hand. "I'm sorry."

The warm touch of his skin against hers produced a flutter in her chest, like a small flock of butterflies had been set free. She curled her fingers around his.

"You've never really told me much about you and Ted. I mean, there was a 'you and Ted' at one point, right?"

She studied the back of Pete's hand. Safer than meeting his eyes. "Yeah. But it was really short-lived and never went anywhere. I was a raw nerve...you know...vulnerable...after the thing with Matt. And then I introduced Ted to my best friend. They were ga-ga for each other from the moment they laid eyes on one another." She smiled at the memory. Happier times. "I always liked Ted, but I just wasn't into him *that* way."

Pete squeezed her hand, but said nothing.

Zoe finally risked looking him in the eye. The butterflies turned into a flock of swallows. She noticed a smudge of barbecue sauce on his chin and reached across the table with her free hand to wipe it away. He caught her wrist and looked at the sauce on her finger. Then he drew her hand closer and kissed the smudge from it.

She inhaled, forgot to exhale, and her breath caught in the flutter within her chest.

And then her cell phone chirped.

Crap.

He grinned at her and released both hands. "You'd better answer that."

As she reached for her purse and her phone, another piercing assortment of musical notes reached her ears. Pete unclipped his own phone from his belt.

Zoe half turned in the booth as she answered hers. Rose's frantic voice wailed at her. "Thank God you answered. I don't know what to do. Logan's gone."

"What do you mean, gone?"

"He's missing. The car's here, but he's not. His cell goes right to voicemail. He didn't leave a note or tell anyone where he was going." Rose's voice dissolved into sobs.

"Don't worry," Zoe said. Ha. Fat chance. "He probably just took a walk to clear his head."

"He's been gone for hours. It's dark out. He would have come home by now."

"Try to relax. I'll be there in fifteen minutes."

Zoe flipped the phone shut and dropped it into her purse. When she turned back toward the table and Pete, he was ending his call, too. His face was a deep shade of crimson.

"What's wrong?" She couldn't take more bad news. Please, don't let it be Logan...

"Someone broke into the evidence room at the station," Pete said. "The computer we confiscated from Sylvia has been stolen."

TEN

Pete wheeled into the lot in front of the police station and jammed on the brakes. He almost snapped the key off in the ignition as he cut the engine. He was pissed. Someone had stolen something from his very own evidence room. Marcy was lying to him. Zoe was lying to him, too. Her face had lost all color when he told her about the break-in, and she'd insisted the call she'd received was nothing.

Bullshit. She knew or suspected something and wasn't telling him.

Officer Kevin Piacenza met him at the office door. The kid's eyes and nose were watery and blood-red. In sharp contrast, his skin appeared rather bluish deepening to dark circles under his eyes.

"You look like crap," Pete told him. "Go home, and take your germs with you."

Kevin responded by dissolving into a coughing fit that forced him to drop into one of the chairs in the room. "I'm sorry, Chief," he wheezed. "I figured you and Seth needed some downtime, so I came in to help." He dabbed at his nose with a wrinkled handkerchief and winced. "When I got here, I found the evidence room door was all busted up."

The pressure inside Pete's head threatened to blow the top of it off. Without waiting to hear more, he headed toward the rear of the building.

The station had been locked up for the night. With only the three full-time officers and four part-timers, one of whom was currently visiting family in Florida, they didn't have the staff to man the station twenty-four hours a day. Hell, most nights, they were lucky to keep one guy on patrol. The state police filled the void when necessary, but Pete and his officers pushed themselves hard and put in too many hours.

The holding cell stood empty, courtesy of Sylvia's attorney arranging bail.

But there was an alarm. Why the hell hadn't the alarm gone off?

The hinges of the steel evidence room door had been removed, and it lay flat on the hallway floor. Too bad it hadn't fallen on the asshole and smashed him.

The area around the lock displayed scrapes and gouges. From the looks of the crumpled metal, someone had used a heavy-duty pry bar to gain access.

Pete stepped over the door and into the room. Gray metal shelves held labeled boxes of evidence from a multitude of cases. Larger items sat on a counter that ran the perimeter of the room. He knew precisely where he had set the computer with its chain-of-evidence tags. The monitor and keyboard remained as he'd left them. But the tower was gone. He glanced around the room on the chance it had been moved.

"I figured you'd want to be the one to dust for prints." Kevin's voice rasped around stifled coughs.

"You figured right." If for no other reason than the powder would likely drive Kevin into a coughing jag that would contaminate the scene. "Get on the phone, and tell Seth to get back in here. While you're waiting for him, write up your report and a requisition for a new door. Then get the hell out of here, and don't come back until you're healthy."

"Yes, sir." Kevin's words followed Pete as he ducked out of the room.

What idiot would lug a computer out through the front of the station, which faced the heavily travelled Route 15? On a hunch, Pete stormed down the hall to the storage room and flung the door open. No one ever left the lights on in there. And yet tonight they burned brightly. He made his way to the back door, keeping vigilant to anything that might be out of place or anything that an intruder might have inadvertently left behind.

The back door was shut. He tugged on a pair of Latex gloves, released the latch, and stepped into the frigid night air.

It only opened from the inside. Yet there was no sign of tampering. No scratches. No pry bar marks.

"Kevin," he called back into the building.

"Yes, sir?"

"Get out here."

Once the young officer arrived, Pete released the door and let it drift shut. The latch clicked. He grasped the handle and tugged. It didn't budge. He tried again. Nothing. The thief might have left through the back, but he didn't gain entrance there.

"Let me in," he shouted.

The door swung open thanks to Kevin. Pete brushed past him and headed for the front of the building. Kevin trailed behind.

In the front office, Pete checked the alarm. "Did you disarm this?"

Kevin shook his head. "It was disarmed when I got here."

Pete noticed that his knuckles hurt and realized he'd been clenching his fists. He knew and trusted his men. Neither Seth nor Kevin would be involved in this. Someone else—someone who had access to the alarm codes—had a hand in this theft.

But who?

Pete's gaze drifted up to the station's lone surveillance camera. Positioned to capture images of anyone entering the front door, it might just hold the answer.

Although Zoe had promised to come right over, she drove straight through Dillard, passing Rose's house. Pete's announcement about the break-in and the stolen computer had given her an idea. She almost hoped she was wrong. However that would mean Logan really was missing.

Half of the farmhouse blazed with light while her half stood in darkness. She stepped quietly onto the back porch and squinted through the lace curtains hanging in her door's window. She thought she noticed a faint glow from the far room. Her fingers tightened on the doorknob. It clicked open.

She burst into the room and crossed to her office. Logan scrambled to shut off a flashlight aimed at the keyboard, but only managed to knock it to the floor with a thud. Both cats bolted to different corners of the room.

Zoe flipped the light switch. Logan froze in mid lunge for the flashlight and blinked at her. If she hadn't been so pissed at him, his sad attempt to hide his presence when he was so obviously busted would have been funny.

"Logan," she began, keeping the timbre of her voice low and—she hoped—threatening. "What the hell have you done?"

His interrupted grab for the flashlight, which had rolled across the ancient, uneven floor, disintegrated into an awkward tumble from the computer chair. He landed on his backside.

"Um," he stuttered. "I—um—wanted to find out what was on the hard drive, but Mom wouldn't let me leave. So I—um—snuck out."

"Sneaking is not your strong suit, kiddo. You're lucky she hasn't called the Marines."

He blushed as he climbed back into the chair. "Sorry."

"Sorry? That's not gonna cut it. How did you get here?"

"I—um—hitchhiked. I know, I know, I'm not supposed to, but—"

Zoe tuned out the boy's babbling as she looked around the room. Hitchhiked? With a stolen computer? "Where is it?"

"What?"

"The computer."

Logan scowled. "Well, it's right here." He pointed to her monitor.

"Not *my* computer. The one you stole from the evidence room."

His face went white.

She started to repeat herself, but stopped. "You didn't take the computer?"

"I took the hard drive. You know that."

Zoe's mind spun like wheels on ice, going nowhere. "But someone broke into the evidence room at the police station this evening and took the rest of it. When your mom called me and said you were missing, I assumed..." As she said it, she knew full well she'd assumed wrong.

"I don't need the rest of it. I've already got the..." His voice trailed off. "Shit."

"Now what?"

"Whoever did take it is gonna find out the hard drive's missing."

"We knew that was going to happen sooner or later," Zoe reminded him.

"Yeah, but cops finding out is one thing. What if—what if Mr. McBirney's the one who took it? When he finds out the hard drive is missing, he's gonna know I'm the one who lifted it and then—" Logan bounced out of the chair and paced across the room, rubbing his forehead. "Shit. He's gonna kill me, too."

Zoe sank into her recliner. She longed to assure the kid that he was way off base and nothing would happen to him. But his panicked stream of thought pretty well mirrored her own.

"We don't know for sure that McBirney stole the computer," she said, trying to convince both of them all was not lost. "And even if he did, why would he automatically think you were the one who removed the hard drive?"

Logan shot her a look that clearly said *Duh.* "Who else would've done it?"

She wasn't sure if he meant the computer theft or the hard drive. It didn't matter. The answer to both was the same. No one.

"This only means one thing." Logan stood a little taller, like one of those superheroes she used to watch with him on TV Saturday mornings.

"What's that?"

"I have to work fast to find out what's on this thing." He strode to the computer, rocking the chair as he flopped into it, almost landing on the floor again.

"Have you had any luck?"

"Well, sort of. But not really."

"Sort of? What's that mean?"

"The restoration program pulled up some files, but I can't open them."

"Why not?"

"Because your computer doesn't have the right kind of accounting software installed on it."

"Oh." Why couldn't something be easy just once? "So we've hit a dead end?"

"Not exactly." Logan cracked his knuckles. "I called a buddy of mine and he has bootleg copies of all different kinds of software. He's gonna get me what I need."

"This doesn't sound very legal."

Logan rolled his eyes. "I've already stolen the hard drive, and you're aiding and abetting or something like that. Don't you think it's a little late to worry about keeping things legal?"

The kid had a point. "So we're stuck until your buddy comes up with this software we need?"

Logan's fingers danced across the keyboard. "Pretty much. But I did find something on here I could open."

At last. Some good news. "Why didn't you say so earlier? Show me."

He clicked the mouse and Outlook opened on the monitor. However, none of the e-mails belonged to Zoe. She leaned over his shoulder for a closer look. Her palms itched with excitement. "This has to be it," she whispered.

"I dunno. I've been reading them, and they're pretty boring. Who cares about how much salt to order for the road department?"

"*You* do if you can't get out to basketball practice because of ice." She roughed up his hair. "Seriously, there's got to be something here." Something worth killing for.

"I know. But there are a ton of messages. Plus the sent ones." He clicked the mouse again. "And the trash can is full, too."

Her cell phone's muffled chirp floated up from her coat pocket. She dug it out and checked the screen. "Rose." *Oops.*

"Thank God." Rose's frantic voice greeted her. "Where are you? When you didn't show up I was afraid something else happened."

"Logan's fine," Zoe said. "I'm sorry. I should have called you the minute I knew."

Rose's weeping came through the line. "Where is he? Where are you?"

"At my house."

Silence greeted her.

"Rose?"

"Your house? What the hell is he doing there?"

Zoe remembered their weak cover story. "He was worried about that computer problem I was having and wanted to try and fix it. I guess he was feeling pretty helpless sitting around home."

The chill in Rose's voice could have left icicles hanging from the phone. "Do not tell me he was hitchhiking again."

Zoe chewed her lip. "Okay. I won't."

Rose responded with a string of profanities. "That boy is grounded for the next year. Bring him home. *Now.* I'm sure your computer can wait until after we bury my husband."

Ouch. "Okay. See you in a few." Zoe stuffed the phone back into her pocket. "As fast as you can," she said to Logan, "show me how to get back into this e-mail program. Looks like I have a lot of reading to do."

Having spent half the night and all morning studying outdated township e-mail correspondence, Zoe came to the conclusion Logan had it right. *Pretty boring.* But buried somewhere among the mind-numbing posts might be the one to explain everything that had happened in the last couple of days.

She noted the point at which she stopped reading around noon. Her shoulders ached from hunching over the computer. Her head throbbed, too, but more from tension than poor posture. And where she needed to be that afternoon and evening would do nothing to improve her stress levels.

Funeral homes freaked Zoe out. Granted, she suspected no one enjoyed spending time there with the possible exception of the funeral director. But every time she walked into one, she flashed back to her eight-year-old self and being told that her dad was inside that shiny, closed box. They never let her see the body. Too badly disfigured after the accident, they said. But how was an eight-year-old to understand? At thirty-five, she still had a hard time grasping the concept of *there one minute, gone the next.*

Now it was Ted's turn. At least the casket was open. It might seem ghoulish to some, but she knew the emotional benefits of seeing for yourself that your father was truly gone.

The public viewing didn't officially begin until two. Family members had been asked to arrive a half hour early for some private time. Honored that Rose and Sylvia had included her in that list, Zoe would still rather be anywhere else for any other reason. Even reading archaic e-mail messages.

She battled her anxiety from the back of the room. Floral arrangements of all shapes and sizes lined the walls, their fragrance choking her.

Across the gulf of muted nondescript carpet, Rose bent over the casket, her head lowered, shoulders shaking. Her mother, Mrs. Bertolotti—Bert to anyone who knew her—flanked her on one side, Sylvia on the other.

Swimming in a suit jacket he had yet to grow into, Logan paced the perimeter of the room. Allison's unnaturally black hair was twisted in a haphazard knot with stray wisps sticking out all over. Zoe suspected it was supposed to look messy. If so, the girl had succeeded in her efforts. She wore a short, plaid skirt and sat knock-kneed in one of the upholstered chairs that edged the room. Her leg bounced in time to the music piped into her brain through ear pods. Thin white wires trailed to the pocket of the pink, puffy winter jacket she'd refused to take off. By all appearances, she didn't plan to stay long.

Zoe closed her eyes to block out the room. But the smell of the flowers and the soft strains of a recorded organ refused to be ignored. They swept her deeper into her childhood trauma. Her father's death. Her mother's attempt to fill the void with a quick remarriage and an eventual escape to Florida. Zoe's own effort to find a father-figure by dating a string of older boys in high school, falling in love with a jerk like Matt and the subsequent betrayal that left her susceptible to the likes of Jerry McBirney.

"You okay?"

Her eyes snapped open. Logan stood before her, a look of concern mingled with despair on his youthful face.

"Yeah." It was a lie, but she couldn't burden him with her anguish. He had his own. Someday, they might be able to compare notes, but not now. Not here. "How are you?"

His jaw clenched, and he managed a quick nod of his head.

She reached out to rub his arm. "I know."

"Have you been over—there—yet?" He motioned toward the casket.

"No." If it were up to her, she'd stay rooted where she was. But he offered his arm. Sucking in a deep breath of courage, she slipped her hand into the crook of his elbow and, leaning on one another, they crossed the room.

"Did you read any of the e-mails?" he said, his voice clandestine.

"Yeah."

"Find anything?"

"No. Like you said, they were pretty boring."

He gave her a little nudge. "Told you."

They exchanged a look. Zoe was grateful, and knew Logan was, too, for the momentary distraction. But it wasn't long enough. As if he were an escort, seating her at a wedding, he slipped her hand from his arm and ducked away.

Bert never looked especially healthy, but she wore the evidence of her recent bout with the flu on her colorless face and in her sunken eyes. Still, she swept Zoe into her arms and whispered, "How sweet of you to come."

Sylvia's embrace came next. Zoe fought off the tears. "I'm so sorry." She choked on the words that seemed insignificant in the face of such grief.

Then she stood face-to-face with Rose. Her childhood friend. Her compadre through it all. A lifetime of joy and sorrow, successes and failures flashed between them without a word. They wrapped one another up in each other's arms and the dam holding back the tears collapsed under the strain.

Zoe dropped into the chair next to Allison who hadn't budged. Members of the community filtered into the room. Within minutes, there was a line out the door. A few gave Zoe a sad nod of recognition. Allison picked at her fingernails.

Zoe drew a deep breath and leaned toward the girl. "I hear the weather forecast for the weekend is calling for a warm up. Maybe we could go riding."

"It'll be too muddy." Allison's voice was flat.

"We've got the indoor arena. It won't be muddy inside."

Allison shrugged.

"Or you could just come over and hang out with Merlin and Jade."

Her sigh was loud and exasperated. "I don't know. Maybe. I'll probably have homework or something." She shifted in her chair away from Zoe. Her body language said, "Leave me alone," clearer than the spoken word ever could.

"Hi, Zoe."

She looked up to find Matt standing over them. In navy blue

Dockers and a muted gray sweater snug enough to complement his broad shoulders and narrow waist, he appeared as boyishly handsome as he'd been when they were in high school. For a split second, she was catapulted into the past and fell in love with him all over again. Just as quickly, the years tumbled back in place. His infidelity and his recent accusations about Ted and Marcy slammed her into the reality of the present. She returned his greeting.

Allison snapped out of her slouch. "Hi, Matt," she said, her voice cheery for the first time in recent memory.

Zoe cast a glance in the girl's direction and recalled Rose's tale of catching her with a high school jock and Ted tossing the kid out and then taking Allison's door off its hinges.

Matt gave a quick nod at the teenager, but kept his attention on Zoe. "How are you holding up? I know this has to be hard on you."

"Not as hard as it is on Rose and the kids." Zoe put a hand on Allison's arm, but she pulled free, jumped to her feet, and stomped away.

Matt scowled after her. "Yeah. I see that."

"Everyone's dealing with losing Ted the best they can." Zoe longed to run after Allison, but sensed the girl needed space. The room was growing increasingly crowded.

Matt took the chair Allison had vacated. "Have you mentioned what I told you to Rose?"

"You mean that her husband may have been cheating on her? No."

He studied his hands. "Not the right time, I guess."

"I don't know if there would ever be a right time. Especially since I don't believe it."

He met her gaze. "You don't?"

Did she? No. Not today. She couldn't permit herself to think of the possibility. And if she put off thinking about it long enough, maybe she'd forget.

"You just don't want to believe it."

She ached to grab him and shake him. Tell him there was no way Ted would be unfaithful. Remind Matt that betrayal was *his* bailiwick. But he wasn't looking at her any more. His gaze had shifted over her shoulder, and his jaw clenched.

Zoe turned to find out what had grabbed his attention. The line of people who'd come to pay their respects extended out the door in the back of the room and into the hallway toward the front of the funeral home, with no end in sight. The person Matt was staring at had just reached the threshold of the room.

Marcy McBirney, wearing head-to-toe black, including oversized sunglasses, clasped a handkerchief to her face as she wept inconsolably.

ELEVEN

The Vance Township Police Station had once again grown quiet. Workmen had installed a temporary door to the evidence room while a new steel door, one without those damned exposed hinges, had been ordered. The technician from the security company had changed the locks and alarm codes. Pete spent the night processing his latest crime scene. The station. *His* station. Having this happen on his watch was damned humiliating.

His hopes of the survcillance camera providing an easy answer were soon dashed. The recording revealed someone of apparently small stature in an oversized coat with a massive hood entering the building, head down. He turned and must have punched the code into the keypad, although all Pete saw was the guy's back. Then, he again faced the camera with his head lowered and bustled down the hallway, out of view. The culprit clearly knew the camera was there and kept his face hidden. Or her face. Pete wagered his suspect was a woman. He also theorized she was wearing a man's coat. And she probably opened the back door so the owner of that coat could gain access without being captured on video.

But there was no way to make a positive ID from what he had. Note to self—find the funds to purchase and install additional cameras.

Wayne Baronick was otherwise occupied with a drug sweep in Brunswick so at least Pete didn't have to deal with him, too. Instead, he seized the opportunity to use some of his old skills from his days with the Pittsburgh Bureau of Police. Vance Township was too small and insignificant to merit a real lab. Trace evidence went to the county crime lab. But Pete had the equipment to process fingerprints and scan them into the computers to run them through AFIS.

For the moment, however, all he needed was a magnifying loop.

Dusting the evidence room for prints had produced several dozen more-or-less usable specimens. The door to the storage room and the back entrance provided a similar number as had the area around the alarm keypad and the front door, but most were too smudged or layered on top of one another to serve any useful purpose. His first task involved eliminating his own prints and those belonging to his men.

As morning faded into afternoon, he grew more frustrated by the hour. Every single print he'd lifted from the evidence room matched either his officers or his own. The bastard—or bastards—had no doubt worn gloves.

Pete's cell phone ringing added to his aggravation.

"Hey, Chief. It's Seth. I'm outside. My key doesn't work."

"I'll be right there," Pete straightened the already perfectly aligned stack of prints and locked the door to the fingerprint lab behind him. Seth gave him a sheepish grin when he let the officer in.

"It's kind of weird to be locked out of your own station."

Pete handed him a new key. "Don't write the alarm code down anywhere. We've had one security breach. I won't tolerate another." He told Seth the code and suggested he figure out some way to memorize it.

"Do we have a suspect yet?" Seth asked.

Pete gritted his teeth. He might just snap the neck of the next fool to ask him that question. "No. If we did, we wouldn't be standing here. We'd be out there making an arrest."

"Yes, sir." His tone of voice indicated he realized it had been a stupid question. "Uh, Chief?"

"Yeah?"

"Could you give me that code one more time?"

Pete rattled it off and left the young officer practicing the numbers on the new keypad. Back inside the lab, Pete studied the useable prints he'd lifted from around the front door. He divided them into two piles. The first were the matches to staff. The second were unknowns. Those he proceeded to scan and run through the AFIS database. Unlike on TV, where quick hits solved cases in under an hour, the real process didn't work that way. He found two hits, but all that came up were a set of numbers that he punched into another computer to match to a potential name. In both cases, the prints matched local citizens who had recently been in the station on legitimate business.

After a break to refill his coffee cup—Seth had made a fresh pot—Pete returned to the lab. He scanned another print and leaned back to wait.

He should be at Ted Bassi's viewing. Not only in his capacity as police chief, but for Zoe. She was holding up remarkably well, but this was hard on her.

Jerry McBirney suspected Marcy had been having an affair with Ted. Interesting. Zoe didn't want to believe it, but the scenario made sense. Marcy's reaction to hearing of Ted's death. McBirney's reaction to her reaction. But why was Marcy sticking to her story, protecting her husband's alibi and therefore him? Or was she merely protecting her own ass? Nice ass, though it may be.

He took off his reading glasses and rubbed his eyes, blotting out all thoughts of Marcy's ass. Do. Not. Go. There.

Instead, he reflected on the blizzard two nights ago and the Buick with Ted's body inside. Was there a link between the murder and this break-in at the station? Had to be. Vance Township wasn't the type of place to have a rash of unrelated crimes. He stared at the stack of fingerprints.

He'd managed to find one lone print in the Buick. Baronick had taken it with him. But Pete had a photocopy of it. Odds were slim, but...

He left the computer running its search and headed back to the evidence room. In the ratty old metal file cabinet in the corner of the room, he hunted for the folder he'd placed there yesterday. Where was it? Tension seized his shoulders and neck. Had the thief taken more than the computer? But, no. There it was. Misfiled, which was normal for Pete. Another reason he missed having Sylvia on the job.

Back in the lab, he picked up the magnifying loop and started back through the stack of unknown prints. Most were obviously not matches. Those were simple to eliminate. Others required closer scrutiny.

Near the bottom of the stack, he came across a smudged partial that had been lifted from the wall next to the front door. Near the keypad. He studied it. He studied the one from the Buick. Back and forth. They were similar. But were they a match?

Yes.

Pete put down the loop, his heart racing. The same person who'd left one lone print in Jerry McBirney's car had also been inside his police station. Could the print Pete held in his hand belong to Ted Bassi's killer?

Leaving Matt sitting on the sidelines, Zoe weaved her way through the crowd. She stopped short of interrupting Rose as she embraced a guy who lived down the street from the Bassis. What did she aim to do, anyway? She couldn't drag Rose out of there before Marcy made it to the front of the line. Besides, Rose had no idea about the affair.

Or did she?

Zoe squeezed her eyes shut against the first twinge of a headache. What was she thinking? There had been no affair. It was all paranoid lies and rumors fabricated by Jerry McBirney and perpetuated by Matt Doaks.

Matt. She should slap him for repeating such nonsense. She turned back toward the direction she'd just come, intent on marching up to him and giving him a good verbal thrashing. However, an elderly woman sat in the chair he'd been in. Zoe surveyed the room. No Matt.

She watched the line inch forward and Marcy with it. The woman's shoulders slumped, and she visibly trembled as she sniffed into her handkerchief.

What was with Marcy's oversized sunglasses? Had the gray skies brightened since Zoe arrived? The indirect lighting of the funeral home definitely did not require them. Zoe studied the woman. Pete's ex-wife. How in the world could she have left a man like Pete for Jerry McBirney? Then again, Zoe, too, had once fallen victim to McBirney's "charm."

When Marcy turned in her direction, Zoe ducked off to the side and pretended to read the tags on the floral tributes.

The line and Marcy advanced. Zoe's headache grew in intensity. Two more people in front of Marcy. Then one.

Zoe watched Rose for any reaction. The last person before Marcy moved on to hug Sylvia. Rose took Marcy into her arms and both women wept. Zoe inched closer until she could hear them over the soft rumble of conversation.

"I'm so sorry," Marcy repeated over and over.

Rose thanked her and patted her on her back.

"Ted was a good man." Marcy whimpered as she eased back from the embrace.

"Yes, he was."

"He'll be missed."

"He already is."

Marcy nodded. "If there's anything I can do. I feel I owe..." The rest was spoken into the handkerchief, and Zoe missed it.

What did she owe? And why?

Marcy moved on to dampen Sylvia's shoulder. If Ted's mother suspected anything was going on, she gave no indication. And Zoe suspected Sylvia would not be able to hide something like that. Nor would she want to.

If there truly had been an affair, Zoe felt confident that neither Rose nor Sylvia knew of it. Relieved, she decided to track down Matt and tell him to keep his lies to himself. Before she had a chance to move, she noticed Marcy give Rose's mother a quick hug and then turn away from the group at the casket. Marcy dabbed her nose and bumped the sunglasses. Wincing, she removed them.

Zoe gasped. Marcy's left eye was purple and swollen. As she touched the handkerchief to it, her gaze met Zoe's and her good eye widened. Marcy rammed the sunglasses back on her face, lowered her head, and disappeared into the crowd.

As Zoe sunk into the nearest chair, memories she'd tried to shove into some dark recess of her subconscious bubbled to the surface. Seeing Marcy's battered face brought back that night so many years ago. A flash of Jerry McBirney—enraged—teeth barred like a rabid dog, eyes bulging, skin red from the booze and the fury. And the huge fist. The impact didn't even hurt. Or she didn't recall that it had. At least not until later when the bruising and swelling set in.

She closed her eyes and lightly touched where her cheekbone had been broken. The physical pain had been nothing compared to the heartbreak that came a few days later.

The volume of the soft murmurs around her notched up, punctuated with some startled exclamations and a wail that sounded faintly like a cat. Stowing that long-ago night to its rightful darkened corner of her mind, Zoe opened her eyes. Rose was wrapped up in a group embrace with a trio of women from the fire auxiliary. But most of the mourners were looking toward the source of the keening at the back of the room. Paramedic instincts kicked in. Zoe bounded from the chair and threaded her way through the mingling crowd. She made it to the hallway in time to spot Allison, still in her pink jacket, breaking free from a grandfatherly gentlemen and running out into the snow. The girl was in hysterics. The older man looked after her, open mouthed.

"That poor child," he said when Zoe approached. "She's just lost her dad. She shouldn't be alone."

"I'll take care of it," Zoe told him. "Thanks."

The line to enter the funeral home stretched out the front door and down the steps. Allison ran as if someone were chasing her.

"Allison!" Zoe shouted after her.

If the girl heard, she didn't respond.

By the time Zoe reached the sidewalk, Allison had turned the corner. Where on earth did she think she was going? And should Zoe go back in and tell Rose?

No. Rose had more than enough to deal with. There was no way Zoe was going to catch Allison on foot. The January wind bit through Zoe's black sweater and twill pants, but she had no time to go back for her coat. She jogged across the street to the parking lot and her truck.

"What do we know about Ted Bassi's murder?" Pete asked his officers.

He paced the conference room. Seth sat on one side of the long table. Kevin, appearing only slightly less feverish than yesterday, sat on the other.

"Besides the fact that County has taken over the case?" Seth asked.

Pete narrowed his eyes at his young officer. "Nobody likes a smartass."

Seth bit back a grin and cleared his throat. "No, sir. I spoke with Ted's neighbors." He flipped open his notepad. "Mostly, no one remembers anything out of the ordinary. But Mrs. Wallace from next door says she saw Ted's truck pull in a little before 8:30 PM. Then she says it left again about twenty minutes later."

"Did she see Ted driving it? Was he alone?"

"Couldn't tell. It was dark. She just noticed the headlights passing her house and thought it odd that he was going out again in the snow.

She said he drove pretty fast for conditions, too."

"What else?"

"That was it. None of the other neighbors noticed anything at all. I also spoke with Rose's mother's neighbors. Both Mrs. Paxton and old Mr. Modic confirm that Rose arrived there sometime between 8:15 and 8:30. Mr. Modic was sitting by the front window and insists he'd have seen anyone leaving the house, but no one did. He gave me a pretty good log of the comings and goings of the rest of the neighbors, though."

Nothing much got past Henry Modic, Pete mused. He thumbed through his own notes. Joe Mendez, who had called in the abandoned car report, swore there wasn't anything there at ten. He'd looked out his window before his favorite TV show came on and there was nothing. He got up to use the bathroom during a commercial break at 10:50 and spotted the car pulled off the edge of the game lands road. When he was getting ready for bed at 11:15, he looked again and it was still there. That's when he called it in. He insisted he didn't see anyone moving around and didn't notice any other vehicles.

"So other than confirming Rose Bassi's alibi, we don't have anything." Pete wished like hell they could locate Ted's missing truck. It might point them in the direction of where the murder had occurred. Which reminded him of the alleged affair. If McBirney had walked in on his wife and Ted...

"Check the parking lot of the Vance Motel for Ted's pickup. And talk to the owners," he ordered. It was a dump, but it was close. "Ask about Monday night."

"What about Monday night?" Kevin said.

Pete hesitated and then shared the rumor of the affair between his ex-wife and the victim.

Kevin managed a whistle. "That provides an interesting motive."

"But not evidence. We need evidence. Blood. Indications of a fight. If you don't find anything at the Vance Motel, call around other area hotels and motels. I want to know if the housekeeping staff had any extra work Monday night or Tuesday morning."

Both Seth and Kevin murmured acknowledgment.

"Next order of business." Pete rapped the tabletop with his knuckles. "Let's go over what we know about this break-in."

* * *

With the Chevy's heater on high, Zoe cruised the residential streets of Phillipsburg. Old but neat homes with crumbling sidewalks populated the neighborhood around the funeral home. The snow plows had been out in force and homeowners had swept or shoveled their walks, so getting around was not an issue.

Where the hell had Allison gone? Did she have a friend nearby? A teacher? Zoe should've gone back inside and talked to Rose. And while she was there, she should have grabbed her coat.

She drove around one block and then another. No sign of the teen in the bright pink jacket. A stop sign loomed ahead. Zoe coasted to the intersection, taking her hands off the wheel to rub some warmth into her arms. She glanced up and down the streets to each side and spotted the girl halfway down the street on the right. Zoe gunned the truck.

Allison leaned against a huge tree trunk, hugging herself. Her face was lowered. If she'd been a turtle, she'd have been tucked deep within her shell.

Zoe pulled to the curb and lowered the passenger-side window. "Hey, kiddo. Need a ride?"

Allison glared at her askance. Mascara-blackened tears streaked her face. "Leave me alone." Her girlish voice failed to carry the anger that her eyes did.

"I can't leave you out here. Come on. Get in. If you don't want to go back to the funeral home right away, we'll drive around a little."

"No." Her voice cracked. She pushed away from the tree and started walking away from the truck.

Crap. It was too cold to chase her on foot without a coat. But Zoe couldn't let her get away either. She slammed the truck into park and cut the engine.

She jumped out and dug behind the seat. Jumper cables, a tool box, a portable tire pump... Under a length of towrope, she found an old musty horse blanket. Not a heavy wool one, but it was better than nothing. She slung it around her shoulders like an oversized shawl and hurried after the girl. Belly straps and buckles swung around her legs, but she ignored them.

Allison made no effort to outrun Zoe, for which she was immensely grateful. She caught the girl a half a block away from the truck and grabbed her arm.

"Will you stop a minute?"

"Why should I?"

Zoe sighed, and a cloud of fog appeared and dissipated between them. "Because I know what you're going through."

"No, you don't."

"Yes. I do. My dad died, too, remember?"

Allison wrenched free of Zoe's grasp, but didn't run away. She jammed her hands into her pockets, her shoulders hunched around her ears. "It's not the same."

Of course it wasn't. Your own pain was always worse than someone else's. But arguing the point wasn't going to help the situation. "Okay. Then talk to me. We'll compare notes."

Allison scrutinized Zoe's odd attire with disdain. "You are so clueless. Everyone is. Nobody knows how I feel. Mom, Grandma, Logan, you...you all treat me like I'm some little kid. I'm not, you know."

Zoe studied her. Black hair and dark eye makeup made her pale skin appear even whiter. Zoe longed to hold her, to cradle her, to tell her to stop trying to grow up so fast. But Allison would never permit it. "I know you're not. And your age is tough enough without something like this happening."

"You don't know what happened. No one does." Allison paused, shivering. Her eyes narrowed. "Except that McBirney guy. He didn't like my dad so he killed him. Everyone says so. That's it. No big deal."

"But it is a big deal. And you're allowed to cry. It doesn't mean you're a baby."

Allison glared at Zoe, her eyes filled with contempt.

The glimpse of anger seething within the teen shook Zoe. What had happened to the sweet girl she'd known all these years? And how could she reach beyond the rage to find her again?

"Please," Zoe said. "Let me help."

Allison stepped back. She unfolded her arms from around herself, her fists clenched. "You just don't get it. I don't want you to help me. I don't need anyone's help. I just want you all to leave me alone. I'd be fine if you'd mind your own damned business." She spun away and stalked off down the sidewalk.

Numb from the cold stinging her legs through her dress slacks and seeping through the horse blanket, Zoe watched her go. At least she headed back in the direction of the funeral home.

What the hell was happening? The girl, so determined to reject the support offered to her, appeared on the verge of a complete meltdown. Allison had been right about one thing: Zoe didn't really know how she felt. The difference between the ages of eight and fifteen was tremendous. At eight, when Zoe lost her dad, she'd been innocent, unaware of the scope of her loss. But at fifteen, Allison was already wracked with angst simply from being on the cusp of womanhood. She'd still been Daddy's Little Girl, her last strong tie to childhood. And now that was ripped from her.

Zoe began to doubt whether family and friends would be enough to see Allison through this heartbreak.

"There was no sign of tampering with the exterior doors and locks," Seth said. "It appears the actor entered through the front using a key and knew the code to disarm the alarm."

"But he didn't have the key to the evidence room," Keith said, his voice deep and raspy.

Pete drummed the table with his pen. "Who knows our alarm code?"

"The three of us and the four part-time weekend guys," Seth said.

"Sylvia Bassi," Kevin added.

Pete couldn't imagine any logical explanation for Sylvia's involvement. "Did either of you mention the code to someone else?"

Both responded in unison, "No."

"Okay. Who else? Think."

Silence settled over the room. Finally, Kevin offered, "How about the supervisors?"

"No." But Pete had started to consider another possibility. One that seemed more and more likely. He kept hoping his officers would suggest some other suspect.

"Someone over on the township offices side?" This came from Seth, referring to the portion of the building used by the zoning officer and the tax collector.

"No," Pete said. They had their own separate entrance and alarm system.

"What about the officers who used to work for the township?" Kevin asked. "The one guy's name was Walter Fanase. The other one left before I was hired."

"Anthony Petrucci," Pete said. "He moved to Colorado two years ago. But it wouldn't hurt to look him up. See if he shared our codes with anyone else. And Walter is with the State Police now. Seth, make some phone calls. Check with Fanase and Petrucci and the weekend guys."

"You think they might be involved somehow?" Kevin said.

"No, I don't. But we need to clear them so we can look elsewhere. Anyone else?"

"What other officers worked here before them?" Seth asked.

"It doesn't matter," Kevin said around a cough. "We were in the old station before that. Different locks."

Pete needed to face facts. There was one other person. Seth and Kevin wouldn't think of her because she had left her job at the department before either of them was hired. Back when both Fanase and Petrucci worked in Vance Township. In this building. Sylvia's former assistant.

Marcy Adams McBirney.

TWELVE

Being Chief of Police came with certain unwritten, but understood perks. Pete took advantage of one now and parked too near the intersection where the curb bore a worn coat of yellow paint. Both sides of the narrow streets around the funeral home were lined with vehicles, including a pair of Vance Township fire engines.

He leaned back in his seat and watched the procession of mourners extend out the front door and down the steps. Would Ted Bassi's killer be brazen enough to put in an appearance?

Only one way to find out.

A blast of biting cold air hit him as he opened the car door. Pulling the collar of his wool coat tighter around his neck, he picked his way across the icy patches on the uneven cobblestones.

Inside the crowded funeral home, strain showed on many faces. A few folks laughed quietly at conversation meant to distract. Several women appeared on the verge of tears. A few men did, too.

A sign at one doorway listed Ted's name. Beneath the sign, a lighted stand held a guest book. Pete picked up the pen and quietly leafed through the pages, checking signatures. The thing read like the county tax register, but there were only a few names that interested him. Matt Doaks, for one. Marcy McBirney for another. Not Mr. and Mrs. McBirney. Just Marcy. Interesting.

Pete scrawled his name on an available line and then made his way through the throng of mourners into the next room. He searched the sea of faces for Zoe.

Ted and Rose's boy stood off to one side, surrounded by other young men. Buddies from school or sports or both. Their Goth daughter with her inky black hair huddled in a chair, shoulders hunched and arms crossed in front of her. Those who sat on either side faced away from her, talking to others.

A half a dozen stoic firefighters, wearing their dress uniforms with black bands around their badges, sat together near the back.

Rose and her mother stood near the coffin, greeting the steady stream of friends, family, and acquaintances offering their condolences. Sylvia had claimed a chair near them. The dark circles under her eyes stood out in stark contrast against her pale skin.

Someone touched his arm. "I wondered if you would make it," Zoe said.

"I was working this afternoon." He cringed as he said it. True or not, it sounded like a lame excuse.

"Anything new with the break-in?"

"Not really. How are Rose and Sylvia holding up?"

Zoe sighed. "Rose is playing the tough guy routine. Sylvia's exhausted." She checked her watch. "I'll be glad when she can get out of here and get some rest."

"You look good." He stumbled over the words. Damn. He was plenty old enough to come up with something better than that.

Zoe blushed. She was damned sexy when she blushed. Maybe that simple compliment wasn't so bad after all. She lowered her gaze and cleared her throat. "Marcy was here this afternoon."

He didn't mention that he already knew. "Was her husband with her?"

"No. Thank God. Hopefully he has the good sense to stay away. He's already given this family enough grief."

"And Sylvia's already given him a black eye." Pete fought the urge to smile. He wished he'd been there to see that.

Zoe scowled, and her lips parted as if to say something. Pete waited, but she must have reconsidered and closed her mouth.

"How did Rose react to Marcy?" he asked.

"No different than with everyone else. If there was anything going on between Ted and Marcy, Rose doesn't know about it."

In his experience, the wife almost always knew when her husband was fooling around. She may not want to admit it, but the darned thing about women—most knew when something was off. Men tended to be clueless. He sure had been.

Of course, there was the possibility that Rose suspected an affair, but didn't suspect Marcy.

"Hello, Chief."

He turned to find the sultry voice belonged to that attorney McBirney had recently hired as township solicitor. The woman in the ridiculous shoes who had been at McBirney's side during the supervisors' meeting. And during the media circus at the station when Sylvia had been arrested. What the hell was her name?

"Elizabeth Sunday, Esquire," she said, as if reading his mind. She extended a hand bearing several glittery rings and long, red nails.

When he took the hand, the intensity of her grip surprised him. "Ms. Sunday. You know Zoe Chambers?"

The lawyer offered Zoe a cool nod. "Such a senseless thing, this murder." Her words were directed to Pete.

Beside him, Zoe stiffened. He caught her hand before she did something stupid. Like slugging the attorney.

"Where's your client?" Pete said.

She raised one eyebrow. "Excuse me?"

"McBirney."

"Oh. I have no idea. And Mr. McBirney is not my client. I represent the interests of the residents of Vance Township."

Several smart-assed comments collided in Pete's brain, begging for their chance in the spotlight, but he decided under the circumstances, silence might be the best alternative.

"I see that Mrs. Bassi has been released from custody," Elizabeth said. "I'm glad. Ted Bassi's death has been such a tragedy for his family. There's no reason she should be incarcerated during this time. It's not like she's a flight risk."

"And it's not like she actually did anything wrong," Zoe challenged.

Pete winced as Zoe's fingers tightened around his. He gave her hand a gentle shake to remind her he was there. She loosened her grip with a quick apologetic grin.

"That isn't up to us to decide, is it, Miss Chambers?" Elizabeth responded. "Well, Chief, it was lovely to see you, as always. If you'll excuse me, I'm going to offer my condolences to the bereaved family." She glided away, hips swaying in a tight skirt. Pete's attempt to avoid staring was only modestly successful.

Zoe's fingers tensed again, redirecting Pete's concentration. "Easy, will ya? That's my hand, not her throat, you're crushing."

"Sorry. I can't believe she'd have the gall to show up."

"She probably considers it a professional courtesy. Besides—and don't break my hand for saying this—but as much as I don't care for her either, most of what she's done has simply been her job."

"Yeah, but it's a job Jerry hired her for when everyone else in the township was happy with our old solicitor. She's another one of Jerry McBirney's puppets."

"Guilt by association?"

Zoe huffed. "Something like that."

Someone bumped them from behind. Pete turned. An elderly gentleman mumbled an apology. Pete realized they were holding up the procession of mourners making their way toward the casket. He smiled his own apology at the man and caught Zoe's elbow, edging her forward.

"What do you think is going to happen to Sylvia?" Zoe asked.

"I wish I knew. I think Judge Mitchell would have thrown the case out if she hadn't used her purse to deck McBirney." While Pete would have enjoyed seeing it, he also wished Sylvia had been smarter than to clobber McBirney in front of the judge.

A pair of women, neighbors of Rose's mother, paused on their way out to exchange pleasantries with Zoe and Pete. A trickle of sweat rolled down Pete's neck. The pack of humanity created more heat than a Pennsylvania coal furnace, and Pete regretted keeping his coat on. At least the line progressed at a steady pace as people appeared eager to get in and get out.

Zoe looked around. "I wonder where Logan went."

The group of high school boys had vanished. "Probably outside to get some air." Pete couldn't say that he blamed them.

"Yeah. A couple of his buddies smoke. They think it's cool."

"Some things never change. Except now to be cool you have to freeze your ass off outside to feed your habit."

Elizabeth Sunday had reached the front of the line. Pete hoped he wouldn't be called in to break up any wrestling matches.

"Sylvia better behave herself," Zoe whispered in his ear, echoing his thoughts.

Rose's solemn expression grew stony when the attorney stepped up to her, offering a hand and a pat on the shoulder. The constant hum of conversation around him blocked his ability to hear the exchange between the women.

Zoe nudged him. "What do you think Elizabeth Sunday, Esquire is saying?"

"Something right out of an etiquette book. Proper and polite."

"And with all the sincerity of a top notch con artist."

"Con artist. Lawyer. Not much difference."

Zoe leaned into him and stifled her laugh against his arm. The innocent display of intimacy stirred an impulse to put a comforting arm around her. He resisted it, but made a mental note to ask her out on a real date when this mess was settled. Not just a cheeseburger at Parson's, but a night in the city. Show her around his old turf.

Pete felt the approach of trouble even before he heard the voice.

"Hello, Chief. I knew I'd find you here," Detective Baronick said.

"And why would you bother trying to find me here?" Any news the county detective had brought could certainly wait for a more appropriate time and place.

"Police business. We need to talk."

"Not here."

Zoe still leaned against Pete's arm, and he felt every muscle in her body tense.

Baronick flashed one of his lady-killer smiles at her, which did nothing to improve Pete's mood. "Hello, Miss Chambers. It's nice to see you again, although I'm sorry it's under these circumstances."

"Did you find Ted's killer?" she asked.

His smile faded. "Sorry. No. This is about the computer theft." He turned back to Pete. "If not here, where? Shall we step outside?"

Elizabeth Sunday had completed her social duties and vanished into the crowd. They were next in line, but the old woman in front of them was weeping in Rose's arms. This could take a while.

"In a minute," he told the detective.

"I'm sorry, Chief, but I'm pressed for time. We busted seven mid-level dealers today and I'll be up all night processing them. I made the effort to drive out here for this, because I thought you might need my assistance."

"In a minute," he repeated. The young detective's arrogance pissed him off even without the added suggestion that Pete's skills were inadequate to deal with local matters.

Baronick scowled. "Fine. I'll wait out front. I trust you'll make it snappy."

The only thing Pete wanted to snap was Baronick's sanctimonious neck. But the detective's fast exit saved them both from the paperwork involved in officer-on-officer violence.

Pete turned to Zoe, intending to apologize, but her face had lost its color. "Are you all right?"

She offered a quick nod and stepped back. "It's the heat in here."

True. Pete's own damp clothing clung to his skin. But he sensed the heat wasn't Zoe's issue. He wished he knew what was.

The woman in front of them released Rose and was embracing Sylvia. He moved forward.

"Chief," Rose said, "I'm so glad you were able to come."

He held her hand, small but strong, and offered his condolences.

"Is there any news? I noticed that detective was here."

"No, nothing about Ted's case."

She sighed. "Did you notice who else was just here?"

"Ms. Sunday. I saw her."

"The nerve of that woman." Rose's eyes glistened with tears.

Pete wasn't sure if they were tears of grief or anger. "You handled yourself with remarkable grace."

"Grace my ass. I didn't want to disrespect my husband's memory by starting a brawl here and now."

Tears of anger. No doubt about it. He smiled and gave her a gentle hug. "Atta girl."

Releasing Rose, Pete moved on to her mother, Bert, a pale woman whose skin now appeared almost blue. Good thing there was a paramedic on the premises.

Sylvia was next. She gave Pete a long, sorrowful gaze. "Tell me this is a nightmare, Pete. Tell me I'm going to wake up and shake my head at the absurdity of it all."

"I wish I could." He embraced his old friend. "I will promise you one thing. We *will* get this guy."

"I know you will. And I know you and the boys are still working on it even though County's taken over the case."

Pete feigned innocence. "I would never go behind the backs of the Monongahela County Detectives Bureau. You know me better than that."

"Of course I do." She winked at him. "Get outta here. Go toss that bastard Jerry McBirney in jail. Preferably the same holding cell I was in."

"Sylvia," he chided. "Did you booby trap my station?"

"I'll never tell."

"I don't suppose you noticed anything odd during the time you were being released?"

"Odd? What's odder than an old woman claiming her personal possessions after being detained for defending the honor of her dead son?"

She had a point. "Someone broke into the evidence room."

Sylvia's face lost its ruddiness. "I-I've been a little distracted," she stuttered. "This is the first I've heard of it. Who?"

"That's what we're trying to figure out. Along with how."

"What did they take?"

"The computer."

"My computer?"

"Well, the one you borrowed and returned."

She curled her lip. "Don't start prettying it up. It's the one I was falsely accused of stealing and had confiscated from my home. That one?"

"That one."

"And now someone else stole it? Can this situation get any more bizarre? You know, of course, it was McBirney who did it."

"What makes you say that?"

"He's covering his behind. There's something on that computer that links him to my boy's murder, and he doesn't want anyone finding out what that is."

Precisely what Pete already suspected. "That's one possibility."

"It's the only possibility, Pete." She stared at him with pleading eyes. "Catch him, will you?"

"I will." He kissed her cheek and turned away before she caught a glimpse of his inner conflict. If McBirney had been behind the break-in, there was little question regarding his accomplice. The smallish woman in the oversized, hooded coat. Pete admittedly harbored resentment toward his ex-wife, but he resisted the nagging voice in his gut telling him she was involved in this burglary up to her beautiful eyeballs.

And if the break-in and theft were connected to the murder...

Pete shook it off. Maybe it wasn't such a bad idea that Baronick take over this case. Much as Pete hated to admit it, he wasn't the most objective investigator at the moment.

His gaze swept the room, searching for Zoe. She'd been at his side until he spoke with Rose. He assumed she'd stepped away to greet other visitors. He wanted to...well, what exactly *did* he want with Zoe? He remembered the sensation of her breasts pressing against his arm. Her fragrance—vanilla and something else earthy—lingered in his nostrils. Maybe it was time he stopped punishing himself for the mistakes he'd made with Marcy. Maybe...

And yet, there was something going on with Zoe, something he couldn't define. He wanted time alone with her, to talk to her and convince her to trust him with her secrets.

But where was she? The room was packed. Still, he knew he could pick Zoe Chambers out of a crowd in any given second.

If she'd been there.

THIRTEEN

Zoe white-knuckled the steering wheel as she approached the farm. Snowflakes caught the headlights, cutting white streaks through the black of night, and the road sported icy patches. While four-wheel-drive had its benefits, braking on ice wasn't one of them. As if to confirm her fears, a dark sedan appeared to have slid off the road a hundred yards or so from the turn onto the farm lane. She slowed and craned her neck to see if someone might be slumped over the wheel. But there wasn't anyone around the car. The driver must have snagged a ride back to town.

Good. She didn't want to deal with a stranded motorist right now. She had enough to worry about. Like how long before the thief discovered all he had was a useless shell? Then, that detective with all his questions showed up at the funeral home. The only solution was to find the truth buried in the hard drive before Ted's murderer figured out where the incriminating evidence was hidden.

She worked the gas feed and the steering wheel, encouraging the old truck to dig in and climb the winding lane to the farmhouse. Bouncing over the ruts and spinning on the hard-packed snow, she made it to her parking spot next to the Krolls' white SUV.

The light was on in the enclosed back porch. Zoe stomped the snow from her dress boots on the door mat. She was about to insert the key into her lock when the Kroll's door at the other end of the porch swung open.

"Zoe? Is that you?" Mrs. Kroll pulled a terrycloth bathrobe tighter around her thin shoulders.

"Yeah, it's me. How are you feeling, Mrs. Kroll?"

The older woman sighed. "Sick of winter. Otherwise, I'm holding up. I'm surprised to see you. I thought you were already in for the night."

"I was at the funeral home."

"Oh. Ted Bassi. Yes. I'm so sorry about that. How are Rose and the kids?"

"As well as can be expected." No use going into details. Especially on an unheated porch with Mrs. Kroll in her pajamas.

"I understand." The landlady nodded. "Well, dear, you know I never like to complain, but that friend staying with you has been rather noisy. Could you please ask them to be a bit quieter?"

"Friend? What are you talking about?"

Mrs. Kroll tipped her head toward Zoe's side of the house. "Don't you have someone visiting? There was some banging around going on a few minutes ago. I thought maybe you were moving furniture. That's why I was surprised to see you pull in." She inhaled sharply. "Oh, dear. If you don't have anyone visiting—oh, dear—perhaps someone's broken in. Should I call the police?"

Logan.

Zoe had assumed the kid had left the funeral home with his buddies from school. Now she realized he'd slipped off once again to come here and work on the computer. Rose was going to skin both of them.

"No, that's okay." Zoe offered her a reassuring smile. "I know who it is. Don't worry."

"Well, good. But do ask him to keep it down, will you?"

"Of course. I'm sorry. Goodnight, Mrs. Kroll."

Once her landlady had disappeared into her half of the house, Zoe braced to give Logan a verbal thrashing. She placed her hand on the door knob and sure enough, it wasn't locked. Throwing it open, she stormed in. "Logan," she called, using her best *I'm Going to Kill You* voice.

The living room was empty. And dark. The door between it and her office was closed. Odd. She always kept that door blocked open. Light filtered under it. A crash and the thud of retreating footsteps sent her heart rate into overdrive. Someone was in her house. And it wasn't Logan.

A burglar? Or Jerry McBirney?

Another door squeaked open. He was escaping through her office's other door into the center hallway. From there, would he burst into the Kroll's side of the house? Or make his getaway by way of the front door?

Zoe charged toward her office and tripped. An indignant yowl filled the room as a disgruntled Merlin bolted for the kitchen.

She hit the door, expecting it to swing wide. Instead, it caught on something. What the hell? She put her shoulder into the door and heaved it open enough to squeeze through.

She gasped at the sight of the room. Her office chair had been flung on its side against the door, no doubt to impede her pursuit of the intruder. The computer tower had been pulled out of its cubby. A side panel had been removed leaving its electronic innards exposed. Disconnected wires sprawled lifeless beside it.

The rarely used front door of the farmhouse screeched open and banged shut. Footsteps pounded across the front porch and faded down the steps.

Zoe paused only a moment to stare at the mess before stepping over it. She charged into the hallway.

Unlike the back porch, the front one was unlit. She hit the switch on the way out, but the light revealed nothing except an expanse of white and a solitary set of boot tracks, which were quickly filling in with fat snowflakes, leading down the porch steps and disappearing across the sloped yard into the darkness. In the distance, she heard a car start.

The dark sedan she'd thought was stuck. She made out the glow of red taillights through the ancient pines that shaded the front yard in warmer months. The whirl of spinning tires digging into ice floated up to her, and the car sped away.

Crap.

She retreated into the house and was met by Mr. Kroll. Jade squirmed in his arms.

"What's going on? Are you all right?" he asked.

"I'm fine," she lied.

"Are you sure? Bernice said you had a noisy friend visiting."

"Yes, well, he's gone now."

"Uh huh." He sounded doubtful. Very little got by Mr. Kroll. But he also made a point of minding his own business. "I suppose you want this back?" He nodded to the cat.

"Please." Zoe relieved him of the wriggling feline who must have seized the opportunity to escape into the rest of the house during McBirney's exit. At least she hadn't followed him out the front door.

"Are you sure everything is okay?" Mr. Kroll brushed cat fur from his sweatshirt.

"I'm sure. Thanks. And sorry for the commotion. Goodnight." Zoe ducked back into her trashed office and closed the door before her landlord could see for himself that everything was definitely *not* okay.

Pete found Wayne Baronick leaning against the Vance Township Police Department's SUV with his arms crossed.

"It's about time," the detective said.

"You didn't have to wait. You could've gone back to Brunswick and dealt with your drug busts."

"I know that's what you'd prefer, but having a theft occur in your own station? Again? I'd think you'd have learned by now that trying to keep this kind of investigation internal isn't the way to go."

Baronick's barb about the ten-thousand dollars in township receipts that had somehow vanished from Sylvia's desk six years ago hit its mark. Pete refused to defend his handling of the old case to the cocky, young hotshot, but recognized he had little choice but to invite County into this one.

The detective smiled, having apparently spotted the capitulation on Pete's face. "How about we sit in your car and you can tell me what happened."

"As if you haven't already heard."

"I'd like to hear it from you."

Pete unlocked the Ford Explorer and opened the passenger door. The last thing he wanted was Baronick's nose in his township business. Especially now. He wanted to sort this out on his own. It wasn't that he wanted to protect Marcy. Not exactly. He didn't want to see her going through the hell of an investigation if she was actually innocent. On the other hand, what did he care if she went through hell? She'd put him through it after all.

Then there was Zoe. Where had she disappeared to? And why? Note to self—force Zoe to tell him what was going on with her.

"Well?" Baronick interrupted Pete's musing. "Are you going to talk to me about the break-in or not?"

Too bad "or not" wasn't really an option. Pete pulled out his notebook and gave Baronick the details he knew. No sign of forced entry at either front or back doors. Door to the evidence room forced. Inventory of the evidence room showed only the confiscated computer tower missing. Trace evidence had been sent to the county lab.

Pete hesitated.

"What?" Baronick pressed.

"I processed fingerprints found around and on the front door. Of those that were usable, most matched my officers, Sylvia Bassi, or local residents who had come to the station on business recently. My men are checking them out, but so far they're all clear."

"Most?"

Pete hesitated, knowing the next words out of his mouth would clinch County's participation in the investigation. "I found a match to a fingerprint lifted from McBirney's Buick."

Baronick choked. "You what?"

Pete glared at him. He was not going to repeat himself when he knew perfectly well the detective had heard him the first time.

"Any idea who they belong to?"

"Not yet."

"There really is a connection between the two cases. Damn. I should have kept that computer with me and logged it into the county evidence locker. Obviously, it would have been safer there."

Pete tried to ignore that last comment.

"Any suspects or leads?" Baronick said.

Besides Marcy and Jerry McBirney? "Nothing solid."

"But your gut's telling you something, isn't it?"

"My gut's testimony isn't admissible in a court of law."

"Come on, Pete. Don't be a hard ass on this. We both want the same thing. To find out who killed Bassi."

"And when I have anything concrete, you'll be the first to know."

"Somehow, I doubt it." Baronick studied him.

Pete held his gaze.

"All right. I guess I'll have to settle for that. For the moment. Anything else you can give me?"

"I've got my men tracking down a couple of former Vance Township officers who had the alarm code to the station. I want to make sure they didn't share the information with anyone else."

"Those codes should have been changed after they left the department. You know that, don't you?"

"The township supervisors didn't feel there was a need for it. No one breaks into a police station. Out? Yeah."

"Well, *someone* broke in, didn't they?"

Pete resisted the urge to tell the detective to go to hell.

"I guess that's it for now." Baronick opened the SUV's door. A rush of cold air flooded the vehicle's interior as he climbed out. The detective leaned back into the car. "Let me know what your men learn. I'll come by the station late tomorrow morning to process the crime scene. You know. In case you missed something." He flashed a dimpled smile and slammed the door.

Pete gripped the steering wheel so tight his knuckles ached. He stared at the parked cars in front of him, watching a man in a dark coat scrape ice from his windshield. White flakes drifted through the night sky in silence. Minutes passed, and Pete got his breathing and his temper under control.

Baronick may have wormed his way into two of his cases. Marcy may have involved herself in a robbery and murder. But there was something else he might still have some control over.

Zoe released Jade who appeared displeased by the new room arrangement. The cat sniffed at the overturned chair and then sulked off to the living room.

Zoe righted the chair and sunk into it to study the carcass of her computer. She couldn't very well call Pete. She already knew his first question. *Why would anyone want your computer?*

Well, you see, we were obstructing justice and hiding stolen property.

Had the intruder succeeded in retrieving the hard drive? Zoe leaned over the upended computer tower and peered at the electronic chips and wires and thingamajigs inside. It might help if she knew what the hell she was looking at.

Something on the back porch thudded. Zoe flinched. Stiffened and listened.

Was she imagining things? Hearing strange sounds that weren't there? Then the firm knock on the back door confirmed her imagination had not run amok. Maybe it was Logan. He would know if her computer had been gutted. Eager, she slipped into the dark living room.

The light on the back porch created a familiar silhouette through the translucent lace curtains.

Pete.

Crap. Any other time, she'd be thrilled to see him. Just not now.

Zoe pulled the door between the rooms shut and flipped the light switch. Both cats blinked at her from their mutual bed on the sofa.

"Don't you check to see who's out there before opening your door?" Pete said as she let him in.

"I could see your silhouette through the curtains."

"Maybe you should consider something heavier. If you can see out, an intruder might be able to see in."

Zoe's forehead tingled with beads of sweat threatening to pop to the surface. Had Pete seen in? Did he know about the intruder? More importantly, had he found out about the computer?

"I'll take that under consideration." She forced a smile and struggled to keep her voice steady. "What brings you out here this evening?"

His gaze swept the room and lingered on the closed office door. He'd been in this room numerous times. Their Saturday night poker gang rotated houses for their games, and she'd hosted them—including Pete—on a regular basis. So he knew she never closed that door.

His eyes locked onto hers.

Act innocent.

Somehow, she didn't think he was buying it.

"You left the funeral home without saying goodbye," he said. "I got worried."

"Sorry. It was so stuffy in there. I couldn't take it anymore. And I figured you were going to be busy for a while."

He held her gaze, unsmiling.

The silence roared inside her head. Zoe broke it first. "Can I get you some coffee?"

A smile finally tugged at one side of his lips. "When have you ever known me to turn down coffee?"

She contained a huge sigh of relief. "Great. I'll make a fresh pot." As she headed for the kitchen, her mind flashed on Pete poking around and wandering into the other room when she wasn't looking. She paused and looked back. Sure enough, he was frowning at the closed door. Her heart thudded against the inside of her sternum so loud she expected the room to echo with it. Think fast.

"Why don't you join me?" she called to him, hoping she sounded just a tad flirtatious. Instead, she feared she sounded as desperate as she felt.

His face softened, and he moved toward her, following her into the antiquated kitchen. He parked himself on a stool in the corner while Zoe opened the canister containing her favorite blend of ground coffee. Maybe they could enjoy a pleasant visit without police matters getting in the way.

"I don't recall ever seeing the door to your office closed before," he said.

Crap.

Her mind raced, and the words came out of her mouth before she had a chance to analyze them. "My heating bills have been horrible this winter. I decided to close off the office and turn down the thermostat in there." Wow. That sounded pretty good. She sneaked a glance at Pete to see how he reacted.

He shrugged his eyebrows and gave a nod. Not that penetrating stare he used on criminals to suck the truth out of them. Good. She turned her attention back to pouring water into the Mr. Coffee.

"We need to talk."

Uh-oh. Maybe not so good. "Sure." She winced at the chirpiness of her voice. "What about?"

He didn't reply. Instead, the stool leg barked against the floor as he stood up and moved to her side. A bead of sweat tickled the back of her neck. He stood next to her. The heat radiating from him made her lightheaded. His breath ruffled a wisp of her hair on her forehead.

"I need you to tell me the truth," he said.

"Truth?" Her voice was almost an octave higher than it should have been.

"You're keeping something from me." A statement of fact. Not a question.

No brilliant retort about heating costs came to her lips. In fact, her brain had shut down, overwhelmed with Pete's closeness. The musky smell of him drove all rational thought into some obscure corner she couldn't access. A line from some otherwise forgotten movie or TV show popped into her head.

Resistance is futile.

FOURTEEN

Zoe didn't dare tell Pete everything. Perhaps part of it. But how much? And which part?

Sentences formed on her tongue, ran through her brain, and died. *I'm helping Logan. To try to find his father's killer.* No. Keep Logan out of it. How could she reveal any portion of what she was hiding without giving up the kid? She had to protect Logan at all costs. For Rose.

For Ted.

Zoe ventured a quick look at Pete who stood in silence, watching her squirm.

"I can't," she said.

"You can't what?"

"I can't tell you the truth."

He scowled. "Why not?"

Zoe sighed and punched the power button on the coffee maker. "If I could tell you that, I could tell you all of it." She turned to face him, locking onto his gaze. "Do you trust me at all?"

He looked at her askance. "Ordinarily? Yeah."

"Then I need you to give me a little space."

"Space? Zoe, this is a murder investigation. I can't give you space when it interferes with me doing my job."

She hadn't considered the position she was putting Pete in. Maybe she should just take him into the office, show him the mess, and confess everything. Let the cops dig through the hard drive from the township computer.

Except she didn't know if the hard drive was still in that mangled jumble of electronics. Or had her uninvited visitor taken it with him?

Either way, Logan would get busted for theft or obstruction of justice or both.

She lowered her head. "I can't. I'm sorry." Without warning, a rush of tears warmed her eyes, and she blinked them away. She'd sworn off crying in front of a man years ago.

Pete wrapped his fingers around her upper arms and drew her to him. "Who are you protecting?"

Once again, she risked meeting his eyes, expecting to read anger or—worse—disappointment. Instead, she saw worry. He was frightened for her.

If he only knew.

Touched by his concern, Zoe lost the battle over control of her tears. "I can't tell you," she whispered. "I promise I will when I can. But I can't right now."

Pete's ice blue eyes bore into hers as if he could extract the information he wanted telepathically. Good thing she didn't believe in telepathy.

Then he pulled her closer. Her body pressed against his. The heat and the smell of him made her dizzy. Her hands found their way to the small of his back. She lifted her chin as he tipped his head, and their mouths met. His warm, moist lips molded to hers. Overwhelmed with a hunger and a longing that flared from some long-hidden corner of her psyche, she forgot to breathe. She sunk into him, aching to hold onto him and this moment for as long as possible. To surrender to his sweetness and strength. His hands slid up to cup her face as if it were made of some fragile thing.

She drank him in. Her mind swam, ungrounded, floating.

And then he eased back, breaking the kiss and the spell.

The mantle clock in the next room ticked off long seconds of silence as the coffee maker gurgled.

Pete opened his mouth, but closed it again. "Be careful," he said at last, his voice less than steady.

Zoe didn't trust herself to speak and gave a nod.

He pressed a kiss onto her forehead and was gone. The coffee maker grew quiet, the pot full. Zoe was left to the sounds of the clock ticking and her heart pounding.

* * *

The following day, after the ordeal of Ted's funeral and graveside services, Zoe had no intention of stopping at the VFW for Ted's bereavement lunch. She'd had all the mourning she could stand. Not to mention the irony of the meal being served in the very location where she'd last seen Ted alive. But the fire engines, draped in black bunting, blocked her truck at the cemetery as she tried to make her escape.

Sylvia caught up to her, rapping on her window. "You're going to eat with us, aren't you?" she said. "There's going to be so much food. And Rose needs you now."

Driven by guilt rather than hunger, Zoe stood in the buffet line prepared by the Fire Department's Ladies' Auxiliary. A mound of rigatoni and a pair of cabbage rolls shared her Styrofoam plate with a helping of salad. Juggling the food, a plastic fork and knife wrapped in a paper napkin, and a cup of watered-down punch, she searched the crowd for Rose and spotted her surrounded by a hoard of well-wishers.

Zoe headed for an empty table, but Sylvia intercepted her and guided her by her elbow to Rose's side. All the others seemed to melt away. Zoe set her plate down and put her arms around her friend.

"I don't know how I'm going to do this," Rose whispered into her ear. "I don't know how to be alone."

"You're not alone. I'm right here."

Rose hugged her tight.

As soon as Zoe released her, a host of friends, family, and neighbors offering their help closed in. Zoe took her plate and fled to a quiet corner where she sat and stared at the food. She'd skipped breakfast and should be starving.

Should be. But wasn't.

Logan slid into the empty seat next to her. His necktie encircled his forehead instead of his throat and the top his oversized shirt gapped open. "Good news." He reached into his jacket pocket and retrieved a square paper envelope. "My man came through for me. I've got the software we need to open those files."

Zoe closed her eyes, but couldn't block out the memory of last night. "That's great. Unfortunately, I think we may have a problem."

He scowled. "What now?"

She told him of the break-in and the attack on the computer.

"Had to be McBirney," Logan said, his voice low.

"That's what I figure, too. I can't tell for sure, but I'll bet he got the hard drive."

Logan chewed his lower lip, and his eyes narrowed in thought. "You're not positive, though. You don't remember what the hard drive looked like?"

"When you showed it to me outside the computer, yeah. But I haven't a clue what it looks like inside the computer."

"Did you touch anything?"

"No. I left it just like I found it." She decided not to mention Pete's visit and the fogging effect he'd had on her brain.

"Good. I told Mom I was going to bring Allison over to the farm after lunch so she could go riding. She said okay and is even letting me borrow the car. I'll check it out when I get there." He slipped the computer disc back into his pocket and gave her an awkward pat on the arm. "It'll be okay."

Zoe watched him walk away, struck by how much he resembled Ted. She stood up and headed for the exit, dumping her untouched plate into the trash as she left.

Sunshine glistened from dripping icicles and melting snow created a sloppy mess on the road. The farm lane, on the other hand, was solid ice. Mr. Kroll had the Massey-Ferguson tractor cranked up and was using the front loader to spread cinders. He pulled out of Zoe's way and waved at her when she returned home.

A quick check of the house confirmed that the intruder had not paid another visit. Zoe had feared the funeral might be a prime opportunity for McBirney to try again. He either had succeeded in stealing the hard drive the previous night, or Mr. Kroll's outdoor activities had discouraged another attempt.

Merlin and Jade, meowing their demands for food, watched Zoe as she changed out of her dress clothes and into jeans and a hooded sweatshirt. Just because she wasn't hungry didn't mean the rest of the household shared her lack of appetite. She made her way down the stairs with the cats racing her to the kitchen.

As she scooped Fancy Feast into two bowls, her thoughts bounced inside her head like a pinball. She had to be at the ambulance garage by four and dreaded the thought of going back to work—her first shift since Ted's death.

Logan and Allison would be there soon. An hour or so in the saddle sounded good. Zoe checked the clock over the stove. One-fifteen. She could take Allison out while Logan worked on the computer and still make it back in time.

She placed the bowls on the floor. Merlin dove into his lunch while Jade sniffed and stared at the mound before her. Then she turned her green eyes upward to Zoe.

"Sorry, sweetie. That's the only choice you get today," she told the feline.

Jade turned and strutted away, parking herself under the stool. The same one Pete had sat on last night.

Pete. What in the world was she going to do about him? The kiss had been incredible. And unexpected. True, she'd imagined what his lips on hers would be like. She'd even permitted a fantasy or two in which things went much further.

But they had been friends for a long time. They worked together, hung out together, played poker together, sometimes met for dinner at one of the local dives. Good friends were hard to come by. Did she want to risk losing this one when her romantic track record sucked swamp water?

Plus, the kiss wasn't even the biggest obstacle between them at the moment. Her secrets threatened to kill off their bond faster than the hint of passion. Pete hated lies. Almost as much as she did.

Maybe Logan would show up and determine the hard drive was gone. And that would be the end of it.

Perhaps that might be the best thing. She and Logan would have to give up.

She could stop keeping secrets from Pete.

The floor vibrated from footsteps on the back porch a moment before a heavy fist pounded on her door.

Masculine voices filtered into the living room. Zoe drew the lace curtain back enough to see Logan standing there, talking to Mr. Kroll.

"Hey, you two," she said as she swung the door open.

Mr. Kroll stomped snow from his boots. "Everything okay in there today?"

"Fine," she assured him. "Are you done with the road?"

"It's as good as it's gonna get right now, I'm afraid. If you'll excuse me, the missus has a pot of soup on the stove that's calling my name."

The landlord headed for the door to his side of the house, and Logan shuffled in, dragging a lumpy backpack with him.

"I thought you were bringing Allison," Zoe said. "Or was that another ruse to get your mother's permission to come over here?" More lies. Just what she needed.

"No. I brought Allison. I dumped her at the barn. That lady who owns Jazzel was out there."

"Patsy Greene?"

"I guess. Anyhow, she was saddling up her horse. She said it's been lame and she wants to see how it's doing. Offered to let Allison ride with her. That's okay, isn't it?"

"Sure." Patsy knew which horses Allison was permitted to use and would take good care of her.

"Cool." Logan deposited his backpack on the sofa and pulled a CD from a side pocket. He nodded at the closed office door. "So how bad is it?"

"You tell me." Zoe led the way into the room.

"Dude," Logan said, dragging the word out into about three syllables. "We're talking seriously trashed."

Zoe held her breath, hoping the hard drive was gone and only slightly ashamed for wishing it.

He dropped to his knees next to the computer tower and peered inside. "Awesome. It's still here. And it's not as bad as it looks at first. Nothing's messed up too much."

So much for being freed of her secrets. The disappointment hit her even harder than she expected. Asshole McBirney. Couldn't even get a simple burglary right.

While Logan tinkered with the computer, Zoe paced the floor behind him. Rearranged a few books on the shelves. Straightened a pair of family photos on the fireplace's mantel.

She needed to get out of the house. "Do you need me for anything?"

He laughed. "No."

If there weren't already so much going on in her head, she might have felt insulted. "I'm going to the barn. Maybe I can catch Patsy and Allison."

"I'll be fine. Can I raid the refrigerator?"

She started to mention that he'd just come from a dinner, but considering it had been his dad's bereavement dinner, she changed her mind. "Help yourself."

Zoe grabbed her parka from the hook next to the pantry, tugged on her boots, and headed out the kitchen door. No one had shoveled the path to the barn, but it was packed down by her own multiple trips along it.

The glare of sunshine nearly blinded her. Squinting, she noted several vehicles parked at the barn. The first mild day after a spell of Arctic cold and snow always brought out the boarders. They would come and play with their horses, brushing them, cleaning out their feet, maybe taking a ride. But only a few chose to muck out their stalls, leaving that to Zoe. She didn't mind. Much.

Inside the barn, silence greeted her. The stalls were empty. She strolled across the indoor arena and opened the sliding door wide enough to gaze out at the pasture. Most of the herd gathered at the three round bales Mr. Kroll had set out last weekend. A few pawed at the snow in search of a rare sprout of January grass. Windstar stood at the stream, dipping his muzzle into the running water.

Zoe made out two mounted figures on the hillside above the pasture, about five hundred yards away. Patsy and Allison were heading toward the neighbor's farm and eventually the back road, a favorite route. If she caught Windstar now and threw a saddle on him after only a token grooming, she might still intercept them on their ride.

She called to her gelding. Everyone's ears perked. If one came, they all came. And with food potentially in the offering, they indeed all galloped toward her.

Zoe slung Windstar's halter and lead over her shoulder, gathered an armload of green, leafy hay from an open square bale, and squeezed through the door into the pasture. She scattered the hay, which appeared more appetizing than the round bales. The fat horses in their fuzzy winter coats dove into it as if they were poor starved beasts.

With minimal effort, she sidled up to her gelding and slipped the halter over his head. She clucked to him and led him to the barn, sliding the door wider to accommodate them both.

The horse followed her to the tack room. She tied him to a steel ring on the wall and ducked inside to grab a bucket filled with grooming tools. Setting it on the ground by Windstar's head, she leaned over to dig through the bucket in search of her favorite stiff brush.

She wasn't aware of anyone else in the barn until a voice behind her sent an icy chill through her soul.

"Hiya, Blondie."

FIFTEEN

It had been twelve years since Zoe last faced Jerry McBirney alone, but the terror seized her as fiercely as if it had been last night. The muscles along her spine turned to ice as memories flooded back. The drunken rage. His face contorted with fury.

She straightened to her full height and turned slowly to face the personification of all her inner demons.

McBirney, wearing a long, dark wool coat and a trace of a smirk didn't much resemble the monster in Zoe's nightmares. The face was older, the creases and lines deeper. But he still wore the same aftershave, and the musky scent gagged her.

"What's wrong? You look scared. I don't frighten you, do I?"

She flashed on the memory of his clenched fist. Thought of Marcy's black eye. She might be able to outrun him, but she wouldn't abandon Windstar with him. She'd learned that lesson all too well when the horse had been a foal. What could she use to defend herself and her horse? She glanced at the bucket holding her grooming tools, trying not to be too obvious. It held only brushes, curry combs, a sponge, and a couple of hoof picks. Not enough to do any real damage.

McBirney laughed. "Relax. I'm not going to hurt you. I just want to talk."

"We have nothing to talk about. Get the hell out of here," Zoe said, pleased her voice didn't quiver.

McBirney took a step toward her and placed a leather-gloved hand on Windstar's rump. "Nice looking horse. What's his breeding?"

As if he didn't know. Protective mother bear instincts kicked in, and Zoe moved forward, slapping his hand away. "Get away from him."

McBirney appeared startled for a moment, and then smiled. "You've always been a feisty one, haven't you? It's one of the things that attracted me to you."

Zoe thought she might be sick. If she were going to throw up, at least she could aim for his shoes.

"I told you I wanted to talk, and I mean it." McBirney grew serious. "It's come to my attention that a lot of people around town seem to think I had something to do with Ted Bassi's death. I did not."

She wanted him out of there. Now. Maybe if she agreed with him, he'd go away sooner. "Okay."

"I mean it. I had nothing to do with that. I know it looks bad. Especially with his body being found in my car and all."

Not to mention the bad blood between them. "I said, okay. Now get out."

"You don't believe me. But think about it. Why would I kill Ted and leave the body in my own car? I'm not stupid."

He showed no signs of complying with her request to leave. A phone hung on the wall by the door, but she'd never make it there in time to place a call without incapacitating him first. Some heavy fence-building tools and blacksmith tools were stored inside the tack room. She might be able to get to them if he were distracted for a moment.

"Why are you telling me this? I have nothing to say about whether or not you're arrested. If I did, it would have happened already."

"I can't talk to Sylvia or Rose, obviously. But you can. And Pete Adams has some personal issues with me that keep him from being objective."

"And you think *I'm* objective?"

"I think you could be."

She choked out a laugh. "Have you forgotten what you did to me?"

McBirney drew a slow breath. "No. Of course I haven't. But apparently you've forgotten that I apologized for it."

"Like that makes it all right."

"I can't be responsible for your being unable to let bygones be bygones."

In that moment, Zoe understood the motivation behind abuse victims killing their abusers. If she'd been able to put her hands on something heavy, she'd easily be able to pummel him to death.

"Bygones? You punched me in the face. Twice. Fractured my cheekbone."

McBirney's eyes narrowed. "I was drunk. And you deserved it."

"Deserved it? No one deserves what you did to me."

"You were a tease. You played me." A tinge of red crept up McBirney's neck to his cheeks.

"I did not."

"You were looking for a sugar daddy."

She gasped, incredulous. "*Sugar daddy*?"

"First you shacked up with Matt until he threw you out—"

"Threw me out? I left *him*."

McBirney sneered. "And then you set your sights on Teddy boy, but he dumped you for your best friend."

"I never set my sights—"

"So you came crawling to me," he said, his tone mocking, "all wounded and pitiful. And needy."

She stepped toward him and shoved him away from her horse. "I'll show you needy, you son of a bitch."

But McBirney threw his head back and laughed at her. "Yeah, you were happy to let me take care of you and buy you pretty things and give you a nice place to stay. But when it was time for you to pay up, you decided to play hard to get."

The night she'd struggled for years to forget slammed into her like a runaway train. After finding Matt in bed with that tramp, she'd left their house and bounced from one friend's couch to another, spending most of her nights with Rose and the kids. When Ted came into the picture and fell for Rose instead of Zoe, she moved out to give them space.

Jerry McBirney had sat next to her at the Elm Creek Horse Auction one night, and they struck up a conversation. His sky blue eyes and quick smile trumped his rough complexion making him attractive if not handsome. Into the ring came a chestnut Quarter Horse mare that was heavy with foal. Zoe fell in love with the horse, but knew she didn't have the money. Jerry offered to buy the mare for her and to board it at his place until she could make other arrangements. Stunned by his kindness, she accepted.

The mare produced a big-boned sorrel colt she named Windstar.

Jerry proposed that she move into one of his spare rooms so she could be closer to the pair. He bought her a new saddle for the mare and a tiny halter for the colt. She cleaned stalls for him and did some cooking and cleaning around the house to earn her keep.

One night, he suggested they go out to eat. Instead of a local diner, he took her into Pittsburgh's Station Square for a dinner cruise on one of the riverboats. Until that night, Zoe always thought he was being kind to a young waif. Having lost her own dad at such an early age, she thought of him as a surrogate, buying her the toys her father hadn't been around to purchase. But on that riverboat, she realized in Jerry's mind, he'd been courting her.

He asked her to dance. She agreed, but pulled away when he drew her close and tried to kiss her. He hounded her all evening, and she struggled to be polite about rebuffing his advances. Finally, he seemed to give up and turned to the bar for solace.

The drive home was silent. Sometime in the middle of the night, Jerry came into her room. She awoke to find him over her, reeking of booze.

"You think I've been feeding you and putting a roof over your head all this time because I'm nice?" she remembered him saying. "I'm not that nice. And now it's time to pay up, Blondie."

His hands crawled over her skin, under her pajamas. She squirmed, fighting to get out from under him, free from his grasp, begging him to stop.

He laughed.

She remembered that laugh.

She remembered her sobs.

In his drunken state, he wasn't able to complete the rape. So instead he battered her with his fists, slamming her face twice.

Zoe had no memory of the pain. Adrenaline and her survival instincts protected her. She managed to catch him off balance after the second blow and got in one of her own, using the small bedside lamp as a club. While he was down, she escaped.

It took two days to line up a stall elsewhere for her mare and foal and a trailer to transport them. She waited until McBirney was gone before arriving at his barn. As soon as she stepped through the door, she knew something was very wrong. The foal's plaintive whinny greeted her along with the sound of thrashing and wood splintering. She ran to the stall to find the mare, glassy-eyed, crashing blindly around the stall, oblivious to her baby.

Zoe barely succeeded in rescuing Windstar without being trampled herself. She secured him in another stall and placed a call to the vet. The mare died five hours later, despite heroic efforts by Dr. Benton. Remnants of her hay told the tale. Clippings from toxic Chinese Yews had been mixed with the alfalfa. McBirney had failed at raping her physically and the beating he gave her left bruises that would heal in time. So he'd taken his revenge in the one way that ravaged her soul as nothing else could.

Twelve years later, Zoe stood toe-to-toe with the man who had orphaned the horse tied next to them now. "You sick bastard. You tried to rape me."

"Your word against mine."

"You beat me."

He shrugged. "Water under the bridge."

She gagged and tasted bile on the back of her tongue. "You killed my horse."

"What? You've gone off the deep end this time."

"You poisoned my mare."

McBirney seemed puzzled. "That mare from the auction? Oh. Yeah. I do remember something about her dying. In my barn. While you were trying to sneak her out without paying your board bill." He rubbed the stubble on his chin. "The way I see it, since you never paid me for the mare or the board, she was mine anyway. So you still weren't out anything. Didn't she have a colt? Whatever happened to him?"

Zoe stared hard at McBirney. Do not look at Windstar. Do not give even a hint.

But it was too late. Realization lit McBirney's eyes. "Aw, so this fine looking animal is out of that mare I bought." He laughed. "*My* mare. That means he's mine, too. Nice looking fellow. He'll look even better in *my* barn."

Zoe's head spun. Was he serious? Legally, did he have grounds? And did it matter? McBirney got what McBirney wanted.

He crossed his arms and studied the gelding with an appraising eye. "I'll be back in an hour with my trailer to pick him up."

Zoe stepped between McBirney and her horse. "No." She hated the desperation in her voice. But what if he did legally have ownership? "I'll pay you." She had no intention of giving him money for her own horse, but she'd be buying time.

"You couldn't afford him, Blondie."

The space behind Zoe's eyes grew cold and still. "I've been boarding *your* horse for twelve years," she said, proud of the calm determination in her voice. "At thirty bucks a month? That should be a good down payment."

McBirney was quicker at math than she was. "That's little more than four grand. A horse like this? I'd have to get no less than ten thousand. You owe me six. And I want it now."

She held her ground, searching his eyes for some hint that he was kidding. She saw none. And she didn't have six thousand. Hell, she didn't have six *hundred.*

A slow smile crept across his lips. "Can't afford it? Let's see. I think we can make a deal."

"What kind of deal?" She expected him to ask her to intervene between him and Pete. Help him get off the suspect list for Ted's death. That's what McBirney had come there for, after all.

But he moved closer. Leaned toward her. His putrid breath hot on her face. "Same deal I wanted from you twelve years ago." His voice was low and lustful. "You and me, Blondie. Only no alcohol this time for me. And total cooperation from you."

The meaning of his words sizzled into her brain. She backed away from him, but he snatched a fistful of her hair. Survival mode kicked in. She tried to knee him. Missed her mark. He laughed, a harsh, triumphant laugh.

She struggled to pry his hand loose. "*Let go.*"

Spooked by the tussle, Windstar tried to bolt. When he hit the end of the rope, the horse attempted to whirl, slamming into McBirney. Staggered, he eased his hold on Zoe's hair. She pulled free, sacrificing a chunk of her scalp in the process, and snatched the only thing within reach—Windstar's bridle. She swung it at McBirney. The steel bit found its mark, catching him across the face.

He yelped and grabbed at his cheek. Zoe dove for the tack room. Her fingers closed around a bottle of fly spray sitting just inside the door. She ran at McBirney, pumping the trigger as fast as she could. The contents weren't lethal, but she knew they stung like hell when you got the stuff in your eyes.

"Bitch!" McBirney screamed as he covered his face. He stumbled and tripped, crashing down on his back.

Zoe leapt to the phone next to the door. She punched in 9-1-1 and waited for the emergency operator to pick up.

"What the hell are you doing?" McBirney frantically mopped his face with his coat sleeve.

"I told you to get out. Next time maybe you'll believe me the first time."

He struggled to his feet. "Fine. I'm going. You don't have to call your boyfriend."

"What is your emergency?" the voice on the phone asked.

"I want to report an intruder."

"No, you don't. I'm out of here." McBirney, his eyes red and watering, waved his arms at her. "And if you insist on calling the cops, I'll have you charged with assault. You can share a jail cell with your friend, Sylvia Bassi." He lurched toward the open door.

As soon as he was outside, Zoe apologized to the operator. "I'm sorry. When the guy saw I was serious about having him arrested, he decided to leave on his own."

"Are you sure you don't want me to send out an officer?"

"Positive. Thanks."

"No problem. If you change your mind or the intruder comes back, don't hesitate to call."

Zoe held onto the phone as McBirney climbed into his car.

He paused with one foot in, one foot out. "And for the record, I was not responsible for killing that horse. Or Ted Bassi." He shook a finger at her. "But you...You had better watch your step."

She hung up the phone when he drove away. Tremors started with her hands and overtook her entire body until her knees buckled. Her scalp burned. She sank to the ground and lost what little lunch she'd eaten.

Pete stared at the scrawls on the whiteboard he'd set up in the conference room, and tried to clear his mind. What was he missing?

Ted Bassi's body had been found in a Buick owned by Jerry McBirney Monday night at 11:35. He had been last seen leaving his home at 8:50. Rankin reported first noticing the car in the game lands at 10:50. That placed his time of death within that two-hour window.

Pete sipped at his coffee and studied the list of suspects. Neighbors placed Rose at her mother's house. The kids had both been at home. Sylvia was the only family member with no solid alibi, having been escorted home after the meeting by her grandkids and Zoe, but then being alone until she showed up at the police station later that night at 11:05. Still, Pete didn't buy Sylvia killing her only son. He'd witnessed her grief firsthand and knew false tears when he saw them. Sylvia's had been real.

So had Marcy's. Had she been having an affair with Ted? None of the local hotels reported seeing either of them Monday night. Or any other night for that matter. She and Jerry McBirney remained on the suspects list with a note that they were each other's alibis and several large question marks.

Physical evidence was noted next. Several long dark hairs undoubtedly belonged to Marcy. They were still at the county trace lab along with the blue fabric Pete had found in McBirney's garage. If it matched Ted's torn jacket, that would place the victim at the prime suspect's home on the night of the homicide.

How had Ted's jacket gotten torn? What was he doing at McBirney's farm? In McBirney's car? And where was Ted's truck?

Pete shook his head. First things first. He picked up the phone.

"Hey, Grace," he said when the county trace evidence tech picked up.

"Pete Adams," came the sandpapery reply. "How the hell are you?"

"I need a favor."

Grace grunted. "You men are all the same. What d'ya need?"

"Do you have anything yet on the Bassi homicide?"

"Jesus, Pete, that stuff only came in this week. I'm still processing evidence from before Thanksgiving."

"I would consider it a personal favor if you could expedite this one case."

"Personal favor, huh?" There was silence at the other end of the line for a moment. "Steak and beer at Galligher's?"

"You got it."

"I'll see what I can do."

The line clicked dead in Pete's ear. Grace was never one for idle chitchat.

Then there was that lone fingerprint on the back of the Buick's rearview mirror. Nothing on the steering wheel. Nothing on the seatbelts or door handles. Nothing. No smudges, no partials. The car had been wiped clean. But the idiot had missed the print he left when he moved the mirror.

Pete swore to himself. If McBirney had been driving the car, he wouldn't have needed to adjust the mirror. Pete had already compared the print against Ted's. No match.

He turned to a second whiteboard, which listed the information on the break-in. The timeline indicated the burglary happened between 4:00 and 5:45 Tuesday afternoon. The suspect list on this one included all the Bassi family, thanks to Sylvia having taken the damned computer in the first place. McBirney was there, too, courtesy of his bizarre interest in seeing the thing out of Sylvia's possession. Pete had scribbled in Marcy's name, too.

Kevin and Seth had phoned the officers formerly employed by the township, but neither one confessed to having shared security codes. Pete didn't buy into either of them being involved in this mess anyway.

Tool marks on the evidence room door jamb and that damned fingerprint were about all they had to go on.

He drained his coffee cup and slammed it down on the table. Who the hell had taken the computer and why? What was the link between it and Ted's death? Everything kept circling back to McBirney.

And Marcy.

Pete rubbed his eyes. What he really needed was to catch a break for once.

The buzzer from the front door sounded. Now what? He pulled the door to the conference room closed behind him and looked at the monitor for the new security camera outside the front of the station. A woman stood there, bundled in a ski jacket. Her face was shielded by oversized sunglasses, but they didn't hide her identity. He studied her, comparing the image with the one from the night of the break-in. Same person? He wasn't sure. Later, he'd sit down and view both side-by-side.

"Hello, Marcy," he said, stepping aside as he let her in.

"I'm sorry to bother you, but I need to talk."

Perfect. "No bother." He escorted her into his office and she sank into a chair without waiting for an invitation.

She kept her head bowed. Her long hair tumbled forward like a veil. Pete eased into the seat behind his desk. He noticed her hands trembling as she reached for the sunglasses and slid them off her face.

"I can't do it anymore," she said, her voice low. "I've been lying to you about Jerry being home Monday night. I can't know for sure where he was, because I wasn't there."

Got him. But Pete's moment of triumph faded when Marcy swung her head to toss her hair away from her face, revealing a swollen and blackened eye. "My God, Marcy."

"I need your help," she said, her voice ragged. "I think Jerry killed Ted."

Zoe's legs felt like over-cooked spaghetti when she finally climbed to her feet. Her mouth tasted like bile and her mind rebelled against efforts to focus. She gazed at her gelding through tear-blurred eyes.

That bastard was going to make some sort of legal claim on Windstar. Was it possible? The horse's registration papers were in Zoe's name and had been his entire life. And McBirney would have too many questions to answer. However he might simply sneak back under the cover of darkness and do something as heinous as he had with the mare all those years ago. That would more closely match his vindictive style.

Another wave of nausea hit her. What if McBirney hadn't really left? What if he'd stopped at the house on the way out?

Logan.

Zoe ran to Windstar who pulled back and showed her the whites of his eyes. "Whoa, boy." She jerked his lead rope free from the tie ring and clucked to the horse. He broke into an easy jog at her side. She crossed the indoor arena with him, opened the sliding door, and slid the halter off his head. The horse took two steps into the slushy snow before taking off at a gallop, kicking up slop as he went.

Zoe tossed the halter onto its hook in the tack room and sprinted back to the house as fast as the snow and her boots permitted. By the time the kitchen door slammed behind her, she was out of breath. Sweat soaked her clothes beneath her parka. She kicked off the boots and thudded through the kitchen and living room to come face-to-face with an ashen Logan at the office door.

"Are you all right?" Zoe asked. "Where is he? Is he still here?"

"Who?"

"McBirney."

Logan shook his head. "Nobody's here. Why? Do you expect him to come back and try again?"

"He *was* back. He came out to the barn."

Logan ran his hands through already tousled hair and his Adam's apple rode the wave of a hard swallow. "Was he alone?"

Was he? "I didn't see anyone with him."

"Where's Allison?"

"She and Patsy are riding."

He gave a quick nod. "Good."

"What's wrong?" Zoe looked past him to the computer. The monitor was black. "Did you find something?"

"No." He said it fast. Maybe too fast. "Nothing."

"But you've shut it down?" Why was he calling it quits so early? She'd expected him to be digging through the old files until she had to run him out so she could go to work.

"Yeah. Uh, something's come up. With a friend of mine. He—uh—needs my help with something. I gotta go. Now." He reached for his coat on the sofa.

"Logan, what's wrong?"

"Nothing." Again, his response came too fast.

"Logan?"

"Are you all right? I mean, did McBirney do anything to you? Do you want me to call Chief Adams for you?"

"You're ducking my question. You found something. What?"

"Seriously. Nothing." Logan shook his head. "I'll come back tomorrow and look some more. Okay?" He tugged on his coat and headed for the back door.

"What about your sister?" Zoe called after him.

"Can you give her a ride home?" he asked without turning.

What was wrong with this kid? "Of course I can."

He paused and met her eyes. "Are you sure you're okay? 'Cause if McBirney hurt you again..."

Zoe spotted Ted's protective nature in Logan's clenched jaw. "I'm fine."

Logan forced a tight smile and closed the door behind him.

Merlin materialized from nowhere and wound around Zoe's ankles. She scooped him up and rubbed his ears while she wandered into the office. What the hell was on that computer?

She deposited the cat onto her recliner and eased into the office chair. Drawing a breath, she punched the power button.

SIXTEEN

Pete clicked his pen and flipped open his notebook. "Were you and Ted having an affair?"

Marcy's good eye grew wide. "No." She lowered her face and her hair fell forward over it again. "But apparently that's what Jerry thought. Since he was sleeping around, he figured I must be, too."

This was news to Pete. "McBirney was cheating on you?"

She drew a deep breath. "Yes. With that lawyer woman."

"Elizabeth Sunday?"

"Uh-huh." Marcy peered up at him, a sheepish grin playing on her lips. "You probably think it serves me right."

He hadn't been going to say it. But now that she mentioned it..."No, I wouldn't..."

"Sure you would. And you'd be right. My marriage to Jerry has been a nightmare right from the start. He was all charm and expensive gifts until we returned home from our honeymoon. Then he had to control my every move. He had to know about everyone I talked to...who I saw. He called me on my cell phone twenty times a day, and heaven help me if I let it go to voicemail."

Pete reached across his desk and swept her hair away from the black eye. "And this?"

Marcy ducked from his touch, letting her hair obscure her swollen face again. "Oh, he was never physically abusive before. Well. Not really."

Pete's jaw ached from the tension. "You mean nothing this blatant before." He fought back a vision of his own hands around McBirney's throat.

She ran her tongue over her lips. "I wasn't having an affair with Ted. But I was seeing him."

"Seeing him?"

"I wanted to leave Jerry. But I was afraid. I knew if I just walked out, he'd track me down."

She didn't say that Jerry would track her down *and kill her,* but Pete sensed that was what she believed.

"We had that little field fire out at our farm last fall. Remember? Well, Ted was one of the firemen who responded. After it was out, he and I struck up a conversation of sorts while they were putting their equipment away. Anyway, he asked me how things were with Jerry. I didn't say anything, but he must have read my mind." Marcy picked at one of her cuticles. "Ted confided in me about what Jerry had done to Zoe and said he was worried about me."

Zoe? What had McBirney done to Zoe? Next time Pete talked to her, he intended to get answers instead of letting his feelings for her distract him.

"We agreed to meet for coffee. I talked. He listened. He had connections in county protective services, and he put me in touch with a discreet divorce attorney." Marcy's voice wavered. "I was making plans to leave Jerry, and Ted was helping me. That's all. There was no affair. But one of Jerry's cronies spotted us together and told him. That was last week." She covered her face with her hands and sobbed.

Last week. And Monday night, Ted's body was found in McBirney's car.

Pete grabbed a box of tissues from the bookcase behind him and set it on the desk. "Who else knew about Ted helping you?"

Marcy plucked a tissue from the box and shook her head. "No one."

"Not even Rose?"

"Oh, yes." She dabbed at her tears. "Rose knew."

"Sylvia?"

"No. I gave Ted permission to tell his wife only because I know firsthand what secrets can do to a marriage." She caught his eye for a moment. "But otherwise, he promised to keep it confidential."

"What do you know about Monday night?"

"Nothing. I was supposed to meet with Ted after the supervisors meeting, but he never showed up. I figured the snow—" Her voice broke, and she pressed the tissue to her mouth and nose.

"Did you try to call him?"

"No. But I wondered why he didn't call me. At least, I did until you showed up Tuesday morning."

"What time did you get home?"

"I wasn't keeping track of time. I think it was around ten or a little after."

"Was your husband home when you got there?"

"Yes. And he was livid."

"Did he hurt you?"

Marcy's left fingers brushed her right upper arm for a moment. "Not really. He broke a lamp, though. Did a lot of screaming. And he made some threats."

"Against Ted?"

"Against me."

Pete didn't realize he was clenching his fists until his pen snapped. Marcy flinched.

"Sorry." He tossed the broken one in the trash and snatched a new one from his desk drawer. "So McBirney was there at ten."

"I'm not a hundred percent sure of the time, but it was about then. Yeah."

"What about the Buick?"

"Huh?"

"Was the Buick there?" How hard a question was it? Yes or no?

Her mouth hung open, and her good eye flitted from one side to the other. Creases deepened in her forehead. "I don't know. It was dark. I wasn't paying attention."

Damn it. "Okay. Forget about that for a moment. What do you know about the computer?"

"What computer?"

Pete almost snapped a second pen. "The one your husband demanded Sylvia be arrested for stealing."

"I don't really know anything about it. Jerry never talks about his work to me. All I know is what everyone else does. From the news."

Pete studied her for indicators of a lie. The physical evidence of battery masked his usual keen ability to read her face. "What about the break-in at the station?"

"I heard about it. That's all."

"When was the last time you came here?"

"To your office?"

"To the station in general."

Her brow puckered into a puzzled frown. "Not since...I haven't been here since before our divorce."

"Don't suppose you shared your knowledge of the station's security with your husband, did you?"

"What? No. Pete, what are you getting at? You think Jerry had something to do with that, too?"

He leaned back in his chair and raised his eyebrows at her in a silent version of "do you?"

Marcy stared at him, her face registering shock. But it dissolved and softened into something resembling surrender. "A week or two ago, I'd have said no way. Now I don't have a clue who I'm married to. But if he had any insider information on station security, he didn't get it from me. Besides, I'm sure you changed everything since I worked here."

Pete rocked forward. He made a silent vow. From now on, he was going to change those codes every other week.

"You're going to arrest Jerry, aren't you?" she said. "I didn't want to believe it at first, but now I know for certain that he killed Ted. Because of me." She buried her face and gave way to hiccupping sobs.

Adrenaline pumped through Pete. Jerry McBirney had motive. The victim's body was found in his car. And now he no longer had an alibi.

Pete's phone rang. Ordinarily, Sylvia would have answered it, and Pete considered letting it go to voicemail. But some locals had never grasped the concept of dialing 9-1-1 for emergencies.

"Excuse me," he said to Marcy as he answered the call.

"Chief? This is Cyril Ramsey."

Ramsey worked with the township's road department. "Yeah, Cyril. What can I do for you?"

"I'm in the plow, out here on Cowden Road about a quarter mile east of the McBirney farm, and I've found a pickup truck over a hill. No one's in it. Must've slid off the road on the ice."

The adrenaline kicked up a notch. Pete flipped back a few pages in his notebook. "You got a license plate number on that truck?"

"Yep."

As Ramsey rattled off the number, Pete matched it to the one Rose had given him. "I'll be right there. Don't touch anything."

"Yes, sir, Chief."

Pete hung up. Ted's truck. A quarter mile from the McBirney farm. And no other houses around. If Ted had run off the road there, and had to walk...

"Yeah," Pete said to Marcy. "I'm going to arrest your husband."

Zoe longed for the day to be over.

The computer yielded nothing. The new software permitted her to open files listing tax records of all the township residents including Social Security numbers. Had she been interested in stealing anyone's identity, she'd have been in heaven. She spent over an hour scanning files, and other than being surprised by some of the locals' stated income, she found nothing of significance.

Nothing worth killing for.

She shut the computer down when Allison came in through the kitchen door. She carried muddy boots, and her cheeks glowed pink from the cold.

"Did you have a good ride?"

"It was okay, I guess. We saw a deer."

"I'm jealous." Damn that Jerry McBirney. On top of everything else, he'd mucked up her chance to get in the saddle on a gorgeous winter day. "Next time, I'm coming with you."

"Whatever." Allison deposited her boots on the rug next to the back door. "Where's Logan?"

Good question. The boy's sudden exit had left a nagging ache in Zoe's gut. "He had to leave. I'm going to drop you off at home on my way to work. Speaking of which, I need to change into my uniform."

Allison plopped into a chair and pulled out her cell phone.

When Zoe came back downstairs wearing her light blue shirt and navy blue trousers with pockets up and down both legs, Allison looked up from the phone. "Could you drop me off at my friend Bethany's house? It's right on Main Street in Phillipsburg."

Zoe studied the girl. She appeared more relaxed than she had since this all began. The ride and fresh air had done her good. "I don't know. Your mom—"

"Call her. It'll be okay. Mom likes Bethany."

"All right." Zoe picked up the phone, harboring a healthy dose of skepticism.

Rose's mother answered on the first ring. She informed Zoe that Rose was asleep thanks to some pills the doctor had given her.

"Bethany?" Mrs. Bertolotti said. "Oh, yes. She and Allison have been friends since grade school. Of course you can drop her off there. Just tell her to call when she's ready to come home."

"Okay. Um..." Zoe hesitated to ask, but couldn't help it. "Is Logan there, by any chance?"

"Logan? No. He called about an hour ago to say he'd be late. Why?"

"Nothing." As long as he'd checked in. "Call me if you need anything."

"Thanks, dear."

By the time Zoe dropped Allison at her friend's front door and pulled into a space in the parking lot across the road from the ambulance garage, the sun had settled low on the western horizon, and the temperature had tanked. In the minutes it took to bustle across the street and into the office, her eyelashes had about frozen.

Trish, the Northern Monongahela County EMS dayshift secretary, was gathering her purse and coat. "Hey, Zoe. Looks like you're in for a busy night. Medic One is en route to Brunswick with a full cardiac arrest and Medic Two just pulled out on their way to a traffic accident on Millers Hollow Road. So you and Earl are up for the next one."

Zoe thanked her. And hoped Trish was right about the busy night. Back-to-back calls all night long might keep her mind off things.

Pete adjusted the angle of the beam of light the lamp threw on his workbench. The carving on the Jaeger's stock wasn't turning out the way he pictured it in his mind. But why should this be any different than everything else in his life?

He'd spent most of the afternoon overseeing the retrieval of Bassi's Ford pickup from where it had rested, almost on its side, over an embankment. Only a half-rotted fencepost kept it from rolling further down the hillside. It was little wonder no one spotted it sooner.

Any evidence outside the truck had been obliterated by the snow. After having the Ford towed back to the township garage, Pete went over the interior of the vehicle, bagging a variety of fibers and hairs, as well as lifting dozens of fingerprints. Unlike the Buick, this vehicle hadn't been wiped clean. Before he'd even had a chance to finish processing the Ford, one of Baronick's cronies had shown up to take possession of the evidence.

Pete set down the chisel he'd been using and fingered the others nesting in an old wooden box next to the muzzleloader. Making a selection, he inspected the blade and tested its sharpness on his thumb.

The phone jangled. He flinched, and a tiny pin drop of blood appeared where the chisel pierced his skin. Guess that one didn't need sharpening after all. He replaced it in its box and reached to answer the phone.

"Chief," came Kevin's voice. "I've got a 2008 Chevy Malibu, registered to Jerry McBirney, parked behind Rodeo's Bar on King's Hollow Road."

"Do you have McBirney?"

"No, sir. The bartender says McBirney was in earlier, but left around four-thirty p.m. No one here's seen him since."

Pete checked his watch. Quarter of seven. Damn it. His head throbbed. "I'll be right there."

He strapped his gun belt on over his jeans and checked his Glock before securing it in its holster. Grabbing a bulky pair of gloves, he slipped into his heavy black jacket.

Pete hated winter. The night air felt every bit as sharp as his chisel's blade and cut into his lungs with each breath. He cranked the SUV's heater onto high, but he was pulling in beside Kevin's cruiser before the first hint of warmth reached him.

The Malibu sat alone next to the dumpster behind the bar. Most of the establishment's patrons parked in the well-lit lot out front. Why was McBirney parked back here?

"No sign of him," the officer said as soon as Pete climbed out of his vehicle, flashlight in hand.

Pete aimed the light at the Malibu's windows and then at the ground. The area had been cleared of snow.

"No footprints," Kevin said. "And no one inside the car. I've tried calling McBirney's cell phone, but no answer. I called his home. Mrs. McBirney states she hasn't seen or heard from her husband since this morning."

Something didn't feel right. Had McBirney left the bar with someone else? Pete strolled around the car, checking each of the doors. All locked. He aimed the light through the driver's window. "The keys are inside."

"Huh." Kevin frowned. "Could be he locked his keys in the car and had to go get another set."

"Possible. Except wouldn't he have called his wife if he needed a spare car key? You just said she hasn't heard from him."

"We need a warrant to search it," Kevin said.

As if Pete needed to be reminded. "I'm not going to search it. I'm going to wait until McBirney comes back and arrest his ass for murder."

"What do you want me to do?"

"Go inside and get me a coffee. Then you can get back on patrol."

"Oh." Kevin seemed disappointed. If Pete hadn't wanted this bust so bad, he'd gladly let the kid sit in a dark police cruiser as the thermometer dipped closer and closer to zero.

What was that? Pete paused and listened for a faint moan.

"What is it, Chief?"

Pete shushed him and held up one finger. There it was again. Low. Soft. Muffled.

And it was coming from the Malibu's trunk.

"Forget the damned coffee," Pete ordered. "Pop that trunk."

SEVENTEEN

The crew room at North Monongahela County EMS sported an eclectic array of furniture that had been donated by various employees. "Donated" meant discarded by dumping it at the ambulance garage. None of the emergency personnel turned any of it down, though. They were thrilled with the donations considering their meager budget limited other furnishing options.

The sofa smelled of dust, but Zoe didn't mind. She knew every lump by heart and knew how to position herself in the proper gully for maximum comfort.

Earl and the crew from Medic One huddled around the ancient television set, grunting and whooping at the Pittsburgh Penguins' game. Medic Two remained out of service at Brunswick Hospital after transporting a teenage male with a possible closed head injury, the result of the traffic accident they'd responded to.

The Red Wings scored, and the guys let out a stereo groan.

It looked like it was going to be a quiet night until the pager tones went off, alerting them to a call from the County Emergency Operation Center.

"I'll get it," Tony DeLuca, crew chief and one of the hockey nuts, hoisted himself out of his chair and lumbered into the office.

Earl stood and stretched. He ambled over to Zoe and booted one of the sofa legs. "Wake up. This one's ours."

"I'm awake." Zoe swung her feet to the floor, sitting up with a yawn.

DeLuca returned a moment later, his face red. "You better get rolling." He waved a sheet of notepaper. "Respond to Rodeo's Bar, thirteen forty-eight King's Hollow Road. Male with multiple penetrating wounds. Undetermined weapon. He's breathing, but unresponsive. The police are on scene. You're asked to go to the rear of the building."

Zoe bounded off the sofa. Earl snatched the paper from DeLuca on their way to the garage.

"You want me to drive?" Zoe asked.

"Nope. I've got it." Earl grabbed his coat from the row of hooks in the garage and headed around to the driver's side.

Zoe shrugged into her parka and climbed into the passenger side. Earl fired up the unit as the behemoth garage door rumbled open.

As they rolled onto Main Street, Zoe picked up the aluminum clipboard and the mic. "Control, this is Medic Three. We're en route to Rodeo's Bar, King's Hollow Road."

"Ten-four, Medic Three. Nineteen eighteen."

Zoe jotted the time on the fresh run report and copied the address and other information from DeLuca's note.

The emergency lights cut swaths through the black night, bouncing off the houses and businesses they passed. Zoe flipped the siren control from high/low to wail as Earl swung the ambulance left at one of Phillipsburg's three traffic signals. They bounced across the rutted railroad tracks and made another left, heading into the countryside.

Penetrating wounds. That could be a stabbing. Or it could mean gunshots.

"What do you think?" Zoe asked. "Bar brawl gone bad?"

"Possible." Earl shot her a grin. "And it wouldn't be the first time. It's your turn to take the lead, you know."

"Only if the police have secured the scene before we get there."

"Chicken."

"You know it."

The unit swayed as they made the hard right onto King's Hollow Road. Zoe braced against the console with one hand and the doorframe with the other.

King's Hollow Road wound its way through a wooded valley, crossing two one-lane bridges along its course. The top speed they could maneuver safely was little more than thirty-five miles an hour. Zoe cut the siren, turning it back on for a few whoops when they approached a blind curve or came up behind another vehicle.

"Medic Three, this is Control."

Zoe keyed the mic. "Go ahead Control."

"Chief Adams requests your ETA."

Zoe checked the dashboard clock. "Estimated time of arrival, five minutes."

"Copy, Medic Three."

Zoe eyed her partner whose face glowed pale green in the illumination of the instrument panel. "Pete wants to know how soon we can be there. That doesn't sound good."

"No, it doesn't. But on the other hand, it seems the cops have things under control so you don't have to worry about leading the way into a barroom brawl."

Small comfort.

Four minutes later, the ambulance rocked side to side as they drove through the potholed parking lot to the rear of the building where two police vehicles sat with their headlights aimed on a car next to a dumpster. Several flares added to the visibility. Even though the cab of the ambulance had only begun to feel the effects of the heater, a trickle of sweat rolled down Zoe's back.

"Control, this is Medic Three. We're on scene."

"Ten-four, Medic Three. Nineteen twenty-nine."

Earl parked behind Pete's SUV and they both leapt out. Pulling on latex gloves, Earl headed directly to the car. Zoe yanked open the patient compartment's side door and grabbed the jump kit and portable oxygen tank. Sirens wailed in the distance.

With the clipboard tucked under her arm, she lugged the equipment between the police cars and took her first good look around. A dark-colored Malibu sat next to the bar's dumpster. Police tape partially encircled the car. The trunk was open and Earl leaned into it, his stethoscope plugged into his ears. Pete and Kevin stood back, watching.

The bar brawl scenario in Zoe's mind began slipping away. It completely lost its credibility when she got close enough to see their patient.

Jerry McBirney, wearing jeans and a flannel shirt, lay curled into a fetal position in the Malibu's trunk. The illumination and shadows cast by the flares and the headlights masked the true colors of the surroundings, but not enough to disguise the sickly pallor of Jerry's swollen face. Or the dark pattern of blood pooling beneath him.

Zoe froze. Was he dead? There had been times when she'd arrived at a scene and hoped the patient showed no signs of life because he was so badly mangled, she couldn't imagine what his "life" might be like if the paramedics succeeded in their mission. This time she hoped the patient was beyond help for a more selfish reason. Heaven help her, she did *not* want to work on Jerry McBirney.

Pete's voice pierced her mental fog. "Zoe."

She shook off the momentary paralysis. "Yeah." She jumped to Earl's side and set the jump kit on the ground, flipping open the clasps. "What have we got?"

"He's alive, but just barely," Earl said. "No response to pain stimuli. Pulse is thready. B.P. is seventy-six over forty. Respiration, twenty and labored."

Zoe stuffed her feelings into some enclosed corner of her brain and scribbled the numbers onto the report. Like it or not, McBirney was her patient and she would do whatever it took to keep the bastard alive.

The sirens she'd heard earlier were louder now, closer.

Earl placed one gloved hand on McBirney's shoulder, the other on his hip and rolled him toward them enough to reveal four small holes in the back of his blood-soaked shirt.

"Bullets?" Earl aimed his question at Pete.

He shook his head. "Looks to me like he was stabbed." He pointed. "See that tear? Looks like the weapon hit a rib and slipped."

"Hard to tell for sure with all that blood," Kevin commented.

"Either way, we have to get him out of there," Zoe said.

Earl released his grip on their patient and dug into the jump kit, pulling out a packet of plastic tubing and a mask. "I'll get him started on O2. One of you guys give Zoe a hand with the gurney."

Pete fell into step with her as she jogged to the back of the ambulance.

"Are you okay?" he asked.

She couldn't afford to think about McBirney beyond what was needed to treat him. "I'm fine."

"Uh-huh." He sounded doubtful.

As they reached the ambulance, another police vehicle screeched into the parking lot, roaring toward them. Unlike Vance Township's cruisers, this one was black with gold reflective lettering. Monongahela County Police. Pete muttered something too low for Zoe to understand. But from the narrowing of his eyes and the set of his jaw, she had a strong idea of what he was saying.

She threw open the back doors of the patient compartment. Each taking a side, she and Pete rolled the gurney out and set it on the ground. She yanked the backboard from its slot beneath the bench seat and a cervical collar from one of the cabinets, and tossed them both on the cot. "Go," she said.

As they arrived back at the Malibu, Earl was adjusting the oxygen to the non-rebreather mask he'd placed on McBirney. Kevin held a stack of sterile gauze squares and a roll of tape, but appeared lost as to what to do next.

Zoe wiggled her fingers into her Latex gloves and snatched a handful of the squares. She ripped the paper covering from the first one. "Tear off some lengths of tape," she told the officer.

He shot her a quick grateful smile and peeled off a foot-long piece.

"Whoa, cowboy. Not that long." She indicated half that length with both her index fingers.

"Oh. Okay."

Glancing up from her work, Zoe noticed Pete charging toward the new arrival and recognized Detective Baronick climbing out of the car.

Earl grabbed scissors and cut open the back of McBirney's shirt. Zoe broke the seal on a bottle of sterile saline solution and poured some of the liquid onto a stack of the 4x4 squares. The rest, she dumped over McBirney's back, washing away some of the partially congealed blood. She tore into another stack of the squares and dabbed his skin as dry as she could. Blood poured from the wounds as fast as she wiped it away.

Bleeding meant his heart was pumping. He was still alive.

For a moment, she questioned whether or not that was a good thing.

"Zoe." Earl's words sliced through her reverie. "Tape."

Kevin held out a perfect length of the stuff. Earl pressed a wad of bandaging to one of the four holes and taped around it. Zoe did the same. Once all the wounds were dressed, Zoe said, "Let's stabilize him and get him out of there."

Zoe fitted the cervical collar around McBirney's neck without looking at his face. Earl and Kevin positioned the gurney and backboard against the Malibu's back bumper.

Pete and Baronick were engaged in a loud, animated conversation. They were far enough away that Zoe couldn't make out more than a few words. She looked at Kevin. "Give us a hand?"

"Yup," he said.

"Okay, kiddies." Earl worked to get a grip on McBirney's shoulders. "Let's make this as smooth as we can."

Zoe maintained traction on McBirney's head and neck. "On three," she said and counted. "One. Two..."

Earl maneuvered the patient's shoulders. Kevin guided his legs. In unison, they muscled McBirney's limp body out of the trunk. Earl secured the patient to the backboard with the straps.

"Grab the O2," Zoe barked at Kevin.

He snatched the small green cylinder of oxygen and handed it to Zoe who positioned it between McBirney's legs.

"You two take him," Earl said. "I'll grab the kit."

Kevin and Zoe wheeled the gurney back to the unit and guided it into the patient compartment. "Is he gonna make it?" Kevin said.

"No one dies in our ambulance," Zoe said. "Earl and I both need to work on this guy. Mind driving?"

"He's on patrol duty," Pete's voice boomed from behind them. "I'll drive."

Zoe caught a glimpse of a muscle popping in his jaw as he stormed past her to the front of the ambulance. She looked over her shoulder at McBirney's car. Detective Baronick and another officer leaned over the open trunk with flashlights aimed inside. The faint wail of distant sirens bounced off the hillsides. Apparently, County had once again taken over.

Kevin pressed his lips together hard in silent communication. Like Zoe, he obviously realized now was not the time to question the chief.

She climbed in beside her patient and flipped the switch for the heater onto high. Earl slid the jump kit into the side door and climbed in, too. Pete claimed the driver's seat. Kevin slammed the back doors and then circled around to slam the side one.

"You're good to go," he shouted, and the ambulance lurched across the parking lot.

Like a well-choreographed dance, Zoe and Earl went about their work, switching McBirney from the portable oxygen tank to the ambulance's supply, slapping the leads for an EKG onto his skin, getting a new set of vitals, listening to the lung sounds. In the bright light of the patient compartment, the grayish blue of McBirney's skin couldn't be dismissed as an aberration created by the poor illumination in the trunk.

Earl touched the patient's neck and met Zoe's gaze. "Pneumothorax," he said.

Zoe took the seat at McBirney's head, the clipboard in her lap. She stared at his face. The left side was puffy and showed signs of bruising. She recalled swinging Windstar's bridle earlier that afternoon and the *thunk* of steel striking flesh. With a shudder, she picked up the radio phone. "Brunswick, this is Medic Three."

After a brief pause, a voice responded, "Go ahead Medic Three."

"We have a male, age forty-six, with multiple penetrating injuries to his upper back resulting in severe blood loss. Patient is unresponsive. B.P. is sixty-eight over forty. Pulse is one sixteen and weak. Respiration is twenty and labored. Lung sounds are absent on the right side. He has distended veins in his neck and is cyanotic." Zoe knew her words translated into bad news made worse by the presence of a collapsed lung.

Earl had pulled out a bag of normal saline even before the doctor at Brunswick ordered them to start the I.V. and do a needle chest decompression. He plugged the tubing into the bag while Zoe repositioned herself at McBirney's side. She tied the rubber tourniquet around the patient's arm and felt for a good vein. Damn it. He'd lost so much blood, there was no way this was going to be easy.

"Can you get it?" Earl asked.

Zoe didn't reply. A bead of sweat tickled her forehead, and it wasn't from the blasting heater. On her third attempt, a red droplet appeared inside the needle. "Bingo," she said.

Zoe finished taping the I.V. catheter in place, and Earl pulled supplies from one of the cubbies to start the needle chest compression.

"Radio Control to let them know we're en route," Zoe shouted to Pete as the ambulance pitched along the potholed road.

Over the roar of the engine and the clanging and banging of

equipment swaying around them, she heard Pete's voice giving the information to the EMS dispatcher.

"Ready?" Earl asked.

"Not really." Inserting a needle into a patient's chest was nerve-wracking enough without the added challenge of performing the procedure in a moving vehicle.

"Do you want me to try?"

Zoe shot a look at her partner. They had worked together long enough to know each other's strengths and weaknesses. Sticking a patient with a needle was not one of Earl's strong points. "I'll do it."

"Okay." Earl swabbed McBirney's upper right chest with Betadine and then leaned back. Zoe inserted a needle between the second and third rib, careful of the angle. She felt a slight give. "I'm at the pleural cavity," she announced. Drawing a deep breath, she advanced the needle further. A whoosh of air escaped. "Got it."

She slid the 14-gauge catheter over the needle and removed it. Earl handed her a Heimlich valve and tubing to finish the procedure.

"Good job," Earl patted her on the back.

"Ha. You're just glad you didn't have to do it."

"You know me too well. Want me to secure it?"

Zoe flopped back onto the bench seat. "Knock yourself out."

The I.V. tubing and bag swung like pendulums inside the patient compartment as the ambulance careened along the dark country road. Zoe braced one foot against the gurney and the other heel against the base of the bench. She clutched the cot's side rail and stared at her patient as Earl finished taping the valve and tubing to his chest.

It had only been a matter of time before *someone* tried to kill Jerry McBirney. But who?

No. She couldn't allow herself to think about that. The man on the cot was just another critical patient. *Do your job, Zoe.* Keep him alive.

Earl moved to the seat at the head of the gurney. Zoe leaned forward to check the flow of the normal saline through the tubing. She clipped her stethoscope into her ears and placed the pad on McBirney's arm, pumping the bulb of the blood pressure cuff. She listened for the weak *thub, thub, thub* as the needle descended the gauge. Nothing. The cardiac monitor showed a rhythm. Rapid and irregular, but a rhythm. She pumped up the cuff again and let the air out slow. Listening.

Watching. Where was it? The needle slipped below seventy. The fluids should be helping by now. Saline might not be a good substitute for blood, but it should at least stabilize his pressure. The needle dropped below sixty.

The cardiac monitor screeched, no longer showing a rhythm. Earl jumped.

"V-Fib," Zoe said.

Earl yanked the defibrillator from its compartment and set it up. Zoe ripped the non-rebreather mask from McBirney's face and placed her ear near his mouth. "No respiration," she reported before grabbing a CPR mask, sealing it over his face, and administering four breaths. She listened again, watching his chest for movement. Nothing.

"Clear," Earl said. Zoe leaned back.

The electrical shock caused the body to buck against the restraints. But the monitor showed no change. No steady *blip blip blip*.

Earl charged the defibrillator again. "Clear."

Again, the shock provided nothing beneficial.

Zoe's own words rang in her ears. *No one dies in our ambulance.*

"Start chest compressions," Zoe ordered as she rummaged through the storage compartments for the laryngoscope and blades.

After sticking a needle into McBirney's chest, intubation was relatively simple. With the endotracheal tube in place, she attached the bag-valve mask and oxygen.

Breathe, you bastard.

"Let me shock him one more time," Earl said.

Zoe knew the defibrillator wasn't going to help. She suspected he did, too. While her partner charged the paddles, Zoe hung a second bag of saline, ready to make the switch when the first one ran dry.

"Still V-fib," Earl announced.

Zoe leaned toward the front of the ambulance. "He's in full arrest," she called to Pete.

In response, he flipped on the siren. The ambulance lurched as it accelerated.

Earl staggered and grabbed for a handrail.

"Here," Zoe said. "You bag and contact Brunswick. I'll do compressions for a while."

He nodded, and they squeezed past each other. He perched on the edge of the seat at McBirney's head, pressing breath into their patient with the bag and reaching for the radio phone. "Brunswick, this is Medic Three."

Zoe braced her feet against the gurney and the bench. She jammed one shin into the cot's side rail and pressed the top of her head against the cabinet above McBirney to steady her. CPR in a speeding ambulance was no easy feat. And Brunswick Hospital was still more than twenty minutes away.

EIGHTEEN

Pete leaned against a low, brick wall outside Brunswick Emergency Department's ambulance entrance, his breath frosted into a cloud in front of him. Medic Three sat silent, a few feet away. At least by driving the ambulance, he had a head start on Baronick, who'd dismissed him back at Rodeo's Bar. Fine. Let the cocky young detective deal with processing the crime scene in sub-zero temperatures.

He was beginning to wonder why he stayed on in this low-budget rural township where he had little choice but to turn over the big cases to County who had the funding and the lab facilities to properly investigate them. Why the hell didn't he ditch this rural police chief gig and go back to Pittsburgh? The only reason he'd moved here in the first place was because Marcy wanted to live in the country.

Marcy.

Pulling out his cell phone, he turned it over and over in his gloved hand. He considered calling her to break the news. But he shoved it back in his pocket. Baronick could handle that, too. There wasn't much Pete could do to protect her at this stage anyway. She was the victim's wife. Automatic suspect number one.

He pushed away from the wall and moved toward the automatic doors, which swung open at his approach. Inside, the emergency department smelled of antiseptic and bleach mingled with the faint aroma of body fluids. Somewhere, an alarm beeped, demanding attention it wasn't getting. A child's unmistakable wail echoed down the hallway.

Pete had helped Zoe and her partner unload McBirney and had watched as they whisked him through the doors, disappearing into the organized chaos. He hadn't followed. Give them time. He'd just be in the way, anyhow. But his curiosity nagged at him. What was going on? Was McBirney dead or alive? He hadn't looked good with the two paramedics working frantically over him the whole trip and then as they rushed him into the hospital.

Pete had no clue where they'd gone. He tugged off his gloves and stuffed them into his coat pockets. Drifting down the hall, he took a glimpse in each room he passed. In one, a young man in baggy jeans held a grungy, bawling child as a sallow-skinned woman reclined in the bed. So that was the source of the wailing he'd heard. Next door, a boy held an icepack to his head while a woman—Pete presumed his mother—paced. The curtains were drawn on the next two, and a pair of Brunswick city police officers flanked the doorway of another room. Pete exchanged a nod of acknowledgement with them.

Medical personnel crowded into the central nurses' station. Two nurses sat, scribbling notes onto records. A lanky male in pale green scrubs squeezed into the space as a petite brunette in white scurried out. A doctor stood in the adjoining glass-enclosed office frowning as he spoke on the phone. Zoe's partner, Earl, stood on the far side of the station, engaged in jovial conversation with an older man wearing dark-rimmed glasses and a white lab coat.

Pete circled the station. Earl spotted his approach. "Hey, Chief. Thanks again for driving."

The bespectacled older man clapped Earl on the shoulder. "I have to get back to work. Take it easy, you hear?" With a nod to Pete, he hurried away.

"Any word on your patient?" Pete asked.

"Nothing new that I'm aware of. He's in room eleven if you want to check on him."

Pete thanked the paramedic and headed down the hallway, dodging harried medical personnel and checking room numbers as he went.

A nurse carrying two I.V. bags of deep red blood bustled past Pete, heading in the same direction, but at a much quicker pace. She ducked into the last room on the left. Room eleven. The curtains were drawn in there, too, but they moved and swayed, indicating some action behind them. Pete paused in the doorway and noted several pairs of feet visible where the curtain failed to meet the floor. The feet shifted and maneuvered around the concealed patient. Grim voices exchanged information in tones too low for him to comprehend the words. But he discerned a sense of urgency in them.

Pete knew better than to enter. He hesitated. Glanced around. The hall cut to the right with more patient rooms on its left. Across from those cubicles, an ambulance cot sporting clean linen was parked. Zoe squatted next to it, her back against the wall, elbows on her knees and face in her hands. Her blonde hair was more disheveled than usual, sticking out on the sides, but flattened on the top from her hat, which lay on the floor.

"Hey," he said softly, kneeling down next to her.

She lifted her face, revealing eyes rimmed in red with dark circles beneath them.

He gave her a smile. "You look like hell."

"Thanks." She buried her face in her hands again, but this time she pressed her palms against her eyes and ruffed up her bangs with her fingers.

"How's the patient?"

She shrugged. "You know as much as I do."

Pete shuffled around until he was side-by-side with Zoe, his back against the wall. But his knees complained too much to mimic her squatting position. Instead, he sat and stretched his legs out. She slid down and did the same.

"What's your professional opinion?" he asked. "Think he'll make it?"

Zoe didn't answer right away. She stared into space, and her face transformed through a succession of expressions from a scowl to a deep frown to something Pete interpreted as fear.

What the hell was she afraid of?

He touched her knee, and she flinched.

"Umm, it's impossible to say." Zoe brushed a hand across her eyes. "You wouldn't think he'd have much of a chance considering the blood loss. But the cold temperatures could've worked to his advantage."

A pair of techs, pushing a portable x-ray machine, bustled into room eleven. The nurse who had passed Pete carrying the blood, another tech, and a solemn young man in a blood-spattered lab coat scurried out, talking in hushed tones as they went.

Pete stared at the doorway. He knew Zoe didn't want to discuss any of this. But he had too many questions, and not much time before Baronick and his posse showed up and booted him back to Vance Township.

"We need to talk," Pete said.

"I know."

Earl rounded the corner. He froze mid-stride when he saw Pete and Zoe. He appeared about to ask a question. But he reconsidered and quietly reversed direction.

"Marcy came to see me earlier."

Zoe met his gaze without saying a word. God, she looked exhausted.

"She said she and Ted were *not* having an affair."

Her eyebrows raised for a moment, then settled. She shifted her gaze to her hands, and a distant smile flickered across her lips.

"She said Ted was helping her get a divorce attorney."

"So it was Jerry who gave her the black eye."

"You knew about that?"

"The black eye? Yeah. She wore sunglasses into the funeral home. I saw her take them off for a moment."

Pete remembered Zoe had mentioned seeing Marcy at the viewing. "Why didn't you tell me about this before?"

"I don't know. I started to, but..." She shook her head.

The X-ray techs rolled their machine out of the room. Within seconds, a man and a woman in scrubs rushed back in.

"According to Marcy, she was afraid of McBirney and didn't want him to know she planned to leave him. He found out she was meeting with Ted and assumed they were having an affair."

Zoe's face softened, and she nodded. "That makes sense."

"So do you want to tell me what you've been hiding from me?"

She stiffened. Her mouth opened, but no sound came out.

A piercing electronic squeal emanated from room eleven, producing a flurry of activity as a team of four charged down the hall and into the glass-fronted cubicle.

"He's arresting again," Zoe said. "They had him back for a while."

Pete watched and listened, expecting someone to come out and pronounce the patient had died. But nothing happened other than one tech leaving and another taking his place.

"They won't call it until after they warm him up," Zoe said.

"Huh?"

"You aren't officially dead until you're *warm* and dead."

"Oh." His mind snapped back to the myriad questions plaguing him. And to something Marcy had said. "What did McBirney do to you?"

Zoe's face went stark white. "What?"

"Marcy told me Ted asked her how things were with her husband, because he knew what McBirney had done to you. What," he asked as he watched her face go from white to almost green, "did McBirney do to you?"

A woman and a man, both in print scrubs, rushed into room eleven. Raised voices drifted out to them.

Zoe pressed both hands against her face and drew in a deep, ragged breath. As she exhaled, her hands dropped to her lap. The fear Pete had read in her face had been replaced with resignation.

"When I was twenty-three, Jerry McBirney tried to rape me."

The story she poured out stunned Pete. From McBirney's manipulative endeavors to charm and seduce a young girl, to the drunken attempted rape, to the vindictive poisoning of her horse. He'd known McBirney was a bastard, but he'd had no inkling of the depths to his evil.

"Why didn't you report it?" Pete asked when Zoe finally grew silent.

Her laugh reeked of desperation. "I was a kid. I'd—been with more than my share of boys all through high school. Part of me—a big part of me—thought I deserved it. Had asked for it somehow."

"No one asks for—"

"I know that. Now. Then? I was confused. Lost. Honestly, I was more upset about him killing my mare than the other stuff. And I didn't think the police would do anything about a dead horse. Besides, I couldn't prove anything. Couldn't prove it then. Can't prove it now."

Some days, Pete hated the way his mind worked. Too many years as a cop made him see things, think things that he wouldn't had he been a civilian. For instance, this whole sad tale should have stirred nothing but sympathy in his heart. Instead...

He knew full well Zoe hadn't stabbed McBirney. There was also the matter of evidence—or lack thereof. But others—Baronick for one— would pounce on her story with nothing short of bloodlust.

"I saw him today," Zoe said, shattering his reverie.

"What? Who?"

"Jerry McBirney. He came to the barn when I was getting ready to go riding. He wanted to convince me he hadn't killed Ted."

The skin on the back of Pete's neck prickled. "What happened?"

She frowned. "We kind of got into it."

Damn it. "What do you mean, *you got into it?*"

"I told him to leave. He wouldn't. He tried his charming, innocent act on me. It didn't work. I reminded him of what he'd done to me. He laughed it off. Said it was my word against his. 'Water under the bridge,' I think he said. He denied having anything to do with my horse." She paused and took a deep breath as if fighting off tears. "Then he threatened to take Windstar away from me."

Windstar?

She must have noticed his confusion. "The horse I have now. His mother was my mare that died." Zoe sniffed. "McBirney claimed Windy really belonged to him. I know he probably couldn't make a claim like that stick in court, but I wasn't thinking straight."

Pete closed his eyes. Why the hell hadn't he left it alone? She hadn't wanted to tell him. He should have respected her wishes.

"I kind of—attacked him."

Pete's eyes flew open. "You what?"

"Well...I offered to pay him off...just to get him to leave me—leave Windy—alone. He claimed I could..." She rubbed a spot on her head and winced. "He suggested a way I could pay that didn't involve money."

"That son of a—" Pete contemplated marching into room eleven and ripping the plugs to every life support gadget out of the walls.

"So I hit him."

Hit him? Pete looked at her slender hands. No bruises. No scrapes. "With what?"

"The only thing I could grab. Windstar's bridle. Well, technically the bit. Then I sprayed him in the face with fly repellent."

Stunned, Pete ran the scene through his mind. The mental image of Zoe going on the offensive with *fly spray* made him laugh, but he camouflaged it as a cough. He wanted to hug this woman. He wanted to take her out to dinner and then bring her home to his bed. He did *not* want to make her mad.

And he sure didn't want to see her arrested for murder.

The cliché about confession being good for your soul might be true, but Zoe wasn't convinced. Pete wanted answers. She hadn't been willing to give up Logan or their investigation into Ted's murder. So when Pete had asked about her more distant past and transgressions, the story had tumbled out. The freshness of the newly re-opened wound made it simpler.

But no less painful.

Nearby, someone cleared their throat. "Excuse me."

Zoe looked up to find an apologetic-looking Earl standing at the corner.

"Sorry to interrupt, but we really need to get back in service." He pointed to his wristwatch.

Zoe climbed to her feet and dusted off the seat of her pants.

Pete stood at the same time. "Mind dropping me off at my car?"

She pictured his SUV parked behind Rodeo's. Would McBirney's car still be there? Probably. With that county detective and his men crawling all over it. Or maybe they'd have towed it away by now.

As if she'd conjured him up by merely thinking of him, Wayne Baronick appeared behind Earl. "Ah. I see the rescue squad is still here. Any news on our victim?"

Victim. Patient. Bastard. Zoe mused on their different perspectives.

"They're still working on him," Pete said.

"Is he gonna make it?"

"It's too soon to tell," Zoe said.

"Doesn't look good, though," Earl added.

Baronick pursed his lips in what must have been an effort to appear concerned. "Well, I drove his wife here. She's out in the waiting room." He turned to Pete. "Do you want to talk to her?"

Pete gave him a wide-eyed innocent look and a shrug. "Why should I? I have nothing to do with this case. She's all yours, Wayne." He clapped him on the shoulder and then turned to face Zoe and then Earl. "Shall we go?"

Relieved to get the hell out of there, Zoe scooped up her hat and grabbed the gurney's framework. Earl stepped up to push from the other end. They steered it past room eleven and had almost reached the exit to the ambulance bay when Baronick called out for them to hold up.

Zoe, Pete, and Earl all turned to see the detective and a doctor, who had been in and out of McBirney's room, heading their way.

"Tell them, Doc," Baronick said.

The grave-faced young man in the blood-splotched lab coat clenched and unclenched his fists. "I'm afraid there wasn't anything we could do. Mr. McBirney did not survive his injuries."

NINETEEN

Zoe let the men sit in the front of the ambulance for the drive to Vance Township. Riding in the back, staring at the empty cot, was the closest she could get to being alone. And being alone was what she needed right now.

Jerry McBirney was dead.

She should feel something. Joy. Relief. Vindication.

Grief?

Instead, she felt apprehensive. The man she'd loathed and feared for over a decade was gone. In theory, he couldn't hurt her anymore. So why was she about to burst into a cold sweat at any moment? Why did she sense McBirney's circle of influence over her life was about to tighten into a noose?

Zoe shivered and leaned over to flip the heater on. There was no happy medium where the ambulance's patient compartment furnace was concerned. You either roasted or froze.

"Are you all right?" Pete called from the front.

"I'm fine," she lied.

Closing her eyes, Zoe spent the rest of the trip oblivious to the conversation in the cab, muffled by the roar of the heater and the clang of the valve wrench against the oxygen tank.

The ambulance jolted to a stop and jarred Zoe from a near-sleep state.

Pete opened the side door, allowing a blast of bitter cold into the patient compartment. He gave her an inquisitive stare. "You sure you're all right?"

Zoe clicked off the heater and stepped out into night air sharp enough to slice through her coat and gloves. "I'm terrific."

"Like hell you are." He took her by the arm and led her away from the ambulance before leaning in close to her ear. "Baronick is going to want to question you. Don't say anything to him. You hear me?"

Baronick? The detective? "Why would he want to talk to me?"

Pete lowered his face to her level so she had no choice but to meet his unyielding gaze.

Zoe tried to swallow, but it stuck in her throat. The conversation she'd had with Pete earlier came rushing back. Her history with McBirney. His threats. Her attack on him. She was going to be a suspect in his murder. Because she'd confided in Pete. Not Pete her friend. Pete the cop.

"You're going to tell Baronick what I told you?"

"Not if I don't have to. And neither are you."

She stared into his face wanting to believe he wouldn't betray her trust.

"I didn't kill Jerry McBirney. You know that, don't you?" she whispered.

Pete touched a gloved thumb to Zoe's lips and cupped her face in his hand. His expression softened. "Yeah. I know that." For a moment, she thought he was going to kiss her again. Instead, he turned and strode to his SUV, parked where he'd left it behind Rodeo's.

Zoe headed back to Medic Three and climbed into the passenger seat Pete had vacated. She leaned forward a bit for a better view of what was now a crime scene. Yellow police tape marked the area. A Monongahela County police vehicle kept vigil. But McBirney's car was gone.

She sat back and closed her eyes.

Earl rested a hand on her shoulder and gave a gentle squeeze. "You want to tell me what's going on?"

"Not now." Zoe drew a deep breath and picked up the mic. "Control this is Medic Three. We're in service, returning to the station."

After two hours of restless sleep, Pete rolled out of bed. He showered, shaved, and dressed, all the while replaying yesterday's events in his mind.

Marcy fingered her husband for Ted Bassi's murder. Yet instead of being the break in the case Pete had longed for, it only created countless new headaches. McBirney hadn't had a chance to refute his wife's accusations. How convenient.

For Marcy.

Zoe's tale only reinforced what a monster McBirney was. Motive wasn't the issue. Hell, it amazed Pete that someone hadn't offed the man years ago.

No. The issue wasn't why. It was who.

Pete unlocked the police station's front door and disengaged the alarm. He checked the clock. Seven-fifteen. Forty-five minutes before he was officially on duty.

He turned up the thermostat, flipped on the light to his office, and glared at the empty coffee pot. Damn, he missed Sylvia. No matter how early he arrived at the department, she'd already be there with a fresh pot brewing.

Maybe with McBirney gone, Pete could get the remaining supervisors to give Sylvia her job back. If she'd take it. Pete would have to work on her.

He popped the lid on the Maxwell House can and peered inside. Empty.

Son of a bitch.

Pete flung the container into the trash can and opened the storage cabinet door. Nothing.

The one and only grocery in Dillard had closed five years ago. He could venture back out into the frigid cold and drive to Phillipsburg. Or...

He stomped into the front office—Sylvia's office—and picked up the mic.

"Thirty-one, this is Vance base."

"This is thirty-one," crackled Kevin's response.

"What's your twenty?"

"I'm on Covered Bridge Lane approaching Route 15."

Damn. That was clear on the other side of the township from Phillipsburg. "Before you come back to the station, swing by the Food Mart and pick up a can of coffee."

"Copy that, Chief," Kevin said, but the jingling bells indicating someone had entered through the front door partially drowned him out.

Pete turned to find Wayne Baronick grinning at him, his hands behind his back. "Out of coffee, Chief? That's a fate worse than death." The detective revealed what he'd been hiding—two cups of Starbucks.

On another day, Pete might have thrown the brew in Baronick's face. Especially considering how pleased the sanctimonious county detective had been last night as he claimed jurisdiction over Pete's crime scene. But Pete needed caffeine. Now. He snatched one of the cups and took a whiff of the aromatic steam.

"You're welcome," Baronick said. "Now, can we talk?"

"About what?" Pete headed for his office, gulping the coffee.

Baronick followed. "Jerry McBirney's homicide."

Pete shook his head. "I'm not on that case. 'Vance Township doesn't have the means to properly handle a homicide investigation.' Isn't that what you said last night?"

"That doesn't mean I don't want your assistance. Besides, I thought you'd be interested in hearing what my guys learned while interviewing the bartender at Rodeo's last night."

Pete settled into his chair and motioned to one across the desk from him.

Baronick made a show of flipping through his notepad. "McBirney arrived sometime after two in the afternoon, not in a very talkative mood. He started with beer. About an hour, hour and a half later, he made a phone call on his cell. The bartender didn't hear the conversation, but said McBirney seemed pleased with himself afterwards and ordered another beer."

"He made a call on his cell? Did you find the phone?"

"No. It wasn't on McBirney, and it wasn't anywhere in the car. I'm working on a subpoena for the records."

"So was McBirney there the whole evening?"

Baronick shook his head. "The bartender said he received a call a little before four. Apparently McBirney didn't like what the caller told him because he switched from beer to whiskey. After a couple of shots, he made another call. The bartender said the joint was getting busy with folks getting off work so he didn't notice how long he was on the phone, but didn't think it was long. After a couple more shots, McBirney paid up and left around four-thirty."

Pete sipped his coffee. Had McBirney met up with his attacker in the parking lot on his way out? Or was that what the killer wanted them to believe?

"We should have some answers as soon as I get my hands on those phone records."

"That's not likely to happen until early next week," Pete said. "If you're lucky."

"I know. In the meantime, I could use your input. You know the people involved. Some of them very well. The bereaved widow McBirney for one." Baronick waggled his eyebrows suggestively.

Pete nearly reconsidered his decision not to make the detective wear the coffee.

He must have sensed Pete's thoughts. "Calm down, Pete. Try not to be so pigheaded about this. We both know you're a better cop than I'll ever hope to be. But local departments simply don't have the budget to effectively handle major crimes. That's just the way it is."

"Stop blowing smoke up my ass, Wayne."

"Your ex-wife wasn't very forthcoming last night. As soon as she got word her husband was dead, she clammed up and demanded a lawyer."

Good for Marcy, Pete thought.

"Don't suppose you know how she got that shiner." The detective sipped his coffee.

"McBirney slugged her."

Baronick choked. He fumbled in his pockets until he found a handkerchief, which he coughed into. "You know that for a fact?"

"I do."

He raised his eyebrows.

Pete knew he was waiting for more, but didn't feel like making it easy on him.

"Okay. How do you know?" Baronick wiped his mouth with the handkerchief before stuffing it into his pocket.

"She mentioned it yesterday when she came in to tell me she thought her husband killed Ted Bassi."

Baronick's eyes grew wide. He set his coffee on the floor and dug his notebook from his jacket. "Maybe you should just tell me everything you know."

As much fun as it was toying with the detective, Pete decided to get it over with. He told Baronick about Marcy's failing marriage, her meetings with Ted Bassi, and McBirney's suspicions.

Baronick didn't say anything for several moments after Pete finished his report. He tapped his pen against his pursed lips and glowered at his notes.   .

Pete sipped his coffee.

"I don't suppose," Baronick said at last, "that you happened to Mirandize Mrs. McBirney?"

"Didn't have to. I wasn't interrogating her. She came in of her own volition to revoke her previous statement that she was home the night Ted Bassi was killed."

"Still. If she gets a good attorney, he'll have any statement incriminating her thrown out. Damn it, Pete. You should have read her her rights."

Pete jiggled the Starbucks cup. Empty. Shit.

"Who else had reason to kill McBirney?" Baronick said.

Who didn't? Pete wasn't about to mention Zoe's late night confession. That left Sylvia and Rose and all the disgruntled township residents McBirney had pissed off during his term in office. And before. "The man had a lot of enemies."

Baronick's eyes narrowed as he studied Pete. "Including you, Chief."

Pete's hand tightened on the empty cup and it crumpled. "What exactly are you suggesting, Detective?"

Baronick scribbled something in his notebook and then closed it and slid it into his jacket pocket. "I'm not suggesting anything. Just stating a fact. Marcy McBirney was a battered wife. You're her ex-husband. Not only did our homicide victim steal your wife years ago, but then he abuses her. Don't suppose you have an alibi for last evening between 4:30 and 6:30, do you?"

Pete wanted to snap an easy answer at the jackass. But the fact was he'd been working on the Jaeger. In his basement.

Alone.

The bells on the door announced someone had entered the station. "Chief?" Kevin called. "I've got your coffee."

Pete glared at Baronick. "I think it's time you leave."

The detective stood. "You're absolutely right. I have a lot of work to do." He extended a hand to Pete. "Thanks, Chief. You've been very helpful."

Pete held Baronick's gaze. He didn't look down at the hand and sure didn't intend on shaking it.

Kevin appeared in the doorway with a plastic Food Mart bag in his hand. "Hey, Detective," he said.

The game of who-blinks-first went on for several long, silent moments. Pete won.

Baronick cleared his throat and turned. He patted Kevin's shoulder as he passed, mumbling a greeting to him.

"What was that all about?" Kevin asked when the bells indicated the detective had left.

"Nothing." Pete tossed the worse-for-wear Starbucks cup in the trash. "Make me a pot of coffee."

Zoe's sleep would have been disrupted by two more calls overnight—had she slept. But both times the pager tones went off, she'd been wide awake, staring at the underside of the bunk above her. By eight o'clock, Friday's daylight shift had shown up. She mumbled goodbyes and ventured into the morning sun.

The sky was crystalline blue and the air so cold that the hairs in her nose froze. She tugged her parka's collar higher, trying to protect her face.

Her truck groaned a bit, but the motor turned over after only minor wavering. She set the heater and the fan on high and flexed her fingers inside her gloves to encourage blood flow.

Jerry McBirney was dead.

All night, that's as far as her brain would venture. But with the light of day burning into the shadows of her mind, she had to consider some hard questions.

Who killed him? What had Logan found on the computer yesterday?

Where the hell had Logan gone?

Zoe shifted into drive and hit the gas. Before she let her mind take off on some ridiculous tangent, she needed the answers to those last two questions. As long as Logan wasn't involved, she didn't care much about the first one.

Except maybe to shake that person's hand.

Five minutes later, she wheeled onto Rose's street and parked in front of her house. As Zoe pounded on the door, she prayed a bleary-eyed Logan would answer.

Instead, a pale, gaunt Rose let her in.

"Have you heard from Logan?" Rose said.

"No. I'd hoped he was here."

"I haven't seen him since he left for your place yesterday after the funeral." Rose's eyes were red and moist, her lips raw and cracked.

Sylvia sat on the couch in the living room. Dark circles shadowed her bloodshot eyes. "Good morning, dear," she said to Zoe, her voice strained and weak.

Zoe leaned down to give her a hug and then turned back to Rose. "He left my house around two. Said a friend needed his help with something."

Rose nodded and started pacing. "He called me and said the same thing. Told me he didn't know what time he'd be home. But when he wasn't back by nine, I started calling his cell phone. It keeps going to voicemail." She threw her hands up. "I spent half the night driving around looking for him, but I don't know where else he could be. I wish Ted were here." Her voice cracked, and she sank into one of the living room chairs.

Zoe knelt at her feet and placed a hand on her knee. "Did you call around to his friends?"

"Of course I did. I called everyone I could think of." Rose brushed a tear from her cheek with a trembling hand.

Zoe hated what she was thinking. McBirney was dead. Logan was missing.

She closed her eyes for a moment. "Have you called the cops?"

"I tried Pete last night," Sylvia said. "Damned voicemail. I left a message, but he hasn't called back. Rose refuses to call 9-1-1."

"I can't," Rose wailed. "I'm afraid. What if...you know...there really is something wrong." She burst into tears. "I can't take it, Zoe. I just buried Ted. I can't lose my boy, too."

Sylvia hauled herself up from the couch and moved to Rose's side.

Her eyes glistened as she rested a hand on her daughter-in-law's shoulder.

Zoe couldn't breathe. She had to tell them. Damn Logan. If only he were home, safe and sound. And innocent. Then it wouldn't be so hard to say the words.

"Jerry McBirney was killed last night."

Zoe noticed Sylvia's fingers tighten on Rose's shoulder. Rose made a sound that was half gasp, half retch. She stared at the carpet. The refrigerator's soft hum in the next room sounded more like a tractor in the midst of the silence.

Sylvia spoke first with a hushed, "Hallelujah." She released her grip on Rose, stood up tall, and stalked into the kitchen. A chair squeaked as she lowered into it. After another silent pause, she slammed her hand on the table.

Zoe flinched.

"How?" Rose said.

"It looked like stab wounds. Punctured a lung. He bled out."

Rose chewed her already raw lip. A parade of emotions marched across her face. Finally, she nodded. "Good."

"Good, my ass," came Sylvia's response from the kitchen. "The son of a bitch deserved a long, suffering death for what he did to my boy." She turned in the chair and met Zoe's eye. "And to you."

Being stabbed and stuffed in a car trunk on the coldest night of the year, left to either bleed to death or freeze to death sounded pretty torturous to Zoe, but she didn't attempt to change Sylvia's mind.

"Anyhow, that's why Pete didn't answer his phone last night. He drove the ambulance so Earl and I could both work on McBirney."

The kitchen chair clattered to the floor as Sylvia staggered to her feet and lumbered into the living room. "You mean you had to work on him?"

"Yeah."

Rose swore under her breath and buried her face in her hands.

Sylvia stared at her. "I hope you didn't try too hard to save the bastard."

"Sylvia," Rose snapped.

"I did everything I could," Zoe said. "Everything I'd have done for anyone else." She felt like she should tack on an apology.

Sylvia shook her head. Then sighed. "Well, yes, of course, you would have to. That's the kind of person you are. Thank heavens he died anyway." She reached for the phone. "I'm going to try Pete again."

The kitchen door slammed, and Sylvia spun toward it.

Rose leapt to her feet. "Logan?"

Allison appeared in the doorway. Like everyone else in the Bassi family, she looked as though she'd put in a long sleepless night. "No. It's me. Isn't Logan here?" Even with her face scrubbed free of its usual heavy make-up, she hardly resembled the little girl Zoe knew and loved.

Sylvia took the girl by her shoulders. "Do you have any idea where he is? Who he might be with?"

Allison's eyes darted from her grandmother to her mother and then to Zoe. "No. I figured he'd be here. I—I don't know." Her face took on a greenish pall. "Oh, my God. Something's wrong. Where is he?"

"That's it." Sylvia released her granddaughter and reached for the phone. "I'm calling Pete. And if he doesn't answer, we're calling 9-1-1."

TWENTY

When Pete answered Sylvia's phone call and said he'd be right there, Zoe offered her goodbyes and ducked out. She didn't feel like another encounter with him. She especially didn't want to be around when Rose reported her son missing. Pete would no doubt put the pieces together the same way Zoe had. Thank goodness he didn't know about Logan and Zoe's attempts at sleuthing. Or the stolen hard drive.

Before turning onto Route 15, she pulled over and shifted into park. She dug her cell phone from her pocket and punched in the coroner's office number. He'd been nagging his part-time deputy coroners to attend more autopsies. She'd assisted on two last summer, but the memory of the stench prompted her to dodge his recent requests. Until today.

She got his voicemail.

"Hey, Franklin," she said after the beep, "this is Zoe. I'm on my way to the morgue. I'd like to observe the autopsy on Jerry McBirney. Maybe even assist. I should be there in a half hour or so." She neglected to mention the desire to see for herself if that brute McBirney actually had a heart. And if he did, whether it was black. She suspected Franklin wouldn't appreciate her humor.

Shifting into gear, she turned right onto Route 15 heading south toward Brunswick. As she passed the police station, her thoughts rolled back to Logan. Maybe he'd phoned and left a message on her machine at home. She would pass the farm on her way. It would take only a minute to find out.

She pulled into the farm lane and hurried into the house. The only message was from her boarder Patsy, who was supposed to feed and clean stalls, but who phoned to say she had the flu. That left the work to

Zoe. She checked her watch. Quarter to nine. Crap.

She punched in Franklin's number again. "It's me. Something's come up and I'm going to be later than I thought. But I still want to attend the autopsy if at all possible. I'll be there as soon as I can."

She rushed through the barn chores and changed into clean clothes that didn't have bits of hay and manure stuck to them. By the time she wheeled the truck back onto the road, her clock read 9:58.

Heavy black clouds rolled in from the west. The radio crackled a weather advisory for late afternoon and into the evening. She punched the power button, silencing the grim predictions. Enough of those played in her brain without any help from the local newscaster.

Paulette greeted her in the back hallway of the Marshall Funeral Home.

"Did Franklin head over to the morgue yet?" Zoe said.

"Oh, dear. I'm afraid he's been there and back. Detective Baronick showed up here at eight o'clock and asked that the procedure be expedited."

Eight o'clock? Zoe sighed. Even if she'd come straight into the city from work, she'd have missed it.

The coroner's assistant gave her an apologetic smile. "He's in his office if you want to talk to him."

Zoe found him at his desk, tapping on his computer keyboard.

"I got your messages after the fact," he said without looking up. "A local politician's death is high priority where the County PD is concerned."

"I understand." Zoe sank into one of the plush chairs across the desk from him. "What did you find out?"

He paused in his typing and gazed at her over his readers. "You were on the crew that brought him in, right?"

"Yes."

"So you know the basic physical condition of the body." He went back to his computer. "Mr. McBirney suffered four penetrating wounds to his posterior upper right quadrant. One of the wounds penetrated the intercostal muscles between the fourth and fifth ribs, missing the scapula and puncturing his lung. Cause of death was exsanguination."

He bled to death. No big surprise. "So they *were* stab wounds?"

"Phillips-head screwdriver."

"What?"

Franklin stopped typing, leaned back in his chair, and removed his glasses. "From the pattern of the tears in the skin, it's my determination that the weapon used was a Phillips-head screwdriver."

Not exactly helpful. Just about everyone she knew had a toolbox and a set of screwdrivers. Even she had one.

"Only one of the wounds penetrated deep enough to be fatal—the one that punctured the lung. The other three attempts hit the scapula and exhibited more tearing, but caused no significant damage. In addition, I found evidence of blunt force trauma to the top of the victim's skull."

Zoe's mind flashed back to another head injury. "Blunt force trauma? The same as Ted Bassi's?"

"Not really." Franklin placed his palm on top of his head. "There was no fracture in this case, but the victim suffered a subdural bleed perimortem. Non-life threatening."

"So he was stabbed *and* hit on top of the head?"

"There were also some soft tissue injuries to the victim's face."

Zoe cringed as she recalled swinging the bridle, striking McBirney with the bit.

"The patterns of bruising would be consistent with a beating." Franklin made a fist.

"Someone punched him?"

"Repeatedly. There was also one other contusion that caused some minor soft tissue damage that was inconsistent with the others. I'd say it happened some time earlier as healing was already evident."

Ah. That would be her contribution.

"This man suffered a violent assault. Possibly multiple assailants." Franklin stared past her and frowned. "And yet, he exhibited no defensive wounds. It doesn't appear he fought back."

"Maybe he didn't have a chance to."

"Perhaps." Franklin slipped his reading glasses back on his nose and rested his fingers on his keyboard. "In any case, I'm afraid Vance Township has another homicide to deal with."

*   *   *

Pete stood inside the doorway of the rear entrance of the Helping Hands Store in Dillard. Mrs. Zellers, who managed the charitable second hand shop, fussed with an errant strand of gray hair that refused to stay in its bun. "The lock's been broken, and there's mud all over the floor. I mopped before I closed up last night. I can't believe someone would break in here and steal from us." Her voice quivered.

Concentrate. A breaking-and-entering call might seem minor to Pete after his previous stop at the Bassi residence, but to Mrs. Zellers, it was huge. "Is anything missing that you're aware of?"

"That's what's so odd. The money box wasn't touched. Not that I leave much here anyway. But the muddy tracks don't go anywhere near the front counter."

"Is there anything else he might have taken?"

She hoisted her shoulders in a mammoth shrug. "Not that I can tell. I'd have to do inventory, but most of our stuff is donations and not worth much. I just don't understand."

Pete leaned over and squinted at the lock. He pulled his glasses from his pocket and jammed them on his face. The tiny scrapes around the keyhole leapt into focus. No pry bar gouges like the ones on his evidence room door.

The muddy tracks Mrs. Zellers complained about were grayish white against the old dark wood flooring. Salt. Not mud. But they did offer a little more to work with. Several distinct tread patterns were evident. He excused himself to go back to his SUV for the camera and his fingerprint kit. If he was lucky, he might get something more than a smudge from the doorknob.

As he trudged through the sloppy parking lot, his mind drifted back to the meeting with Rose, Sylvia, and Allison. Two frantic women and a girl, who had already lost a husband, a son, and a dad, were now forced to report a missing teenager.

Logan was seventeen. Pete suspected any other kid that age would be hanging out with friends, oblivious of his parents' concerns, trusting in his own immortality. But Logan wasn't any other teen. He'd just buried his father. And the prime suspect in that case had turned up dead the same night the kid disappeared.

Pete opened the back of the SUV and pulled out the canvas bag with the bulging pockets. Then he slammed the door and lugged the bag back to the store.

He'd asked them all the standard-issue missing-person questions. He knew what the kid was wearing the last time Rose had seen him—blue plaid flannel shirt, jeans, blue and white Blue Demons high school jacket, winter boots. He knew the car Logan was driving—his mom's silver Ford Taurus. The three women—grandmother, mother, and sister—had provided him with a list of friends and hang-outs.

While he'd let the Bassi women believe he'd pay special attention to the case because of his friendship with Sylvia, in truth, he feared he might be looking for a killer.

Mrs. Zellers hovered nearby as Pete dusted for prints. He held little hope he'd find anything clear enough to prove useful. He photographed the salty tread marks. Nothing noteworthy about them. Work boots would be his guess. About a size ten and a half or eleven.

"Try to do an inventory of your stock, and get back to me if you find anything missing," Pete told her as he packed the camera in his bag.

"Of course."

"And..." He pointed at the lock. "Get that changed. Now."

"Yes, sir. Thank you, Chief."

He tossed his bag in the back of the SUV and climbed behind the wheel. His full attention returned to Logan Bassi, and he shuffled through the notes he'd taken an hour ago. He had damned little time. He needed to find the boy before Baronick caught wind of the disappearance. Once that happened, Logan would be assigned the official role of murder suspect instead of missing person. Sylvia and Rose would go on the defensive and clam up. And a seventeen-year-old kid would become the center of a Monongahela County Police Department manhunt.

Pete hated the thought of being the one to arrest Logan. Sylvia would despise Pete until her dying breath. But the kid stood a better chance with someone who knew him than with one of those county boys.

Maybe Logan wasn't guilty. But then why the hell was he running? Or was he? Were Rose's fears plausible? Had something happened to him, too? Pete had a gnawing sensation in his gut that either way, this would not turn out well for any of the Bassi family.

Zoe parked in front of the Bassi house. Rose's car—the one Logan had borrowed—wasn't there. Crap. She punched his number into her cell phone, but the call went straight to voicemail. What teenaged kid turns his cell phone off?

Sylvia answered the door. Dark bags draped beneath her bloodshot eyes. Deep creases etched her forehead. She'd aged ten years in the last twenty-four hours.

"Have you heard anything?" Zoe tossed her coat over the back of a kitchen chair.

"Nothing. Rose is out of her mind. I don't think she's slept in a week." Sylvia led the way to the living room. "And on top of everything else, Allison is sick."

"Sick?"

"She's come down with the bug Rose's mom had earlier in the week. Poor kid's been locked in the bathroom throwing up for almost an hour."

Zoe glanced around the empty room. "Where's Rose?"

"Here." She appeared in the hallway, looking even more haggard than she had a few hours earlier. "I was making some phone calls. No one's seen or heard from Logan."

Zoe crossed the room and enfolded her friend in a hug.

Rose shrank against her. Then she pulled away. "This can't be real. None of it." She shuffled to the couch and collapsed onto it.

Zoe sat next to her, and took one of her hands in both of hers. "What did Pete say?"

Sylvia settled into one of the armchairs flanking the couch. "He gave us a speech about teenagers and how they lose track of time."

"And he said Logan's too old for an Amber Alert," Rose said.

"But he took all the information and is going to look for him."

Zoe understood what Pete was up to even if Rose and Sylvia were too distracted or too unwilling to face it. Logan was a suspect in McBirney's death. Pete would use the missing kid angle to look for him without alerting anyone else. Especially that Detective Baronick guy.

"So did you get a chance to watch them cut Jerry McBirney's heart out?" A hint of Sylvia's old sparkle glimmered in her eyes.

"I was too late."

"What a shame."

Rose made a face. "I can't imagine watching something like that anyway."

As if to punctuate the sentiment, the unmistakable sound of retching drifted from the back hallway.

"Poor Allison." Sylvia shook her head.

Someone pounded on the door, and all three women jumped.

Rose's shoulders sagged. "It's not Logan. He wouldn't knock."

"I'll get it." Zoe beat Sylvia to her feet and headed for the kitchen. She peeked through the curtain and feared she might join Allison cuddling up to the toilet.

Detective Wayne Baronick.

Zoe hesitated. She should warn the others. *Don't mention Logan's missing.* On the other hand, if the detective already knew, he'd find their evasion highly suspicious. But did they really want the entire county police force looking for a frightened kid? A police force that not only didn't know and care about Logan, but who believed him capable of murder?

Baronick pounded again. "Mrs. Bassi, it's the police. Please open the door."

"The police?" Rose staggered to her feet.

"I don't recognize the voice," Sylvia said. "It's not any of *our* boys."

"It's Detective Baronick," Zoe mouthed. Then she swung the door open, but stood blocking the entrance. "Hello, Detective."

He eyed her. "Zoe, isn't it?"

She suspected he knew very well who she was. "This isn't a good time."

"I promise to be brief." He stood his ground, grinning at her.

Maybe he'd catch what Allison had.

Zoe stepped aside, letting the detective enter. She followed him into the living room. Over his shoulder, she made a zip-the-lips motion at the two women. If only they were psychic and could read her thoughts.

"Have you found my son?" Rose blurted.

Crap.

Zoe circled around the detective to stand between Rose and Sylvia. Baronick's face was frozen in that toothy smile. His version of a poker face, Zoe imagined.

"Your son's missing?"

Zoe caught both women's hands and gave them a wrenching squeeze. If they'd been sitting at a table, she'd have kicked them in the shins.

Sylvia winced and eyed her. Zoe gave a slight head shake.

"Didn't Chief Adams let you know? Logan's been missing since yesterday afternoon," Rose said.

"Really?" Baronick dragged the word out.

Zoe pictured a python being thrown a rat.

"And Chief Adams knows about this?"

"We spoke to him earlier," Rose said.

Zoe cleared her throat. "But the chief doesn't believe he's missing so much as he's being a typical teen. Probably having a grand time with his buddies and forgot to call home."

She met Sylvia's gaze. The older woman's eyes had narrowed, her jaw clenched.

Bingo. She got it.

"I'm sure that's all it is. He's with a friend," Sylvia said, her voice as smooth and rich as bourbon.

Rose shot her a look.

"He'll be home before long. I'm certain of it," Sylvia told the detective.

"You think so? Well, that's good." His eyes shifted to each of them. "Actually I was hoping to have a chance to speak with Rose about a few things. Alone. But since you have company, maybe we can meet another time."

"Oh, that's not a problem," Zoe chimed in. Let him stay there and chat up Rose a while. Zoe wanted to get a head start on finding Logan anyhow. Giving Sylvia's hand a gentle pat, she said, "We were just leaving."

"We were?" Sylvia said.

"You just got here." Rose's mouth and brow were pressed into a dazed frown.

"I'll stop by later." Zoe released Sylvia's hand and pulled Rose into a hug. "Walk us to the door?"

Baronick wasn't smiling any more. He scowled as he watched the interaction between the women. "While I'm in the area, I'd like to make time to speak with both of you, too. Is there a time I could stop by your homes that would be convenient?"

Sylvia puffed up her ample bosom. "I'm heading home now to take care of a few things. Two doors down, but I'm sure you know that."

"Yes, ma'am, I do."

"Then stop in when you're done here."

Zoe wondered if Baronick knew that Sylvia's purse should be registered as a lethal weapon.

"Thank you." The smile was back. "I'll do that."

Zoe tugged both Sylvia and Rose into the kitchen with her.

"What's wrong with you two?" Rose said in a ragged whisper as they pulled on their coats.

Zoe put her arms around her and spoke into her ear. "He thinks Logan's disappearance makes him look guilty of McBirney's murder."

"What? That's absurd."

Sylvia shushed her and joined in a group hug. "Just don't say anything. He's working on a murder case. Two murder cases. His only interest in Logan is as a suspect."

They pulled apart and made a silent pact with their eyes.

"Call me if you need anything," Sylvia said.

"I'll stop by later." Zoe patted Rose's arm.

"Um. Excuse me," Baronick called from the living room. "Zoe, you didn't tell me when would be a good time for us to talk. I've been looking forward to getting to know you better."

His smile brought back the python image to Zoe. Only now, *she* was the rat.

TWENTY-ONE

Pete was having no luck. He'd been to the high school. Logan Bassi was on the excused absentee list, but Pete had them check anyway. The school secretary looked up the boy's class schedule and sent a student office-helper—a bored-looking girl with pink hair and a pierced lip—to confirm his absence.

As expected, he wasn't there.

Pete left his card in case anyone spotted Logan.

The sky had turned a deep steely gray, and a few snowflakes drifted through the air with the promise of more. The temperature had climbed into the low thirties, but that only set the stage for another snowstorm.

Pete checked his notes and pulled out of the school's parking lot. He made stops at the homes of several of Logan's friends. No one claimed to have seen him since the funeral. And none of them led Pete to believe they were lying.

Zoe's hand rested on the doorknob of Rose's kitchen door. So close to freedom, and yet she felt trapped. Baronick had only learned of Logan's disappearance minutes ago—thanks to Rose and Sylvia and their big mouths—and he hadn't placed any phone calls since he'd arrived, so Zoe still had a shot of tracking the kid down before all hell broke loose. If she could only escape the detective's questions.

"I have a busy day ahead," she said.

Baronick's smile vanished. "I do need to speak with you about a few things, and it'd be better to take care of this sooner than later."

"Are you placing me under arrest?"

"What?" He scoffed. "No. Of course not."

"Then if I'm not under arrest, you can't detain me."

The smile crept back onto his face. "I don't want to arrest or detain you. I just want to chat. Why make it difficult? I could sure use your cooperation." His gaze shifted to Rose and to Sylvia. "All of you. We all want the same thing, after all. To find out who killed Jerry McBirney."

"Not really," Sylvia muttered under her breath.

Zoe snorted.

"What was that?" Baronick said. "I didn't hear you."

"I said Zoe has to go to work." Sylvia's voice rang out.

"I'm aware that she's on duty tonight. But not until four o'clock," Baronick said.

A chill snaked its way down her spine. The detective knew her schedule. That couldn't be good. "Um, yes, but I also manage the farm where I live. I have work to do there before my shift begins."

"Fine. Then let's talk right now, so you can be on your way. Is there somewhere I can buy you a cup of coffee?"

"In Dillard? No."

The detective glared at her. "There's coffee at the police station. We could go there."

Sylvia cleared her throat. "You said she wasn't under arrest."

"She's not."

But if Sylvia built up her usual head of steam, Zoe feared they might all end up at the station. "Okay, just wait a minute. If you're that intent on talking to me right now, we can sit in my truck. You won't even have to spring for coffee."

He nodded. "That'll do." He turned his attention to Sylvia and Rose. "Ladies, I'm sure you can find something to occupy your time. I'll get to you both shortly."

"You know where to find me," Sylvia said. Without giving the detective a chance to argue, she snatched her purse from the chair where she'd left it, and pressed past Zoe, out the door.

Rose's eyes appeared glazed. Too little sleep and too much stress had left her bewildered.

Zoe took her hands. "Go check on Allison. Make sure she's okay."

Rose gave a quick nod, glanced at Baronick, and headed for the hall.

"Allison? The daughter? She's here?"

"She's in the bathroom, throwing up. She caught the flu from her other grandmother. Very contagious." Zoe faked a big smile. "I hope you've had your flu shot, Detective."

From the look on his face, she guessed not.

Baronick followed her down the snow-covered sidewalk to her truck and slid into the passenger seat without further invitation. She climbed behind the wheel and turned the key to get the heater running.

"How well did you know Jerry McBirney?" Baronick opened his notebook.

Too well. "I've lived in Vance Township all my life. So did he."

"Did you get along with him?"

"No one did."

"So you didn't like the man?"

She took a breath. "Do I need an attorney?"

Baronick shrugged. "I don't know. Do you?"

The python-and-rat thing came back to her.

"Let's try something else. Do you have any idea who might have wanted him dead?"

"Probably lots of people. I told you no one liked him." Zoe wondered at what point she was incriminating herself. Logan. Rose and Sylvia. "You should pick up a copy of the minutes from the supervisors' meetings. He wasn't what you might call 'popular' with his constituents."

Baronick made a note. "That's a very good idea. I'll do that. Thanks for the help."

Zoe relaxed. Maybe she really could steer the investigation somewhere—anywhere—other than Logan's direction.

"When was the last time you saw Mr. McBirney?"

Tension bit into her shoulders again. "Um. He came to my barn yesterday afternoon."

"*Your* barn?"

"The one I manage."

He grinned at her. "The one I'm keeping you from. Sorry."

What was with this guy? Good cop, bad cop all rolled into one?

"Can you remember what time he was there?"

"About one-thirty."

"And how long did he stay?"

Too long. "Fifteen, twenty minutes maybe."

"Really?" He sounded amazed. "What was he doing there? Did you invite him?"

"No. He just showed up." Tread lightly. "He wanted to convince me that he wasn't responsible for Ted's murder."

"And did he?"

"Hell, no."

Baronick chuckled and nodded. "And it took him twenty minutes to try to convince you? And you to say no?"

Sweat beaded under Zoe's bangs. She turned the heater down. "He could have tried for an hour. I'd still not believe him."

"I understand." He flipped back a few pages in his notebook, scowling. Then he flipped forward again. Without looking up, he said, "So tell me about the night Jerry McBirney tried to rape you."

Between stops, Pete patrolled the streets of Vance Township, searching for that silver Ford Taurus. He found several, but none matched Rose Bassi's license number. He ran them anyway. Just in case. But every one of them was clear.

Damn it. Pete had been seventeen once. Where would he hide if he wanted to disappear? Winter made it tough. The ice cream joints and the parks were closed for the season. He made a loop past them anyway. Just in case.

The two area campgrounds were both closed. Not to mention it was too cold to sleep out. But he drove through them.

Just in case.

Nothing.

The nausea that hit Zoe had no connection to Allison's flu. How the hell had Baronick found out about that? Pete? No. Pete wouldn't tell him.

Would he?

Pete *was* a cop after all.

No. He hadn't shared the news of Logan's disappearance with the detective. He certainly wouldn't have betrayed her.

But who else knew? It wasn't something she'd shared with many. Ted and Rose. And Sylvia. They'd been her family back then. No one else.

"Ms. Chambers? Are you all right?"

"I'm fine." She swallowed back the bile that seared her throat. "And I'm done answering questions without a lawyer."

Baronick tapped his pen on the notebook. "I don't blame you. I understand it was pretty ugly. But, okay, you don't want to talk about it. We'll change the subject."

Zoe swallowed. She needed water.

"Tell me about Logan Bassi's disappearance. When was the last time you saw him?"

"I'm done." Her brain spun out of control. "Get out of my truck."

"Why? I'm just trying to help find the boy. His mother and grandmother are obviously distraught by his disappearance."

"Yesterday," Zoe said. "I saw him yesterday."—*true*—"At Ted's funeral."—*half true*—"We were all there." *True.*

Baronick made a notation. "Do you think the loss of his father might have gotten to him? Made him run off? Maybe he needed some space."

"Maybe. I have to go. I've got work to do. Please get out of my truck."

"Did Logan feel as strongly as you do that Mr. McBirney is responsible for his dad's death?"

Zoe drew a deep breath, chasing the fog from her brain. She turned to face the detective and fixed him with her best *I-mean-business* stare. "I can't speak for anyone else. You'll have to find Logan and ask him." She failed to mention that she intended to find him first. "Now, get out of my truck. Because I'm going home. If you don't get out now, you can come to the farm with me and muck out stalls. But don't expect me to give you a ride back to your car."

Baronick sighed. "Really, Zoe, it would be so much easier on everyone if you'd just cooperate."

"Yeah. Easier on you. Either arrest me or get out."

He gave a troubled shake of his head and closed his notebook. "You have to know this doesn't look good for you. Or for Logan. Innocent people don't try to hide things."

"Goodbye, Detective."

He opened the door and stepped out.

She watched as he sloshed back up the snowy sidewalk to Rose's door. Rose met him there. With the windows up, Zoe couldn't hear the conversation, but it appeared that she had no intention of letting the detective back in. He held his hands palm up, apparently imploring and cajoling her. A minute later, he turned and headed back toward the street.

Yay, Rose.

Baronick looked up at Zoe as he reached the end of the walk. Probably wondering why she was still sitting there if she were in such a hurry to get back to the barn. But he didn't come any closer to the truck. Or his car. Instead, he turned and headed down the street toward Sylvia's house.

Zoe cut the engine and jumped out, jogging to Rose's door.

She swung it open before Zoe had a chance to knock. Rose caught her arm as she slipped out of her coat and hauled her into the living room. "What did he ask you?"

"About McBirney. Who might have killed him. When I saw him last. That sort of thing."

"Anything about Logan?"

"Yeah. I told him I saw him yesterday at the funeral. That's all. Then I kicked him out of my truck."

"Nothing else?"

"Nothing."

"Good." Rose sank to the floor and stretched out on her back, covering her eyes with her forearm. "I want the cops to find my boy. But..."

"You didn't answer *any* of Baronick's questions?" Zoe sat down next to her.

"No. Sylvia called me on my cell phone, and we agreed we'd both send him packing. I can't think straight."

"Me either. How's Allison?"

"In bed. Poor kid looks like death. Not much of a fever, though."

"That's good."

Only the soft rumble of the furnace interrupted the silence for several long moments. Then Zoe remembered what she needed to do.

"I have to find Logan," she said.

"Before that detective does." Rose pushed herself up to sit cross-legged. "Do you think Pete believes Logan had something to do with McBirney's death?"

"Yeah, I do."

Rose rubbed her eyes. "I'm so stupid. I'm terrified my son's hurt. Lying in a ditch somewhere, bleeding, maybe dead. And the cops think he's hiding because he killed a man? How moronic is that?"

Zoe longed to comfort her best friend. Tell her everything would be okay. Logan wasn't hurt. And he wasn't hiding from the law.

Rose must have seen the doubt in her eyes. "Zoe? Oh, my God. You think he did it, too. You think he killed that bastard."

"I don't know." Zoe swiped away a rush of hot tears. "I don't want to believe he's hurt. What else is there? Honestly, if he did kill McBirney, no jury would—"

"Convict him? That's what you were going to say, isn't it?" Rose leapt to her feet. "I can't believe you. He thinks of you as an aunt, for crying out loud. You helped me raise him. How can you even consider—" Her voice broke, and she covered her face with both hands. "Get out."

Zoe stood, her head reeling. "What?"

"You heard me. Get out. Get the hell out of my house and don't ever come back." Rose stormed out of the room.

Zoe's knees threatened to buckle. She couldn't catch her breath. This wasn't happening. None of it. Ted wasn't dead. Logan wasn't missing. Rose didn't despise her.

The kitchen door slammed, and Sylvia bustled in. She took one look at Zoe and froze. "My God. What's happened? Logan?"

Zoe shook her head. "No." She sucked in air. "I gotta go." Brushing past Sylvia, she stumbled out into the gray afternoon, barely noticing the fat snowflakes pelting her tear-streaked face.

She had to find Logan. And if she wanted Rose to forgive her, she needed to prove him innocent.

Snow covered the edge of the road, but the pavement remained wet. The tires of Zoe's truck hissed against the slop as she drove back to the farm.

She'd stopped at a couple of Logan's friends' houses only to learn they hadn't seen him. They had, however, seen Chief Pete Adams, who was also looking for him. She'd prefer to have been there ahead of Pete instead of trailing his efforts. At least no one mentioned Detective Baronick.

She considered calling Pete, but if he'd had any luck, she figured she'd have heard about it. So Zoe decided to search the only place he wouldn't know to look—her computer. That's what Logan was doing the last time she or any of them had seen him. He'd found something there. Something that sent him off—where? To meet McBirney? Or somewhere else? She had to know.

The fat snowflakes had turned the farm into a Currier and Ives print, coating the grass and the pine trees in pristine white. The path to the farmhouse's back door was becoming slick, forcing Zoe to pick her way down the slight hill. As she approached the enclosed porch, she heard voices. Mrs. Kroll's laughter rung out.

Zoe's landlady and Matt Doaks were perched on the wooden bench, sharing a chuckle.

"Matt? What are you doing here?"

"I came to talk to you. You weren't home, but your charming neighbor's been entertaining me."

Mrs. Kroll patted him on the arm. "Such a nice young man. You should come around more often."

Only if you want to date him. "What did you want to talk to me about?" Zoe said.

He motioned to her door. "Mind if we go inside? I've been keeping Mrs. Kroll out here in the cold for too long."

"It's no bother. I'm quite toasty." Mrs. Kroll pulled the afghan she wore as a shawl tighter around her bony shoulders.

"Matt's right. You don't want to get a chill." Zoe glared at him. "Let's go inside."

He helped Mrs. Kroll to her feet.

"It was nice meeting you, Matt." The landlady batted her eyelashes at him like a coquette and excused herself, hobbling off to her half of the house.

"I think your neighbor was flirting with me," he said as Zoe unlocked her door.

"And you love it."

"I love all women. All women love me."

"Not all."

He grinned. "If I want them bad enough, yeah, they do."

Zoe fought her gag reflex as she stepped aside and let him pass. How had she ever fallen for him?

Matt stood in the middle of the room and turned in a complete circle, taking it all in. "I like what you've done with the place. What do you call this style? Early American garage sale?"

"Shut up." Zoe slipped out of her coat and pulled off her boots.

"Seriously. It's—homey."

"What the hell do you want?"

He approached her, moving like a panther stalking a gazelle. She planted her feet and crossed her arms in front of her. Her insides shifted away from him, as though all her internal organs were plastering themselves against her spine. But she wasn't about to give him the satisfaction of winning this game of chicken.

Matt stopped inches from her, his face tipped downward toward hers. His warm breath smelled vaguely of chocolate. "Do you have any idea how beautiful you are?"

Zoe avoided looking at those baby blue eyes. Those dimples. Some distant memory of loving the jerk stirred low in her gut. Far away from her brain. She clenched her fists. "Just tell me what you want and leave."

He brushed a finger against her cheek. It lingered on her lower lip before curling under her chin, tipping her face up. "Every time I see you, I realize all over again what an ass I was."

"Finally. Something we can agree on." She hated the slight tremble in her voice.

"Isn't there some small chance you could forgive me? I never loved anyone the way I loved you. And I know you feel the same way, Zoe. We could be so good together."

The distance between his mouth and hers lessened. Where had all the air in the room gone? His lips parted, and he leaned in.

Forget the damned game of chicken. "No." Zoe bobbed away from him and darted behind her dining room table. "If you have something to say—some reason other than this stroll down memory lane—then just say it. I'm not having a very good day, and you're the last thing I need right now." She pressed her fingers to her lips. Why had she told him, of all people, that she was having a bad day?

"Why? What's going on? Oh. Of course." He thumped himself on his head. "The funeral. How is Rose holding up? Are the kids okay?"

"They're great."

"Really? This ordeal has to be hell for them. They're lucky to have you."

Good old Matt. She could always count on him to rub salt in her wounds. Even when he didn't realize he was doing it.

He prowled around the room, studying the framed photos on her mantle—Allison, several years ago, on a pony next to Zoe on Windstar; a Bassi family portrait; and an old picture of Zoe with her mom and dad before he'd died. Then Matt crossed the room, glanced into her office, and stopped next to a set of shelves holding a cheap CD player and her meager music collection. "I see your taste in tunes hasn't changed."

What the hell was he doing? "What's this all about? Are you so bored that you need to come here and harass me for the afternoon?"

"Something like that." He ambled back to the sofa and flopped down on it, stretching out his long legs. "I've come to realize that I miss what we had all those years ago. I'm tired of fooling around. I keep thinking about settling down, and the only woman I'd want to do that with is you."

Zoe searched his face for some sign that he was joking. Or stoned. "What happened? Your latest bimbette dump your ass?"

He chuckled and shook his head. "Come on, Zoe. At the very least, let me be your friend again. That would be a start."

She looked at the clock. Crap. She still had barn work to do. "I don't have the time or energy to be your friend. Maybe you could knock on Mrs. Kroll's door, though. I'm sure she'd enjoy the company. Now, I really need you to get out of here. I still have to clean stalls before my shift."

"You're on duty tonight?"

"Yes."

"All right." He sighed and climbed to his feet. "While I'm here...We're having an emergency board of supervisors meeting tomorrow afternoon at two o'clock. I imagine you heard that Jerry McBirney died."

"I heard."

"We're having a meeting to reorganize the board. I thought you'd like to know."

"That's it?"

"It doesn't have to be." He gave her that boyish, flirtatious, cock-eyed grin that melted girls' hearts. Both young and old.

"Yeah, it does." She nodded toward the door. "Bye."

He shoved his hands in his pockets. "Okay. But I'll see you tomorrow, right? At the meeting."

"Maybe."

"You'll want to be there. We've got some big surprises in store. Trust me."

"Trust you?" She bit off a laugh.

"When did you get so cold?"

"When I walked in on you and that slut in my bed."

He winced. And then he left.

Zoe exhaled. She looked at the clock. Matt's visit hadn't left her much time. But maybe she could still squeeze some luck out of this crappy day and find something—anything—on the computer to help locate Logan.

TWENTY-TWO

Once school let out, Pete checked the rest of the list of Logan's friends. One of them thought he might have spotted Logan at the JV basketball game the night before, but he couldn't be sure. Pete suspected the kid was on something, with his eyelids at half-mast, and made a note to keep an eye on the boy.

By five o'clock, the roads were beginning to glaze over and snow continued to fall. Pete had depleted all his ideas of where a kid would hide and considered the strong possibility that Logan was no longer in Vance Township. Maybe he'd headed into Brunswick.

The mall.

If Pete was seventeen and trying to disappear, he'd go to the mall in Brunswick, where every teenager in Monongahela County hung out. On a night like this, the parking lots would be largely deserted. Spotting a silver Taurus—or any vehicle—would be simple.

Pete headed for the police station, his shift over. He planned to drop off the evidence from the break-in at the Helping Hands Store, stop at home to change into his civvies, and then drive to the Brunswick Mall. Sears was having a sale on tools. If he happened to pick up a missing teen in the process, so much the better.

As he wheeled into the Vance Township PD lot, he noticed a vehicle in his spot. An unmarked black Ford sedan that he recognized as Baronick's.

Seth sat on the edge of what had been Sylvia's chair. "He's in your office," the young cop said. "I told him he should wait in the conference room, but he wouldn't listen."

Pete waved a hand at him. His office door was closed. Without knocking, Pete entered and found the detective making himself at home in Pete's chair, poring over a file.

"If you're going to set up camp in my station, you might want to do it in the conference room," Pete said. "More space."

"Thanks, but I'm fine." Baronick motioned to the seat across him. "I'm glad you're here. I've spent the day chatting with your local citizens and could use your help sorting through my notes."

Instead of taking the chair Baronick had indicated, Pete moved around the desk and stood over the detective.

"You knew the Bassi kid was missing," Baronick said.

It wasn't a question so Pete didn't answer it.

"Any thoughts?"

"About what?"

"The missing Bassi kid." Baronick finally looked up. "Any luck locating him?"

"Not yet."

"So what do you think? Is he another victim? Or a suspect?"

"What I think," Pete said, "is that you're in my chair."

The detective met his gaze. The young hot shot probably fancied himself to be a master poker player. But Pete caught the minuscule muscle twitch beneath his right eye.

Seth appeared in the doorway and froze.

Keeping his eyes on Baronick, Pete said, "What?"

"I've got a call. Vehicle accident out on Oak Grove Road. No injuries."

"So go."

Seth vanished, obviously not eager to get in the middle of this pissing contest.

Baronick's twitch turned into a full-blown blink. He gathered his papers and vacated Pete's chair, taking a seat in the one he'd motioned to earlier.

Pete reclaimed his desk, rearranging his mess to suit him. Sylvia always said no one but Pete could find anything there, and that was the way he wanted it.

"So about the Bassi kid?" Baronick said.

"He left without telling his mother where he was going. What teenaged boy hasn't done that at one time or another?" Pete didn't buy his own words for a moment, but wasn't about to throw Sylvia's grandson to the wolves. Especially this wolf.

"And that's all there is to it?"

"As far as I've been able to tell."

Baronick shrugged. "As I mentioned, I've been chatting with a number of your local citizens. They're a fascinating bunch. Everyone seems to know everything about everybody around here."

"Anybody tell you who killed Ted Bassi or Jerry McBirney?"

"Not exactly. But I've learned some interesting tidbits, and I've been able to compile a list of potential suspects."

"Really?" Pete crossed his arms in front of him and leaned back. This should be entertaining.

"On the surface, it would seem everyone loved Ted Bassi with the notable exception of Jerry McBirney. Did McBirney kill Bassi and then someone else took revenge on McBirney? Possibly. On the other hand, no one had much good to say about McBirney. I have a sense there's going to be considerable dancing on his grave once he's in the ground."

"Can't argue with anything you've said so far."

"I did come up with one strong suspect for both murders. One person with motive, means, and opportunity." Baronick beamed as though he'd just discovered the cure for cancer.

"And who might that be?"

"Marcy McBirney."

"Marcy? What motive does she have for killing Ted Bassi?"

"Crime of passion. They were having an affair."

"No, they weren't. Ted was helping her find a divorce attorney."

"I'm sure he was. The man didn't want his lover married to someone else." Baronick snickered.

It struck Pete that he hadn't questioned Marcy's version of the story. He hadn't wanted to.

"But your ex-wife isn't my only suspect. As I mentioned, it's possible we have two killers. Supposing Jerry McBirney killed Ted Bassi, then I have two—make that three—other suspects for the McBirney homicide." Baronick held up one finger. "The boy. Logan Bassi. Getting revenge for the murder of his father."

Pete cringed. He feared the same thing, but hoped more than anything to find evidence to the contrary.

Baronick held up a second finger. "Zoe Chambers."

Pete choked. "What?"

"I discovered that she and McBirney have a rather nasty past, including an attempted rape."

Pete held his poker face. How the hell had Baronick found out about that? Did he know the rest of it? McBirney's visit to her at her barn? The threats? If he didn't, Pete wasn't going to be the one to tell him. "That's two."

Instead of holding up the third finger, Baronick folded both hands together and rested them on the desk. "My third suspect is still in love with McBirney's widow, even though he's divorced from her. That would be you, Chief."

"Visibility sucks," Earl said.

Zoe, content to leave the foul-weather driving to her partner, squinted into the night. With the exception of the black sky, everything was white—the surface and the edge of the road, as well as the curtain of snow sweeping across Medic Three's headlights. Her nerves played hell with her gut. The night was too eerily similar to Monday, and she kept seeing Ted's body in that Buick.

"Are you all right?" Earl said. "You're awfully quiet this evening."

"I'm fine." She wasn't. The computer had refused to offer any indication of what sent Logan off to who-knows-where. She'd made it up to the V's in the tax records. The clue was probably buried in old lady Zuckerman's file.

Or she'd missed it completely.

Plus Logan still wouldn't answer his cell phone. She stared out the window at the blizzard. Where the hell was he?

The radio crackled. "Medic Three, this is Control. What's your 10-20?"

Zoe reached for the mic, but paused. "Good question. Where are we?" They were returning to the garage from Brunswick Hospital on Route 15 after a cardiac run, but her mind had drifted and one snowy bend in the road looked the same as another.

"We're coming up on the intersection with Mays Road," Earl said.

"Thanks." She keyed the mic. "Control, this is Medic Three. We're about a half mile north of Mays Road on Route 15."

"Medic Three, respond to a vehicular accident with injuries. Route

15 approximately two miles north of Dillard. Fire-rescue has been notified."

"Copy that. Medic Three en route."

"Eighteen forty-two."

Zoe grabbed the clipboard and started filling out a new report while Earl flipped the switch for the emergency lights.

"It's gonna be like this all night," Earl predicted. "No one wants to give up their Friday night drinking with their buddies just because the weather's a little bad."

"A little?"

The ambulance fishtailed as Earl maneuvered around a sharp bend, but he managed to maintain control.

A minute later, they rolled past the farm. Zoe looked up at her house. It was completely dark. Odd. She hadn't left any lights on in her half, but the Kroll's half was always brightly lit.

They came up behind a slow moving car and Earl whooped the siren at the driver.

"Watch," Zoe said. "He'll panic and run off into a drift."

Instead, he stayed squarely on the road, but slowed down even more. "Hold on." Earl tapped the siren again and then pulled out and gunned it around the car.

Another mile and Zoe made out the orange glow of flares through the white lace curtain of snow. "There."

"Got it."

She radioed in to Control and jotted the time on the report.

As they eased up to the scene, Zoe assessed the view before them. One car, a dark colored sedan with the front end caved in against a utility pole, which was snapped off at the point of impact. Wires sparked and crackled and were all that kept the pole from coming all the way down.

Ah-ha. That explained the darkened farmhouse.

A second car was pulled off the road on the far side of the smashed one, its headlights adding to the illumination provided by the flares.

Zoe and Earl climbed out of the ambulance. Sirens wailed, and an air horn blasted in the distance. Snow pelted her in the face, and she pulled her hood over her head. Grabbing the jump kit from the back, she half ran, half skated toward the car.

A figure leaned into the car's open driver's door, his back to her. He straightened and turned, taking a step toward them, catching the light of one of the flares. His hands and the front of his coat were dark with blood.

"Oh, my God," Zoe gasped. "Pete."

Pete realized instantly what Zoe was thinking. "No," he said. "It's not my blood." He wiped his hands on his bomber jacket. Damn. Another one for the trash. "He's got a head laceration. It's bleeding like a mother, but I don't think it's that bad. His leg, on the other hand..." Pete wanted to warn her who "he" was, but she rushed past him before he had a chance.

He'd been on his way to Brunswick to investigate his mall theory. The roads were treacherous, but the idea of that kid being out in this weather—not to mention Sylvia at home on the verge of a stroke worrying about him—was more than enough incentive to take the risk.

The crash must have happened mere minutes before he came upon it. He almost broadsided the damned car since it blocked both lanes. Smoke poured from under the wrinkled hood. He'd grabbed his fire extinguisher, a flashlight, and his cell phone and ran to the passenger door.

Pete aimed the light through the window. The driver, his face bloody, shielded his eyes from the beam, but Pete recognized him.

Matt Doaks.

Pete hit the smoldering engine with the fire extinguisher and called in the accident to the EOC. Then he wrestled the driver's door open to get a better look. He was greeted with a moan.

"Chief Adams," Doaks said through clenched teeth. "Man, am I glad to see you."

"Where are you hurt?" Pete took in the wilted airbag drooping from the steering column and noticed Doaks was wearing his seatbelt. So he wasn't a complete moron.

"I don't know. My chest hurts, and my head's throbbing. And I can't move my right leg."

Pete aimed his light toward Doaks' feet. The left leg seemed okay, although wedged under the dashboard, which was considerably closer to the driver than it was before impact. However, the right shin appeared to have an additional angle to it besides the normal ankle and knee joints.

"Don't move. I called 9-1-1."

"I smell smoke."

"Fire's out."

Doaks swiped a hand over his face, and when he looked at the blood, he let out a yelp. "Holy shit. I'm bleeding."

"Scalp wounds do that. Don't worry about it."

"*Don't worry*? How much blood does a person have?"

"Enough. What have you had to drink tonight?"

"Nothing. I guess I hit an icy patch. One minute I'm driving along. The next, I'm spinning and—" He made an explosion sound and spread his fingers wide. Then he winced. "Ow."

"Not a good night to be out," Pete said. "Where were you headed?"

Doaks pressed a hand to his head. His face contorted with pain. He took a couple of shuddering breaths. Then he relaxed a bit. "I'm sorry. What did you say?"

"Where were you going that couldn't wait for better weather?"

"I was supposed to meet a friend in Brunswick." He made a feeble attempt at a grin. "You know. A female friend. Hot enough to melt all this snow. Damn. My head's killing me."

"Consider yourself lucky that your airbag deployed or that statement might be truer than you realize. As it is, looks like you're going to miss your date."

"I need to call her. Don't suppose you've seen my cell phone?"

"You'd better wait until you get to the hospital for that."

Pete left Doaks searching for his errant phone. As he lit and set out the flares, he heard a short blast of siren in the distance and a moment later, the ambulance had arrived.

"Matt?" Zoe was saying. "What the hell are you doing out here?"

Pete didn't catch Doaks' response.

Earl pulled a penlight from his cargo pants and checked their patient's pupils. Zoe caught Doaks' wrist, eyes on her watch.

Pete turned his attention to the red emergency lights sweeping through the veil of snow about a half mile down the valley. The throaty sirens of the fire engine echoed off the hillsides. A minute later, the truck braked to a stop behind Pete's car. Seth pulled up behind them. Fire fighters swarmed around the wreck, conferring with Zoe and Earl and dragging equipment from the truck.

"Hey, Chief." Bruce Yancy, captain of the Vance Township Volunteer Fire Department approached him lugging a Port-a-Power in one hand like it was a lunch box. He extended the other gloved hand toward Pete, who took it and winced. The big, burly man had a grip that could crush a steel beer can with minimal effort. "You responsible for putting out the engine fire?"

"Sorry if I invaded your territory."

"No problem. We'll just have to sign you up with the Fireman's Association." Yancy's laugh matched his size.

These guys loved their work.

"Poor bastard did a number on that utility pole. Both electric and phone lines are down. Course that's nothing compared to his car." Yancy patted the Port-a-Power. "Especially after we cut it open to get him out."

Seth, wearing a reflective vest over his parka and a fur-lined hat with earflaps, shuffled up to them. "Hey, Chief. What have we got?"

"Matt Doaks."

The young officer swore. "Another township supervisor? How bad?"

Not as bad as Jerry McBirney. "He's conscious and alert. Worrying about standing up his girlfriend."

Yancy chuckled and slapped Pete on the back. "I'll let you boys do your job, and I'll go do mine. Maybe we can get him out of here in time to make his date."

Not from the looks of that leg, Pete thought as the fire captain hustled off.

Pete and Seth took up positions to direct the minimal traffic. Two more fire trucks arrived. Firefighters set up lights and proceeded to carve up Doaks' car like a Thanksgiving turkey. From his post, Pete watched Zoe and her partner in the heart of the frenzy, working to stabilize and immobilize the patient. A shout went up as they wedged open the car enough for the paramedics to ease Doaks onto a backboard and the gurney.

Zoe and Earl started to push the cot through the snow, but Doaks waved one hand in a frantic gesture. Zoe leaned over him, her ear close to his face. Then she turned back to the car and leaned inside. After a moment, she straightened up and returned to Doaks.

Pete watched as she winged Doaks' cell phone at him.

TWENTY-THREE

"The nerve of that bastard," Zoe muttered after she and Earl deposited their patient into a cubicle at Brunswick Hospital's emergency department.

"What's frosted your ass?" her partner said.

That was a good way to describe how she felt. Only a few hours ago, Matt had been pleading for her to take him back. Claiming he was ready to settle down. Then he turned around and asked her to find his cell phone in the mangled wreckage of his car so he could call his *date* and let her know why he was a no-show.

"Just Matt being Matt," she said. Earl already knew enough about her sorry excuse of a past with the jerk. She decided not to bore him with more recent developments.

"Is he hitting on the nurses already?" Earl grinned at her.

"Something like that. Do me a favor? Take care of the clean linens for the gurney, and I'll make a coffee run. I'm buying."

"Hey, I never turn down free caffeine. You're not planning on detouring out to McCluskey's Bar for a little vodka to add to it, are you?"

"Vodka? Hell, no. Whiskey." Zoe winked at him as she headed for the double doors, slapping the square silver button on the wall to open them.

She made her way through the mazelike hallways toward the employees' lounge, and reflected on the moment they'd arrived at the accident to find Pete covered in blood. *Not again,* she'd thought. One of the curses of working for a small, local ambulance service was pulling up to a scene only to discover she knew the patient. This week there had been Ted, and McBirney, and then Pete. On top of all that had happened, Pete being hurt was too much.

But, no. It wasn't Pete. It was Matt. Yet another man from her past.

Another set of automatic doors swished open for her, and she made her way through the maze of hallways to a pair of elevators. As she waited, her mind drifted to Logan. Where was he on this nasty night? Was he safe?

Was he alive?

Zoe closed her eyes. Which was worse—Logan being found guilty of McBirney's murder and sentenced to life in prison, or being dead?

The elevator dinged and her eyes flitted open. The doors parted. She stepped inside and pressed the button for the third floor.

A few minutes later, she entered a minimalist cafeteria and lounge. A half dozen assorted hospital employees sat at the Formica tables, eating, drinking, and chatting. A skinny young man with hollow eyes stood behind the counter by the cash register. Zoe contemplated buying him a cup of coffee, too. He looked like he needed it more than she or Earl did.

"How's Doaks?"

Zoe spun to find Pete behind her. He wore a different coat...one that wasn't blood-soaked. But this one looked too lightweight for the weather...probably an all-purpose spare he kept in his car. His hair was wet from melting snow, and she bit back an urge to reach up and brush away the lingering droplets. "They're taking x-rays and running tests. It's pretty obvious his right leg's broken. His pupils were equal and reactive, so my guess is his head injuries are superficial."

He motioned for her to step up to the counter. "How about you? I saw you chuck his cell phone at him. Not standard procedure for handling trauma victims."

He'd seen that? How embarrassing. "Matt has a knack for knowing how to push my buttons. But I'm fine. What are you doing here? Do you suspect he was drinking?"

"Not really. I was coming into town anyway, and I wanted to check on you." He nodded to the skinny kid. "Two large coffees. My treat."

"Actually, I said I was buying for Earl, too."

"No problem. Make that three." Pete pulled out his wallet and counted the bills. The skinny kid made change and handed them three large foam cups.

They moved to another counter that held five coffee pumpers.

"Why were you driving into Brunswick in this weather?" Zoe said as she waited for Pete to fill the first cup.

"I'm still trying to track down Logan Bassi."

Her heart leapt into high gear. "Did you hear something about where he might be?"

"No." Pete handed a full cup to her and started on the second. "No one knows anything. It's like the kid crawled into a hole somewhere and vanished."

She hoped it was a warm, dry hole. "What makes you believe he's in Brunswick?"

"Just a hunch. I've checked everywhere I can think of around home. So I thought about where I might go if I were a seventeen-year-old."

"And?"

"I thought of the mall." He handed her another cup.

Why hadn't that occurred to her? Logan and Allison always met their friends at the Brunswick Mall.

Pete fit a lid on his coffee, and Zoe doctored Earl's with half-and-half and sugar, gave it a stir, and snapped lids on it and on hers.

"I don't suppose *you* have any idea where he might be?" Pete said.

"No."

He gave her a look that suggested he didn't believe her.

"Honestly. I don't. I've been trying to find him all day, too. Rose is pissed at me, and I figure finding Logan might be the only way to get back into her good graces."

He sipped his coffee as they headed for the door. "Why is Rose mad at you?"

Zoe froze. She was verbally painting herself into a corner with Pete again. But if Logan was guilty, did keeping their secret matter anymore?

Then she remembered something else. Not only was Rose mad at her. Zoe was mad at Pete.

She opened her mouth to give him hell, but nothing came out. Where to start? Should she accuse him? Or ask him why he betrayed her trust to that detective? He was just being a cop, after all. The person she should be angry at was herself for opening up to him. She clamped her jaw shut and plunged past him, into the hallway.

"Hey," Pete called after her. With his long legs, he'd caught her in three strides. "What's going on?"

She stopped again, this time spinning to face him. "Baronick questioned me this morning. He wanted to know about the night McBirney tried to rape me."

Pete's jaw tightened.

"You told him about what I said to you last night. How could you? I thought you were being a friend, but instead you were just being a cop." The pain of betrayal poured from her. Afraid she'd burst into tears if she said any more, she stumbled away, heading back to the elevators.

Pete caught her again. "I didn't tell Baronick anything. Whatever information he has, he didn't get it from me."

Zoe eyed him. Maybe she was once again being a sucker. But she needed to trust someone. And Pete had always been the most trustworthy man she knew. "Who then? Rose and Sylvia wouldn't have said anything. Ted and McBirney are both dead. No one else knew about it."

"What about Doaks?"

"I never told him. He knows I despised McBirney, but he doesn't know why."

They reached the elevators. Thankfully, no one else was there.

"Maybe McBirney told Doaks?" Pete pressed the down button.

Zoe laughed. "McBirney claims—claimed—he did nothing wrong, but I still doubt he told anyone about that night." *If for no other reason than no man would admit to another that he couldn't complete "the act."*

The steel doors slid open with the chime of a bell.

"Someone else knew." Storm clouds brewed in Pete's eyes. "Marcy knew."

They stepped into the elevator.

In the chaos surrounding McBirney's emergency department cubicle last night, Zoe hadn't processed everything Pete had told her. Now, she struggled to recall. Marcy and Ted weren't having an affair. Ted was helping her because he knew what McBirney had done to Zoe. Ted must have told Marcy about it.

With Zoe's head spinning, the reedy young man who passed in front of the elevator doors as they slid shut nearly escaped her notice. It took a second, then two, then three, before it registered. Even then, she doubted her own eyes.

Logan?

She dove for the open button , but with a cup of hot coffee in each hand, she was limited to jabbing at it with her elbow.

"What are you doing?" Pete said.

On a third attempt, she hit the right button and the doors slid open. She charged through them. Looked left, then right. Caught a glimpse of someone rounding the corner, heading away from her. "*Logan*," she called.

Whoever it was didn't reappear. Clutching the coffees, Zoe galloped after him, ignoring Pete's shouts from the elevator. Brew slopped, burning her hand, but she barely noticed.

She skid around the corner to find a pair of nurses, heads bent over a clipboard one of them was holding. Startled, they looked up at her. "Did you just see a boy run past here?" Zoe asked.

They exchanged glances, shrugged, and shook their heads.

Between the nurses and Zoe were two patient rooms. She set both cups of coffee on the floor next to the wall and entered one of them to find only a frail, elderly gentleman sleeping, his mouth open, his dinner tray untouched. She turned and crossed the hall to the other room. Two white-haired women occupied it. One was watching television. The other had company—a younger couple with a pair of kids. Everyone gave Zoe questioning looks. She apologized, excused herself, and backed out.

"Zoe?"

She wheeled, coming face to face with Pete.

"What's going on?"

"I—" She swallowed. "I thought I saw Logan. I guess my eyes were playing tricks on me."

Pete shot a questioning look toward the nurses, but they again shook their heads. "Looks that way. Come on. Let's go back."

Zoe collected her coffee and followed him back to the elevator. Clearly her imagination had conjured up the very person she so badly wanted to find. She took a deep breath to clear her brain. What had they been talking about? Oh. Yeah. "So you didn't say anything to Baronick?"

The doors opened onto the hospital's lower level.

"About you and McBirney? Not a word," Pete said. "You didn't kill him, did you?"

Zoe jerked her head up to find a grin tugging the corners of his mouth. "No. I didn't kill him. I did assault him with a bit and bridle. And fly spray. But that's the extent of it."

"All right then," he said and turned left off the elevator.

She paused a moment before following. Her mind wandered up three floors to that young man who looked so much like Logan. Once again, she dismissed it as tricks of a stressed mind. What the hell would Logan be doing at the Brunswick Hospital anyway?

Pete rolled out of bed and checked the clock. Not yet six a.m. He had Saturdays off. No reason to rise so early. But as usual, he hadn't slept more than a couple of hours. Might as well be up and productive rather than lying around staring at the ceiling.

The mall idea had been a bust. Thanks to the snowstorm, the stores had closed early. The hallways were deserted. Metal gates barred most of the storefronts. He made a loop around the parking lot, checking on the few stranded cars, but nothing matched Bassi's Taurus. He followed a PennDOT salt truck home along Route 15. The going was slow, but safer than passing it and battling the snow and ice.

The drive gave him time to ponder these two damned murder cases. And the one common thread that connected them.

Marcy.

Married to an abusive, manipulative bastard with a long history of violence, she definitely had a motive for McBirney's death. Ted Bassi's? She claimed they weren't having an affair. She claimed they were friends, and he was helping her plan her escape from her husband.

But did Pete believe her? That question had nagged him long after he returned home and well into his sleepless night.

He shuffled into the bathroom and stepped into the shower letting the stream of hot water pelt his face, hoping it would wash his ex out of his brain. Mineral deposits coated the showerhead, and stray jets sprayed in various directions. Maybe he could spend his day off fixing it. He made a mental list that included a trip into Phillipsburg to the hardware store for plumbing supplies.

That plan had faded by the time he finished brushing his teeth and made his way to the kitchen. Sunshine flooded through the blinds, all that much brighter from reflecting off a good two feet of snow.

His phone rang when he was halfway through his second cup of coffee. The home phone, not his cell phone, which told him it wasn't the officer on duty.

"Good morning, Chief. This is Matt Doaks."

"How's the leg?" Pete asked.

"If it weren't for the pain killers, I imagine it'd be sore as hell. Hey, I wanted to thank you for helping me out last night. I really appreciate it."

The standard reply, "Just doing my job," rolled off his tongue without effort.

"The other reason I'm calling is to let you know we're having an emergency supervisors' meeting this afternoon. Two o'clock at the VFW. I thought you'd probably want to be there."

"This afternoon? Are you up to it?"

"I'm not saying I won't be under the influence. I'm not driving, by the way." Doaks chuckled. He sounded *very* under the influence at the moment. "But the fact is we need to make some hard decisions now that Jerry McBirney's gone. We don't want the township left swinging in the breeze. Can I count on you to be there?"

Pete agreed, and Doaks hung up with a too-cheery farewell.

After draining the coffee pot, Pete collected his quilted Carhartt coveralls from a peg by the backdoor and pulled on an old pair of boots. He stepped outside, grabbed the snow shovel from the porch, and inhaled the crisp, clear morning air.

The road in front of his house had been cleared by a township snowplow, leaving the end of his driveway packed with an extra foot of heavy, gray muck. He started in front of the garage door and dug his way out.

The work felt good. Hard on the back, but the perspiration and the labor cleared his mind.

He wanted to take Marcy at her word, but couldn't. There were too many lies in their past. She'd told him that Ted's wife knew about their meetings. So he would make a point to stop in and talk to Rose. He'd inquire about Logan, too. Had she heard anything from him?

Remembered some detail that might help locate him?

And what was going on between Rose and Zoe? Those two were tighter than sisters, yet Zoe mentioned a rift.

Pete finished clearing his short driveway and started on the sidewalk. Sweat trickled down his back under his t-shirt.

A car made the turn onto his street and approached at a crawl. He recognized Baronick's unmarked black sedan. The detective pulled up in front of him and cut the engine.

"Morning, Chief," Baronick said as he climbed out. "I hear you had a little excitement last night."

Pete leaned on the shovel. "I suppose you're going to tell me I should invite you in on that case, too."

Baronick grinned as he slogged through the mound of snowy muck. "No. Feel free to handle all the traffic accidents you like." His face grew serious. "I've just come from talking to Fratini."

"What does our illustrious district attorney have to say?"

"He agrees with me that you need to stay clear of this investigation."

"Which one? The Bassi murder? Or the McBirney murder? And let's not forget the break-in at my police station."

"All of it. You and I both know there's a connection. Might even be the same person responsible for all three. But you're too close to it to be effective."

"Too close? It's a small township. If I'm not permitted to investigate any crime in which I know the suspect or the victim, I might as well tender my resignation right now."

Baronick waved a hand as if shooing a fly. "That's not it, and you know it. This is for your own good and for the case's." The detective moved closer and lowered his voice. "Your ex-wife is high on the suspect list. So is Zoe Chambers, and word has it you're friendly with her."

The way Baronick said "friendly" made it sound sordid. Pete expected him to wink. If he did, Pete would lay the sanctimonious jerk out cold.

Baronick might have guessed as much. He didn't wink. "Anything you uncover involving either woman is going to put you in a real bind. And if you don't find anything, it looks suspicious, too. Like maybe you didn't try hard enough."

The urge to belt the guy intensified.

"And I'm not even touching on your own motive to kill McBirney. I know you didn't do it. But the DA doesn't know you as well as I do."

"I'm sure you did your best to plead my case."

"I'm not here to arrest you, am I?"

"I don't know, Wayne. Are you?"

Baronick stepped back and shook his head. "Of course not. But stay away from this case. If you happen to hear anything, don't act on it. Call me. Let me handle the investigation. For your own sake. When we make an arrest, we don't want the case tainted by insinuations of misconduct. Have I made myself understood?"

Pete still longed to sucker punch the bastard, but he had to admit he might not be the best person to deal with Marcy. "Understood."

"Good." Baronick headed back to his car, then paused before getting behind the wheel. "And off the record, I'll do my best to keep you in the loop."

"Uh-huh."

Baronick drove off, made the turn, and headed up the hill to Main Street. Pete picked up shoveling where he'd left off, noting the detective had neglected to specifically order him off the missing Bassi boy case. Perhaps the omission had been a mere oversight. If so, Pete knew he'd better meet with Rose sooner rather than later.

Before Baronick realized his mistake and added that one to the keep-away list, too.

TWENTY-FOUR

Sylvia answered the door at Rose's house. "Pete. It's good to see you," she said, closing it behind him. "I'd ask if you've heard anything about Logan, but I can tell by your expression that you haven't."

Pete removed his hat and tugged off his gloves. "You can read my face now, can you?"

Sylvia's laugh was more of a huff. Her skin had faded to shades of white and gray with dark bags under her bloodshot eyes. "I should warn you, Rose is in bad shape. Allison's sick as a dog. Can't keep any food down. With Logan missing and Ted...It's more than a body should have to deal with." Her voice cracked.

"I'll keep it brief."

He followed her into the living room. The drawn curtains blocked out the bright sunshine, leaving the room in twilight darkness even though it wasn't yet noon.

Rose appeared in the hallway. She stiffened when she spotted Pete. "What's *he* doing here?" Then she softened for a moment, her shoulders wilting. "Oh, my God. Have you found Logan?"

"No. I'm sorry. I don't have any news on him."

She bristled again and crossed her arms in front of her. "Then I want you to leave."

"Rose," Sylvia chided. "It's Pete."

"I don't care. He's a cop. No better than that detective who was here yesterday. They all think Logan's involved in McBirney's murder." Her eyes glistened, and her lip trembled. "Even Zoe thinks so."

Ah. That explained the rift between Zoe and Rose. But why would Zoe think the kid was guilty?

Sylvia slipped an arm around Rose's shoulders. "Now, now. You don't really believe that."

"She said as much." Tears streamed down Rose's face. "My best friend. After all the time she's spent with my kids over the years. How could she think such a thing? Logan adores her. He spent hours over at her place trying to fix her damned computer this week." Rose crumbled against Sylvia.

Pete leapt toward them, catching Rose and helping Sylvia ease her into a chair in the living room where she doubled over and sobbed. He knelt at her feet. The last thing he wanted to do was intrude on her grief more than he already had. But he had to find out about Marcy. "I need to ask you something."

Rose sniffled and looked up. "Will the answer find my boy? Or clear his name?"

Pete drew a breath. Not exactly. As much as he hoped to find proof that Logan was innocent, his questions for Rose only served to clear another suspect of the crime.

She must have read the answer in his face. "No. I'm done answering questions. I'll tell you the same thing I told that detective. You want any more answers from me, you haul me down to the station and let me call my attorney. Otherwise, we're done." She pushed him away and climbed to her feet. Swaying for a moment, she held up a hand when he reached to steady her. "Sylvia, show Chief Adams the way out. I have to check on my daughter."

Rose disappeared down the darkened hallway.

"I'm sorry, Pete," Sylvia said. "I told you. She's a mess."

"Are you staying with her?"

"I'm taking turns with her mother. But Bert's still not feeling all that great either. Damned flu."

Pete started for the door. Marcy had said only Rose knew, but maybe…"Sylvia, do you know anything about Ted and Marcy?"

"Ted and Marcy? What do you mean?"

"Did they know each other? Socialize? Did Ted talk about her?"

"You make it sound like—Pete, if you're suggesting what I think you're suggesting, I'm going to be as angry with you as Rose is."

He placed a hand on each of her rounded shoulders. "I'm not suggesting anything. I'm just asking. And from your response, I'll take that as a 'no.'"

"Ted was a good boy." Tears welled in Sylvia's eyes.

Pete decided he'd better get the hell out of there before he made yet another woman cry. He leaned down and planted a kiss on Sylvia's cheek. "Yes. He was."

He pulled on his hat as he headed for his car. Rose hadn't given him the answer he was looking for. But she did give him something else without realizing it—more questions for Zoe. Like what was wrong with her computer that required Logan's assistance right after his father had been killed?

Pete suspected he knew the answer. And he didn't like it much.

Zoe parked in the freshly plowed VFW parking lot, away from the other vehicles arriving for the meeting. She turned off the ignition and leaned back in the seat.

Last night, she'd taken three more runs into Brunswick Hospital. Each time, she'd made an excuse to escape the Emergency Department and prowl the hallways in search of that young man who resembled Logan. She needed to prove to herself it wasn't him. But the look-alike remained as elusive as the real missing boy.

With Matt nursing a broken leg, Zoe assumed the emergency meeting would be cancelled. However, when she came in from her barn chores that morning, she found his message on her cell phone's voicemail stating he was home, and the meeting was on. And that she absolutely needed to be there.

Why? She couldn't imagine. As she sat in the parking lot staring at the VFW building, a week's worth of memories flooded her brain. One week. If she could only turn back the clock one lousy week. Ted would be alive. Logan and Allison would be tormenting each other. Rose would still be her best friend. She'd even accept McBirney's revolting presence in her fantasy. A small price to pay for all being right with the world.

A knock on her driver-side window jarred her back into reality. Sylvia, bundled in a blue wool coat, cast a tight smile at Zoe through the glass.

"I'm surprised to see you here." Zoe slid down from the seat and slammed the door.

"I was invited." Sylvia rolled her eyes. "What's your excuse?"

"Pretty much the same thing." She glanced around for Rose.

"She's not coming." Sylvia took Zoe's arm, and they picked through the slush toward the building. "Rose and her mother are sitting with Allison."

"Is she feeling any better?"

Sylvia shook her head. "If anything, I'd have to say she's worse. I think we'll take her to the urgent care center at the hospital if she doesn't show improvement soon."

"Any word from Logan?" The mention of the hospital brought him back to the forefront of Zoe's mind.

"No. You know that boy had nothing to do with McBirney's murder, don't you?"

Zoe wished she could give Sylvia the response she wanted. "I just hope he's okay."

Sylvia scowled at her. "That's not a real answer."

"It's the only one I have."

Matt Doaks intercepted them, sweeping along on crutches. He held up his right leg, encased in a plastic and Velcro brace, to avoid the slop. "Hello, ladies. I'm glad you could both make it."

Sylvia grunted.

"I don't know why you're so insistent on my being here," Zoe said.

He winked. "You'll see." Then he swung away, maneuvering the crutches like a pro.

"I'd like to see him hit an icy spot on those things," Sylvia said.

The mental picture of Matt sprawled on his back, crutches askew, forced a snicker from Zoe.

"You know what's going to happen here today, don't you?" Sylvia said.

They started forward again. "Not a clue."

"This is Matt Doaks' big coming out party. With McBirney gone, Doaks will claim the throne of Chairman. He wants everyone here to witness it."

Zoe fought her gag reflex. Matt? Chairman of the township supervisors? Was that better or worse than McBirney? At least he wasn't the brutish monster McBirney had been. But she had strong reservations about Matt's leadership skills and judgment.

She held the door for Sylvia to enter the VFW and then followed. Inside, the crowd wasn't quite as large as it had been on Monday night.

Men and women in coveralls and boots milled about. The soft rumble of assorted conversation filled the room, punctuated by an occasional boisterous laugh.

Sylvia drew an audible breath. Her face had lost the ruddiness of winter's chill, and her lower lip trembled. Zoe took her hand and squeezed. She knew what Sylvia was thinking because she felt it, too. Less than a week ago, Ted had been in this room. Two days ago, lunch had been served here following his burial.

"I don't know if I can do this," the older woman whispered.

"You don't have to. Do you want me to take you home?"

Before she could reply, several locals surrounded them, offering Sylvia hugs and condolences. Zoe escaped the circle of well-wishers and stepped into line to sign the attendance sheet.

Howard Rankin and Matt sat at the head table. The two surviving supervisors. Howard, the voice of reason. Matt, Jerry McBirney's puppet.

Elizabeth Sunday perched on the edge of a chair at the end of the table. She appeared a bit disheveled. Stray wisps of hair hung in front of her face. She wore a bulky turtleneck sweater and wool pants with flat boots. Not her usual urban chic style.

Zoe signed the roster. She checked on Sylvia and saw that she was flanked by friends. The smile on her face told Zoe she'd be fine. So she slipped into an empty seat at the end of the third row. Far back enough to hide. Close enough to the door to make a quick exit.

The crack of the gavel against the table drew everyone's attention. Matt stood and cleared his throat. "Find a seat, folks. We have a lot to cover and none of us wants to spend our entire Saturday here."

"Most of us don't want to spend any of our Saturday here," a hefty man with a scraggly brown beard grumbled as Zoe swung her legs out of the way so he and his buddies could sidle into the chairs next to her.

Sylvia, escorted by her lady friends, crossed the room to find seats in the first row. After a couple of minutes of chairs squeaking and groaning and clanging against each other, the room settled into near silence, which was broken by the clank of the door opening.

Pete walked in. He leaned against the wall in his usual spot and folded his arms across his chest. Zoe searched for some sign on his face about Logan, but he was in poker mode.

"Okay," Matt said. "I'm calling this emergency meeting of the Vance Township board of supervisors to order. Before we go any further, I'd like to call for a moment of silence for our fallen comrade, Jerry McBirney."

The room fell quiet. Zoe shifted in her chair. Fallen comrade? Matt made McBirney sound like a war hero. She looked up and noticed Pete watching her. A hint of smile flickered across his lips, and then he broke the contact. A rush of heat spread across her shoulders and settled around her neck.

Matt cleared his throat again and thanked everyone. "Now. For our first order of business. Howard and I have been talking on the phone since the news of Jerry's passing reached us, and we've come to a decision. It's my great honor to introduce to you, our new chairman of the board of supervisors—Mr. Howard Rankin."

The crowd broke into a raucous round of applause with a few whistles and whoops thrown in. Zoe wished she could see Sylvia's face. The bearded man and his pals clapped and smiled. "Maybe there's hope yet for this township," one of them said, echoing Zoe's thoughts.

Matt sat down, and Rankin climbed to his feet.

"Thank you. Thank you," the new chairman said. "Let me just say I intend to pay close attention to the wishes and needs of the residents of Vance Township. I want to keep all lines of communication open. Now, I want to turn the floor over to township solicitor, Ms. Elizabeth Sunday."

The attorney stood and faced the audience. She tucked an errant strand of hair behind her ear. "In keeping with the good news, I am pleased to report that the township is dropping its complaint against Mrs. Sylvia Bassi."

The news might have held more weight if the evidence against her hadn't been stolen. But it brought another round of applause nonetheless.

"And," Sunday said, raising her voice above the crowd noise, "on behalf of the supervisors, I wish to apologize for the board's regrettable actions in this matter." She turned to Sylvia. "Mrs. Bassi, I'm truly sorry for the pain and stress we've caused you."

"Don't that beat all?" the bearded man said to the guy next to Zoe. "A lawyer making apologies."

"Ain't that one of the signs of the apocalypse?" the other man said, and they all chortled.

"Thank you, Ms. Sunday," Rankin said as she reclaimed her chair. "Next. We have a seat up here to fill. We'll hold a special election in May to fill the vacancy, but in the meantime, Matt and I will appoint someone to the post for the next four months. We've talked at great length about this and have given it much consideration." He paused and looked at Matt, who smiled and nodded. "We're in full agreement that we've made an excellent choice. The person we'd like to appoint as interim supervisor is Zoe Chambers."

TWENTY-FIVE

For a moment, the room fell silent. Or Zoe lost her sense of hearing. She wasn't sure which. When the applause and shouting filtered into her consciousness, it sounded muted at first, as though she had fallen into a deep lake and was hearing the din through the water.

Someone clapped her on the back, snapping her out of her fog. The hooting and whooping blasted into her brain.

What the hell just happened? Supervisor? *Her?* Was this a joke? She must have heard wrong.

"What are you waiting for?" the bearded man said. "Get up there."

Apparently she'd heard right. Zoe climbed to her feet and made her way to the front of room. She caught Pete grinning at her.

When she reached the front table, Matt motioned to the chair next to him.

"Don't I get a say in this?" she whispered loud enough that both Matt and Rankin could hear her.

Rankin laughed.

Why was he laughing? She wasn't kidding.

She eased into the chair and gazed at the faces before her. They appeared pleased. This was madness.

As the room quieted, Rankin said, "You all couldn't hear her, but Ms. Chambers asked if she gets a say in this."

"No," someone shouted, bringing a round of snickers from the crowd.

Rankin turned to Zoe. "How about you humor us and just try it out for today. So we can handle some official business. If you don't like the fit, we'll talk later."

Matt leaned closer and whispered in her ear. "It'll be harder to bitch about our actions when you have a hand in them."

She pulled back and eyed him. He gave her the killer grin that had charmed the pants off many a female over the years. In response, she fixed him with a glare, hoping to convey her immunity to his alluring ways.

"We'll definitely talk later," Zoe said loud enough this time so that everyone could hear.

Another wave of chuckles swept the crowd.

"Okay, let's get down to serious business," Rankin said. "After receiving many questions and complaints from township residents in recent months, I move to relieve Elizabeth Sunday from her duties as township solicitor."

"What?" the attorney snapped. "You can't do that."

Suddenly, Zoe liked this new gig.

"Yes, ma'am, we can," Rankin said.

Sunday leapt to her feet and a few more stray wisps escaped her French twist. "Matt. You promised me I'd keep this job."

Matt scrunched his mouth together and shrugged.

Zoe wondered exactly when and where he'd made that promise.

"I'm sorry, Liz," Matt said. "I second the motion."

"A motion has been made and seconded. All in favor?"

Silence fell over the room. Then Zoe noticed both Matt and Rankin staring at her. "Oh," she said. "Aye."

"Motion carried," Rankin said. "We thank you for your service, Ms. Sunday."

At that point, he dismissed her and moved to rehire old Reginald Scoffield who had been the township solicitor for decades before McBirney had unceremoniously replaced him. That motion also passed.

Zoe leaned back in the chair. Maybe this supervisor's thing wouldn't be so bad. Maybe she could tolerate sitting next to Matt for a handful of meetings until a permanent replacement could be elected. Undoing all of Jerry McBirney's reckless decisions was the most fun she'd had in ages.

The door clanked open, and Wayne Baronick slipped in. He claimed a spot on the wall next to Pete.

Rankin shuffled some papers in front of him and took a swig from a bottle of water before continuing. "Okay. Next. Um. It's been brought to my attention..." He looked toward Baronick and Pete with an expression Zoe couldn't quite interpret. Desperation? Regret? Anxiety? "Chief Adams, I've been informed that—well—that you have some personal issues with regards to Jerry McBirney's murder investigation."

"Personal issues?" Pete echoed. "What the hell are you talking about, Howard?"

Rankin's hands trembled as he reshuffled the papers.

Zoe leaned toward him. "What personal issues?" she asked in a rough whisper.   .

Rankin glanced around the room. Shielding his mouth with his hand he replied, "It's been brought to our attention that Chief Adams is something of a suspect in the case."

Zoe choked. Pete? A suspect? She felt like she had walked into the middle of a movie. And not even the movie she'd purchased the ticket for. None of it made sense.

Pete pushed away from the wall. "Howard?"

Rankin raised his voice so everyone could hear. "I don't want to get into specifics in a public forum. But it's clear that you should not be working this case."

Pete made a deliberate quarter turn to face Baronick who failed to meet his gaze. Pete continued to study the detective, but his words were directed at Rankin. "I'm sure it's also been brought to your attention that I'm not *on* the case."

"Yes, but we've been told you're working it anyway. And that can't be permitted. It's a conflict of interest, and it puts the entire case in jeopardy. There are too many legal implications to allow you contact with the evidence or the witnesses." Rankin, who'd been reading from the papers in front of him, looked up.

Pete said something to Baronick too low for Zoe to hear. A muscle in Baronick's cheek twitched.

"I hate doing this, Pete," Rankin said. "But I'm afraid I must move that the board of supervisors suspend you—with pay—until further notice."

Zoe looked at Matt, expecting to see surprise on his face, too. But there was none. He knew about this all along. And he'd dragged her into the middle of it, making her part of the team of henchmen offering Pete up for sacrifice.

"I second the motion," Matt said.

"All in favor say 'aye,'" Rankin said.

Matt and Rankin both said, "Aye."

"No," Zoe said.

"Opposed?"

"Hell, yes, I'm opposed," Zoe said loud enough that her voice reverberated.

"The word is 'nay,'" Matt whispered.

For a moment, she visualized jumping to her feet and tackling him. Slug him in the nose. Maybe break his other leg. Instead, she glowered at him and dropped her voice into its lowest, most threatening range. "Nay."

"The vote is two for the motion, one opposed. Motion carries. Chief Adams, you are suspended from duty pending further investigation." Rankin cracked the gavel against the table, and the room erupted.

The moment Howard read the words, Pete knew who had provided them to him. At least he'd been able to tell Baronick exactly what he thought of him before storming out of the meeting.

Suspended. Son of a bitch.

"Pete, wait."

Damn it. Baronick had followed him into the parking lot.

"Pete. Chief Adams. Wait."

Pete spun so fast the detective almost slammed into him. "You can't call me 'chief' anymore. I'm under suspension."

"For crissakes, Pete. Listen to me. You're still the chief. I just need you to step aside until I clear this case. At least officially."

"What do you mean—'officially' clear it?"

"No. I need you to step aside—*officially*." Baronick caught his arm, a move which made Pete consider breaking his fingers. "Look. I'm doing you a favor. The conflict of interest thing is legit. That you might make even a half-ways competent lawyer question evidence in the case is fact. You know that. If you use your head and think about it, you know that."

Pete knew he wanted to use the detective for a punching bag. But the gleam in Baronick's eyes sparked Pete's curiosity.

"You're off the case," Baronick went on. "You're basically on paid vacation. I've seen to it that you have a ton of free time on your hands.

What you do with that free time is none of my concern." He raised an eyebrow. "*Capice?*"

Pete understood. He studied the young detective's grinning face. So that was it. Baronick was behind the whole suspension ruse, but with the intention of giving Pete free rein. Maybe the kid had some redeeming value after all. "Yeah. I got it."

"Good. And if you happen to stumble into anything interesting while you're on vacation..."

"You'll be the first to know."

Pete heard someone call his name and turned. Zoe sprinted towards him from the building.

"I've got to get back to work," Baronick said.

"Good idea," Pete said. Zoe might just have a bottle of fly spray in her purse, and the detective might well be her next victim.

She jogged up as the detective ambled away. Her skin was flushed from the cold, and her breath framed her face like a veil. "I don't see any blood or bruises," she said. "But I didn't get a good look at Detective Benedict Arnold. Did you give him a black eye?"

"No. Not yet. Is the meeting adjourned? Or did you walk out?"

"It's over. Firing you was the final bit of business on the agenda." Zoe's mouth trembled. "I'm so sorry about that. I can't believe they roped me into the middle of it. I think McBirney has taken possession of Howard Rankin's soul."

Her indignant rage brought a smile to Pete's heart. "It's all right. I'm not fired, after all. Just suspended."

"Close enough. I could just shoot Matt." She crossed her arms in front of her and cocked one hip. "I'm quitting the board."

"You were just appointed."

"I don't care. Mine will be the shortest political career in the history of mankind."

"I think you should stay." Pete caught her scowl. "You know the old saying. Keep your friends close..."

"...Keep your enemies closer."

"Think of it as being a spy. You'll have the inside track on what Howard and Matt are scheming."

A spark lit her blue eyes, and one corner of her mouth tipped upward. "Spy? Well, when you put it like that..."

Pete took her hand. "Do you have a few minutes? I need to talk to you."

Her fingers tensed. "What about?"

"Logan. And your computer."

If Pete had dropped a hundred-pound anvil on Zoe's chest, she'd have been able to breathe easier than hearing the words "Logan" and "computer" coming from the chief's lips. He knew. She wasn't sure how much he knew, but he'd put enough of it together to making lying about it pointless.

Township residents filtered out of the VFW, buzzing about the meeting. A few called to Pete, expressing outrage and concern. He waved at them.

"Walk me to my truck," Zoe said.

"How did you get the stolen computer?" Pete asked as they strolled through the sloppy parking lot.

"Logan brought it to me."

"Logan broke into the police station?"

"What? No. Just the hard drive. He removed it before you guys confiscated the computer from Sylvia's house. He installed it in my computer, and we've been trying to find whatever must be on it to compel McBirney to kill Ted."

"But what about the break in at the station?"

"I had nothing to do with it. Neither did Logan. He had no reason."

Pete stopped and glared at her. "You mean to tell me the computer we had in evidence—the one that was stolen—"

"Was basically a hollow shell." Zoe finished the sentence for him. "Yep. That's what I'm telling you."

His frown melted into a smile. "So whoever broke into my station got absolutely nothing for his troubles."

"That about covers it. However, he figured it out. And he figured out where the hard drive was."

The smile vanished. "What happened?"

"That night you came to my house." Zoe's throat tightened. She wasn't sure if the sensation arose due to the memory of the invasion or the memory of his kiss. "The night you noticed my office door was closed…It was closed because McBirney had broken in and opened up the computer. I must have interrupted him before he had time to remove the hard drive. He ran out the front door and down the hill to the road."

"You're sure it was McBirney?"

"Who else would it have been?"

"Did you *see* him?"

Zoe thought back. "No. I just heard him rummaging around and then footsteps running away. It was dark. But I'd spotted a car parked along the road when I was coming home. I thought at the time someone had gotten stuck in the snow and abandoned the vehicle. But when McBirney ran off, I heard the car start up."

"What kind of car?"

"Dark sedan. Nondescript."

"License number?"

Crap. Why hadn't she paid more attention? "I'm sorry."

Pete moved toward her truck, tugging her along with him. "That's all right. You said he broke in? How? I don't recall the lock being damaged."

"It wasn't. In fact, when I first realized someone was inside, I thought it was Logan. He knows where I hide the key."

Pete jerked her to a stop again. "He knows where you *hide your key*?" He released her hand and gave her shoulders a shake. "You hide a key? Zoe. Have I taught you nothing?"

She preferred Pete's concern to his contempt and grinned. "Sorry."

"As soon as you get home, you're going to call someone to get the locks changed and you're not going to hide a key anywhere. Do I make myself clear?"

"But McBirney's dead. He's not coming back."

Pete's eyes narrowed at her. "Zoe."

"All right already. I'll change the locks."

"Good girl." He slipped an arm around her shoulders and continued the final few yards to her truck. "How did McBirney know where to look for your key?"

Her mind spun. How *did* McBirney know about her key? "I…don't know. I guess someone must have told him. Or he snooped around and found it." Pete was right. Hiding a key was a stupid idea.

"Who would have told him about it?"

"I have no idea."

He gave her *that look*. Scowling eyes, pinched mouth. A wordless tongue-lashing. Then he made a sound deep within his chest that was half exasperated sigh, half growl. "Okay. What did you and Logan find on the hard drive?"

The anvil fell on her chest again.

"Zoe?"

"I wish I knew. Logan came over Thursday after the funeral. He was working on the computer when I was in the barn with McBirney. When I got back to the house, Logan seemed—I don't know—*strange*. He insisted he hadn't found anything. But I had a feeling...He said he had to go meet a friend. That's the last time I saw him." Hearing the words out loud made it all too real. Was Logan capable of murder?

They reached the truck and the driver's side door. Pete squinted into the distance, his jaw clenched.

"I know I should have told you. But I didn't want to get Logan into trouble with the law on top of everything with his dad. I honestly thought we'd find something on McBirney and turn it in to you then."

"You shouldn't have taken it on yourself."

"At least you can't arrest me now that you've been fired." Zoe nudged him, hoping to make him smile again.

"I'm only suspended. I can still arrest you."

A vision of handcuffs and jail cells crushed any remaining breath from her body. She searched Pete's face for any sign that he was joking. Damn his dry wit. Damn his poker face.

"But I'm not going to," he said after a lengthy silence.

Zoe's knees threatened to dump her onto the slush-covered gravel, and the air she'd been lacking rushed into her lungs.

Sylvia trudged up to them. "I'm glad to see you two are still speaking. Pete, I don't know what those idiots are thinking."

His face held its scowl. "Don't worry about it. Zoe, have you been able to find anything on that computer? Any clue what Logan might have found?"

"What?" Sylvia asked.

"No. Nothing. But I'm kind of technologically challenged."

"That's what I thought. We need someone who knows their way around those things to help us out."

Us?

"What are you two talking about?" Sylvia demanded. "What about Logan?"

From across the parking lot, someone called Pete's name. Zoe spotted Baronick waving frantically with one hand, holding a cell phone to his ear with the other.

Pete sighed. "I'd better go find out what he wants." He squeezed Zoe's shoulder. "There's only one person who knows that computer." He shot a glance at Sylvia, and then turned back to Zoe. "Tell her what you told me. Everything. When I get back from talking to Baronick, the three of us are taking a ride to your house."

"What's going on?" Sylvia said as Pete walked away.

"Do you want to sit inside my truck? It's a long story."

"No, I don't want to sit down. Just start talking, missy."

By the time Zoe had made it half way through the tale, Sylvia changed her mind and accepted the offered seat. By the end of the recounting, she'd deflated. Her shoulders sagged with the weight of more despair than any one person should ever have to endure.

"Logan didn't kill that bastard," Sylvia said, but without the old steely conviction.

"I hope not," Zoe said.

A sharp rap on her window made her flinch. She turned to see Pete. From his grim expression, she knew neither she nor Sylvia wanted to hear what he had to say. Zoe opened the door and swung around to face him.

"Baronick just got a call. They found Logan's car."

"Where?" Sylvia's voice carried both hope and terror.

"In the parking garage at Brunswick Hospital."

So it *had* been Logan outside the elevator last night.

"The hospital?" Sylvia said. "Is he all right?"

Pete shook his head. "They haven't located the boy yet. Just the car. There's no record of treatment. The police are searching the hospital property."

"Well, that's something. Thank God." Sylvia reached over and patted Zoe's knee. "You need someone to search that old hard drive. I'm your woman. Let's go. I need to find something to prove my grandson didn't have anything to do with McBirney's murder." She sat back and buckled her seatbelt.

"You two go on. I'll follow you in my car in a few minutes." Pete stepped back, but held Zoe's gaze.

There was more. Something Pete wasn't saying in front of Sylvia. And whatever it was, Zoe knew it was devastating.

TWENTY-SIX

Damn that Baronick. The son-of-a-bitch nixed Pete's demands to drive to the hospital and view the Bassi kid's car. Worse still, the detective was right. Pete was under suspension for a reason. There had to be no suggestion of impropriety. No hinting by a skilled defense attorney that someone on the case may have reason to tamper with evidence. At least Baronick was keeping Pete in the information loop.

And the information sucked.

Pete parked next to Zoe's truck and picked his way through the slick, melting snow to the farmhouse's back door. A mound of the mushy white stuff slid from the porch roof to the ground with a splat. He took a cautious glance up to make sure he wouldn't be buried under a mini avalanche before stepping onto the enclosed porch.

Zoe answered the door before he had a chance to knock. "You didn't try to call me, did you?"

"No. Why?"

She shook her head. "My phone's still dead, thanks to Matt's little fender-bender last night. So, what's going on? I could tell there was more to it than you said back there."

"Where's Sylvia?"

"She's on her cell phone with Rose. Seems Allison has gotten worse, and Rose is taking her—where else? The Urgent Care Center at Brunswick Hospital."

Damn it. Well, hopefully the place was big enough that Rose wouldn't bump into the county investigators. "I need you to show me where you keep this hidden key." In truth, he needed Zoe out of the house, away from Sylvia.

Zoe frowned, but closed the door behind her as she stepped onto the porch. "It's right here." She reached up to the top of the doorframe and felt around. Biting her lip, she admitted, "It's gone. I guess McBirney kept it."

Pete pulled out his pad and made a note. Ask Baronick to check McBirney's personal effects. "Change the locks."

"I already told you I will. Now what is it? Did they find Logan?"

"No." Pete drew a breath. "But they found bloody clothes in the backseat. They match what Rose told me he was wearing when he left the house on Thursday." Another thought occurred to Pete. The break-in at the Helping Hands Store. He made another note to follow up with Mrs. Zellars about her inventory. He suspected the only things missing were a pair of pants, a shirt, and a coat.

"Whose blood?" Zoe said. "On the clothes. Logan's?"

Pete doubted it. "Don't know yet. Everything is on its way to the county crime lab."

Zoe sank back against the door.

"It would be best to not mention this to Sylvia," he said.

Zoe gave a nod and turned to let them both inside.

Sylvia sat in Zoe's office at the computer. She looked up when they entered. "I wondered what you two were doing."

"Anything new on Allison?" Zoe said.

"Just what you already know. Rose'll call me as soon as she knows anything."

Pete stripped off his coat and hat, dropping them on the sofa in the living room as he passed by. "Have you found anything yet?"

Sylvia shook her head. "Just a lot of stuff that should have been deleted and written over long ago. I hate to say it, but McBirney's complaints had some validity. Township residents' tax records. Social Security numbers. I should have been more careful."

"But being proven right isn't a reason for Jerry McBirney to kill Ted." Zoe leaned over her shoulder and studied the screen.

"No, it isn't," Sylvia said. "I'm still looking."

Pete's cell phone rang.

"You owe me that steak dinner at Galligher's," said the raspy voice on the other end of the line.

Pete left Zoe hovering over Sylvia's shoulder and slipped into the living room. "Grace. What have you got for me?" he asked the lab tech.

"Actually, I think you owe me dancing after dinner, too. Baronick would can me if he knew I was calling you with this before contacting him."

"Just tell me what you found."

"That blue fiber? It matches the material in Ted Bassi's jacket."

"That places Bassi in McBirney's garage."

"Not so fast. This is a good news, bad news sort of thing. It's also a match to the jacket Baronick brought in this morning from the Bassi kid's car, although there aren't any holes in that one. The point is the fabric is from any one of thousands of Phillipsburg Blue Demons high school jackets floating around. Or more precisely, any one that has a rip in it. I can't definitively match it to the tears in Ted Bassi's coat, but I can't rule it out either. The evidence isn't conclusive."

"Terrific," Pete muttered. "Anything on the blood-stained clothes?"

There was silence on the line for a moment. "Are we on for dinner and dancing?"

"Grace, you know I don't dance. What about the blood?"

"You don't play fair, Pete Adams. It'll take weeks to get the DNA results, but I can tell you the blood type on the clothes and on the screwdriver match the victim, Jerry McBirney. And we lifted several smudges and one lovely useable print from the screwdriver handle." There was a pause. "It's a match to Logan Bassi."

Pete closed his eyes. Damn it. "Any matches to the prints from McBirney's cars?"

"Not yet. Sorry."

"How about the evidence from Ted Bassi's pickup?"

"Good God, man. You ask for the moon. I haven't gotten to the trace evidence yet. So far the prints all match family members. But I'm still working on it."

"Steak and a beer," Pete said. "No dancing."

"I'll take what I can get." The lab tech clicked off in his ear.

He slipped the phone into his pocket and swore under his breath. Logan's print was on what might prove to be the murder weapon. Baronick would love that. But something felt off about it.

When Pete returned to Zoe's office, Sylvia was leaning toward the computer monitor as her fingers danced over the keyboard. Zoe looked up with a glint in her eyes. "Was that anything important?"

"No." Burdening them with the latest news wouldn't help at this point. "Did you find something?"

"Maybe." The tension in Sylvia's body reminded him of a cat, ready to pounce on a sparrow.

"Well?"

"Gimme a minute," she snapped.

He looked at Zoe who shrugged.

Sylvia clicked the mouse, studied the monitor, clicked again, and spent a moment reading what appeared on the screen. "Well, I'll be damned."

Zoe leaned over her shoulder and Pete edged closer, squinting over Sylvia's head.

"Crap." Zoe's voice was little more than a hoarse whisper.

"What?" Pete demanded, fumbling for his glasses.

"I was looking through the local income tax records and noticed that seven or eight years ago, Jerry McBirney's business was doing a slow nosedive. Then suddenly, everything turned around. As though it had gotten a shot in the arm. I didn't know what to make of it. Then I started snooping through some of the old e-mails in here." Sylvia looked up at Zoe, but dodged Pete's eye.

"And?" he prompted.

"You're not going to like this," Sylvia said.

He realized his glasses were in his coat pocket in the other room. "Damn it. Just tell me what the hell you found."

"Remember the ten thousand dollars that went missing six years ago?"

Of course he remembered. Up until the break in at the station, it had been the single most embarrassing moment of his career. Tax season and the township deposit had vanished. One of his officers had been assigned to take the money to the bank, but no one admitted to seeing it. Or taking it. Pete had interrogated everyone with access to the station. He'd come up empty, but the resulting internal tension led to his two top men, Fanase and Petrucci, leaving the township.

Sylvia drummed her fingers on the mouse pad. "There are a series of e-mails here over a period of a month or so. They're between Jerry McBirney and..."

"And?"

"Marcy."

Six years ago. Marcy had still been Pete's wife. And she'd been assistant police secretary. Sylvia was right. He wasn't going to like it.

"McBirney complains about his finances and how he needs an influx of capital to get his business back on its feet. Marcy mentions the daily deposit and how it just sits on her desk until an officer picks it up and runs it to the bank." Sylvia clicked the mouse and read another e-mail. "It's all here. McBirney put her up to it, but Marcy's the one who took the money."

"I vaguely remember this," Zoe said. "The checks were never recovered, right?"

"Right. The thief probably burned or shredded them. But there was enough cash to give McBirney the boost he claimed to need." Sylvia shook her head. "Marcy. I can't believe it. She came to me a couple days after it happened, asking if I had the deposit slip. Claimed since the money wasn't on her desk, she assumed someone had already taken it to the bank."

Pete turned away from the computer. Not only had Marcy cheated on him, left him for that son-of-a-bitch McBirney, but she'd stolen money from the township he'd been sworn to protect. When he'd been all of ten feet away in his office. He remembered questioning her about it. But back then he hadn't believed his wife capable of lying.

"Are you sure?"

"It's all right here." Sylvia's voice had softened. "I'm sorry, Pete."

No wonder McBirney had wanted the computer back.

"Ted found out, too, didn't he?" Sylvia said. "He confronted McBirney. That bastard killed my boy to keep his own butt out of jail."

Her scenario made sense. But it didn't resolve all the questions spinning through Pete's mind. If McBirney was the killer, did he have an accomplice? What else was Marcy guilty of? Sweet, vulnerable Marcy. Then, the question Pete knew better than to ask out loud.

Had Logan found these files?

A merry jingle broke the silence, and Sylvia snatched her cell phone from the desk next to the keyboard. "It's Rose," she announced.

As Sylvia answered the call, Pete motioned Zoe into the other room.

"If this is what Logan stumbled across, it doesn't look good, does it?" she whispered.

"No. It doesn't." Pete relayed the information about the blood on the clothes.

Zoe squeezed her eyes shut and rubbed her forehead. "But we still don't know for sure. Like you said. DNA will take weeks."

"A fingerprint they found on the screwdriver belongs to Logan."

She sunk down onto the sofa and covered her face with her hands.

He longed to reach out and touch her shoulder, but thought better of it. She seemed so fragile at the moment that his mere touch might cause her to crumble to pieces.

Everything that was going wrong in the lives of those he loved traced back to his own failings. As a cop. As a husband. He had to make things right somehow before he offered his heart—or even small comfort—to someone else.

Sylvia staggered through the doorway, her face gray. "Pete, can you drive me to Brunswick Hospital?"

Zoe brushed a hand across her face and leapt to her feet. "What's wrong?"

Sylvia opened her mouth, but no sound came out. She closed it and licked her lips before trying again. "It's Allison."

"Oh, my God." Zoe grabbed Sylvia's arm. "What's happened now?"

"She's missing. Rose left her in the examination room to get her something to drink and when she came back, Allison was gone."

"I'll go with you," Zoe said.

"No." Sylvia patted Zoe's hand. "Rose is upset. It's better for you to stay here. If Pete will take me."

Zoe bit her lip. She looked at him, her eyes moist with tears she tried to blink away.

"Of course," he said. "Let's go."

As Sylvia collected her coat and purse, Pete tipped his head to bring his mouth close to Zoe's ear. "Are you going to be all right?"

"Yeah. Are you?"

He responded with a short, noncommittal laugh before grabbing his coat and following Sylvia out the door.

* * *

Zoe watched Pete close the back door behind him as he and Sylvia left. Then she sank into her office chair, still warm from Sylvia's time there. Over the past week, Zoe's world had imploded around her. In the last hour, it had gasped its last breath. Ted was gone. Logan was most likely responsible for Jerry McBirney's death. All because she had permitted him to use her computer to play detective.

Detective. Not judge. Not jury. Not hangman.

Damn kid.

Now Allison was sick and missing. Rose was falling to pieces, but didn't want Zoe around to offer support. Instead, Rose blamed Zoe for everything. And why not? Other than Ted's murder, she'd had a hand in each and every aspect of Rose's heartbreak. Not to mention Pete's suspension.

Merlin sauntered into the room and sprang uninvited into Zoe's lap. She rubbed a velvety ear between two fingers, and the cat purred in bliss.

"At least you still love me," she said.

He made two circuits of her lap before settling down for a nap.

Zoe stared at the computer screen and the e-mail message it displayed. McBirney had a lot of nerve, accusing Sylvia of theft of township property.

Another question arose. Why hadn't she found this series of messages when she'd spent the better part of Tuesday night searching the e-mail archives? Squinting at the screen, she noticed Sylvia had opened a subfolder titled "Personal" that Zoe had overlooked.

What else had she missed?

She rested her hand on the mouse and ran the curser down the list, pausing on one with simple initials for a title. "A.B."

Scratching Merlin's head with her free hand, Zoe clicked on the new discovery.

The list of the inbox messages that popped up was recent. The most current one was dated only a week ago. Logan had claimed he didn't use the slow, obsolete computer. But someone had.

Zoe stared at the list. She recognized a few of the senders' names including Bethany, Allison's friend. So Allison had made use of the computer even if her brother hadn't.

One of the other names jumped out at her. What the fuck? Zoe scanned down the list. There it was again. And again.

Matt Doaks.

Zoe clicked on one with the subject line "Sexy" and read.

Loved the pix. U R so hot. Can't wait to C U tonite. Love, Matt.

She gagged. Pictures? She clicked on the Sent folder and found a message from Allison to Matt, dated a few hours prior to the one she'd just read. Subject line: Pix. When Zoe opened the attachment, the image swam in front of her eyes, and she blinked to clear her vision and her mind.

Allison sprawled across a bed, naked, in a pose suitable for *Penthouse*.

Zoe slammed her hand down on the mouse to close the file, but mistakenly opened another. In it, Allison, still nude, had company. Matt.

Zoe didn't miss this time. She closed the program and shut down the computer.

Had Logan seen those? And if he had, why the hell was Jerry McBirney dead instead of Matt Doaks?

TWENTY-SEVEN

From the corner of his eye, Pete watched Sylvia worry an already shredded tissue. She said nothing the entire ride to Brunswick, but the occasional tear-laden sigh escaped her.

He made a left from Main Street onto Flannigan, which swept in a wide bend before climbing the hill to the hospital's front entrance. As soon as he came out of the turn, he spotted the pair of Monongahela County police vehicles flanking the driveway and a team of officers blocking it.

Pulling up to them, Pete rolled down his window and showed his badge.

"The hospital is in lockdown," the senior officer told him. "A teenaged suspect in a homicide may be on the premises, and his sister is missing."

Sylvia broke into loud sobs.

"I know." Pete gave the officer a hard scowl. "I have their grandmother with me. Where's Detective Baronick?"

The officer asked him to stay put and turned away to muffle his conversation over his radio. A moment later, he turned back and directed Pete to a side entrance before ordering the other cops to let him through.

County police vehicles, Brunswick city police, and the Pennsylvania State Police had surrounded the hospital. Officers stood at each door. Flashing red and blue strobes reflected off the building's marble and glass façade.

"You'd think they had Jack the Ripper cornered here," Sylvia muttered.

Pete started to tell her the police presence was simply an effort to locate two missing kids. But he knew better than to bullshit Sylvia.

He spotted Baronick standing on the sidewalk, talking on a cell phone and pulled into a spot marked for doctors only.

"Stay here until I find out where Rose is," he said.

"You just want to find out what's going on without me being around to hear."

"A little of that, too. Yeah."

But she obeyed, crossing her arms in front of her chest.

He climbed out of the car, surprised by the relative warmth of the air. A steady *drip drip* of melting ice and snow from the roof punctuated the rumble of idling engines, the static of radio transmissions, and the murmur of conversation. Pete caught Baronick's eye as he approached, and the detective held up one finger while he finished his phone call.

"I didn't expect to see you here, Chief." Baronick tucked his phone into a pocket. "And by that I mean you *shouldn't* be here."

"The kids' mother called Sylvia. I was with her and offered to drive. What's going on?"

Baronick eyed him askance. "No sign of either of them. We've towed the car to the garage to finish processing it. For all we know, the boy never set foot inside the hospital. His sister disappeared from an exam room while the mother stepped outside for a minute. We've locked the place down, but so far there's no sign of her."

"Where are you keeping Rose?"

"One of the family waiting rooms. But not so fast. It's your turn. Any chance the grandmother knows anything? Maybe one of the kids called her?"

Pete thought about the old e-mails on the computer. He really didn't care to share that bombshell with Baronick just yet. "She doesn't know anything about the whereabouts of either of the kids." That much was the truth.

"You're sure?"

"I'd stake my career on it."

"Have you managed to come up with anything else?"

Pete considered his options. "It's too soon to tell."

"Come on, Pete. You know the deal. You're suspended. I agreed to look the other way when you snoop around, but you have to keep me in the loop."

"I will. Just give me a chance to ask a few questions. I don't want to send you off on a wild goose chase."

Pete watched Baronick's face. Was he buying it?

"I want to hear from you by tomorrow morning," the detective said.

"Deal."

"And then I want everything you have. Wild goose chase or not. Got it?"

"Got it. Now let me get Sylvia in to see her daughter-in-law."

Pete waved Sylvia over to the door while Baronick hailed one of the county patrol officers to usher them inside.

The police presence was less noticeable once they entered the hospital. "Did you find out anything?" Sylvia whispered as they followed their escort.

"They haven't seen either Logan or Allison. That's it."

"Maybe Logan didn't have the car. Maybe someone else took it." A fleeting look of hope crossed her face, but faded to concern. Pete knew she'd followed that thought to a conclusion he'd already considered—one that placed Logan in the position of victim rather than suspect.

They both remained silent until the young officer directed them toward a door with a simple, "In there."

Pete nodded to him and opened the door for Sylvia.

The small windowless room held two faded sofas, a pair of well-worn upholstered recliners, and a round table surrounded by stained plastic and chrome chairs. A niche in one corner housed a coffee pot and baskets containing packets of sweetener, stirring sticks and creamers. Rose sat slumped on one of the sofas, her mother next to her. Two plainclothes officers occupied the recliners. One of them stood when Pete and Sylvia entered.

Sylvia bustled to Rose's side, but she didn't look up.

"Have you heard anything?" Bert asked.

"No. Sorry," Pete replied.

Sylvia sank into the sofa and rubbed Rose's back. "You poor child."

Rose sat up, and Pete tried to remember the last time he'd seen such grief on a person's face. She opened her mouth to speak, but broke into a wail instead. Bert and Sylvia cradled her from each side, and she folded forward over the blue jacket in her lap.

Pete raised an eyebrow at the cops, both of whom had returned to sitting. They gave a simultaneous minute headshake. Still nothing to report.

"Where could she have gone?" Bert said. "She left her coat. It's cold out. She couldn't have left the building."

"Was she in a hospital gown?" Pete said.

"No. She hadn't changed into it yet."

Rose gave a shuddering sob and sat up again, weaving as though she might tip in any direction at any moment. "My babies," she whimpered. She hugged the high school jacket to her, then held it up by the shoulders, laid it on her lap, and smoothed it before folding it with expert precision.

Something about the coat caught Pete's attention. "May I see that?" he said, keeping his voice soft.

Sniffling, Rose held the bundle out to him.

He carried the jacket to the table and unfolded it, spreading it out. The blue and white Phillipsburg Blue Demons jacket matched the ones worn by Allison's brother and father with a few minor differences. It lacked the blood of Logan's coat and the shredding of Ted's. However, just above the waistband on the back, was a tiny hole the size of a nail head.

"What is it?" Sylvia said.

Pete's mouth went dry. "You say this is Allison's jacket?"

"Yeah. Why?" Bert said.

He looked at the three women. Two worried grandmothers and a distraught mom. He looked at the coat and the hole. Evidence. "There's a chance the detectives could use this coat to help find her." He hated lying.

"You mean like have one of those search dogs get her smell from it?" A ray of hope sprung into Bert's eyes.

That sounded reasonable. "Something like that."

A cell phone rang, and Sylvia rummaged in her purse.

"But it's all I have of my baby," Rose whimpered.

Bert patted her knee. "Let him take it, sweetheart. If it'll help them find her..."

Sylvia found her phone and answered it.

Rose frowned, sniffed, and nodded. "Okay. If it'll help. Take it."

Pete bundled the jacket under his arm and headed for the door.

"Pete, wait." Sylvia's voice sounded strangled.

He turned around to see her holding her phone out to him. Her eyes were unblinking. He tried to decipher the expression on her face. Excitement? Maybe. Terror? Possibly.

"It's for you," she said.

He crossed the room and took the phone from her, but she offered no clue, verbal or physical as to the caller's ID.

"Hello?" he said.

"Chief Adams," came a vaguely familiar voice on the other end. "This is Logan. I need to see you. I want to turn myself in, but only to you."

The photographs of Allison and Matt were burned into Zoe's brain. She closed her eyes, and they became more vivid. She paced the floor of the old farmhouse, trying to think straight.

She wanted to pummel Matt. What the hell was wrong with that idiot? Allison was a kid. Fifteen years old. Had he gone insane? And what was she going to do about it? Call Pete? No. He was busy with Sylvia and Rose.

Zoe stopped in the middle of her living room and thought of Matt's visit. Only yesterday, he'd stood in this very spot and suggested they could be so good together. Was that before or after he'd asked about Rose and the kids?

Bastard.

Zoe jammed her feet into her boots and snatched her coat from the hook on her way out the door.

The sun was sinking low on the horizon. The unseasonably mild temperatures had melted away much of last night's snow, leaving patches of brown grass and mud peeking through. Zoe fought the slick footing up the slope to her truck and climbed in.

The roads were clear and dry except for patches of water running across. She pressed hard on the accelerator, ignoring the posted speed limit along Route 15. By the time she pulled up in front of Matt Doaks' house, the dusk-to-dawn lights were blinking on.

Zoe slid down from the driver's seat and shivered. The

temperature had already taken a tumble.

Matt's car was gone, and the windows of the small, gray walkup were dark. It had been years since she'd stood in this spot, gazing at the house they'd once shared. An outside spotlight shone on the concrete sidewalk. Wilting mounds of snow edged it. A trio of shrubs acted as sentinels at the base of the wooden steps leading up to a deck on the front of the house.

Zoe drew a breath. The cold air felt crisp and refreshing compared to the flames licking her brain. She put a hand on the railing and climbed the steps. At the front door, she hesitated and then knocked. Nothing happened. No lights came on. No sound of footsteps. She knocked again. As she watched and listened, a thought sprouted and grew.

How long had Allison been missing? Was there any chance she might have come here? Small details such as how she would have gotten to Matt's house hid behind the shadow of Zoe's sudden intense notion that the girl might be hiding inside.

Zoe ran her fingers along the top of the doorframe. Did Matt still keep a spare key there? He'd been the one who started her hiding a key in that spot. She touched cold metal. At least some things didn't change. She jammed the key into the lock and let herself in.

The house smelled remarkably clean for a bachelor pad. The only illumination came from the streetlight outside. She made out the forms of a sofa, coffee table, and chairs, but waited for her eyes to get used to the dark. "Allison," she called.

No reply.

"Matt?"

The swish of tires on pavement broke the silence. Was Matt coming home? Zoe watched at the door, but the approaching car failed to slow and passed by on the road below.

Within a few moments of standing in the silent living room, Zoe became accustomed to the low light. Details of the room grew more evident. A television sat in one corner. A laptop occupied a desk against the back wall.

The laptop that held Allison's correspondence and photos?

Zoe resisted the urge to smash it. "Hello?" she called. "Is anyone home?"

She wandered toward the kitchen in the back of the house. The cabinets and countertops looked unchanged, but the table and chairs were different. Her hand went to the light switch she knew was on the wall, and she flipped it, flooding the room with light.

While the house smelled clean, the kitchen didn't appear to have been on the maid's list. The soles of Zoe's boots stuck to the greasy floor and the counter felt tacky. Wincing, she wiped her fingers on her coat. She turned and inspected the room, unsure of what she was looking for. Evidence that Allison had been there? Or maybe Logan?

Almost a dozen pill bottles perched like soldiers on the kitchen table. Zoe picked one up and read the label. Vicodin. The prescription was in Matt's name. Probably for the broken leg. But, no. It was dated weeks earlier. She checked a second one. Oxycontin. Dated two weeks ago and almost empty. The others were for more of the same or similar painkillers. All in Matt's name, all prescriptions written from several different doctors and filled at a half a dozen different pharmacies.

Damn Matt. She'd believed he'd long ago kicked the addiction that began with that blown knee in the high school championship game. The one that had destroyed his basketball career and put an end to his athletic scholarship. When had he started the pain meds again? Or had he ever really been clean?

Then she spotted it. Amidst the prescription bottles on the kitchen table lay a familiar key ring advertising Figley's Feed Store and a brass house key. Her key. She grabbed it, clutching it hard as though it might try to escape. What the hell?

Pieces fell into place in Zoe's mind. Matt was behind the computer theft. He knew those photos were on it. The break in at her house? It wasn't McBirney at all. It was Matt. He knew she kept a spare key on the doorframe and took it. When she interrupted him, he fled and came back later. But Mrs. Kroll interrupted him.

That perverted bastard.

She stared at the key. And the drugs. Damn. It was all evidence. Or would have been if she hadn't touched everything. Well, she wasn't going to leave her key here for him to try again. Not when she hadn't changed the locks yet. She stuffed it in her jeans pocket.

Should she search the rest of the house? No. Better to get the hell out of there before Matt returned. There had been many times in her life when she'd wanted to kill him, but never as strongly as right now.

She flipped off the light switch and crossed to the front door. Unlike Matt, she remembered to return his key to its rightful spot above the door.

Stars blinked in the clear sky above, promising a bitter cold night. Already, ice had skimmed over those damp spots. Zoe clutched the railing and picked her way down the steps to avoid a quick ski run without the skis. At the bottom, she fumbled in her pocket for the truck key.

Something shiny in the snow next to the sidewalk caught her eye. The overhead spotlight reflected off a chunk of glistening ice between the shrubs. Or was it? Zoe squatted down for a closer look. Ice? Or a fragment of glass?

No. Not a fragment, but a lens. An eyeglass lens.

A bass drum could not have made as much noise as the pounding of her heart. She reached for the lens. But stopped. She'd already contaminated the evidence in the kitchen. Not again.

Shaking fingers located her cell phone. Somehow, she steadied them enough to punch in Pete's number.

Pete found Baronick where he'd left him in front of the hospital. He demanded and received a large evidence bag into which he stuffed the folded up coat. As he marked the tag, he explained to the detective what it was.

"I'll have Grace take a look at it," Baronick said. "Good work."

Pete glared at him over his reading glasses.

"Where are you headed now?" Baronick said.

Pete double-checked the information he'd written. "Back to Vance Township." No sense mentioning the detour he intended to take along the way. He handed the bag and the pen to Baronick, who added his signature to the chain of evidence.

"I'll let you know when we locate the Bassi kids," the detective called after Pete, who waved an acknowledgment.

He didn't know where the girl was, but Logan was waiting for him at a pizza joint a half-dozen blocks away.

Those six blocks happened to be through one of the worst

neighborhoods Brunswick had to offer. Once-grand Victorian houses, now reduced to derelict fire hazards with broken windows and boarded-up doors, lined the streets along with abandoned storefronts and weedy vacant lots. Sylvia would have had a stroke if she'd known her grandson had trod these sidewalks. But Russo's Pizza sat on a corner of Main Street where the transition from slum to university campus began. Logan blended in with the college kids hanging out on a Saturday evening.

Pete slid into the booth where Logan nursed a cola and a slab of cold pizza. The kid's eyes were rimmed in red and underlined with dark circles. His knuckles were bruised and swollen.

"You look like hell," Pete told him.

Logan made a feeble effort at a smile, but failed. "Thanks for coming."

"Of course I'd come. Where have you been these last two nights?"

"I spent one night in the high school. I slipped in during a JV basketball game and hid in one of the bathrooms until everyone was gone. Then I drove here. But I kept seeing cops and security guards everywhere I went. I ended up at the hospital. Pretended I was visiting some sick dude. Swiped some food off a tray that someone didn't want. Slept in the trauma unit's waiting room with a bunch of other people. No one says anything when they think you've got family being treated."

Pete had to admit, it was pretty damned ingenious. Better than the mall, which cleared out at closing time. "Your sister was at the hospital earlier, and now she's missing. What do you know about that?"

Logan took a long swig from his cola. "I saw her."

"Where is she now?"

He shrugged. "I don't know. Honest. I don't. She got really pissed at me and took off."

"Why is she pissed at you?"

The boy squirmed in his seat. "I told her I wanted to turn myself in. She didn't want me to."

A waitress interrupted them and asked if Pete wanted anything. From the frown on her face, he gathered Logan's cola and cold pizza weren't adequate rental for the space they occupied. He ordered coffee and a whole pepperoni pizza to go.

After she left, Pete leaned forward. "You mentioned turning

yourself in on the phone. What exactly is it you're turning yourself in for, son?"

Logan blinked and a stream of tears rolled down his cheeks. He swiped them away with the sleeve of his shirt and gingerly rubbed his inflamed knuckles. "It was me. I killed Mr. McBirney."

TWENTY-EIGHT

Pete leaned back in the red vinyl bench seat and watched the kid fight to blink away tears. Some confessions came hard. Some came easy. Some, like this, came too easy. But as he watched Logan Bassi pull himself together, Pete's gut told him the boy wasn't lying.

Damn it.

"You know I have to take you in," he said.

Logan gave a quick nod that was punctuated by Pete's cell phone ringing.

He expected to see Sylvia's name on the caller ID, but the screen displayed ZOE instead.

"I can't talk right now," he said by way of a greeting.

"I found something." Zoe sounded breathless, panicked.

"What?"

"An eyeglass lens. I think it's Ted's." The phone beeped and Zoe swore under her breath. "My battery's almost dead."

"Where are you?"

"At Matt Doaks' house. Outside. A bunch of prescription painkillers and my missing house key was on his kitchen table."

Her words tumbled into and over each other in his head. "Matt Doaks?"

Logan slammed both palms down on the table. "Who is that?" he demanded.

"Is that Logan?" Zoe said.

"Both of you, shut up," Pete snapped. "Yes, it's Logan."

While Zoe was thanking God in Pete's ear, Logan appeared on the verge of climbing over the table. "Who is that?" he repeated.

"It's Zoe."

"Did she find the pictures on the computer?" Logan said.

"Yes," Zoe shouted.

What the hell was this? A conference call?

Her phone beeped again.

"What pictures?" Pete said.

Logan opened his mouth to answer, but Pete held up a finger to silence him.

"Anything you say can and will be used against you in a court of law, so shut up." The kid was a minor. And Sylvia's grandson. Pete wasn't about to step over—or even anywhere near—the line on this one. "Zoe? *What pictures?*"

She proceeded to tell him about the e-mails and the attached photos she'd stumbled across after he'd left with Sylvia. That son-of-a-bitch Doaks.

"So I came over here to—I'm not sure exactly what. Beat the crap out of him, I suppose. But he's not here. I let myself in—"

"You what?" Pete said. "Zoe."

The waitress appeared and set a cup of coffee in front of Pete.

"I used to live here. I know I shouldn't have, but it didn't feel like breaking in. I knew he hid a key the same way I do."

"That goes both ways. He knew where to find yours, too."

"Right. Only I put his key back where I found it. He kept mine. Anyhow, when I was leaving, I spotted something shiny in the snow next to the sidewalk at the base of his steps. It's an eyeglass lens. I haven't touched it."

"And you say Doaks isn't there?"

"Not yet."

"Okay. I'll get someone over there right now. You get out of there before Doaks shows up."

"I'll wait until the cops get here," she said.

Damn Zoe. "Don't argue with me."

"If I spotted this thing, Matt might, too—" The phone beeped again, followed by silence.

"Zoe," Pete shouted into the phone. "Zoe?" He let out a growl. Who the hell was on duty? Saturday. That would be Nate Williamson, one of the part-timers. He punched in the number.

"She found the pictures?" Logan asked.

Pete glared at him without answering. When Nate picked up, he ordered him to Doaks' house. "Run every red light, break every speed limit, but get there *now*," he told the officer.

Pete picked up the cup of coffee and took a long sip. What he really needed was bourbon, but caffeine would have to do. Many questions plagued him at the moment, but one nagged at him more than the rest. "I have to ask you. These pictures were of your sister and Doaks, right?"

Logan lowered his head. "Yeah."

"So why did you kill McBirney?"

He shifted in his seat and chewed his lip. "Because he was raping my sister."

Zoe plugged the cell phone charger into her truck while she sat shivering and waiting for the cops. She prayed that Matt wouldn't show up before they did. What would she do then? Could she put on a sufficient act to keep him distracted? Pretend she was flirting with him? The idea nauseated her. When the Vance Township police cruiser rolled up next to her, she released the breath she'd been holding for what felt like hours.

A gust of wind caught her full in the face as she stepped out of the Chevy. She pulled up her hood, holding it tight to her ears. Officer Nate Williamson, who was big enough to have played linebacker for the pros in his younger days, approached her.

"Whatcha got?" he asked.

Zoe led him to the base of the stairs and pointed to the lens poking out of the dirty snow and ice.

Williamson squatted and frowned at it. "Did you touch it?"

"No."

"You sure?"

"Very sure." She considered reminding him that she was a deputy coroner and knew about crime scene security. Then she remembered picking up the pill bottles and pocketing her key from Matt's kitchen table and decided to simply confirm that she hadn't tampered with the evidence.

Williamson retrieved a camera from the cruiser and started snapping photos. Within minutes, a county car rolled in, and two detectives in long black coats climbed out. One of them conferred with Nate while the other drew Zoe aside to ask her questions. Her name, her address, her phone numbers. Why was she here? Where all had she gone inside the house? What had she touched?

She reluctantly admitted to entering the house, emphasizing that she used to live there. Instead of dreading Matt's return, she now prayed for it. What if something had happened to him? There she was, having been in his house with intent to…What exactly?

It didn't matter. If anything happened to Matt, she would definitely be at the top of the suspect list.

Again.

While the county detective didn't appear pleased with much she had to say, he didn't arrest her. Instead, he told her to go home, and he'd contact her later.

Zoe's fears about the road surface were alleviated when she eased up behind a yellow PennDOT truck. She hung back, watching the de-icing material scatter from the back of the vehicle and coat those wet spots that had turned treacherous. A mile shy of home, the salt truck turned onto a side street, leaving Zoe to fend for herself the rest of the way.

Mr. Kroll had salted the farm lane, too, and Zoe's pickup climbed the hill with minimal effort. She didn't let off the gas when she reached the house. Instead, she chugged to the top of the hill and then coasted toward the barn. She needed to check the animals and welcomed the momentary distraction.

Light shone from the stall windows and seeped out from around the big sliding doors at the end of the barn. Odd. All of the boarders knew to turn off the lights on their way out. There were no cars or trucks parked in front. Apparently, someone had left before dark and not realized the lights were still on.

Pete leaned back in the booth, stuffing down his rage as he listened to Logan's story and jotted notes.

"I went there to confront Doaks about what he'd done to my sister, but when I got there I found them in the bedroom." Logan shuddered. "Allison was—was naked—and McBirney was on top of her with his fist drawn back." Logan clenched his own fist. "McBirney had gouges in his back. Holes. He was bleeding real bad. There was blood everywhere. And Allison was holding a screwdriver." His voice cracked.

Pete reached across the table to grip the boy's arm for a moment. "You're doing fine, son. Take your time."

Logan nodded. Ran a trembling hand through his hair. "I tackled McBirney. Shoved him off my sister. We crashed into the wall and I—I started beating on him."

He paused, breathing hard. Reliving the experience, Pete guessed.

"Next thing I know, Allison pulled me off him. She was crying and—and I didn't know what to do."

The boy fell silent. Pete gave him a minute to regroup before gently prodding. "What *did* you do?"

Logan's eyes grew dark. "I noticed Doaks standing there, and I tried to cover up my sister. I was gonna pound him like I'd done with McBirney, but Allison started saying how Doaks had saved her. And that she loved him." Logan grimaced as if the words tasted foul in his mouth. "Then Doaks started going on about how he knew I wanted to talk to him about Allison, but we had to take care of this situation first." Logan made air-quotes around *situation*. "He said we couldn't let anyone find out Allison killed McBirney, and I'd helped finish him off. So he gave me the screwdriver to get rid of, and he was gonna see that Allison got cleaned up, and then he was gonna get rid of the body. It was stupid. I never should have left her there with him. But he kind of made sense at the time, you know? We had to protect Allison. No one could know. And—and..." The boy put his head down on the table, his shoulders quaking with silent sobs.

Pete rubbed his eyes hard. Too bad he couldn't blot out the mental picture of what the kid had gone through. Both kids. Sylvia's grandchildren. How the hell was he ever going to make this all right?

Zoe nosed her truck up to the big door and cut the engine. The chill of the night air stung her face as soon as she stepped out of the Chevy. She bustled to the smaller door and let herself through.

Someone had brought the horses in and a few nickered at her entrance. The barn smelled of fresh hay and warm horseflesh. The animals hadn't been in their stalls for long—no earthy aroma of manure tickled her nose.

Zoe crossed to the message board on the feed room wall. Whoever brought the horses in should have noted whether they'd grained them or just fed hay, as well as any special attention anyone might need. But the most recent note was from the morning. Not only had one of her boarders left the lights on, they'd neglected this duty, too.

She moved to Windstar's stall and looked in at him. The water bucket was full. He had plenty of hay. But his feed pan was empty.

"So have you had your supper yet or not?"

He gazed at her with his soft brown eyes, wisps of hay sticking from between his lips.

"You'd lie to me anyway, and say you hadn't just to get more." Zoe reached in and stroked his face.

"I fed him."

Zoe wheeled to find Allison standing in the doorway to the feed room. An oversized black bomber jacket draped from her narrow shoulders. The sleeves swallowed up her arms, hanging well below her fingertips. Her skin appeared gray and her eyes dull and sunken in. With her stringy black hair framing an expressionless face, the teen looked like an extra in a zombie movie.

Zoe grabbed the teenager's shoulders. "How did you get here? Are you okay?"

Allison's gaze didn't meet Zoe's eye. "I hitchhiked. Like Logan. But don't be mad. I got everyone in and fed them. All by myself." Her voice was little more than a whisper. "Water. Hay. And grain. I followed the chart about who gets what. Did I do okay, Aunt Zoe?"

"You did great, sweetie." Zoe bent down, trying to place her face in Allison's line of vision. But the girl still stared blankly downward.

"Good. I wanted to get one thing right before..."

Zoe caught the girl's face between her gloved hands and leaned in until their noses almost touched. "Allison. Are you all right? Allison?"

Something hit the ground with a soft thud. The teen swayed and crumpled into Zoe.

"Allison?" Zoe wrapped her arms around the girl and was thrown off balance. Zoe managed to break the girl's fall as they tumbled to the dirt. "Allison!"

"I've screwed up everything." The girl's voice was so weak Zoe doubted she'd have heard her if she hadn't been cradling her in her arms. "Tell Mom I'm so sorry."

"Allison, what's wrong with you?" Kneeling in the dirt, Zoe repositioned the girl's left arm that had twisted awkwardly in the collapse. That was when Zoe noticed a dark splotch on her brown gloves. She tugged one off and touched it with her cold, bare finger. The finger came away red and sticky.

Zoe ripped her other glove off and began a frantic search of Allison's limp body. Her scalp and neck were fine. Zoe unzipped the too-big jacket. When she grabbed the cuff of the sleeve to pull it off, the fabric was warm and sickly wet to the touch. Skinning the coat from Allison's arm revealed ugly red gouges across a dainty wrist.

Zoe spotted the knife—one usually kept in the tack room for cutting open bales of hay or bags of feed—lying on the ground next to her. That's what she'd heard hit the ground before Allison toppled.

"My God. What the hell have you done?" Zoe whispered between chattering teeth. She yanked the second sleeve off to find more gashes, deep enough to reveal tendons. Blood streamed from both of Allison's wrists, forming puddles in the dirt.

The girl met Zoe's gaze. Her face contorted. "I'm sorry." Her frail voice broke in a sob. "It's all my fault." She squeezed her eyes shut, and tears trickled down her cheeks. "Daddy. I'm so sorry. It's my fault he's dead." Her voice deteriorated into disjointed mumbling. "Awful...Logan...stabbed...McBirney..."

The girl was making no sense. Zoe quelled her desire to ask questions and instead, shushed her. She needed to get help and to stop the bleeding. "You lie still," she told Allison as she edged her knees out from under the girl's head and lowered her to the ground. "I'll be right back."

Zoe leapt to her feet and dug in her pocket for her cell phone. Nothing. She checked the other pocket and came up empty. Crap. It was in her truck on charge. She sprinted to the phone by the entrance and snatched the receiver from the hook. The familiar hum of a dial tone was noticeably absent. The lines were still down. One more thing to thank Matt Doaks for.

The call to 9-1-1 would have to wait.

She darted into the feed room. From a metal cabinet in the corner, she gathered a box of sterile gauze pads, a roll of cotton and two rolls of Vet Wrap, tossing everything into an empty bucket. On her way back to Allison, she grabbed a wool horse blanket and a pair of splint boots.

Dropping to her knees beside the girl, Zoe set the bucket to the side and covered Allison with the wool blanket, leaving her lower arms exposed. She examined both wrists. The slash on the left one looked deeper, so she started with it.

"Allison? Try to stay awake, okay?" Zoe ripped open several packets of gauze four-by-fours and slapped them on the gouged flesh, then covered them with a layer of cotton. "Talk to me. You said Logan stabbed McBirney?"

Allison's eyes opened, rolled back, then focused. "No. Not Logan. Me. I stabbed him. And Matt."

"You stabbed Matt?" Pressing hard with one hand to quell the bleeding, Zoe grabbed a Vet Wrap with the other, tearing into the packaging with her teeth.

"No." Allison closed her eyes. Took a breath. "Matt stabbed him. Then I stabbed him. I killed him."

Zoe anchored an end of the self-sticking bandage with her thumb and began winding it around Allison's wrist and forearm the same way her mind struggled to wind around the idea of what these grown men had done to Rose's kids. As her hands did the work, her mind clicked back to Doc's autopsy report on McBirney.

Only the one wound penetrated deep enough to be fatal—the one that punctured the lung. The other three attempts hit the scapula and exhibited more tearing, but caused no significant damage.

Would Allison have the strength to stab McBirney with enough force to kill him? Zoe contemplated the girl's thin arm as she bandaged it and decided not likely. But Matt?

Yeah.

Zoe pressed the end of the Vet Wrap in place. A dark patch of blood had already appeared through the bandaging. She picked up the stiff leather split boot and buckled it over the dressing. Ordinarily used to protect and stabilize a young horse's fragile leg bones, the brace would also immobilize Allison's wrist and add more pressure to the wound.

Zoe stepped over her to work on her right arm. "Allison?"

The girl gazed unfocused into the distance.

"Why did you do this to yourself?"

Her lower lip quivered. "Matt. I thought he loved me. He *said* he loved me."

Zoe fought back a primal scream. Those pictures on the computer. Those e-mails. And years ago, the image of walking into her bedroom—hers and Matt's—to find him with that bimbo from the Tastee Freez. A collage of perversion danced across her brain.

"I knew if I said anything to anyone, he'd get in trouble. I loved him, so I never said a word." Allison's sob-ravaged voice hiccupped. "He didn't mean to kill Daddy. It was an accident. Daddy came to drag me away from him. Said Matt would go to prison. They fought. Matt tackled him and they both fell down the steps. It was—it was like Matt was riding a sled. And the sled was Daddy." She made a sound like a laugh. Or was it a cry?

Zoe's hands trembled as she finished buckling the splint boot over the second bandage. The visual Allison painted sickened her. She longed to scoop this child up into her arms.

Allison drew a watery breath around her tears. "And now he wants to break up with me. He didn't say so yet, but I can tell. He's tired of me." She sniffed. "I love him so much. I told him I'd kill myself if he left me and he said 'go ahead.' He said that would solve all his problems."

Zoe shushed her and leaned over to give her a hug without disturbing her bandaging job. "It's okay now," she whispered. But she knew she needed to get EMS there or it most definitely was *not* going to be okay. "Allison, where's your cell phone? Is it in your coat?" Zoe didn't wait for an answer. She grabbed the bloodied jacket and rammed her hand into one pocket. Nothing. She detected something in the second one before she reached inside. But what she dug out of it wasn't a phone. It was a bottle of pills. A match to those she'd found at Matt's place. And it was empty.

"Allison? Did you take these? Allison?"

A faraway smile played on the girl's lips. "Matt's my candy man."

Zoe swore. It wasn't just Matt's charm and good looks that bound the girl to him. He was supplying her with prescription painkillers. Her flu wasn't the flu. He'd cut her off, and she'd been in withdrawal. Zoe stared at the empty bottle as one question screamed inside her brain. Was Allison overdosing in addition to bleeding out?

"Listen, sweetie, I'm going to go out to my truck for a second to get my phone. Then I'm going to call for help. I'm not going to let you die."

"I don't wanna die," Allison wailed.

"I know." Zoe rearranged the wool horse blanket so that it covered Allison's arms and tucked it around the girl's face and ears, too. "You stay still, okay? I'll be right back."

"Okay."

Zoe jogged to the door and let herself out into the frigid cold night. She crossed her arms, tucking her bare hands under them until she reached the Chevy. The door handle was so cold it stung her fingers to touch it. She jumped up onto the seat and searched the dash for her phone. It wasn't where she usually put it. Must have fallen off. Her fingers located the charger plug inserted into the cigarette lighter, and she reeled it in. The coiled cord bounced back at her without the weight of the cell phone on the end.

What the hell?

She leaned down to search the floor, feeling under the seat in the dark.

"Looking for this?"

Zoe banged her head on the steering wheel as she bolted upright. Standing next to her truck in the light cast by the dusk-to-dawn lamp, holding her phone in his hand, was Matt Doaks.

TWENTY-NINE

Pete placed a call to Baronick and arranged to meet him at the Monongahela County Police Headquarters. The detective was already waiting when Pete led Logan into the building.

"Didn't waste any time getting here, did you, Wayne?" Pete said.

"Hey, you tell me you're bringing in a fugitive, and I drop everything to accommodate you." Baronick flashed a smile that made Pete wonder how much he'd spent on those veneers.

Beside him, Logan cringed.

"I need to talk to you a minute," Pete told the detective.

"Sure." Baronick waved over two uniformed officers. "Place this young man under arrest, gentlemen. Put him in the interrogation room, and I'll be along shortly."

Logan gave Pete a frightened, helpless look over his shoulder as the two officers ushered him away.

"Okay, Pete. What is it?"

He hadn't told Baronick about Logan's "confession." The kid was underage and hadn't had legal representation. The entire story would be thrown out of court in a heartbeat. "Tread lightly on this one. He's a kid. A good kid. And he's been through hell this week."

"I hear you. But if he killed a man, I can't look the other way."

"I'm not suggesting you do." A headache began to creep up the back of Pete's skull. "Just don't steamroll him. Now, what's going on at Doaks' place?"

"No sign of him yet. My men are still at his house. The eyeglass lens they found might be a match to the one missing from Ted Bassi's frames or it may not. Even if it is, it may not be enough to get a search warrant. I need that hard drive from your girlfriend's computer."

"She's not my girlfriend." If Pete could share Logan's story, they'd have no problem obtaining a warrant. McBirney had been killed in that house. Besides, Pete wanted to see Zoe's computer, too. He'd tried to call her from the HQ parking lot, but got no answer on her cell phone.

"That's not what I've heard." Baronick chuckled. "Anyway, I haven't been able to reach her. I need the photos you told me about to get a warrant for Doaks' house."

Where are you, Zoe? "Wasn't she at Doaks' place when your men got there?"

The toothy grin faded. "Yeah. Those idiots sent her home. But they figured we'd be able to contact her if we needed something."

"Keep trying." Pete didn't add that he would, too. "I have a stop to make first, and if you haven't reached her by then, I'll swing by her place on my way home."

The glass double doors behind them whooshed open, letting in a blast of icy air and an even icier Sylvia Bassi, dragging a beefy, gray-haired man in a suit behind her.

"Where's my grandson?" Sylvia demanded.

"He's waiting in interrogation, Mrs. Bassi," Baronick said. He nodded to the man beside her. "Mr. Imperatore."

"I see you know my attorney." Sylvia clutched her purse against her chest. Pete hoped she didn't decide to use it as a weapon again. "He's also my grandson's attorney."

"I assumed as much," the detective said.

"And I would very much like to speak with my client, Detective Baronick." The attorney gave one of his sleeves a tug.

"Give me a second, and I'll take you back." Baronick drew Pete aside. "I suppose I have you to thank for leaking the kid's arrest to the grandmother," he whispered.

Pete smiled. "I told you not to steamroll him. Sylvia will make sure that you don't."

Baronick squinted at him. "Just let me know if you hear from Zoe Chambers."

"Will do." Pete turned to leave, touching the brim of his ball cap and nodding at Sylvia.

She nodded back.

God help Wayne Baronick.

The half-hour drive to Vance Township from Brunswick offered Pete time to ponder recent events. Logan's confession wasn't the end of it. Pete thought of the old saying about the tip of the iceberg. There was a helluva lot of crap still hiding under the surface.

Starting with Ted Bassi's killer.

Pete wasn't willing to believe he had two totally separate homicides on his hands. If he bought into Logan's story that he and Allison had been responsible for McBirney's death—and the more Pete thought about it, the bigger that *if* became—did he still have a killer running loose? Pete could understand Logan attempting to protect his sister. But no way did that boy have a hand in killing his father.

Allison, however...

Pete shifted in the driver's seat. He hated the idea, but something about it rang true. Allison Bassi had been acting more bizarre than usual since Ted's death. They'd all written it off to grief. Was it something more? There was that blue fiber in McBirney's garage that matched her school jacket. The one with the hole in it.

And, of course, there was Matt Doaks. He'd never liked the guy, but always chalked most of that up to Zoe's past with the bastard.

Jealousy. First he'd suspected McBirney of Bassi's murder, largely because of Marcy. Now, he was doing the same thing with Doaks because of Zoe. Baronick may have been right to take him off this case. Not that he wasn't up to his neck in it anyway.

Where to go first? Pete wanted to talk to both Marcy and Zoe. He dug his cell phone from his coat pocket and tried Zoe's home number only to be greeted with a busy signal. Her cell went directly to voicemail. Damn it, Zoe. Get off the phone. Well, at least she was at home.

He slowed and made a sweeping left turn off Route 15 onto Mays Road. Treacherous glossy black patches dotted the road that was more gravel than blacktop. The afternoon's thaw made the back roads passable, if not entirely safe. At the top of the hill, he swung right onto Cowden Road and followed the ridge all the way to McBirney's farm.

Pete had expected the long winding farm lane to be a mess without McBirney and his tractor around to plow it. Instead, the lane was clear—almost in better shape than the township road he'd driven in on.

Lights brightened the farmhouse's kitchen windows. Pete parked next to the back stoop and cut the ignition. He contemplated his next action, reminding himself that he was under suspension. Picking up his cell phone he punched in Nate Williamson's number.

"Chief?" Williamson said when he answered.

"What's your twenty?" Pete said.

"I'm still hanging out at Matt Doaks' house."

"Anything new there?"

"No, sir. The county crime scene unit has processed outside. Now we're waiting around for Doaks to come home. Maybe he'll let us in without a warrant." From the tone of Williamson's voice, he wasn't optimistic of that happening in this lifetime.

"Are you available, or do the county guys want you to stay put?"

"Uh, no. I'm just hanging out. What do you need, Chief?"

Pete smiled. He knew what Williamson was doing. Hoping to be present for some excitement on a long boring night. Arresting a widow probably wasn't in the same category as waiting for a sexual perv to put in an appearance. "Head over to Jerry McBirney's farm. I may have some work for you to do."

"Copy, Chief. On my way."

Pete tucked the phone back into his pocket and stepped out of his car. The porch light flipped on. Good thing he hadn't been counting on the element of surprise. Marcy opened the door as he raised his fist to knock.

"Pete," she said. "I wondered who was pulling in so late. I'm a little jumpy now that I'm out here all by myself."

"You should get a dog." Or maybe not. If she was in jail, her protection would be handled by the state.

Marcy escorted him into the kitchen. "Coffee? Or do I need to ask?" She smiled.

"Do you have any made?"

"There's a cup or two left in the pot. It's cold, but I can nuke it."

"Thanks."

While she bustled around the kitchen, pulling a mug from the cabinet, filling it from a large pot, and placing it in the microwave, Pete took a seat at the table.

"What brings you out here tonight?" Marcy asked. "If you're here to ask me about Jerry's death, I'm afraid you'll need to contact my attorney."

"No. I need to ask you some questions, but not about your husband's murder."

The microwave beeped, and Marcy removed the steaming mug, placing it in front of Pete. Then she settled into the chair across from him and folded her hands on the table. He studied her face. The swelling had shifted downward, making her jaw line puffy, and the bruising had turned more yellowish green than black and blue.

"Your face looks better."

Her good eye twitched, but she said nothing.

He sipped his coffee. "At what point in our marriage did you start sleeping with McBirney?"

She blanched. "What?"

It was Pete's turn to say nothing. Instead, he watched her expressions run the gamut.

"Why would you want to know that?" she said.

He shrugged, wanting to appear nonchalant. Don't accuse her too early. Make this seem like a normal conversation. "Curious. With everything that's happened in the last week, lots of old memories have surfaced. I quit my job with the Pittsburgh Bureau of Police to move here because you wanted a quieter life." He managed a short laugh.

Marcy leaned back in her chair, resting her hands in her lap. "You think we'd have ended up differently if we'd stayed in the city?"

It was a question Pete had considered innumerable times over the years. "Maybe. What do *you* think?"

She pressed her lips together and stared over his shoulder a moment before letting her gaze come back to his. "I never liked the city. You knew that. I wanted space and fresh air to raise kids—" Her voice broke.

He resisted the urge to reach across the table to her. Their shared memory of two miscarriages wasn't the direction he'd intended this discussion to take. Get back on track. "So you weren't happy in Pittsburgh. You obviously weren't happy here either. Not with me."

Marcy squirmed in the chair. "Why are we talking about this now?"

"Because we were never able to talk about it before."

She took a noticeably deep breath and exhaled. "Okay. I don't think it was so much that I was unhappy with you. After we lost the two babies, I wasn't happy with myself. When we didn't get pregnant again,

I thought getting that horse would fill a void. I'd always wanted a horse. Ever since I was a little girl. It was just happenstance that I stumbled across Jerry's ad for stall space in the paper. It wasn't like I planned to find a kindred spirit when I decided to board Comanche here."

Pete clenched his fists. "Kindred spirit? At least you aren't calling McBirney your soul mate."

"I thought he was. At first. Jerry and I both loved long rides in the woods. You were too busy with work to spend time at the barn. Or with me anywhere for that matter."

"So that's when you started sleeping with him?"

Marcy stood and crossed to the sink, where she grabbed a towel and began drying the few dishes parked in the drainer. "Not right away. But, yeah, over time."

"Were you sleeping with him when he went through his financial problems?"

A glass clattered into the sink and shattered. She gripped the edge of the counter until her knuckles turned white.

Pete stood and moved next to her, where he could see her face and the tortured series of expressions that danced across it. "Or did the affair start after he managed to bail himself out?"

She stiffened, her jaw set. "If you're insinuating that I only agreed to sleep with Jerry after he came into some cash—"

Her feigned indignity disrupted his attempt at indifference. "No, not at all. I'm just wondering whether you started fucking Jerry McBirney before or after you stole the township's receipts to fund his bad financial choices."

Marcy spun to face him. Even her bad eye had widened, showing white all around. "How did you—"

Pete's cell phone rang. Hoping this was finally Zoe returning his calls, he dug the phone from his pocket. The number on the screen wasn't Zoe's, though.

"It may be nothing, but I thought you'd like to know," said the gravelly voiced lab tech, when he answered.

"What've you got, Grace?"

"It's still too soon to have DNA on the hairs recovered in the vehicles, but I've looked at them under the microscope."

"And?"

"There were several long dark hairs found in Ted Bassi's pickup that were dyed."

Goth girl Allison. No big surprise there. "That's it?"

"Would I be calling you if that were all?" Grace gave a snort over the phone. "There were also long dark hairs found in the Buick. The ones from the passenger side headrest were from a natural brunette."

That would be Marcy.

"But," Grace continued, "there were also long, dark hairs found in the trunk. Dyed ones. They match the ones in the pickup."

"Thanks, Grace." Pete snapped the phone. What the hell were Allison's hairs doing in Jerry McBirney's trunk? Before he had a chance to make sense of it, his phone rang again. "Yeah, Nate?" he answered.

"I'm at the end of McBirney's lane. What do you want me to do?"

Pete eyed his ex-wife, who was leaning against the kitchen counter, pressing a dish towel to her face. He realized this was the first time in all the years he'd known Marcy that her tears hadn't cut into his heart. Instead, his gut told him trouble lurked elsewhere. "Have you had any word from county about Doaks or Zoe?"

"Nothing on either of them. You think something's happened to Zoe?"

"I hope not. Come on down to the house. I need you to take Mrs. McBirney in for questioning."

Marcy staggered to a chair and dropped into it, weeping into the towel she held to her mouth.

Pete snapped the phone closed.

"How did you find out after all these years?" Marcy whispered.

"That computer that your husband made such a fuss over. Your e-mail exchanges are still on it."

She swore and put her head down on the table.

Pete crossed to the door and watched the headlights from the township's second cruiser sweep down the lane toward the house.

"What's going on with Matt and Zoe?" Marcy said.

He turned to find her sitting up, wringing the towel in her hands, a look of total defeat on her battered face. "Huh?"

"I heard you on the phone asking about them. Has something happened?"

"I don't know. The county police have some questions to ask Matt."

"What kind of questions?"

What the hell difference did it make to Marcy? "I think you have enough problems of your own to deal with right now. You don't need to worry about Matt Doaks."

"I know." Her voice sounded like a child's. "It's just that Matt and Jerry are—were good friends. He had dinner here quite a bit."

Something whispered in the back of Pete's brain. The jumble of puzzle pieces struggled to click into place.

Keys.

Doaks knew where Zoe hid her house key.

Hidden keys.

One of the things that never made sense to Pete was the lack of a car key in the Buick. He'd assumed McBirney had driven the car out into the game lands that night and left it and Ted's body, but brought the car keys home with him. It had never felt right.

A knock at the door indicated Williamson had arrived.

"You say Matt and Jerry were good friends," Pete said.

"Yes," Marcy said.

"Did Jerry ever loan the Buick to Matt?"

"Yeah. Matt's old car kept breaking down last summer. Jerry let him use the Buick whenever he wanted."

Williamson knocked again. Pete parted the curtain and held up a finger. In the porch light, he made out the officer's nod.

"Marcy, did Matt know about Jerry's spare key?"

"Spare key?"

"The one he kept on a nail in the garage. He showed it to me that morning I came here to question him about Ted's death. Jerry couldn't locate it at first."

"Oh. Yes. Jerry showed it to him so he didn't have to bother one of us every time he needed to borrow the car."

Damn it.

Pete yanked the door open so fast that Williamson flinched. "Chief?"

"Take Mrs. McBirney into custody. Charge her with theft of township property."

"Like Sylvia Bassi?"

Not quite. "Just do it." Pete broke into a sprint toward his car.

"What's up?" Williamson called after him. "What's wrong?"

Maybe nothing. Maybe everything. "I'll call if I need you." Pete pressed Zoe's cell number into his phone as he leapt behind the wheel of his vehicle.

"Come on, Zoe. Pick up."

He turned the key and the engine roared to life.

Zoe's voicemail greeting played in his ear. Pete snapped the phone shut and rammed it in his pocket. Shifting into gear, he jammed his foot down on the accelerator.

Damn it. The phone lines were still down to Zoe's house. That's why he'd been getting a busy signal there. He should have gone to her place first. If anything happened to her...

THIRTY

Matt Doaks made a ridiculous sight, propped up by crutches, his right leg and foot encased in that Frankenstein boot. Zoe might have found his appearance nonthreatening—bordering on humorous—except for those pictures on the computer, that empty pill bottle, and what Allison had just told her about his involvement in Ted's death.

A gust of wind drove icy pellets of snow into Zoe's face. She blinked and squinted, keeping an eye on her cell phone, cradled in Matt's gloved left hand. "Give me the phone," she said, keeping her voice low and calm.

"This?" Matt held it up. "What do you need it for?"

Her mouth had gone dry. Should she tell him the truth? That Allison lay inside, slowly going into shock from slicing her wrists? Not to mention possibly overdosing on his drugs? Did he harbor any real feelings for the girl? Or was what Allison claimed he said the truth? That her death would solve all his problems.

Zoe couldn't take the chance. Best to pretend she didn't know anything about any of it. "Just give me the damned phone." She made a grab for it, trying to appear more playful than desperate.

As she expected, he held it out of her reach and grinned. That's it. Let him think this was a simple game of keep-away. She jumped, making the attempt appear half-hearted. Let him believe the scramble was all in fun, keep him off-guard, and then kick that bad leg out from under the bastard.

At least that was her plan.

He laughed at her ineffective jump and twisted slightly to the right. Now.

She shifted her weight to one foot and started to swing the other back. But before she could sweep it forward again, he twisted his body hard to the left, bringing his arm and fist around.

The blow sent Zoe sprawling. The impact of the frozen ground hurt worse than Matt's punch.

"You bastard," she sputtered, rubbing her jaw.

As she watched, Matt dropped her cell phone to the ground and mashed it with the tip of one of the crutches.

"There are cops crawling all over my house," he hissed. "Why do I think I have you to thank for that?"

She worked her way up to her knees. He *thought* he had her to thank. He didn't *know*. Play dumb, Zoe. Find out what he *does* know. "Cops? Why the hell would there be cops at your place?"

"Gee, I don't know." Now he was the one playing dumb. "Maybe because some lying little brat decided to run to her Auntie Zoe and tell tall tales."

So that was how it was going to be. His word against Allison's. Zoe sat on her knees, touching her cheek with her fingertips. Her mind was too busy to register pain. How did he know Allison had come running to her? "I have no idea what you're rambling on about. What are you doing out here, anyway?"

"You've seen the pictures," he said. It wasn't a question. "I knew that punk Logan couldn't keep his mouth shut."

"Logan didn't tell me anything. I found them myself. You really are a sick bastard." She shifted off her knees, into a squat, keeping her eyes on those crutches. If she sprung at him, he might club her with one of them, but she should be able to tackle him and gain some control over the situation.

Matt's laugh sounded like a cough. "Are you kidding me? You've seen how that girl dresses and struts her stuff. She came on to me, I'll have you know. I was working on the addition to the high school, and she kept hanging around me, wearing those tight shirts that showed off her chest. And those tight jeans with that sweet ass." He gave an orgasmic moan.

Sickened, she braced to push off.

But before she could spring, Matt reached into his coat pocket and brought out a revolver. "Don't do it, Zoe." He placed the tip of one crutch against her shoulder and shoved.

She toppled sideways, but caught herself before she hit the ground a second time. "Why don't you just get the hell out of here, you son of a bitch?"

He heaved a melodramatic sigh. "Oh, but I can't. Don't you see? You've discovered my secret. I can't—I *won't* go to jail for sex crimes. You know what they do to guys branded as sex perverts in prison? Now get up. I'm freezing my ass off. Let's go in the barn."

Zoe obliged. Slowly. Her eyes were no longer glued to the crutches, but to the black handgun, barely visible in the darkness, except for the reflection from the light high on the outside of the barn. "Matt, you don't need that thing." She forced her voice back to its low, calming tones. Like she'd use on a scared colt. Or a psych patient.

"Shut up and move." He motioned toward the barn door.

She took small steps. Time. She needed time to think. Allison was inside. Obviously, Matt held no affection for the girl. How would he react when he saw her? Could Zoe afford to risk finding out? What could she do to stop it?

She should have taken him out when she had the chance.

At the door, Zoe stopped. She turned to face Matt. And the barrel of the gun. For a moment her breath caught in her throat.

"Inside," he said. "I'm freezing out here."

She forced her gaze from the revolver's muzzle to Matt's eyes. Had they always been that crazed? She swallowed against a hard, dry lump in her throat. "Look, Matt. I don't want to get you into trouble. No one else has seen the stuff on the computer. Let's you and me go back to the house. I'll give you the hard drive, and you can do whatever you want with it. That was you—breaking into my house that night—wasn't it?"

He huffed. "Yeah. But you came home too early. I figured you'd be at the funeral home until they closed up. Then when I tried again, your nosy neighbor lady caught me on the porch. And I was going to give it one more try while you were on duty Friday night, but then..." He motioned to his leg.

"You were on your way here to break in when you wrecked?"

"Yep." He grinned. "And you came to my rescue. You and Pete Adams. Ironic, huh?"

That would be one word for it. "Okay. So let's do it now. I'll let you in, and you can take the damned thing. It's been nothing but trouble this whole week."

He appeared to be considering it. Once she had him away from the barn and Allison, she could figure a way out of this.

"And you'd keep quiet?" he said.

"Absolutely. I mean, you're right about Allison. Rose was telling me about finding some jock in her room and taking the door off the hinges. You can't be blamed for being drawn to a sexy young thing like that. Especially when she's throwing herself at you." Gag. Zoe wanted to go home and wash her mouth out with Clorox.

Did he buy it? Maybe, maybe not. But the enticement of getting his hands on that hard drive might be enough to move this party away from the barn. And Allison.

"Okay," he said.

"Okay?"

"Yeah. Okay."

Zoe fought to keep the relieved sigh from being too obvious. She moved away from the doorway.

"Except..." The chill in Matt's voice made the bitter January temperatures feel balmy. "I want to know what you've got in that barn that you don't want me to see."

Zoe's breath caught deep in her chest. "Nothing." She feared she'd said it too quickly. "Come on, Matt. That hard drive is the only real evidence against you. Who's going to believe a whacked-out Goth girl's word against yours? You're a respected businessman. A township supervisor."

"But *you* know."

"I know nothing," she cried. "A lawyer would call it hearsay. Take the damned hard drive, and get the hell out of my life."

Long seconds passed with only the sounds of the wind moaning and dead tree branches rattling. Zoe fought the urge to glance at the gun. Hold his gaze. Look sincere. She didn't even blink at the burst of wind-driven snow crystals that pelted her in the face.

His expression wavered. Softened. For a moment, Zoe clutched at the hope that she'd reached him. But then he gestured at the barn with the gun. "Inside."

A sob threatened to break free from Zoe's chest. Defeat weighed heavy on her sagging shoulders as she turned. Matt propped both crutches under one armpit to keep the gun leveled at her.

As the barn door creaked open, Allison's plaintive voice called out, "Aunt Zoe?"

"I'm here, honey." Zoe stepped inside with Matt right behind her.

"Allison? What the—?" Matt halted for a moment, apparently startled by the lump on the ground covered by a horse blanket. "What happened?"

Allison made a feeble attempt to turn her head. "Matt? Is that you?"

He crutched past Zoe, keeping enough distance that she dared not attempt a tackle. Not when he had the gun aimed at the girl under the blanket. He stopped next to Allison and looked down at her, his mouth pressed into a questioning frown.

"It is you," Allison said. "You came to save me."

"Not hardly." The words slipped out before Zoe could catch them.

Matt shifted the gun into the same hand as the crutches. But it was still aimed precariously at Allison. He leaned down, and with his free hand, swept the blanket aside. He straightened and laughed. "What the hell do you call this? You bandaging a kid or a horse?"

While his attention was locked on the bizarre sight of a young girl with Vet Wrap and splint boots on her arms, Zoe edged closer. Not that she had a clue as to what she'd do, but she needed to protect Allison. Somehow. "Because of you, she cut herself."

"You slashed your wrists?" he said to Allison.

She struggled to sit up. Wiggled and strained, but couldn't lift herself up. "I'm sorry."

"Yeah. Me, too." Matt grunted. "You should have done something that would've worked."

Gun or not, Zoe considered jumping the snake.

He held up the revolver. "See? This would work much better than a knife."

A knife? Zoe's mind flashed on the knife dropping from Allison's hand into the dirt of the barn floor. Where had it gone?

Allison started weeping. "You're going to shoot me? I thought you were here to save me. I thought you loved me."

Matt shook his head and looked at Zoe. She snapped her attention from searching the ground to him. "Kids," he said. "Where do they come up with these stupid ideas?"

She'd had the same stupid idea once.

"So what's your plan?" Zoe said. "You're going to kill both of us?"

"I don't have much choice, do I?"

"You could let us go. I'll still give you the hard drive. Without hard evidence, no jury will convict you. But you kill us? Then you've got murder charges to deal with."

He studied Allison who was growing paler and shivering harder by the moment. Zoe took the opportunity to inch a little closer to where she thought the knife had fallen. Unfortunately, Matt happened to be standing at that spot. With her luck, he was standing on the damned thing.

"I'm afraid it's too late. Maybe before Ted Bassi stuck his nose in my business. But now?"

Allison's weeping became louder. Matt lifted the gun, pointing the muzzle at the girl.

"No," Zoe said in her best authoritative voice. Keep him talking. Keep him off kilter. "If you're planning to kill both of us, you'd damned well better shoot me first."

"Huh?"

"Because the second you shoot her, I'm going to jump your ass and beat you to death with your own crutches." She'd told him a lot of lies that evening. This, however, was gospel.

His hand lowered a bit.

Now for the buying-time part. "If you're going to kill me anyway, I'd like to go to my grave with some answers. I know you didn't plan to kill Ted, but if it was an accident and not murder, why not just call 9-1-1?"

Matt swung the gun toward Zoe. "Do you honestly expect me to fall for the oldest ploy in the book? Keep me talking until help arrives?" His deep laugh carried to the barn's rafters.

She stared at the gaping black muzzle of the gun. As angry as she was about Ted, about Allison, about every time Matt or any man had betrayed her, at that moment, the only thing she could process was she did not want to die. "It's no ploy." Stay calm. Play to his ego. "I know you're smarter than that. Or are you? Everything would have been so much simpler if you'd just called the cops in the first place."

"Simpler? Are you kidding? I could just hear the questions. *What was Ted's daughter doing there? What were you and Ted arguing about?"* Matt shook his head. "I couldn't let the cops find his body at my place. So I enlisted Allison's help and together we loaded Ted's body into my trunk. She followed me in her dad's pickup over to Jerry's place. At least, she followed me until she ran the thing off the road."

Just when Zoe thought Matt couldn't sicken her any more. Not only had he killed Ted in front of his daughter, he'd made her help him dispose of the body and cover up the crime.

Zoe risked looking away from the gun to check on the girl. How was she reacting? She wasn't. Her eyes were closed. Her lips were tinged with blue. She wasn't shivering any longer. Allison needed an ambulance. And she needed it now.

Zoe forced down the rising panic. "What about Jerry McBirney? I thought you were friends."

"No. You thought I was his lap dog. Isn't that what you said?"

The menace in his voice brought her focus back to the gun still aimed squarely at her head.

"After the incident at the supervisors' meeting, I figured Jerry was an easy alibi. Everyone would believe he'd killed Ted. The investigation wouldn't go any further."

Matt had been the one to feed her the information about Ted and Marcy's affair. And Zoe had swallowed it whole.

"If only I'd gotten my hands on that computer." A wistful note crept into Matt's voice. "Stupid girl. I can't believe she didn't erase those e-mails."

For a moment, Zoe thought he was going to kick Allison's unconscious form. Gun or no gun, she braced, ready to pounce on him. Instead, he gave a little hop on his good foot. As he moved, Zoe spotted it. He *had* been standing on the knife. Half buried in the dirt floor, only the brown leather hilt was exposed.

Don't look at it. Don't draw his attention to it.

"Then what?" she said. "Did Jerry find out you were framing him so you had to kill him, too?"

Matt kept the gun aimed at Zoe, but shifted his gaze to Allison. "He called me. Said he wanted to meet me at Rodeo's, but this one..." He nodded toward the girl at his feet. "This one phoned me and insisted we get together."

Matt's gaze stayed on Allison. The gun drifted off target. Zoe eyed the knife on the ground and inched closer, hoping he wouldn't notice and bring a sudden and deadly end to his reminiscences.

"I called Jerry and told him I'd be late," Matt went on, "but the son-of-a-bitch apparently couldn't wait. He showed up and caught us."

"You really ought to lock your doors," Zoe quipped and regretted it immediately.

Matt swung back to her, and once again, she stared down the gun's barrel. "You're a smart ass, aren't you, Zoe? You're right. Allison isn't about to cause me any more problems. Hell, look at her. She's probably dead already. You, on the other hand...I should definitely shoot you first."

The combination of cold and terror seeped through Zoe's coat. She hugged herself to quell the shivering. If she had any fragment of hope to save Allison and herself, she had to stay steady. Matt was right about the girl. She looked dead. Except for the miniscule movement in her chest. Whatever Zoe was going to do, she had to do it soon.

And she had to *not* get shot.

"You don't have to do this," she said.

"Oh, yeah, I do. It's something I've wanted to do for a long time. You don't even know how bad or how long I've hated you."

"Huh?" This wasn't going in a direction she expected or liked.

"I've despised you from the moment you walked out on me."

"Me? Walked out on you? You cheated on me. Hell, you didn't lock the doors back then, either."

"I told you that girl meant nothing. I loved you. But you were so high and mighty. You refused to forgive me. Instead, you started seeing other guys. Ted. Jerry. I wanted to strangle you every time I saw you with someone else."

The man was certifiable. Zoe wanted to tell him so, but the words froze in her throat.

Matt laughed. "You wanna hear the funniest part? I got you back and you didn't even know it was me. You blamed good ol' Jerry. See? He's been my scapegoat for years."

Her eyes fogged for a moment as the realization of his words sunk in. "What do you mean?"

"That precious horse Jerry bought and boarded for you. He didn't poison her. I did. I was sick of seeing you shacking up with that old reprobate. All because he bought you a fucking horse. Hell, I'd have bought you a whole herd if I knew that's what you wanted. Getting rid of her wasn't hard. I'd trimmed my hedges—our hedges—and snuck a handful of the clippings into her hay. A tasty treat."

Matt's hedges. The toxic Chinese Yews at the base of his steps where Ted had died. Where she'd found his eyeglass lens. McBirney may have been a pig and a scoundrel. But he wasn't the monster Zoe had always thought. Matt Doaks was the monster.

Her knees gave out on her, and she sunk to the dirt. Her stomach heaved, but she swallowed back the bile. Her vision cleared, becoming sharper than she'd ever known.

The knife lay only five or six feet in front of her. Matt stood another foot or so away. Allison's skin was turning gray, her breath barely discernable. Somehow, Zoe knew Matt was watching her every move. *Look away. Just one second, that's all I need. Look away.*

"So what happened when Jerry walked in on you and Allison?" she said.

"Oh," Matt said, reminded of the story he'd been telling. "The old cuss wanted a piece of the action. Can you believe it? He'd figured out about how his car came to be found with Ted's body in it and was furious. But he had a price for keeping quiet. He wanted to share the girl."

Okay, so Jerry was a monster, too.

"He was all set to do sweet Allison when Logan walked in. That kid was ready to hand me my head, but then he saw what Jerry was doing to his little sister. It kind of distracted him if you know what I mean." He laughed again.

Through the laughter, Zoe heard something. A car. The distant crunch of gravel in the lane. Not close to the barn. Not yet. And Matt apparently hadn't noticed.

"But Logan didn't kill Jerry. You're the one who stabbed him," she said.

"Who told you that?"

Zoe wasn't about to give up Allison. "The coroner's report. You stabbed him with a Philip's head screwdriver. The cops know, Matt. You aren't going to get away with it this time."

His eyes were on her. Damn it. Look away.

"It wasn't me." Gone was the lilting laugh. Instead Matt's voice became shrill, reeking of guilt. "When they find that screwdriver, my prints won't be on it."

"What did you do? Wipe it clean and then hand it to Logan?"

All signs of good humor had vanished. Dragging the crutches with him, Matt took an uneven step toward her, his face ugly in its rage. But all Zoe saw was the yawning maw of his gun.

The sound of tires on gravel grew louder. Zoe willed her hands to be still. No trembling. Her muscles tensed. She knew she'd only get one chance. To Matt, she hoped she looked like she was collapsed on her knees. In reality, she was crouched and ready.

The vehicle outside pulled up to the barn. Matt's eyes shifted. A car door slammed. Matt wheeled toward the sound. The gun barrel followed his gaze.

And Zoe sprang.

THIRTY-ONE

Pete passed an unfamiliar car edged off the lane several yards from the barn and parked next to Zoe's truck. The Chevy's driver's-side door stood open. But no Zoe. As he stepped away from his car, the sharp crack of a gunshot shattered the country stillness, followed by a shriek.

He ducked behind the pickup's open door. With one hand, he released his sidearm from its holster. Something on the ground caught his eye. A smashed cell phone. Zoe's? In an instant, every sense became sharper. Details leapt into his consciousness. He focused on the barn, the smaller door, flanked by two larger ones. The light seeping out beneath them and through the windows along the side of the building. He watched for any hint of a shadow indicating movement inside.

He listened, too far away to hear clearly. The sound of a car passing on the road below made the effort even more difficult. But he thought he made out the rustling of movement. And perhaps...sobbing?

He punched 9-1-1 into his cell phone.

God, was he too late?

"Shots fired," he rasped when the operator picked up. "Vance Township Officer needs assistance. Kroll farm on Route 15. At the barn."

He hung up.

Where was Zoe? Was she hurt? Or worse?

He knew damned well he should wait for back up. He also knew there wasn't time. In a crouch, he picked his way across the gravel to the barn. The metal sheeting would do squat to stop a bullet. Don't think about it. He pressed his shoulder into the edge of the doorway and reached out, pounding on the door. "This is the police. Throw out your weapon and come out with your hands where I can see them." He hunkered down and moved back, sighting his weapon on the doorway.

"Pete." It was Zoe's voice that called to him. "Help us! He's unarmed." Her voice sounded odd. Strained. Was she being forced at gunpoint to lure him in?

Pete stepped again to the side of the door, this time testing the knob. It offered no resistance. He swung the door wide and stepped into the opening, his weapon in front of him.

The scene before him made him lower it.

Zoe knelt over Matt Doaks who was moaning and squirming. Zoe's hands were pressed against his blood-soaked thigh. Next to them lay a motionless Allison covered with a dusty horse blanket.

"Call an ambulance," Zoe shouted at him. "Two patients. Tell them to call in Life Flight. And expedite it."

Already, sirens wailed in the distance. Pete redialed the emergency operations center and added the request for a medical response.

"Where's the gun?" he said.

She tipped her head. "I kicked it over there." Then she nodded toward Allison. "And the knife is there, next to her."

"Knife?"

"It's a long story. I'm sure I'll have to repeat it a few dozen times."

"So give me the short version for now."

"Matt killed Ted."

"I know."

She looked up at him. "You *know*?"

"Well, I pretty much figured it out before I headed over."

"He's been supplying Allison with drugs, too. And I'm fairly certain he was the one who administered the fatal stab wound to Jerry McBirney." She turned back to her patient, bearing down on the wound. "That's what happened, isn't it, tough guy?"

Doaks yelped. Pete bent over him. The punk looked as though he was on the verge of bursting into tears. A thought occurred to him. "Hey, Doaks. How'd you get the alarm codes to my police station?"

Doaks whimpered. "Allison. She'd seen Sylvia punch them in and remembered them. Then she lifted the old lady's key, let herself in the front door, and opened the back one for me."

Son of a—

Pete turned back to Zoe. "But what happened here?"

"He intended on killing Allison and me," Zoe said. "He had the gun. Allison had cut her wrists. Bad. Attempted suicide."

Pete eyed the girl. Maybe more than just attempted.

"She dropped the knife she used, but Matt didn't see it. I did. So when he got distracted by the car—you—I grabbed the knife and stabbed him."

Doaks let out another girlish wail.

Pete moved to where the gun lay and leaned down to get a better look. "He had a gun and you had a knife?"

She gave him a tired grin. "I know what you're gonna say."

He said it anyway. "Don't you know? Never bring a knife to a gunfight."

"Very funny. Now take your sense of humor into the tack room and get me some bandages out of the cabinet in the corner."

Three months later, daffodils and crocuses offered a burst of spring color at the base of the VFW's flagpole, and the air carried a tease of warmth. Zoe stood in the sunshine, taking advantage of a night off duty and the rare rain-free day.

"Ready to play township supervisor one last time?" Rose strolled toward her.

"Oh, yeah. If I've learned nothing else in the last few months, I do know I never want to go into politics." Zoe opened her arms, and her friend stepped into the quick embrace.

"That's too bad, you know? You and Sylvia together on the board? That would bring back the entertainment value to these meetings."

Zoe raised a hand, acknowledging Howard Rankin, who passed by the women on his way inside. Howard would no doubt keep the chairmanship. Joe Mendez, who had taken over the seat vacated by Matt Doaks, was a shoo-in to keep it when the residents voted in three weeks. And Sylvia was running for Zoe's slot with her blessing. Funny, no one had tried to talk Zoe into putting her name on the ballot. "The world isn't ready to handle the two of us overseeing anything. Not even a little rural government like ours."

Rose snickered, and Zoe contemplated how glad she was to see her old friend coming back to life.

"How are the kids?"

Rose shoved her hands into her jeans pockets and lifted her face to the sun. "They're going to be okay. Mr. Imperatore is pushing for some community service for Logan and feels the DA will go for it. All he really did was punch McBirney. Matt's the one who stabbed him."

Zoe breathed in the spring air and nodded.

"I hear you were in to see Allison this afternoon," Rose said.

Zoe watched a couple of local residents wander in from the parking lot. "Yeah. She looks great."

"Like her old self. Almost. Her hair is back to auburn. But there's a lot of stuff going on behind her eyes. Don't you think?"

Zoe hooked her arm through Rose's and bumped shoulders with her. "Give her time. She's been through hell. Matt had her completely under his spell. She's got to learn to reclaim her power."

Rose looked at Zoe askance. "I talked to her on the phone before I headed over here. She told me what all you said to her. Thanks."

Zoe stared into the distance, but instead of Dillard's boxy houses, she was seeing Allison seated in that place. They called it a treatment facility. The brightness of the room had surprised Zoe at first. She'd expected dull and gray, but that description seemed to be reserved for the patients.

They'd talked about Matt, their mutual mistake. Zoe had shared her Jerry McBirney experience with Allison. "Even though it happened all those years ago, I was still afraid of him. I believed he could still hurt me. I gave him that power over me."

Allison had bobbed her head in understanding. "That's how I feel. I let Matt do things. Helped him get away with..." Her eyes glistened, still not quite able to speak about the night her dad died in front of her eyes. Zoe took her hand. Allison squeezed it and went on. "I let Matt and his pills take something from me. I let Matt take *me* from me."

Zoe cupped the girl's face in her hand. "But you can still take *you* back. He doesn't own you. He can't hurt or control you anymore."

Of course, the fact that Jerry McBirney was dead while Matt Doaks was only locked up awaiting trial didn't help. But Allison had seemed comforted by the words.

"Good evening, ladies." Pete's approach interrupted Zoe's reverie. He'd been reinstated within days of the incident in the barn, and the sight of him in his uniform stirred all Zoe's muddled emotions. At least some things remained the same.

"Hi, Chief," Rose said. "Come for the show?"

"What show?"

"I was just telling Zoe I wished she'd run against Mendez and stay on the board." Rose nudged Pete with her elbow. "Don't you think she and Sylvia would spice up the meetings again?"

Pete chuckled. "I don't think the township could handle them both."

"See? That's what I told her," Zoe said, enjoying the easy banter. "Besides, I kind of like dull supervisors' meetings. I think the hottest topic on tonight's agenda is Joe's push to finally get the signage on the new highway changed."

As soon as she said it, she wished she hadn't. Memories of that bitter January night silenced all three of them.

"Here comes Sylvia," Rose said, breaking the strained hush. "Talk to you two later."

Zoe watched her friend jog down the sidewalk toward Ted's mother.

"How are you doing?" Pete's voice was low enough that no one else could hear. Even though there wasn't anyone else around.

"I'm...okay. How about you?"

He gave a noncommittal shrug. "We've missed you at poker."

Zoe studied the cracked sidewalk. A bug, testing the viability of spring, explored the pebbled concrete surface.

She'd been avoiding Pete while sorting through her boatload of emotional baggage. Was she an awful person for being glad she hadn't managed to save McBirney? Was it horrible that she felt the world benefited from his absence in it? And then there was Matt. How could she have ever been attracted to that murderous cad? Why hadn't she seen him for what he was—both years ago when he'd poisoned her mare and more recently when he'd poisoned the soul of her best friend's young daughter?

Plus, Zoe had heard rumors of a reconciliation between Pete and his ex-wife and been too afraid to find out what truth there was to them. She hadn't intended to ask, even now, but heard the question come from her lips anyway. "How's Marcy?"

Pete turned to stand shoulder-to-shoulder next to Zoe, and gazed at the same Dillard houses she'd just been looking at. His arm brushed hers. "You know she put the farm up for sale?"

"I heard." She'd also heard Marcy had escaped litigation for stealing township funds. Something about statute of limitations.

"She's moving."

Did Zoe want to know? Not really. "Where?"

"Can you believe it? Back to Pittsburgh."

Zoe choked on her surprise. Those gossip mongers at the station lied. "Wasn't it Marcy who..."

"Wanted to move away from the city. Yeah." He shot a quick glance at her, and she caught a glimpse of a grin. "Ironic, huh?"

But that was only half the question. "So, are you moving back, too?"

He threw his head back and laughed. A wonderful, full-bellied laugh. "No," he said. "I'm not moving back to the city. I admit I thought about it for a while when County was having all the fun with my evidence. But I'm sorry to tell you. Vance Township is stuck with me for a police chief."

Howard Rankin poked his head out of the VFW door. "Hey, Zoe. Are you coming? I want to get this meeting started."

"I'll be right there."

Howard ducked back in. Pete caught her arm. "I'm not staying for the meeting. Somehow, I don't think a police presence is needed here tonight."

"Oh." She covered the flicker of disappointment that threatened to add a whine to her voice. "Okay."

He stepped away. Then turned back and tucked a strand of hair behind her ear. "Poker Saturday night?"

For the first time in a very long while, Zoe managed a smile untainted by fear or doubt. "Count on it," she said.

ANNETTE DASHOFY

Annette Dashofy, a Pennsylvania farm gal born and bred, grew up with horses, cattle, and, yes, chickens. After high school, she spent five years as an EMT for the local ambulance service. Since then, she's worked a variety of jobs, giving her plenty of fodder for her lifelong passion for writing. She, her husband, and their two spoiled cats live on property that was once part of her grandfather's dairy. Her short fiction, including a 2007 Derringer nominee, has appeared in *Spinetingler*, *Mysterical-e*, and *Fish Tales: the Guppy Anthology*. Her newest short story appears in the *Lucky Charms Anthology*.

Henery Press Mystery Books

And finally, before you go...
Here are a few other mysteries
you might enjoy:

LOWCOUNTRY BOIL

Susan M. Boyer

A Liz Talbot Mystery (#1)

Private Investigator Liz Talbot is a modern Southern belle: she blesses hearts and takes names. She carries her Sig 9 in her Kate Spade handbag, and her golden retriever, Rhett, rides shotgun in her hybrid Escape. When her grandmother is murdered, Liz hightails it back to her South Carolina island home to find the killer.

She's fit to be tied when her police-chief brother shuts her out of the investigation, so she opens her own. Then her long-dead best friend pops in and things really get complicated. When more folks start turning up dead in this small seaside town, Liz must use more than just her wits and charm to keep her family safe, chase down clues from the hereafter, and catch a psychopath before he catches her.

Available at booksellers nationwide and online

Visit www.henerypress.com for details

DOUBLE WHAMMY

Gretchen Archer

A Davis Way Crime Caper (#1)

Davis Way thinks she's hit the jackpot when she lands a job as the fifth wheel on an elite security team at the fabulous Bellissimo Resort and Casino in Biloxi, Mississippi. But once there, she runs straight into her ex-ex husband, a rigged slot machine, her evil twin, and a trail of dead bodies. Davis learns the truth and it does not set her free—in fact, it lands her in the pokey.

Buried under a mistaken identity, unable to seek help from her family, her hot streak runs cold until her landlord Bradley Cole steps in. Make that her landlord, lawyer, and love interest. With his help, Davis must win this high stakes game before her luck runs out.

Available at booksellers nationwide and online

Visit www.henerypress.com for details

BOARD STIFF

Kendel Lynn

An Elliott Lisbon Mystery (#1)

As director of the Ballantyne Foundation on Sea Pine Island, SC, Elliott Lisbon scratches her detective itch by performing discreet inquiries for Foundation donors. Usually nothing more serious than retrieving a pilfered Pomeranian. Until Jane Hatting, Ballantyne board chair, is accused of murder. The Ballantyne's reputation tanks, Jane's headed to a jail cell, and Elliott's sexy ex is the new lieutenant in town.

Armed with moxie and her Mini Coop, Elliott uncovers a trail of blackmail schemes, gambling debts, illicit affairs, and investment scams. But the deeper she digs to clear Jane's name, the guiltier Jane looks. The closer she gets to the truth, the more treacherous her investigation becomes. With victims piling up faster than shells at a clambake, Elliott realizes she's next on the killer's list.

Available at booksellers nationwide and online

Visit www.henerypress.com for details

DINERS, DIVES & DEAD ENDS

Terri L. Austin

A Rose Strickland Mystery (#1)

As a struggling waitress and part-time college student, Rose Strickland's life is stalled in the slow lane. But when her close friend, Axton, disappears, Rose suddenly finds herself serving up more than hot coffee and flapjacks. Now she's hashing it out with sexy bad guys and scrambling to find clues in a race to save Axton before his time runs out.

With her anime-loving bestie, her septuagenarian boss, and a pair of IT wise men along for the ride, Rose discovers political corruption, illegal gambling, and shady corporations. She's gone from zero to sixty and quickly learns when you're speeding down the fast lane, it's easy to crash and burn.

Available at booksellers nationwide and online

Visit www.henerypress.com for details

ARTIFACT

Gigi Pandian

A Jaya Jones Treasure Hunt Mystery (#1)

Historian Jaya Jones discovers the secrets of a lost Indian treasure may be hidden in a Scottish legend from the days of the British Raj. But she's not the only one on the trail...

From San Francisco to London to the Highlands of Scotland, Jaya must evade a shadowy stalker as she follows hints from the hastily scrawled note of her dead lover to a remote archaeological dig. Helping her decipher the cryptic clues are her magician best friend, a devastatingly handsome art historian with something to hide, and a charming archaeologist running for his life.

Available at booksellers nationwide and online

Visit www.henerypress.com for details

THE AMBITIOUS CARD

John Gaspard

An Eli Marks Mystery (#1)

The life of a magician isn't all kiddie shows and card tricks. Some-times it's murder. Especially when magician Eli Marks very publicly debunks a famed psychic, and said psychic ends up dead. The evidence, including a bloody King of Diamonds playing card (one from Eli's own Ambitious Card routine), directs the police right to Eli.

As more psychics are slain, and more King cards rise to the top, Eli can't escape suspicion. Things get really complicated when romance blooms with a beautiful psychic, and Eli discovers she's the next target for murder, and he's scheduled to die with her. Now Eli must use every trick he knows to keep them both alive and reveal the true killer.

Available at booksellers nationwide and online

Visit www.henerypress.com for details

PORTRAIT OF A DEAD GUY

Larissa Reinhart

A Cherry Tucker Mystery (#1)

In Halo, Georgia, folks know Cherry Tucker as big in mouth, small in stature, and able to sketch a portrait faster than buck-shot rips from a ten gauge -- but commissions are scarce. So when the well-heeled Branson family wants to memorialize their murdered son in a coffin portrait, Cherry scrambles to win their patronage from her small town rival.

As the clock ticks toward the deadline, Cherry faces more trouble than just a controversial subject. Between ex-boyfriends, her flaky family, an illegal gambling ring, and outwitting a killer on a spree, Cherry finds herself painted into a corner she'll be lucky to survive.

Available at booksellers nationwide and online

Visit www.henerypress.com for details

FRONT PAGE FATALITY

LynDee Walker

A Headlines in High Heels Mystery (#1)

Crime reporter Nichelle Clarke's days can flip from macabre to comical with a beep of her police scanner. Then an ordinary accident story turns extraordinary when evidence goes missing, a prosecutor vanishes, and a sexy Mafia boss shows up with the headline tip of a lifetime.

As Nichelle gets closer to the truth, her story gets more dangerous. Armed with a notebook, a hunch, and her favorite stilettos, Nichelle races to splash these shady dealings across the front page before this deadline becomes her last.

Available at booksellers nationwide and online

Visit www.henerypress.com for details

PILLOW STALK

Diane Vallere

A Mad for Mod Mystery (#1)

Interior Decorator Madison Night has modeled her life after Doris Day's character in *Pillow Talk*, but when a killer targets women dressed like the bubbly actress, Madison's signature sixties style places her in the middle of a homicide investigation.

The local detective connects the new crimes to a twenty-year old cold case, and Madison's long-trusted contractor emerges as the leading suspect. As the body count piles up like a stack of plush pillows, Madison uncovers a Soviet spy, a campaign to destroy all Doris Day movies, and six minutes of film that will change her life forever.

Available at booksellers nationwide and online

Visit www.henerypress.com for details

CROPPED TO DEATH

Christina Freeburn

A Faith Hunter Scrap This Mystery (#1)

Former US Army JAG specialist, Faith Hunter, returns to her West Virginia home to work in her grandmothers' scrapbooking store determined to lead an unassuming life after her adventure abroad turned disaster. But her quiet life unravels when her friend is charged with murder – and Faith inadvertently supplied the evidence. So Faith decides to cut through the scrap and piece together what really happened.

With a sexy prosecutor, a determined homicide detective, a handful of sticky suspects and a crop contest gone bad, Faith quickly realizes if she's not careful, she'll be the next one cropped.

Available at booksellers nationwide and online

Visit www.henerypress.com for details

KILLER IMAGE

Wendy Tyson

An Allison Campbell Mystery (#1)

Philadelphia image consultant Allison Campbell is not your typical detective. She's more familiar with the rules of etiquette than the rules of evidence, prefers three-inch Manolos to comfy flats and relates to Dear Abby, not Judge Judy.

When Allison's latest Main Line client, the fifteen-year-old Goth daughter of a White House hopeful, is accused of the ritualistic murder of a local divorce attorney, Allison fights to prove her client's innocence when no one else will. But in a place where image is everything, the ability to distinguish the truth from the facade may be the only thing that keeps Allison alive.

FORGIVE & FORGET

Heather Ashby

Love in the Fleet (#1)

When Hallie McCabe meets Philip Johnston at a picnic, she is drawn to his integrity. He is a gentleman. But also an officer. From her ship. Aware of the code against fraternization between officers and enlisted, Hallie conceals her Navy status, hopeful she and her secret will stay hidden on their aircraft carrier until she can figure out a way for them to sail off into the sunset together.

Caught in an emotional firestorm, Hallie faces a future without the man she loves, a career-shattering secret from the past, and the burden of being the one person who can prevent a terrorist attack on the ship she has sworn to protect with her life.

Manufactured by Amazon.ca
Bolton, ON

12717811R00168